The Precipice

ALSO BY PAUL DOIRON

The Bone Orchard

Massacre Pond

Bad Little Falls

Trespasser

The Poacher's Son

The
PRECIPICE

Paul Doiron

MINOTAUR BOOKS
NEW YORK

THE PRECIPICE. Copyright © 2015 by Paul Doiron. All rights reserved. Printed in the United States of America. For information, address St. Martin's Press, 175 Fifth Avenue, New York, N.Y. 10010.

www.minotaurbooks.com

Library of Congress Cataloging-in-Publication Data

Doiron, Paul.
    The precipice : a novel / Paul Doiron. — First edition.
        pages ; cm. — (Mike Bowditch mysteries ; 6)
    ISBN 978-1-250-06369-4 (hardcover)
    ISBN 978-1-4668-6868-7 (e-book)
    1. Game wardens—Fiction.   2. Young women—Crimes against—Fiction.
3. Murder—Investigation—Fiction.   4. Missing persons—Investigation—Fiction.
5. Wilderness areas—Maine—Fiction.   I. Title.
    PS3604.O37P74 2015
    813'.6—dc23
                                                                        2015013520

Minotaur books may be purchased for educational, business, or promotional use. For information on bulk purchases, please contact the Macmillan Corporate and Premium Sales Department at 1-800-221-7945, extension 5442, or write to special markets@macmillan.com.

First Edition: June 2015

10 9 8 7 6 5 4 3 2 1

For my friend and teacher, Ron Joseph

Outside are the dogs and sorcerers and the sexually immoral and murderers and idolaters, and everyone who loves and practices falsehood.

—The Book of Revelation

The Precipice

PROLOGUE

There is a sign at the southern entrance to the Hundred Mile Wilderness. It is made out of rust brown wood and painted with white letters, and it sends a stern and unmistakable warning to all who enter:

> Caution. There are no places to obtain supplies or help until Abol Bridge 100 miles north. Do not attempt this section unless you have a minimum of 10 days' supplies and are fully equipped. This is the longest wilderness section of the entire Appalachian Trail and its difficulty should not be underestimated.

The last photograph we have of the two women shows them posed beside this sign with their arms around each other, looking more like sisters than college friends who have hiked together from Georgia to Maine. Their faces are deeply tanned from months in the sun, and they are dressed in well-used backpacking gear—bright synthetic shorts, patterned bandanas rolled around their necks, and heavily scuffed boots. Samantha Boggs is wearing a tie-dyed shirt: a wannabe hippie. Missy Montgomery has on a pink tee with the words MONSON: BY THE SHORES OF LAKE HEBRON. They are both smiling like bridesmaids at a wedding.

We know that the photograph was sent at 11:33 A.M. on Sunday, September 7, by a Samsung Galaxy smartphone. It traveled via

I

cell tower and satellite down the eastern seaboard to their parents, who lived less than five miles from one another in the wealthy community of Buckhead, in the North Atlanta suburbs. Samantha and Missy had e-mailed home many similar pictures since they'd set off on their journey seven months earlier. This one just happens to be the last we have of the two women before they vanished. And we will probably never know who took it.

The accompanying message said they would be in touch when they arrived at Abol Bridge, on the West Branch of the Penobscot River. Cell service is spotty throughout the Maine Highlands, but the *Thru-Hikers' Companion* (the bible of the AT) said there was a pay phone at the campground store from which they could reliably call home. Samantha and Missy told their parents not to worry; the so-called wilderness was not as dangerous as it sounded. The path crossed logging roads that had been built since the Appalachian Trail was first blazed in 1937. And besides, they were sure to encounter other hikers along the way, including friends who were following the same rugged route from Springer Mountain to Baxter Peak—a journey of roughly 2,200 miles, which the young women intended to finish before the last week of September.

Samantha and Missy said it would take ten days to cross the Hundred Mile Wilderness. They told their parents to expect a call on September 17. The families waited—and waited—and now three more days had passed since the hikers should have arrived at Abol Campground. But still there was no call. Finally, on September 20, the parents gave in to their growing fears. They used the Montgomerys' political connections to mobilize a massive search on their behalf in the distant Maine woods.

Which was how I came to be involved in the case.

In my four years as a Maine game warden, I had practiced search-and-rescue drills in all seasons and in all weather, and I had taken my skills into the field on more occasions than I could count. There was no aspect of my job that was as rewarding as finding a living person. And there was no experience as heartbreaking as following the calls of ravens to a flyblown corpse that had once been some-one's daughter or son, father or mother.

At the Advanced Warden Academy, my search instructor told me, "You will experience strong emotions. Do your best to ignore them."

What he meant, I have come to believe, is that passion blinds you to the truth before your eyes. It causes you to miss important evidence. In the rush to find a missing child, you step on the bent blades of grass she left while wandering away from home. If you hope to find a lost person, you need to set aside your emotions. But how do you remain calm when a toddler is lost near a raging river? Or when two hikers vanish without a trace on the most heavily traveled trail in the country?

The truth is, no training exercise ever prepares you for the mood swings you go through when you are hunting in a remote place for actual human beings who might or might not be alive, and you realize that their fate is entirely in your hands.

At the start of a search, best-case scenarios still seem possible. Maybe one of the women twisted an ankle, you think, and they are hobbling back to civilization. Or they simply wandered off a moose path that they mistook for the main trail and ended up mired in an alder swamp, from which you can still rescue them. They might not be in the woods at all. You'd be amazed how many "lost" people are found drinking in bars, eating in restaurants, and sleeping in motel beds, unaware that the state has mobilized a massive search on their behalf because they didn't have the self-awareness to check in with worried friends and family members. In those early hours, you tell yourself that any crazy thing might yet happen.

I

I got the call about the lost hikers at the start of what was supposed to be a romantic weekend with my girlfriend.

Stacey Stevens and I had been dating for only four months and hadn't yet gone away together to the sort of place where a man takes a woman in the hope of impressing her. But I had rented a small, outrageously expensive cottage on Popham Beach, down at the mouth of the Kennebec River. There was a fisherman's co-op nearby where we could buy lobsters and clams to steam on the propane stove, and a fancy inn farther down the road where we could have a dress-up dinner if we got tired of cooking. The screen door of the cottage opened onto a sandy path that led through dune grass to a mile-long beach with views of Seguin Island in the hazy blue distance. I had visions of sunbathing and skinny-dipping.

Things hadn't started well. As I was carrying in the luggage, I was bitten on the arm by a greenhead. Then we discovered that the plumbing didn't work, and I had to wait for the property manager to come while Stacey took a book down to the beach to read.

"You sure you don't want me to wait with you?" she asked.

"No, you should go ahead. What are you reading, by the way?"

She held up a hardcover volume with the title *Chronic Wasting Disease in White-Tailed Deer.*

"I've heard it's a real page-turner," I said.

"Ha, ha, ha," she said with a smile. She put on her sunglasses and went barefoot down to the beach.

Stacey was a biologist with the Maine Department of Inland Fisheries and Wildlife, the umbrella organization for the Warden Service. She lived and worked near the New Brunswick border, where I had once had a patrol district. Over the summer, I'd been transferred to Division A, near Sebago Lake, in the southern part of the state, which had turned our relationship into a long-distance affair before it had really even begun. It was now a five-hour drive for us, door to door, although Stacey happened to be a pilot and had borrowed her old man's floatplane to come visit me.

She was a couple of years older than I was, almost thirty, with hair the color of mahogany and eyes the lightest shade of green I'd ever seen. She had high cheekbones, which she'd inherited from her mother, and a strong jaw, which she'd gotten from her father. She was thin, but not in an unhealthy way, not to my eyes at least. Her natural expression seemed to be one of guarded suspicion, but on the rare occasions when she laughed, her whole body shook. It was as if she worked so hard at repressing her enthusiasm that it came out with the force of an earthquake. I wished I could hear her laugh more. Her parents were such cheerful and optimistic human beings, I knew that she must be one, too. If I worked hard enough at loving Stacey, I was certain she would open up in time.

Her father, Charley, was a retired Warden Service pilot who still volunteered whenever we needed another pair of eyes in the sky. He and his beautiful wife, Ora, had practically adopted me when I was a rookie warden in desperate need of personal and professional guidance.

I'd been infatuated with their youngest daughter from the moment we'd met, but she'd been engaged to another man, the heir to a multimillion-dollar lumbering concern. When I'd revealed that he was tangled up in some bad business, Stacey had called off the engagement. The experience had soured her on men in general and me in particular. Finally, in June, I had mustered up my confidence and asked her out, secretly believing I had no chance in the world. To my surprise, she'd said yes.

Four months later, I was still praying that she would recognize we were soul mates. Stacey Stevens was everything I had ever wanted in a woman. We both loved the woods, and we shared the same disregard for authority, especially when it came unearned. She was smart and capable and feisty as hell. But there seemed to be a chasm between us I could find no way across. The beach house was my best effort to bridge it, and already I could see that I might need a new plan. We'd driven separate vehicles to our romantic getaway, so we hadn't even had that carefree time in the car together.

When she returned from the beach an hour later, her skin was browner than before, she smelled pleasantly of coconut suntan lotion, and I was still waiting for the property manager to fix the pipes.

"How much is this place costing you for the weekend?" she asked.

"You don't want to know."

"I don't think you're getting your money's worth here, Bowditch. I hope you're not bankrupting yourself."

I half-smiled and looked at my bare feet.

"What?" she said.

"I have a confession to make. It's kind of embarrassing." I gulped down a mouthful of air to prepare myself. "I have a trust fund."

"No way!"

"My stepfather set it up for me after my mom died last year. I didn't want to take the money, but Kathy Frost convinced me. She said, 'You're such a Catholic martyr. Give half to charity if you're feeling so guilty about it.'"

"I'm going to guess which charity you gave it to. PeTA?"

"Very funny." Stacey and I were both hunters. "I gave it to the Wounded Warrior Project."

"Because of your friend who was wounded in Afghanistan?"

I didn't like to think about Jimmy Gammon, who had come home from war disfigured beyond recognition and in constant agony, or the way he had chosen to die. "The way this country treats its veterans is a disgrace."

She came over, grabbed the back of my head with both hands,

and slipped her tongue into my ear. Her breath was hot against my neck. "Have I ever told you how sexy your righteous indignation is?"

I cocked an eyebrow. "Are you teasing me, Stacey?"

"No, but I'm about to. Come with me."

That moment, as if on cue, the manager appeared at the screen door. He was a slow-moving and seemingly unapologetic character, and he banged around in the crawl space beneath the building for ten minutes before emerging with a wrench in his hand and a head wispy with spiderwebs.

"You're all set here," he said in a heavy Maine accent.

"So how about knocking a couple hundred dollars off the rent for the inconvenience?" said Stacey.

"Do you want me to leave the wrench?" the man replied.

"I'm serious, champ," she said. "How about a discount?"

"Enjoy your stay."

"Gotta love the customer service in this place," Stacey said with a full-body laugh after the manager had driven off in his minivan. "Now, where were we?"

She took my hand and pulled me into the little bedroom. It was wallpapered in seashell patterns and painted in soft beach colors.

I sat down on the mattress, and the springs made a rusty, complaining sound. "At least the bed isn't broken."

She tugged her T-shirt over her shoulders and head. "Not yet," she said.

The first time Stacey and I had slept together was the most intense sexual experience I'd ever had. The second time was even more exciting. By this point in our relationship, however, I'd begun to realize that our physical intimacy was fast outpacing our emotional intimacy.

I tried to make a joke out of it as we lay together now, listening to the pounding waves through the open window.

"You know, Stacey, sometimes I wonder if you're just using me for sex."

She ran a hand through my crew cut. "Oh, poor you."

"I'm not complaining!"

"You'd be the first man in history who ever did, Bowditch."

Before I could say another word, she slid off the mattress and disappeared into the shower.

I lay on my back, watching the breeze ruffle the thin cotton curtain. The midday sun angled in through the window and touched my groin and bare legs with its warmth. I could taste the salt air on my lips.

I was so positive that she was the love of my life, that the two of us were meant to be together, and yet she seemed content that we remain intimate strangers. Even her playful habit of calling me by my last name seemed like an attempt to hold me at bay.

My cell phone rang in the living room. I grabbed my jeans from the floor and pulled them on.

It was my new sergeant, Jason Ouellette, apologizing for interrupting my weekend. He said that two hikers had gone missing on the Appalachian Trail and asked if I could make myself available to assist with the search. The Hundred Mile Wilderness was a solid three hours' drive north of Popham Beach, in the remote Moosehead Lake region. While it wasn't unusual for wardens to be summoned to far-flung locales, the sergeant's request suggested a need for extra manpower that went well beyond the ordinary.

I heard the shower stop in the bathroom and felt a pang, not so much at the thought of losing hundreds of dollars on the beachhouse rental as for the missed opportunity to make inroads with Stacey.

"Can you come?" asked Ouellete.

"Of course," I said.

Stacey stepped out of the bathroom with a terry-cloth towel wrapped around her body. I signed off with the sergeant and tucked the phone in the back pocket of my jeans.

"What's wrong?" she asked.

"Two women disappeared in the Hundred Mile Wilderness.

They're thru-hiking the AT, and they were supposed to talk to their parents in Georgia three days ago. It doesn't sound good."

Some of the color seemed to drain from Stacey's suntanned face and she sat down, almost as if her legs had given way, on the edge of the pale sofa.

"They just graduated from Pentecost University," I said. "Have you heard of it? I never have."

"It's a Christian school down south. How old are they?"

"Twenty-one and twenty-two."

Her hair was dripping in her face, but her almond-shaped eyes had glazed over, as if she had fallen into a trance.

"What is it?" I asked. "Are you OK?"

"I was twenty-one when we hiked the Long Trail in Vermont, my friends and me."

I had a feeling that she was referring to the three women I'd met earlier that spring in the village of Grand Lake Stream, including her former girlfriend, Kendra. "Did something happen to you?"

Her pupils tightened into focus, but she still seemed shaken. "No."

"Then what is it?"

"We met some creepy men that week. But there were four of us. I can't imagine what would have happened if it had just been me and Kendra."

Stacey was a pilot and a scuba diver, a crack shot with a rifle or a pistol, and she could track the blood trail of a dying moose through an impenetrable swamp. As a wildlife biologist, she went alone into all sorts of dark places, and it had never occurred to me to worry about her. But her wavering tone made me wonder if something bad really had happened to her on the Long Trail and that for some reason she was unwilling to admit it. The thought that she might be keeping a secret troubled me.

"I don't have to volunteer for this," I said. "I can stay here with you."

She frowned, as if I'd just uttered some drunken nonsense. "You have to go, and you know it."

I glanced at our luggage, which was sitting where we'd left it beside the door. At least we hadn't unpacked. "I've already paid for the cottage. You can stay if you want."

"Not while those girls are missing."

"Maybe they'll show up tonight and I'll be able to turn right around and come back here."

She pushed the wet strands of hair out of her eyes and stood up, clutching the towel tightly above her breasts so it wouldn't drop. She returned to the bedroom without meeting my gaze again.

"I wouldn't bet on it," she said, her voice hard with certainty.

2

About five hundred people are reported missing in Maine each year. Most of them are found somewhere between twenty-four and forty-eight hours later. The Bible students—as the media ended up referring to them—had been missing for nearly two weeks when we got the call.

Two weeks. Too late.

Those four words were running in a loop in my head as I adjusted the sweaty straps on my canvas rucksack and looked up the forested mountainside at the rapidly receding back of my search partner—an improbably able-bodied volunteer whom I'd met earlier that afternoon at the command post. The two of us had driven in my patrol truck from the North Woods village of Monson to a distant logging road where we could intersect the trail closer to the midsection of the Hundred Mile Wilderness. Despite my best efforts at making conversation, he'd barely spoken a word to me on the hour-long drive, preferring to stare out the window at the blur of green trees through which we were traveling.

I assumed my youthful athleticism was why I'd been assigned the legendary Bob "Nonstop" Nissen and sent to check the remote Chairback Gap lean-to for signs the women might have stopped there. But as soon as the two of us had set off on the access trail to the shelter, I knew this middle-aged man was going to kick my ass. He was well past fifty, but he could scramble up a sheer cliff like a Barbary ape. Most wilderness rescue volunteers use trekking poles, or even climbing axes, to steady themselves, but Nissen preferred to use his big calloused hands to pull himself up the mountain, going on four limbs at times. He had skin so sun-browned, it seemed to be turning to leather; and he was wearing safari shorts, which showed off calf muscles the size of grapefruits. His climbing boots were made by La Sportiva, one of the best and most expensive brands in the world, which told me a lot about the man's priorities.

Now I watched him disappear around a clump of lichen-crusted boulders.

Since we'd started climbing an hour earlier, Nissen hadn't so much as glanced back in my direction. He seemed to view our assignment less as a search-and-rescue mission and more as a personal competition. His sole purpose seemed to be getting to the top of Chairback before me.

Back in Monson, while we were packing our supplies, the officer in charge had told me how Nissen had gotten his unusual nickname. For more than two decades, he'd held the record for the fastest "unsupported" thru-hike of the Appalachian Trail—sixty-one days from south to north, carrying his own supplies, without the assistance of another human being. He'd recently lost his title to a young trail runner from Virginia, but I could easily imagine Nonstop coming out of retirement to regain his former glory.

Perspiration had soaked the brim of my black duty cap and was now streaming freely into the corners of my eyes. I'd left my olive green ballistic vest and button-down shirt back at the truck. I was now dressed in green cargo pants and a black T-shirt with the words GAME WARDEN printed on the back. In place of the L.L. Bean hunting shoes I normally wore, I'd put on a pair of Danner climbing boots. I'd even locked my SIG Sauer .357 pistol in the glove compartment. It felt unsettling to be in the wild unarmed.

The skies were gray and darker in the west; the forecast called for late-afternoon thunderstorms. The hot, humid air surrounded me like a damp towel thrown over my head. The September woods were still lush and green on certain north-facing hillsides but sunburned and dry as kindling in other places. Both the thermometer and the calendar indicated that this was a summer day, but I had noticed a swamp maple glowing red in one of the wet ravines—a harbinger of autumn soon to come. A broad-winged hawk soared high above the treetops, crying its thin cry. The raptors had begun their southbound migration.

Stacey teased me about being a "compulsive noticer." I was like a cat, she said, easily distracted by every crawling bug and fluttering leaf. What could I do? It was who I was. And I thought it made me good at my job.

Five hours earlier, I'd been relaxing in bed beside her, feeling the cool sea air on my skin and listening to the rhythmic crashing of the waves. Now here I was in the sweltering mountains, trying to keep pace with a freak of nature. As much as I loved the forest, the appeal of mountain climbing for its own sake had always eluded me. I could understand why some people—especially those who lived in cities or suburbs—might feel the urge to hike the Appalachian Trail, but for someone who essentially lived in the Maine woods, as I did, there was no need to embark on a two-thousand-mile journey to commune with nature.

On the drive up, I'd kept picturing the dazed look in Stacey's eyes when she'd told me about hiking Vermont's Long Trail with her friends. I was more and more certain that she was withholding something from me about that experience. She'd mentioned meeting "creepy men" in the woods. God knows, there are plenty of them out here, I thought. My search partner among them.

When I had finally worked my way around the clump of boulders, I was surprised to find Nissen seated on a log, waiting for me. He had taken off his shirt, displaying a brown torso so venous and devoid of fat that it looked like a textbook illustration for the human circulatory system. There was a small crucifix tattooed in green ink between his pectoral muscles. And he was eating a banana that he had removed from the fanny pack he wore slung around his narrow hips.

"You hanging in there?" he asked with an expression that didn't seem overly concerned with my answer.

I nodded, unable to utter an actual sentence in reply. My lungs burned as if I'd inhaled smoke from a campfire. It annoyed me that I couldn't keep pace with a man old enough to have been my father.

Nissen had interesting hair: dark brown in color and cut in a style that fell somewhere between Moe of the Three Stooges and early Paul McCartney. His head was triangular in shape, narrowing to a stubbled chin. He had enormous brown eyes, like an arboreal creature that had evolved to see in the dark.

"I'm used to hiking alone, so sometimes I go too fast," he said.

"Wouldn't it have been easier to come up the AT rather than bushwhacking like this?" I reached for one of my water bottles and unscrewed the lid.

"Easier, yeah. But this shortcut is faster. Besides, I thought you'd prefer slabbing."

"Slabbing?"

"Going around the summit. There's a precipice near the top that's a bitch to climb."

I didn't appreciate the insinuation that I wasn't up to the challenge. "We should be looking for signs of Samantha and Missy rather than just racing to the top. Blowing our whistles, too."

He stuffed the remainder of the banana into his mouth and then carefully rolled up the peel and tucked it into his fanny pack. "Until we get a look at the logbook in the Chairback Gap lean-to, we won't even know if those girls made it this far. First order of business is narrowing down the PLS, right?"

The abbreviation stood for "point last seen." In the jargon of search-and-rescue, it indicated the place on a map where a missing person had last been positively identified. I hated to admit it, but Nissen was right about the futility of examining every rock and leaf for signs of the two college kids. The reason we'd been sent on this quick ascent up Chairback Mountain was to help refine the search area. Normally, we would have been part of a bigger group, but the officer in charge—Lt. John DeFord—had deployed teams to do quick checks, called "hasty searches," of the trail registers. Other squads were rushing to inspect the lean-tos at Logan Brook and Potaywadjo Spring, farther north, in hopes that Samantha and Missy might have left messages there.

Nissen sprang like a jack-in-the-box to his feet. He was probably no taller than five-seven. "Do you want to rest some more while I go ahead?"

"No, I'm good."

"I don't want to push you too hard."

I clenched and unclenched my fists. I couldn't tell if he resented being partnered with an inferior climber or if he was just an arrogant son of a bitch. Anyone who hikes two thousand miles alone isn't likely to be a people person.

When he turned around, I observed that his bare back was heavily scarred between the shoulder blades, the skin pink and welted, whereas the rest of his skin was brown. It was almost as if he'd suffered a bad burn in the distant past. Or maybe he had a tattoo removed, I thought.

I was about to remind him that the Warden Service was running this search, when the breeze brought the sound of a distant engine to my ears. Squinting into the sunshine, I caught sight of a small floatplane flying over the summit of Chairback Mountain. It was a private Cessna—not part of our Aviation Division—but I recognized the two canoe paddles lashed to the pontoon cross braces.

"You know who that is?" Nissen asked.

"A friend of mine," I said with a smile.

Stacey must have called her father after I'd left the beach house. I should have known the old pilot would have gassed up his plane the moment he heard two young women were missing in the wilderness. The thought of Charley Stevens joining the search filled me with new hope and gave my heart a much-needed jolt of adrenaline. I matched Nonstop Nissen step for step the rest of the way up the mountain.

3

The lean-to perched on a steep hillside in a notch between the summits of two mountains, Columbus and Chairback. Like most shelters along the Maine section of the Appalachian Trail, it had been built in the Adirondack style: three walls made of skinned cedar logs and the fourth open to the elements. A corrugated metal roof did a serviceable job of keeping out all but the worst wind-blown rain. A rake hung from a nail on the side, to be used to sweep up the campsite.

I stood with my hands on my hip bones, huffing deep breaths. My quads and hamstrings felt twitchy. The light shimmering through the canopy of leaves overhead gave everything a sickly green pallor, even the skin on my arms. Somewhere in the trembling treetops, a red-eyed vireo sang a broken series of notes, then fell silent.

Given the heat and the approaching thunderclouds, I'd expected we might find people at the shelter. It was peak season on the AT as thru-hikers pushed themselves to climb Mount Katahdin before Baxter State Park closed in mid-October. The lean-to slept six camp-ers, and there were bare, beaten patches of dirt in the forested area where others had pitched their tents over the summer. But there was no one to be seen.

Nissen crouched by the fire ring—a circle of scorched rocks near the structure's missing wall—and thrust his fingers into the mound of charcoal and ashes.

"Still wet." He showed me his blackened fingertips. "Someone doused a fire this morning."

"Why don't you check the privy," I said.

His scowl told me what he thought of my suggestion. "Let's have a look at the register before we start poking around the shit house."

I'd worked on many search-and-rescue operations, including those involving the Appalachian Mountain Club and Outward Bound, and without exception, I'd found the volunteers to be professional and obliging. I'd never encountered anyone with the self-importance of Nonstop Nissen. When we got back to the command post, I intended to talk with Lieutenant DeFord about him, but there was no point in getting into a pissing contest now.

He wiped his hands on his powerful thighs, leaving dark smudges, and rose from the ground. Our climb hadn't even winded him. He frog-jumped up inside the lean-to before I could take a step in his direction. I couldn't see what he was doing, but a moment later he stuck his head out of the shadows and said, "They were here."

"How do you know?"

"Because they signed the logbook."

I slipped the straps of my pack off my greasy shoulders. Then I unzipped the outer pocket, removed my point-and-shoot camera and my palm-size flashlight, and followed Nissen into the shelter. At the outer edge of the raised platform was a round log on which to sit while you laced up your boots. The wood had been worn smooth and shiny from hundreds of hikers resting their backsides on it. I sat down on the log and swung my legs around until I was facing the interior. Then I crawled forward to meet him. He handed me the trail register, a simple spiral-bound notebook. Up close, I got a whiff of his body odor; it wasn't musky like normal perspiration, but pungent, as if he'd recently gorged himself on onions.

It was cool and dark beneath the roof, and I couldn't understand how Nissen could read anything unless he had the eyes of a lemur. I switched on my SureFire and shone the beam onto the open page. There was an entry, written in purple ink, dated nine days earlier:

We have our own private shelter tonight. A full moon is shining almost as bright as the sun. We fall asleep serenaded by coyotes. They sound even closer than the last time.

The entry was signed "Naomi Walks" and "Baby Ruth," which, we'd been told, were the pseudonyms Samantha and Missy had adopted for their journey. The practice was widespread on the Appalachian Trail. Thru-hikers chose colorful trail names for themselves or were given them by other backpackers.

"'Serenaded by coyotes.'" Nissen's breath was as sour as his sweat.

"'They sound even closer than the last time,'" I recited.

"When was the last time?"

Not having seen the women's earlier log entries, I had no idea.

"I need to photograph this." I started to back out into the open air. "How about you check that latrine now."

"What am I supposed to look for? Used tampons?"

"Why don't you put up some posters while you're at it," I said.

I reached into my backpack and found a few copies of a flyer that Lieutenant DeFord had hurriedly printed out in the Warden Service's mobile command unit. Each search team had been ordered to tack them up at its assigned lean-to. It showed the photograph of Samantha and Missy taken beside the warning sign at the edge of the Hundred Mile Wilderness. The word MISSING was printed in big letters across the top, followed by a description of the two women—their ages, heights, and weights—with instructions for anyone with information to call the Maine State Police.

"Use this." I handed him the staple gun I kept in my truck to put up NO HUNTING signs. My fingers were all swollen from the hike up the mountain.

Nissen grunted but obeyed.

Back in Monson, a representative from the Appalachian Trail Conservancy had told us we would have intermittent cell service between Cloud Pond and Chairback Gap. But when I tried my phone, I had no coverage. I could only assume the approaching thunderstorm was interfering with the transmission. I'd hoped to contact the next team of searchers to the north.

Lieutenant DeFord had assigned another group to check the next lean-to on the trail, ten miles away on the steep approach up White-cap Mountain. If they discovered that the women had signed in at that shelter, we would keep shifting the search area deeper into the Hundred Mile Wilderness. If there was no record of their having arrived at the Carl A. Newhall shelter, then Chairback would become the point last seen, and we would concentrate our attention on the ten-mile stretch between the two campsites.

I sat on the log at the edge of the platform, taking pictures of the diary pages. We would want to talk with anyone who might have encountered Samantha and Missy in the past two weeks, and so we needed to match trail names with actual people. Some of the pseudonyms were really far-out:

> *The Incredible Hunk*
> *McDonut*
> *Sassy Frassy*
> *Dogmom*
> *Daddy Shortlegs*
> *Swedish Meatball*
> *Doughboi*
> *El Chupacabra*
> *Hetty-Mae*

Almost every search-and-rescue operation has a component that wardens don't emphasize to the friends and family of the missing persons—at least not at first. People don't just drop off the map because a compass breaks or they take a wrong turn down an unmarked trail. Sometimes they choose to vanish because they have broken laws or because they are on the run from dangerous situations, usually involving drugs and guns. Other times, they disappear because they've met the wrong person on the trail.

Samantha and Missy were wholesome-looking young women who had ventured into a place largely empty of other human beings: a wilderness where cell phones didn't work and you could scream all night without being heard. There wasn't a person involved in this search who didn't share the same dark fears about what might have happened to them.

While I'd been taking pictures, the sky had turned slate gray and the wind had stopped abruptly, as if someone had switched off a giant fan. The sudden stillness seemed eerie. Very often, you get these quiet moments before electrical storms. I wished I had thought to stuff a rain jacket into my pack. Nissen and I wouldn't leave this mountain without being drenched. Under normal circumstances, I would just have waited out the rain inside the shelter (better to hold tight than break a leg sliding down a muddy path), but time was of the essence, especially since we had already lost so much of it.

As I was putting my point-and-shoot back into its neoprene pouch, I realized Nissen should have returned by now. The privy was down the hill from the lean-to—out of sight and, more important, out of smell. But not that far.

"Nissen?"

I heaved the rucksack onto my shoulders again and made my way through the thigh-high underbrush toward the outhouse. A rumble of thunder sounded in the west and rolled across the forest treetops, a crashing wave of sound.

The privy was a shabby little wooden structure with a half-moon window and a sign nailed beneath it: LATCH DOOR WHEN LEAVING OR PORCUPINES WILL EAT THIS BUILDING. Whoever had made the sign had carved chomp marks in it as a playful joke. The door was closed, per instructions.

"Nissen?"

I took a peek inside and got a whiff that made my eyes water and my throat tighten. Someone had scrawled "Help! I'm out of mountain money!" on the back of the door. It was trail lingo for toilet paper. I backed away from the stinking structure and glanced back toward the lean-to. The situation was challenging enough without my having to chase down my search partner, too. I blew on the emergency whistle I was wearing on a lanyard around my neck and waited.

"Up here!" Nissen's voice came from somewhere south of the shelter.

I trudged up the hill, doing my best to avoid trampling the young firs and spruce trees pushing through the fallen needles. A raindrop landed with a splat on the bridge of my nose. A moment later came another clap of thunder, this one considerably closer to Chairback.

I met Nissen on the trail, hurrying north toward the lean-to. To my surprise, he had acquired two companions, a man and a woman. They were a middle-aged couple, both dressed in the traditional garb of older thru-hikers: floppy-brimmed hats, packable raincoats (black for him, purple for her), shorts that showed off their muscular legs, and dirty boots. The long, lumpy packs on their backs looked like they weighed a hundred pounds each.

"These folks came from Cloud Pond," said Nissen.

"What's going on, Warden?" the man asked, bracing himself on two trekking poles.

"We're looking for two missing hikers. They would have been heading north from Monson." I removed a copy of the MISSING poster from my back pocket. "Have you seen them?"

The man, who had a thin nose and thinner lips, studied the photograph. "I don't think so." He handed the paper to the woman.

"Naomi Walks and Baby Ruth," the woman said, reading the trail names aloud. She was a full head shorter than her partner and had black hair with a dramatic white streak in it that made me think of Cruella de Vil. "I remember reading their entries in some of the logbooks. They quoted the Bible a lot in their notes."

"We're atheists," the man explained.

"Agnostics," the woman said.

I took out my notebook and pen. "Can I get your names?"

"Rick and Connie Chalmers," she said. "We're from Sacramento."

The rain had picked up, and a gale-force wind had begun to blow.

"Are you thru-hikers?" I asked.

The husband nodded his head. "We did the Pacific Crest Trail three years ago and thought we'd come east."

"And you're sure you never met these women on the AT?"

"They seemed to be about a week ahead of us the whole time," said Connie. "Judging by the dates in the trail registers, I mean."

The temperature had dropped twenty degrees in the past five minutes. Cold gusts were bouncing around the tops of evergreens, shaking loose pine cones. Dead branches clattered onto the forest floor.

Rick Chalmers hunched his shoulders reflexively against the rain. "What do you think happened to them?"

"We don't know," I said. "They were supposed to call their parents from Abol Bridge three days ago."

"Oh, dear," said Connie.

"Warden, would you mind if we talked out of the rain?" Rick pointed with his aluminum walking stick at the shelter.

I glanced at my wristwatch and saw that it was six o'clock. We had another hour of daylight, not accounting for the premature darkness arriving with the storm. Even if we left Chairback Gap immediately, Nissen and I would still find ourselves negotiating a murky, rain-slick trail. Lightning flashed again over my shoulder. Involuntarily, I found myself counting the seconds before I heard thunder. I barely got to two. The explosion nearly knocked me off my feet.

"That sounds like a good idea."

The Chalmerses and I ducked our heads and made for the shelter, but Nissen took his time. The sudden plunge in temperature had left me shivering, as if I'd just taken a bath in ice water. He hadn't even bothered to put on his shirt. The rain seemed to bounce off his bare skin.

When we were all under the overhanging roof of the lean-to, Connie said, "We'd been hoping to make the bunkhouse before the storm arrived, but we were lucky to get this far."

I wiped the wet brim of my cap and shook the water from my hand. "What bunkhouse?"

"Hudson's Lodge," said Nissen. "It's a few miles north of here, along the old AT route."

"The *Companion* says they have a bunkhouse where you can stay for a dollar a night if you do work," said Rick.

Lieutenant DeFord hadn't mentioned the lodge in his briefing.

"It just opened last year," said Nissen with a sneer. "'In the Heart of the Hundred Mile Wilderness' is their marketing slogan."

I had to assume DeFord would have contacted the owners to see if Samantha and Missy had passed through during the previous two weeks. It was protocol to call all the local fishing guides, logging companies, and sporting camps—anyone with a business inside the search radius.

I showed the Chalmerses the logbook inside the shelter and asked if they knew any of the thru-hikers who had signed their trail names. Daddy Shortlegs and Swedish Meatball were a friendly older couple from the Midwest, they said. The others they knew only from their logbook entries.

"We're not the fastest ones out here." The man smiled at his wife.

"My trail name is Turtle," she said. "He's the Hare."

Rain fell in sheets off the lean-to roof. It felt like we were inside a cave behind a waterfall, looking through a diaphanous curtain of water. Out of the corner of my eye I saw Nissen squatting on his heels at the edge of the platform. He had his scarred back to us and was staring out at the tempest, as motionless as a gargoyle. Every now and then, a blue flash of lightning would light up the forest like a strobe, and the sky would crack open overhead. I tried to forget the fact that we were two thousand feet up and miles from the nearest road.

I left the Chalmerses a poster to show other hikers and told them to call the number listed if they encountered anyone who had seen Samantha and Missy. I was about to step down off the log at the edge of the shelter when Connie said to Nissen, "Have we met before?"

"No," he said, then leaped out into the pouring rain.

Connie turned to her husband. "Doesn't he look familiar?"

"I don't remember faces," Rick said.

I said good-bye to the Chalmerses and jumped down into the mud. I expected that I might have to whistle for Nissen again, but I found him standing to one side of the lean-to, out of the wind.

"You ready to head back to Monson?" he asked.

"Not yet," I said. "I want you to show me this bunkhouse."

"What for? The lieutenant would have called Hudson's Lodge already. The girls won't be there."

I started off into the cold drizzle without answering him.

4

The storm chased us down the mountain. Every few minutes, another blue flare went off, and a deafening shock wave rolled across the landscape. I could feel the reverberations in the walls of my heart.

The dusk had come early with the clouds, and the downpour had turned the path into a rushing streambed. It was like running blindfolded down a sluiceway. The beam of my headlamp bobbed along in front of me as I tried to keep my balance. I wasn't always successful. My pants were smeared with mud.

Half a mile down, we came upon a sugar maple that had been cleaved in two by a thunderbolt. The exposed heartwood looked like a black slash. Charred and broken branches lay scattered among the exposed roots and smoking leaves. When lightning strikes a tree, the electricity travels through the sap, and the superheated liquid explodes the living plant from within. If the previous weeks had been any drier, we might have found ourselves cut off from my truck by a newborn forest fire.

Nissen didn't bother with a flashlight. Those lantern eyes of his seemed to function perfectly well in the shadows. He moved by grabbing a sapling and then swinging his body forward until he could grasp another with his free hand. It felt like I was trying to keep pace with Tarzan of the Apes. Once again, I found myself outdistanced. I didn't know what he planned on doing when he reached the bottom, since I had the only set of keys.

I stopped in a sheltered crevice between two boulders and took a swig from my water bottle. I'd nearly drained both of the quart containers on my climb up Chairback. It felt strange to be soaked to the skin and yet so dehydrated at the same time. An hour earlier, I'd been on the verge of heat stroke; now I was goose-pimpled from the cold. Every warden has seen fatal cases of hypothermia in the middle of summer: swimmers who overestimate the warmth of a spring-fed pond, mountain climbers who wander into pouring rain above the tree line. All it takes is enough cold water to depress your body temperature ten degrees. There are so many ways a person can die in the woods.

Including murder.

Most of the thru-hikers I'd met on the AT had been great people, but I had a friend who worked as a ranger in Baxter State Park, at the trail's terminus, and he had told me about the increasing amount of drug use he was seeing in his campground. Pot and booze had been the traditional intoxicants of choice among the White Blazers (named for the color of the markers along the path). Hallucinogens, too, of course—the Appalachian Trail had long attracted hippies and the younger people who emulated them. But in recent years, crystal meth had started appearing in Maine, brought up in backpacks from the South, where it was epidemic in the hollows of the Great Smoky Mountains. "I've seen methamphetamine turn a normal guy into a werewolf," my ranger friend had told me one night over a crackling campfire: a horror story for twenty-first-century America.

Add to that the local creeps who lived within spitting distance of the trail—the poachers, predators, smack addicts, recluses, robbers, and Doomsday preppers—and it was a wonder there weren't more homicides.

But it wasn't my responsibility to compile a list of suspects for a crime that might not even have taken place. My only job was to gather information for Lieutenant DeFord and report back. With luck, Samantha and Missy had already stepped out of the woods, unharmed and embarrassed by all the fuss.

Then I remembered Stacey's warning. "I wouldn't bet on it," she'd said.

I stuffed my Nalgene bottle into the rucksack, readjusted the headlamp on the brim of my dripping cap, and set off in pursuit of Nissen. The legendary trail runner was also earning a place in my personal rogues' gallery.

I'd parked my patrol truck behind a stand of shrub willows at the edge of a clearing. Like any good warden, I prided myself on knowing how to hide a vehicle from prying eyes—an essential skill when your job involves sneaking up on poachers—but Nissen had had no trouble finding the truck again in the gloom. The wiry little man was sitting on the hood, swinging his legs like a bored kid in church. He'd finally put on a shirt: a blue-and-gold baseball jersey with the University of West Virginia mascot on the front. His alma mater, I assumed.

"Thanks for waiting," I said.

"You're welcome," he replied without a hint of sarcasm.

The temperature had begun to climb again now that the storm had passed through, and the mosquitoes were out enjoying the evening. I slapped at my neck but missed the insect feeding on me, then swatted at my arm and missed the next. The bugs seemed not to want to bite Nissen, despite the invitation of all that exposed skin.

I reached into my pocket for my cell phone.

"You won't get a signal here." Nissen slid off the truck. "There won't be anything until we get over to the lodge."

I needed to report what I'd found atop Chairback to Lieutenant DeFord. And I still hoped to connect with the team that had gone up Whitecap Mountain. I wanted to hear what they'd discovered at the next lean-to. After a minute of searching, the NO SERVICE message appeared again on the illuminated screen. I put the phone away and beeped open the truck.

Nissen climbed into the passenger seat and let in a squadron of mosquitoes before he closed the door. I tried every channel on the police radio, but all I heard was static. The heat coming off our wet bodies caused the windows to fog up instantly, and I had to run the blower to clear them. There was nothing to do but wait until the defogger did its job on the windshield.

"So what's the deal with this new lodge?" I asked.

"What do you mean?"

"I have the sense you don't approve of it."

Nissen had a disquieting habit of conversing without making eye contact. "They've got a chef there and bathrooms in most of the cabins. You can go stand-up paddleboarding and everything. It's *real* nice."

"So you don't like it because you're a purist?"

"Nothing is pure on the trail anymore," he said, "least of all the fabled Hundred Mile Wilderness. You're lucky you don't get hit by a logging truck crossing the KI Road these days. And Gulf Hagas has basically become just another tourist attraction. Someone should sell T-shirts."

Gulf Hagas (rhymes with Vegas) was a spectacular ravine nearby with hundred-foot slate cliffs and a series of stomach-dropping waterfalls carved by the West Branch of the Pleasant River. It was commonly, but inappropriately, nicknamed "the Grand Canyon of the East." I'd hiked the Rim Trail when I was a student at Colby College and had nearly slipped over the edge trying to impress my girlfriend with my foolhardy fearlessness.

"We're not going to find those girls holed up in the bunkhouse," Nissen said, "so why are we going over there? Who exactly are you looking for?"

"Any of the other names I found in the Chairback trail register."

The air inside the cab of the truck smelled worse than a locker room now, but the blowers had cleared a sliver at the base of the windshield. I shifted the transmission into reverse and backed carefully out of the bushes. My pickup was a brand-new black GMC Sierra, which I washed and waxed every weekend. It was inevitably going to get scratched and battered, but this was the first nice vehicle I had ever been assigned, and I intended to baby it as long as I could.

"So what's your story, Nissen?" I asked.

He cocked his head as if to shake water out of his ear. "What do you mean?"

"What do you do for work when you're not out searching for lost hikers?"

He paused, as if the answer was a state secret he was forbidden to disclose. "I'm an apiarist."

"You mean a beekeeper?"

"That's what the word means. I have a few bee yards with three hundred hives. I sell honey and beeswax, but the big money is in pollination services."

"And you make decent money doing that?" I asked.

"Probably more than you make."

"That wouldn't take much," I remarked, as if he hadn't intended the insult. Maybe the poor guy's autistic, I thought. I could never tell the difference between someone with Asperger's syndrome and a garden-variety misanthrope. I tried to be charitable.

"I have a booth at the Big E in Springfield, Massachusetts, next week. I usually clear ten grand there."

This was the nickname of the month-long Eastern States Exposition, the largest agricultural fair in New England. The Warden Service had a traveling display it set up there, featuring taxidermy mounts—deer heads, moose antlers, stuffed fish—confiscated from poachers; it was called the "Wall of Shame." Something like half a million people attended the Big E, I'd heard.

We rumbled down the narrow tote road in the dark. The truck shook back and forth as it traversed a path of stones bulging up from the weeds. I heard branches scraping the sides of my vehicle and rocks bouncing against the undercarriage. So much for babying my new truck.

"What did you do before you started keeping bees?" I asked.

"This and that," he said.

"Do you live in Monson?"

"No, Blanchard."

It was the next town to the south—even deeper in the boondocks. "Any family?" I asked.

"It's just me and my shadow. Hey, I like to keep my privacy, you know?"

I'm a curious person by nature, and sometimes I go too far asking questions. Normally, I would have apologized for the intrusion, but with Nissen, there seemed to be no point in making the gesture.

After a while, the logging trail dropped us onto the gravel thoroughfare Nissen had mentioned. The KI Road sliced across the Hundred Mile Wilderness from one side to the other. From the village of Brownville, it traveled west past the old foundry at Katahdin Iron Works (for which the road was named), then paralleled the rapids of Gulf Hagas before it climbed up and over the Longfellow Mountains, ending at last in Greenville, on the shores of Moosehead Lake. There were checkpoints at both ends maintained by the North Maine Woods Association, but the gatekeepers were essentially toll takers and did little to police the wild lands.

I rode the brake hard down a hill, watchful for deer and moose that might leap from the trees, and saw in my headlights the sudden reflection of parked vehicles in a lot up ahead, where the Appalachian Trail crossed the road. If we'd kept following the path instead of bushwhacking down the mountain, Nissen and I would have ended up here. I counted two GMC warden trucks, two Toyota pickups, one Ford Explorer SUV, and one Subaru BRAT. The vehicles belonged to the searchers who'd gone up Whitecap Mountain.

"Is this the ford across the Pleasant River?" I asked.

"On the other side is the Hermitage," Nissen said. I recognized the name. It was a historic stand of old-growth white pines, some hundreds of years old. "Then the trail follows Gulf Hagas Brook up the mountain. It's roughly nine point nine miles from Chairback Gap to the Newhall shelter."

I grinned. "Roughly nine point nine miles?"

But Nissen didn't get my joke.

As I pulled into the unlit parking lot, the door of one of the black GMCs opened and a short blond woman climbed out. I would have recognized Warden Danielle Tate from a mile away. Five-four, square-shouldered, and hands perpetually clenched into fists, as if to show the world she was ready for battle. She was just twenty-four and a recent graduate of the Advanced Warden Academy.

Dani Tate belonged to what I thought of as the new breed of Maine game wardens, who saw themselves as law-enforcement officers first and foremost. They tended to identify more with state troopers and county deputies than with the older wardens, who could remember a bygone era, the time before deer hunters were required to wear blaze orange and when logs were still being driven down the timber-clotted rivers each spring.

Because of my age, I was often lumped in with this younger crowd. The truth was, I'd always emulated the woods-wise veterans who had never graduated from college but could follow the path of a fleeing poacher across bare stone in the middle of the night. Charley Stevens had once described me as the "youngest old fart he'd ever met," and I'd taken it as a compliment.

Tate stared directly into the glare of my beams, as if daring me to run her down. She had gray eyes like pebbles from a streambed and a flat face that seemed plain except on the random occasions when she chose to display one of the most dazzling smiles I'd ever seen.

A rumor was going around—started no doubt by my former sergeant, Kathy Frost—that Dani Tate had a crush on me. I'd been mortified when I heard it, not because I didn't like her, but because I feared Stacey might become jealous, and I didn't want to give my girlfriend another excuse to hold me at arm's length. Tate seemed like a good person and potentially a great warden. (She'd memorized every chapter and paragraph of the Maine code of fish and wildlife laws the way some people do the Bible.) But in my opinion, she could have stood to lighten up a little.

I pulled alongside her and rolled down the window. "I didn't know you were part of this, Tate."

"Are you kidding? Where else would I be?" She peered past me. "Who's that with you?"

My passenger surprised me by thrusting his hand out. "Bob Nissen," he said.

"Nonstop Nissen?" Dani asked.

"The one and only. Pleased to meet you. What's your name?"

So Nissen was only a selective mute, depending upon the sex of the other person.

"Tate," Dani said. "What did you guys find up on Chairback?"

"The girls were there nine days ago," I said. "They left a diary entry in the logbook. I took a picture of it and the rest of the pages in the journal. I'm going to e-mail my photos to Lieutenant DeFord when I get a signal."

"I've been getting one intermittently at the top of the hill to the west. You might try up there."

With the engine off, I could hear the river. The ford was at a flat-water area below the churning plunge pools of Gulf Hagas and was often impassable. During periods of heavy rain, the Appalachian Mountain Club deployed a ranger to prevent hikers from wading to their deaths.

"Why did DeFord station you here?" I asked.

She exhaled hard, flaring her nostrils. "Communication. The lieutenant said he needed someone to drive out if there was a problem getting a cell signal."

It must have galled Tate to be left behind while the other wardens got to climb a dangerous mountain in the dark. The woman was the walking definition of *gung ho*.

"Did you hear from the team on Whitecap?"

"Yeah," she said. "I guess there's always a decent signal up above the tree line."

"What did they find?"

"Nothing in the logbooks. Samantha and Missy always left a

journal entry at every shelter where they spent the night. Sergeant Ouellette's team checked the lean-tos at Newhall and Sidney Tappan and came up dry. I doubt the next team is going to find anything at Logan Brook."

I felt the hairs on my arms rise. "That makes Chairback Gap the point last seen."

With this new information, we had succeeded at narrowing down the search area. Unfortunately, the valley between Chairback and Whitecap mountains spanned dozens of miles of cliffs and ravines. It also included the deepest river canyon in the state of Maine and a pathless track of old-growth pines.

Worse yet, this interval was bisected by a heavily traveled road, so it wasn't just thru-hikers whose names would need to be added to the list of potential suspects. It was anyone who might've driven down the KI Road in the past nine days. If you were a sexual predator studying the map of Maine, looking for the most advantageous place to abduct two unsuspecting women, you might very well choose this artery through the heart of the Hundred Mile Wilderness.

5

The thunderclouds had broken apart just as quickly as they'd formed, but there was a gauziness to the night sky that made the stars look fuzzy, as if I was viewing the constellations through a nylon mask.

"I thought I'd head over to Hudson's Lodge," I told Dani Tate.

"What for?"

"I'm curious about something."

Her expression hardened. "Shouldn't you be heading back?" she said, making no effort to hide her disapproval. "Besides, Lieutenant DeFord already talked with Caleb Maxwell. He's the manager at Hudson's. Some of his people are up on Whitecap with Sergeant Ouellette. Maxwell says Samantha and Missy never stopped at the bunkhouse."

"I want to talk to the other hikers," I explained. "Now that we know that Chairback was the PLS, it makes sense to ID the people who stayed at the shelter before they scatter. I have the list of trail names, and we're going to need to find out who these people are in real life."

As a rookie, I'd nearly been drummed out of the service for sticking my nose where it didn't belong. I still had a reputation for over-enthusiasm when it came to the investigative aspects of my job, but I was working hard to establish myself as a trustworthy officer. Frankly, though, I didn't care whether Danielle Tate liked my decisions or not.

Her reply surprised me. "That makes sense."

Maybe there's hope for her yet, I thought.

"I'm going to keep trying to raise DeFord. If you talk to him first, let him know what we found."

"Ten-four," she said. "You should be able to use the lodge's phone and computer if you don't get a signal on your cell. They've got a pretty high-tech setup at that place, from what I hear."

Nissen made a snorting sound to remind me what he thought of the new ecolodge.

"Thanks," I said.

"Hey, Bowditch." She took a step toward the truck.

"Yeah?"

She took a long time to answer. "Never mind."

I rolled up the window to keep out the bugs and regretted the decision instantly. I wondered when the last time was that Nissen had used antiperspirant—or soap, for that matter.

At the top of the hill above the ford, my phone began to buzz. I brought the pickup to a halt and checked the signal. There was a single bar of coverage—not enough bandwidth to call DeFord or send him photographs, but enough to release the backlog of messages that had piled up while I was climbing the mountain and which were now belatedly arriving.

Most of them I ignored, but at the bottom of the list of missed calls was Stacey's number. As usual, she had chosen not to leave a voice-mail message. I held up the lighted screen of my smartphone and tapped her number. For a moment, it seemed like I might be able to make a connection. But the satellite had passed on, and all I heard was the hollowness of a dropped call.

The drive to Hudson's was shorter than I'd expected; essentially, we circled the base of Chairback Mountain from east to west. Signs directed us to the lodge from the KI Road and then down a hill. The trees parted at the bottom, and we crossed a wet meadow that had been flooded by beavers. A swollen brook ran through a culvert beneath the road, the surface of the water shimmering like a tarnished mirror. Then we entered the forest again. As we descended another hill, ruts in the gravel gripped the tires of my truck and refused to let go until I gave the wheel a jerk. After a minute, we entered the well-manicured grounds of the lodge. I followed the signs to the manager's house, which was tucked into a grove of pines below the guest parking lot.

As we pulled up to the illuminated path, a black Lab came bounding out of the shadows. For a split second, I feared the dog might claw my truck, but there was a whistle from the house, and the animal slammed to a stop. A man emerged from the front door and stepped from flagstone to flagstone to avoid the puddles left by the rain. The first thing I noticed was that he was wearing bright red Croc sandals.

Nissen and I got out of the truck. I could smell a lake somewhere nearby and heard the sound of water running in ditches: the aftermath of the storm.

"Sorry about Reba," the man said. "She's the world's oldest puppy."

The Lab wagged its tail so hard its hindquarters shook.

"You've trained her well, though. I'm Mike Bowditch. Are you Caleb Maxwell?"

"The last time I checked."

He was long-limbed and carried himself with the looseness of a professional surfer. He had blond hair, parted in the center and pushed back behind his ears, and was wearing leather bracelets around both of his wrists and a braided necklace around his throat. He had on a flower-patterned shirt and a pair of jeans cut off below the knees like denim culottes.

"Do you know Bob Nissen?" I asked.

"Oh, I know Bob," Caleb Maxwell said with a cold smile. When he pivoted toward the halogen light, I could see wrinkles around his blue-green eyes, which made me think he was older than I'd first assumed. Early forties maybe. "He and I go way back. How's the book going?"

Nissen stared off into the trees without answering.

"Bob wasn't a fan of our building the lodge," Caleb said. "He let his feelings be known at some public meetings we had in front of the Land Use Regulation Commission, nearly torpedoed us. Before that, he and I were on the Moosehead SAR team together. Do you remember the lost snowboarder on Big Moose Mountain, Bob?"

"I remember," Nissen muttered.

"So what's going on with the search for those two girls?" Caleb asked. "I wanted to help out, but we've got a full house tonight, and I needed to stay on-site. I haven't heard from my crew since they left. I know Josh went with some wardens up Whitecap. And Addie was supposed to meet up with another team at the base of Chairback."

"That was us," I said. "We ended up going up the backside of the mountain to the shelter."

"That's a hellish path! I'm surprised you didn't break a leg."

"Will this Addie be all right?" I asked.

"She's a wilderness first responder. She probably hooked up with the others. So is there any news?"

Since we'd just met, I decided not to take Caleb Maxwell into my confidence. We seemed to share a similar opinion of Nissen, though, which suggested his instincts couldn't be all bad.

"I was hoping to talk to the thru-hikers you have staying here," I said. "Or anyone else who might have been up on Chairback recently."

He fiddled with the rope necklace around his throat. "The Cains from Hartford booked all eleven of our cabins for a family reunion. They just arrived yesterday, and they spent today out on the water before the thunderstorms hit, so I doubt they'll be of help."

"Paddleboarding?" Nissen asked.

"Yeah. Why?"

"Who's staying in the bunkhouse?" I asked.

"We've got eight thru-hikers tonight." Caleb kept his eyes on me rather than on Nissen. "I'll take you down there if you want."

"That would be great," I said.

"Reba, come!"

He led us along a damp and winding path that cut through the evergreens. Without my headlamp, I could barely make out Maxwell's broad shoulders in the darkness ahead of me, but he seemed not to need a light. The tangy, almost acidic smell of wood smoke hung in the air. Ahead, I could hear voices muffled behind walls.

We emerged from the trees into a grassy clearing that contained a single building. It was fashioned entirely of cedar logs that hadn't yet weathered. I could hear people talking and laughing inside the bunkhouse as we circled around to the front. There was a heap of wet backpacking gear piled outside the screen door.

Caleb rapped once with his knuckle on the frame and peered inside. "Is everyone decent?"

"Define *decent*," came a young woman's voice, followed by mostly male laughter.

As I stepped through the door, my nose was treated to an amazing bouquet of aromas: wood smoke from the stove, floral shampoo (or maybe soap), burned coffee, the steamy smell of drying sleeping bags, muddy boots that stank from within and without, bug repellent, the distinctly sweet odor of consumed alcohol being exhaled, and some sort of freeze-dried curry dish being heated on a propane camp stove.

I counted seven people at first glance, five men and two women, neither of whom was Samantha Boggs or Missy Montgomery. One of the guys, a bearded dude with a red bandana tied around his head, took one look at the gun at my side and threw up his dirty palms.

"I didn't do nothing!"

More laughter.

"Come on, people," said Caleb. "Warden Bowditch is here about those two missing women I told you about."

Instantly, the room went silent. The sensation I'd had of crashing a college party disappeared with a *poof*. They all knew how

43

serious the situation was. Two members of their community were in trouble.

I handed the poster of Samantha and Missy to a man seated in his boxer briefs on the nearest bunk. "Do any of you recognize them? Their trail names are Baby Ruth and Naomi Walks."

One woman, an attractive but disheveled strawberry blonde, raised her hand as if I were her college professor. "I've seen their names in the logbooks."

"Did you meet them?"

"No."

The piece of paper circulated. I watched each hiker study the photograph. Thousands of people hiked the AT each summer, and it was probably asking a lot to hope that this group had overlapped with Samantha and Missy. The two missing women had been days ahead of these hikers for most of the trek.

The poster came back to me, and I gave it to Caleb. "Can you post this for me in the lodge?"

"No problem."

Despite being almost as young as most of the people in the room—and younger than a couple of them—I felt uncomfortably old as I directed myself to the group again. "If you do come across these women, you need to call nine-one-one or contact the Appalachian Mountain Club. Did any of you spend the night at the Chairback Gap lean-to?"

"We did. Night before last." A tan young man with a patchy beard pointed at the strawberry blonde. "I'm El Chupacabra and she's Hetty-Mae. We came down here for a shower and a real meal."

"Are we in trouble?" asked the young woman.

"We're just trying to make sure we don't waste our time chasing down the wrong people. Can I see some identification, please?"

The man and the woman took out their wallets. They were made of hemp.

Caleb loomed over my shoulder. "Wait a minute. Where's Mc-Donut?"

I glanced up from photographing the couple's driver's licenses.

"He's taking a shower," someone said.

"Again?" said Caleb. "We practice water conservation here."

I recognized the trail name from the Chairback logbook. "Who's this McDonut?"

Maxwell rolled his eyes. "A kid from Massachusetts. He sprained his knee coming down Chairback and hobbled in with an Ace bandage wrapped around it. He's been in no hurry to leave. I think he likes it here too much."

"How long ago did he show up at the lodge?" I had a feeling I knew the answer.

"Eight days ago," Caleb said.

It was the day after Samantha's and Missy's last logbook entry.

6

Hudson's Lodge was an impressive building made of unweath-
ered logs, new cedar shingles, and lots of glass. Lemon light
streamed through the windows, attracting swirling clouds of moths
and caddis flies. Nissen and I followed Caleb Maxwell up a rough-
hewn series of steps—immense flagstones embedded in the earth—
to the double doors.

"He's got all the fucking lights on, too," Caleb said under his
breath.

I wiped the mud from my boots on a steel grate before stepping
inside the lodge. Nissen did not.

"This is quite a place," I said.

"It's a state-of-the-art green building," Maxwell said, as if it
were a rehearsed speech he gave to new guests. "You can't see them
in the dark, but there are solar panels on the roof. And all the toilets
are composting. The lodge is heated by groundwater from a six-
hundred-foot-deep well. We try to conserve as much energy and water
as possible, and we recycle everything we can." He paused in an
entry decorated with trail maps and informational posters. "Hey,
McDonut!"

"In here!"

The room to the left had several comfortable chairs, arranged
around a fieldstone fireplace and a Jøtul wood stove so hot the
air above it rippled with heat. Low coffee tables were littered with
magazines: *Orion, Backpacker, AMC Outdoors*. There was no wall

between the sitting area and the brightly lighted dining hall, where a wet-haired man was eating GORP from a glass container and reading one of the magazines he'd picked up in the lounge. He looked young, somewhere in his early twenties, and the bottom half of his face was covered with light brown scruff that was almost but not quite a beard. On the table beside him rested a sweat-stained and sun-faded sombrero.

"Do you remember what I told you about energy conservation, Chad?" Caleb said in his camp counselor tone.

The young man rose stiffly to his feet, and I saw that he had a blue brace on his right knee. He brushed the crumbs off a faded T-shirt with the slogan DON'T SMOKE (SHITTY) WEED. If he was a thru-hiker, he was one of the pudgiest I'd ever seen. The miles had done little to melt the fat from his stomach, chest, and back.

"Oh, shit, bro. I came up here to take a shower and lost track of time." His big head wobbled back and forth on his neck when he spoke, as if his neck muscles were weak. "Hey, I know you!"

I realized that he was looking past me at Nissen.

"You two know each other, too?" I said, wondering how I'd lived this long without hearing Nissen's name.

"Everyone on the trail knows who Nonstop is. The guy's like a living legend. Good to see you again, sir." He gave a military salute.

Nissen grunted and glared off in another direction.

"This is Warden Bowditch," said Caleb Maxwell.

I put on my Officer Friendly face and crossed the stone floor until I was standing across the table from the soft-bodied hiker. "Do you mind if I ask you a few questions?"

"Um, that depends, I guess. Am I in trouble? I didn't mean to leave the lights on."

"The light police is another department."

His openmouthed expression told me he didn't understand that I was joking. I indicated that he should sit down again. I settled into a chair opposite him. The dining room still smelled of roasted turkey.

"I'm hoping you can help me with some information," I said.

"Sure thing, bro." His blue eyes appeared glassy, and the blood vessels around the irises were engorged. Even having just showered, his body gave off the skunky aroma of marijuana.

"Let's start with your name."

The smile returned, bigger than before, and he tapped two fingers against the brim of the sombrero on the table. "They call me McDonut."

"He means your real name," said Caleb Maxwell.

"Oh!" the young man said. "It's McDonough. Chad McDonough."

I held out my palm to him. "Can I see some identification, Chad?"

He looked at my open hand, as if not quite grasping the request, then began fishing around in the many pockets of his cargo shorts until, after several false attempts, he located a battered wallet stuffed with receipts. He opened a flap and held out a driver's license, which gave his address as North Adams, Massachusetts. In the photograph, he was clean-shaven and his wavy brown hair was cut short in frat-boy style. His height was listed at five-eleven, his weight at 240 pounds. Was it possible to gain weight hiking the Appalachian Trail?

I set the license on the table and got out my point-and-shoot.

"Do you guys want some coffee?" Caleb asked.

"Thanks."

The lodge manager disappeared into the kitchen. A moment later, I heard the sound of water running from a tap into a pot.

McDonough watched me closely from across the table. "Is everything cool here, sir?"

"Caleb says you've been here eight nights. Where are you coming from?"

"Um, Monson."

"Are you a thru-hiker?"

"No, man, I'm a section hiker."

"That means he's doing the trail in pieces," Nissen offered from

49

across the room. He said this in the way someone might refer to a habitual drunk driver.

McDonough seemed oblivious to the other man's contempt.

"Easy does it, right? I'm not hard-core like that dude." He waggled a thumb in Nissen's direction, as if they were old friends. "So what's going on? Is there some sort of emergency?"

"We're looking for two missing hikers," I said. "They would also have been heading north from Monson." I removed the well-wrinkled copy of the MISSING poster from my pocket and unfolded it so he could have a look. "Have you seen them?"

He squinted at the piece of paper. "Oh shit."

"You recognize them?"

I could feel my heart swell with blood. Based on everything I'd learned so far, Chad McDonough might have been the last person to see the women alive.

"They never told me their real names." McDonough returned the flyer to me, grease-smudged from the GORP he'd been eating. "Did something happen to them?"

"Well, they're missing," said Nissen from behind me.

I removed my notebook from my pocket. "When was the last time you saw them?"

His bleary eyes drifted away from mine, and he raised a hand to count with his chubby fingers. "Nine—no, ten days ago."

"Where?"

"Back at Cloud Pond. We stayed together in the shelter there. Drank a little beer, talked about Georgia, where they're from. I was a lifeguard on Jekyll Island once. Best summer of my fucking life."

"Was anyone else with you at Cloud Pond?"

"There was another dude, but he slept in his tent outside. He came in after dark and was gone before we woke up."

I leaned my elbows on the lacquered tabletop. "Can you describe him for me, Chad?"

"Didn't really see him. He put up his tent beyond the edge of the firelight. Some people are just antisocial. You learn to respect their privacy. We're all out here for different reasons, you know?"

"Do you remember what color the tent was?"

"Red, I think." His tongue pushed between his lips, then slipped back out of sight. "Is he a suspect or something?"

I realized that I was getting ahead of myself. "Let's go back to the beginning. Where did you meet Samantha and Missy?"

"In Monson."

"At Shaw's?" It was a legendary boardinghouse frequented by thru-hikers.

"No, we couldn't get in because it was Saturday. We stayed at the other place, Ross's."

"Ross's Rooming House?"

"Yeah, we had dinner together. The girls were studying French because they were going to Africa—one of those countries where they speak French—to become missionaries after they summited Katahdin. I told them I wanted to practice my *français, s'il vous plaît*. I spent my junior year in Paris. They thought I was a pretty comical character, I guess."

"What do you mean?"

"I asked in French if they had any pets back home, because I miss my dog, Einstein, and it turns out *pet* is the French word for 'fart.'" He grinned. "Naomi almost fell out of her chair, she was laughing so hard."

"That must have been embarrassing."

"Hell, no, bro. Back in high school, I was voted class clown. It's my greatest achievement to date."

"So you set off the next morning into the Hundred Mile Wilderness? That was on Sunday, the seventh?"

"I don't know the date, but I remember it was Sunday because the girls wanted to know if there was a church in town. But we ended up cruising out to the trailhead together. We kept leap-frogging each other at first. They'd rest for a while, and I'd pass them. Then

I'd rest for a while, and they'd pass me. The last time I saw them was at Cloud Pond. I was hoping we'd end up in the same lean-to, and we did."

"They weren't into you, I take it."

McDonough leaned back so hard in his chair that it scraped across the pine floor. "I'm a gentleman. I don't kiss and tell."

I couldn't imagine two Christian women engaging in a ménage à trois with this oaf. "Tell me more about this man in the red tent."

He ran his hand through his wet hair, undoing the work he'd previously done with a comb. "He showed up after dark. It was hard to see anything beyond the firelight. He might have said hello to one of the girls—I think it was Naomi—and then he just crawled inside his tent."

I glanced up from my notes. "What do you mean he might have said hello to one of the girls?"

"She was out using the facilities. When she came back, she gave a pretend shiver, like he was a weirdo. You know, her eyes were wide."

"Did she seem frightened?"

"No, just like he was an odd individual. You meet a few out on the trail." His eyes darted over my shoulder. "Right, Nonstop?"

Nissen stood with his back to us still, arms crossed, silent as a statue.

"So the man in the tent didn't sign the Cloud Pond logbook?" I said.

"Not that I remember."

In all likelihood, it meant his name wasn't among the ones I'd found in the Chairback register, either.

"If you never got a good look at him, how did you know his tent was red?"

"I had to get up in the middle of the night to drain my vein. I had a few brews I bought at the store in Monson. I must've seen the color in my headlamp."

"And in the morning he was gone?"

"I had kind of a hangover, so I decided to sleep in."

"What about Samantha and Missy?"

"Naomi woke me as they were packing up, wanted to see how I was doing." Clownish circles appeared on his cheeks, as if the memory embarrassed him. "The truth is, I had to yack a couple of times. I think it was because I was so dehydrated. I decided to stay another night there."

"So you didn't run into them again?"

"No, they were a day ahead of me. I saw that they made it to Chairback Gap, because they wrote in the logbook. You should go up there and check it out."

Nissen startled me by speaking. "We just came from Chairback."

I flipped through the photographs I'd taken. When I came to the entry the women had left in the trail register, I passed the camera to McDonough. "Does this look like their handwriting?"

I saw his lips move, as if he needed to sound the words out. "Yeah," he said. "Huh. That's weird."

"What's weird?"

"That stuff about the coyotes. We heard them howling at Cloud Pond. Baby Ruth had read in a book that wolves sometimes attack women who are having their periods. I had to explain that coyotes weren't the same as wolves. Naomi said, 'If one of them gets too close, I'll Mace it in the face.' She had this pink canister of pepper spray. You don't think the coyotes followed the girls to Chairback?"

"No."

"Now you've got me scared to go back out there," McDonough said, "and I'm not even having my period."

"When *are* you leaving, Chad?" asked Caleb Maxwell. He'd returned with a pot of coffee and a pitcher of half-and-half. He poured a cup for me and offered one to Nissen, who just ignored him.

"Soon." McDonough lifted his braced knee to show us. "My leg still hurts."

I took a sip of coffee. "How did you injure it?"

McDonough shrugged. "Sprained it coming down Chairback.

Slipped and fell off one of those big wet rocks. Thought I'd torn my ACL at first, because it hurt like a motherfucker."

"Were you wasted? Is that why you fell?" Nissen asked.

"No, I wasn't wasted." The young man flicked his eyes at me in annoyance.

"What the fuck are you even doing out here, *McDonut*?" There was a sneer engraved on Nissen's face. "You don't belong on the trail."

"Relax, bro."

"Don't call me 'bro,' monkey mouth."

I held up my hand in a stop signal. "Knock it off, Nissen."

"Two girls are missing, and all he cares about is stuffing his hole and getting wasted."

"Did you just call me a monkey?"

"I called you a monkey mouth."

"Take it easy, Chad," said Caleb.

McDonough kicked over his chair as he rose to his feet. "Fuck you, old man. I don't give a shit who you are."

Nissen balled his right hand into a fist as he crossed the room in several quick strides. I reached out and grabbed his wrist; it was as hard as rawhide. The man might have been in his mid-fifties, but I wouldn't have wanted to get into a wrestling match with him.

"Calm down," I said. "Both of you."

"He insulted me!" The circles on McDonough's cheeks grew darker as they filled with blood.

I didn't let go of Nissen's arm until he had settled back on his heels.

"Finished?" I said.

"I don't feel like talking anymore," McDonough said, putting on his ridiculous sombrero. "I'm going to bed."

I pushed my chair away from the table and stood up. "So which way are you headed from here? In case I need to contact you again."

"Nobo."

Caleb translated. "He means northbound."

"It might take me a while," McDonough said, "but I'm going to make it to the top of Baxter Peak even with my bum knee."

"I appreciate your cooperation, Chad." I tried to sound friendlier than I felt.

"I hope you find those girls, sir," he said. "They're really cool chicks. Not your usual Bible-thumpers."

Giving Nissen one final glare, the fat young man stumped out of the dining hall.

After I'd heard the door slam, I said, "What the hell was that about?"

"Guys like him desecrate the trail," said Nissen. "They're an offense to everything the AT stands for."

"He's just a kid, Bob," Caleb said.

"And you can go to hell, too, Maxwell," Nissen said before he also stormed out into the night.

Caleb shook his head in disgust before raising the coffeepot at me. "You want another jolt?"

"Sure," I said. "This is turning into a long night."

Nissen had called Chad McDonough "monkey mouth." The only other person I'd ever heard use that expression was a convict at the Maine State Prison. The term is jailhouse slang for a person who yammers on about nothing. Just when I thought I was beginning to get a handle on Nissen, he slithered again from my grasp.

7

I asked Caleb if I could use the lodge's telephone to contact Lieutenant DeFord, and he led me through a sparkling metal kitchen to an office tucked behind the reservation desk. He turned on the computer in case I needed it, then left me alone. I seated myself in his mesh-backed office chair and dialed the number at the command post.

"DeFord."

"This is Bowditch. I'm at Hudson's Lodge. I haven't been able to get a decent signal before now."

"What did you find?"

"Samantha and Missy stayed at the Chairback Gap lean-to nine nights ago. They left an entry in the logbook. I've taken pictures of it and will send them to you now. I ran into Dani Tate at the ford across the West Branch of the Pleasant River, and she told me that the team that searched the next two shelters didn't find any evidence they'd been there."

"I just got a text from Tate. It's looking like Chairback Gap was the point last seen."

"There's something else, sir. I found a hiker who claims to have spent the night with them at Cloud Pond."

He took a moment to answer, probably counting back in his head. "When was this?"

"Ten days ago. His name is Chad McDonough. He's twenty-three, from North Adams, Massachusetts."

"What's he been doing since then?"

"Staying at Hudson's. Caleb Maxwell told me he came in with a sprained knee and has been hanging out here until it healed. McDonough's trail name is McDonut."

"How in the world did you locate this guy, Bowditch?"

I told him about the trail names I'd found in the Chairback logbook and how I'd come to the lodge hoping to ID some of the thru-hikers. Then I recounted my conversation with McDonough.

"What's your take on him?" the lieutenant asked.

"I'm not sure," I said. "He comes across as this guileless pothead, but I think he lied to me about a few things in his past. He has a temper, too. This whole McDonut persona might be an act."

"Send us his identification information, and we'll check him out. Do you still have Nissen with you?"

I fought the urge to ask why I'd been assigned the misanthrope. "Yes, sir."

"Head on back to Monson. Report in at the RV when you get here. I'm going to move the circus back up to Greenville tomorrow. It makes sense to be closer to the point last seen."

"I'll be there in an hour," I said.

"Drive safe. We had a fatal in Rockwood a couple of hours ago. The driver hydroplaned off the road, slammed into a tree. That's no way for anyone to go."

"I'll be careful."

"Get yourself a cup of coffee," he said. "Stay alert."

I didn't know DeFord well, never having served under him, but he struck me as a good lieutenant. He was on the young side for the job—early forties—but he projected a confidence that didn't feel phony and had received more decorations for heroism than any warden in the service. People talked about him as a future colonel, and I could easily envision him in the big chair. The current holder of that office, Timothy Malcomb, had taken over in an acting capacity while the commissioner conducted a search, and he had also made

it known he didn't want the position long-term. (Nor was he a favorite of Maine's hot-tempered governor.) Maybe DeFord had the
political instincts to survive in the capital snake pit. If he hoped to
rise to the colonel's office, he would need to find Samantha Boggs
and Missy Montgomery first—preferably alive. There had been a
time in my life when it would've shocked me to think that someone
might use a crisis to advance his career interests. I'd wised up a lot
since those days.

I removed the flash card from my camera and slid it into a port
in Caleb's computer. I opened my Web mail, typed a short message
to DeFord, and attached the photographs. Then I hit Send.

I hadn't felt this exhausted since the Criminal Justice Academy.
Boot camp had been only five years ago, but it seemed like another
lifetime. I was older, in any case.

Caleb Maxwell had one of the neatest desks I'd ever seen. There
was a careful stack of yellow and pink forms—receipts for food ship-
ments, etc.—in a wooden box beside the computer keyboard, and
he had taped the five-day weather forecast to the wall. The sole personal effect was a framed photograph that showed Caleb embracing
an athletic-looking woman with short brown hair and exception-
ally white teeth. The picture had been taken against a background
of blue sky and rolling green mountains. Both Caleb and the woman
looked healthy and happy, but there was something about the photograph that made me think it represented a sad memory.

It was late now, and wherever Stacey was, she was probably
asleep. I tried to convince myself she was still at the beach house,
lying in the bed we'd shared earlier. I imagined that the window was
open and the sea breeze was fluttering the curtain. But I knew she
hadn't stayed.

My first serious girlfriend, Sarah Harris, would have preferred
to be awakened, rather than not hearing from me. Most women
seemed to be that way. But not Stacey. Her frequent silences discour-
aged me from interrupting them. I wanted to believe that there was

no special significance behind her decision not to leave a voice-mail message earlier. She knew I would be in touch when I had something to report. It wasn't a lack of concern on her part.

I leaned back over the keyboard and opened the browser to my Web mail program again. Using two fingers, I typed an e-mail to her:

> Dear Stacey,
>
> I saw that you had called but decided not to wake you. No sign of the missing women yet. I found an entry in a trail logbook that proves they were at a shelter on Chairback Mountain 9 nights ago. But they seemed to have disappeared after that. I don't know what to think at this point, but I don't have a good feeling. My search partner is a jerk named "Nonstop" Nissen, who once held the record for the fastest thru-hike of the AT. I'm writing from a new ecolodge called Hudson's in the Hundred Mile Wilderness. I tracked a thru-hiker here named "McDonut," who seems to have had contact with Samantha & Missy. He's another piece of work.
>
> I saw your dad's plane earlier, and it lifted my spirits. I'm not sure how long I'll be up here. I'm hoping you're still at Popham. It would make me happy to think so, but I'll understand if you decided to leave. I wish I were there with you now.
>
> —Mike

I hit Send and sat there for five minutes, waiting for a reply that never came, before I gave up and shut down the computer.

I found Caleb Maxwell in the sitting room, warming his hands over the woodstove. His mind seemed elsewhere. He flinched when I spoke his name, as if he hadn't heard me walk up behind him.

"Thanks for your help," I said.

"Is there anything else I can do?"

"I'm sure Lieutenant DeFord will be in touch to let you know."

"The thought of those girls disappearing up on the mountain is pretty damned awful."

"Yeah."

"I always felt like I was making a difference back when I was on the search-and-rescue team," he said. "These days, I'm not so sure."

"What happened between you and Nissen?" I asked.

"I was just busting his balls. He seems to bring it out in me."

I knew what he meant. "What's this about Nissen writing a book?"

"It's called *Death on the Appalachian Trail,* and it's an encyclopedia of all the crazy ways people have kicked the bucket on the AT. You know—falls, hypothermia, drowning, murder."

Since Caleb was opening up, I thought I'd satisfy my curiosity. "You mentioned some incident with a snowboarder."

Caleb fell silent for a moment. When he spoke again, there was a quiver in his throat that hadn't been there before.

"A kid went off the trails at Big Moose Mountain. There was a pretty bad snowstorm that night. Our team was called in to help the wardens and the ski patrol. We thought the kid might be playing a prank—like he was really hiding somewhere. His friends said he always talked about those survival shows on TV. I guess I convinced myself it was a stunt he was pulling because he wanted attention. The next morning, we were doing a grid search of one of the glades on the back side of the mountain, using ski poles to poke down under the new snow. Nissen was the one who found his snowboard. He called us all over, and there was this boy's dead face peeking out from under the crust. His skin was sparkling. That's one of the things I'll never forget, the way it reminded me of diamonds."

A piece of burning wood snapped, popped, and sizzled in the stove.

"What was the other thing?" I asked.

"How happy Nissen seemed—like he'd just proven that he was the best searcher on the mountain. The fact that this poor kid's parents were back at the lodge didn't mean anything to him. He just kept grinning."

On the drive out, Nissen sat silently in the passenger seat. At one point, I thought he might have fallen asleep, but when I looked over, I saw his enormous eyes glowing green in the dashboard light.

We headed west on the KI Road, bound for the town of Greenville, which was the closest thing to civilization in this part of Maine. The road followed a deep notch cut into the bedrock by the Pleasant River. The thunderstorm had opened new potholes in the gravel, and muddy puddles exploded across my headlights, smearing the glass. I was probably going too fast, but I was in a hurry to be rid of my passenger and his foul stench. The static on my police radio began to fade as we crested the mountains. I turned up the volume, but there wasn't anything new.

About a mile from the North Maine Woods gatehouse, we came upon an animal sitting in the wet road. If I hadn't known better, I might have mistaken it for a wolf. Its fur was reddish brown, with a black streak down the back, and I could see the muscles ripple beneath the skin when it scratched one of its pointed ears. I knew that canids tend to be curious by nature—I'd had red foxes approach me in the woods, as tame as dogs—but I'd never encountered a coyote this brazen.

"Maybe it's rabid," I said.

"It doesn't look sick to me."

I honked my horn, but the animal remained seated on its haunches, staring straight at the truck with eyes that shone like lamp-lighted brass fixtures. I tried my blues, to no avail. Finally, I flung the door open and stepped out, resting my hand on the grip of my sidearm. Before I could take three steps, the wild dog gave a sudden leap and disappeared into the roadside bushes.

I returned to the pickup, remembering Samantha's and Missy's ominous note about coyotes. I could tell from Nissen's expression that the troubling thought had occurred to him, as well.

"That's a strange coincidence," I said.

"I don't believe in them anymore."

8

With the help of another cup of coffee I purchased at a late-night convenience store in Greenville, I managed to make it back to Monson without flattening my truck against a telephone pole.

The village of seven hundred people was surrounded by forest, except where the paved road went through, and had once been a busy way station for travelers headed to Moosehead Lake and Mount Kineo. Thoreau had passed through town in 1846 and made note of a pair of moose antlers, fastened to a post, that functioned as a road sign directing travelers north to Greenville and south to Blanchard. Later in the nineteenth century, a Welsh immigrant discovered black slate in the ground and made a fortune digging the first of what would become many quarries in the Monson woods. A chain of rectangular pits—some flooded, some not—followed the seam in a northeasterly direction from Lake Hebron into the forested highlands. Locals will proudly tell you that the gravestones of both John and Jacqueline Kennedy in Arlington Cemetery were carved out of Monson slate. But the mining industry, like so many others in Maine, had long been in decline.

The town's commercial hub now consisted of a lakeside post office, a general store that doubled as a gas station, a redemption center that paid out a nickel apiece for bottles and cans, and a surprisingly out-of-place Louisiana Cajun restaurant—all strung along a main street where few travelers bothered to stop, because what was there worth stopping for? Many of the downtown buildings had plywood over their windows or faded FOR SALE signs tacked to their doors. Two had been converted into competing places of worship, John the Baptist Missions and the Lake of the Woods Tabernacle, as if faith were the only growth industry left in town. The latter of these churches had one of those changeable letter signs on which the resident preacher had spelled out his message for the week: NO ONE WHO PRACTICES DECEIT SHALL DWELL IN MY HOUSE—PSALMS. The building was a clapboard fire trap, with an external staircase and a roof that looked primed for collapse. If it was indeed the Lord's house, I wondered who would choose to dwell in it.

The Warden Service had commandeered the Monson municipal building for the search. When I'd driven past the lopsided wooden structure earlier, I'd noticed that the clock above the firehouse doors was broken, the hands frozen at 11:55. It seemed like an unnecessary metaphor.

"Do you want me to drop you somewhere?" I asked Nissen.

"My van's parked in back."

I turned left off Route 15 and plunged down a hill to the field where DeFord had set up his temporary headquarters. The mobile command post was a streamlined black vehicle nicknamed "the RV," due to its resemblance to a Class C motor home (although no one would have mistaken it for your grandfather's Winnebago). A communications array bristled from the roof, and inside, state-of-the-art computers ran GPS mapping software to assist search-and-rescue missions.

When we'd left, the lot had been jammed with all sorts of emergency vehicles: warden trucks, state police cruisers, patrol cars bearing the insignia of the Piscataquis County Sheriff's Department, a lone ambulance just in case. Most of them had scattered for the night, leaving tire marks in the flattened grass. But a few remained.

DeFord had also sent most of the volunteers home after dark; it was standard procedure in these operations. A few diehards had pitched their tents at the edge of the woods; others slept on air mattresses in their truck beds or in the backs of their Subaru wagons. The Salvation Army wagon still had its door open, light and steam spilling out into the darkness, so the cook could serve hot coffee and beef stew to the night shift.

I parked my patrol truck in a vacant spot, turned off the engine, and let out a deep breath I hadn't realized I'd been holding. Without a word of thanks, Nissen hopped out and walked away. Just when I thought the man couldn't be any ruder, he found a new level. I watched him zigzag through the parked trucks and cars to a white Woodstock-era VW camper van. A giant honeybee was painted on the side, along with the name of his business—Breakneck Ridge Apiary.

"You're welcome," I said aloud.

My sore legs had stiffened from sitting in the truck for an hour. The ground was swampy from the thunderstorm and squished beneath my boots. I rapped on the side door of the mobile command post. Then the door opened, and I found myself looking up at Sergeant Kathy Frost.

"Speak of the devil," she said.

Kathy had been my field training officer and was still my best friend in the Warden Service. She was in her fifties and had bobbed hair the color of butterscotch and a spray of freckles on her nose and cheeks. Instead of wearing a regulation uniform, she was dressed tonight in flannel and denim.

Five months earlier, she had been shot by a sniper outside her farmhouse in Appleton and had lingered in a coma for days, fighting for her life. She'd lost her spleen during surgery and probably pieces of other organs. The last time we'd spoken, she had still been on forced convalescent leave. The purple rings around her eyes told me she was far from healed.

"What are you doing here?" I asked, practically stuttering out the words.

She gave me a wink. "I'm in charge of the K-9 team, remember?"

"There's no way they've let you return to duty."

"Come in already. You're letting in all the bugs."

I had so many questions for her, but there were half a dozen officers seated around the gray plastic table in the center of the RV. It was the wrong moment for us to catch up.

The confined space glowed with computer screens and smelled of fresh-brewed coffee. A projector threw a topographical map against one of the beige walls, showing the Appalachian Trail between Chairback Gap and Whitecap Mountain. Icons indicated the locations of the lean-tos, and a dotted line traced the meandering trail.

Lieutenant DeFord turned from a conversation he was having with a state police detective and glanced up at me from his chair. He had a boyishly handsome face, dark blond hair cut close to the scalp, and a physique that verified the stories of his having almost made the Olympic biathlon team but for an ACL tear.

"Bowditch," he said. "Glad you made it back in one piece."

"We had a little rain up on Chairback, sir."

"There was lightning popping everywhere down here. I wondered whether you and Nissen would even be able to get off the mountain tonight."

"Nissen doesn't seem easily fazed."

A few subtle smiles from the assembled officers told me that Nissen's reputation preceded him.

"The same could be said for you." DeFord indicated a chair at the table. "Do you know everyone here?"

There were four other wardens, including Kathy, all of whom I knew, plus the state trooper, a detective sergeant, who was dressed in a blue T-shirt and blue tactical pants tucked into black boots, and whose name, I was told, was Brian Fitzpatrick. Another man—lean, black-haired, wearing a dress shirt and tie, suit pants, and shiny shoes—sat quietly in the corner. The lieutenant passed over him without introduction.

DeFord fetched a bottle of Poland Spring water from the refrigerator for me. "So, we've been going over the photos you sent. Why don't you fill in the details for us."

It took me fifteen minutes to describe what I'd found at the shelter and recount the conversation I'd had with Chad McDonough. Midway through my monologue, one of the overhead fluorescents began to flicker, throwing a jumpy light on the assembled faces. Both Fitzpatrick and the warden investigator assigned to the case—an affable gray-haired guy named Wesley Pinkham—interrupted me frequently.

"What was your take on McDonough's state of mind?" Sergeant Fitzpatrick asked. He worked out of the Maine Information and Analysis Center. "You said he seemed stoned?"

"He had a strong odor of marijuana on him."

Fitzpatrick crushed a piece of hard candy between his molars. "Did you search him for drugs?"

"I thought it was more important that I establish trust. When he told me he'd hiked with Samantha and Missy, I wanted to learn everything I could from him."

"That was the right move," said Wes Pinkham.

Except for the handgun and badge on his belt, Pinkham looked nothing like a game warden and everything like the branch manager of a savings and loan. He had thinning hair held in place with pomade, a stomach that overflowed his belted chinos, and aviator glasses that had last been in vogue—well, I wasn't sure how long ago, but not since before I was born. I could imagine that his average Joe appearance (Little League umpire, president of the Lions Club) might have helped when he went undercover to purchase illegal cuts of deer meat from poachers.

The lieutenant asked Wes Pinkham to bring up on the computer projector the photo I'd taken of Chad McDonough's driver's license. We studied the magnified image on the wall. McDonut seemed so clean-cut in his Massachusetts DMV photograph.

"Did you believe that he was telling the truth about the girls?" Sergeant Fitzpatrick asked.

The detective had a reddish gray buzz cut that looked like it would become curly if he ever grew it out. His complexion was pale, but there was a rosy blush on his cheeks that suggested he might've enjoyed a nightly nip—or had before he found the program. He had an accent that sounded as if he'd grown up in South Boston.

I wasn't sure what Fitzpatrick wanted to hear. I glanced at Kathy, seated beside me. She winked again, as if telling me to trust my instincts.

"I think he might have been lying about some things," I said, "but not about Samantha and Missy. The kid definitely has an edge to him, but he didn't strike me as dangerous."

"We ran a background check on McDonough," Fitzpatrick announced, "and he was suspended from UMass after being accused of sexual assault."

I had the sense that he'd been waiting to ambush me with that information. I became aware of the black-haired man watching me with the intensity of a predator. His eyes were so black, they seemed to be all pupil.

"Was he convicted?" I asked.

"Criminal charges were never brought," said Fitzpatrick. "The girl was intoxicated herself and didn't have a complete memory of the night. The DA couldn't proceed with the case, but the school decided McDonough should take a year off, until she graduated."

"If he was involved with Samantha's and Missy's disappearance," I said, "I have no idea why he would hang out on the trail. Why wouldn't he have gotten the hell out of there?"

The mysterious black-haired man in the corner spoke for the first time. "Did it occur to you that he might've been making up this 'man in the red tent' to divert attention from himself?"

"It occurred to me, yes."

"Do you want to bring him in for an interview?" DeFord asked Pinkham. "At this point, we still don't have evidence of a crime, so we can't call him a material witness."

"Tell him his help will be invaluable in finding the two girls," the warden investigator said. "Make him feel like everyone is depending on him."

"We're going to need to track down all the other names on the list Bowditch gave us," said Sergeant Fitzpatrick.

Kathy tilted back in her chair. "Personally, I'd start with the Incredible Hunk."

"You think he sounds like a suspicious character, do you?" Pinkham asked with a sly grin.

"I just want to see if the man lives up to his name."

Everyone smiled except Fitzpatrick and the man in the corner, whose name I still didn't know. Despite her ill health, Kathy was making a brave effort to participate. I couldn't help worrying that she might be pushing herself too hard. Her skin was the color of parchment.

A BlackBerry vibrated on the table. The lieutenant picked it up. "DeFord."

The rest of the room fell silent while he had his conversation.

I leaned my head close to Kathy and whispered, "You should be home in bed, getting your strength back."

"Now you're the one giving lectures?"

DeFord ended his call and put the phone back on the table.

"Samantha's and Missy's parents are on their way up here from Georgia," he said. "They're flying into Greenville tomorrow morning on a private plane. The commissioner wants us to meet them at the airstrip."

I didn't envy the lieutenant. Searches were difficult enough to manage without having powerful people second-guessing every decision.

"Do you want me to call Deb Davies?" asked Kathy.

"I think you'd better," said DeFord.

The Reverend Davies was one of the Warden Service's two chaplains. Whenever we got word that an Alzheimer's patient had wandered off into a blizzard, or a canoe had overturned on a lake and the paddlers were missing, or a snowmobile had crashed into a tree and the driver had been found lifeless, his limbs bent in impossible directions—whenever death, in other words, had become more than just a possibility—she would be summoned.

Samantha and Missy might yet turn up alive, but someone would need to stand vigil with the waiting, worrying parents, and it made sense for it to be a minister. I was just relieved it wouldn't be me. My prayers so rarely came true.

9

Lieutenant DeFord took me aside and rested a hand on my shoulder. It felt as heavy as lead.

"You look exhausted, Mike. We've booked rooms at Ross's. Go get yourself a good night's sleep, and we'll see you back here in the morning."

It was the same boardinghouse where Samantha Boggs, Missy Montgomery, and Chad McDonough had spent their last night in Monson. All I knew about the place was that it catered to thru-hikers this time of year. As long as the beds were free of bugs, I'd happily accept whatever was offered.

"Hope you don't mind having a bunk mate," said Kathy with a shit-eating grin I didn't understand. I'd lived in a dormitory at the Maine Criminal Justice Academy and shared cabin bunkhouses with wardens over the years. I had no expectations of privacy in my job.

She followed me out into the humid night, closing the door of the RV quickly behind her to keep the bugs out. There was a bright halogen spotlight on the back of the fire station, but otherwise the parking area was pitch-black except for the glowing tents set up by the searchers along the perimeter of the lot. In the dark I couldn't read her expressions at all.

"What was that about?" I asked.

"What?"

"The comment about the bunk mate."

"Oh, you'll see."

I decided to let the matter slide. Whatever her private joke was, she could tease me about it in the morning. A mosquito landed on the meaty part of my hand, but I squished it before it bit me.

"I don't think it's a good idea for you to be here," I said. "You should be at home recovering."

"There are two young women out there who seem to be lost," she said, but she was unable to disguise her weariness. "I'm pretty good at finding people. And DeFord could use my help."

I couldn't deny that the search would benefit from her expertise. Kathy had headed up the Warden Service's K-9 team almost since its inception; for years she'd tracked down missing persons with her coonhound, Pluto, and schooled other wardens in the mysteries of dog handling. But Pluto had died earlier that spring, shot by the same psycho who'd wounded Kathy, and she hadn't yet adopted a puppy to train. Kathy claimed she was waiting until she had returned to full health, since teaching a young dog to follow a human scent across all kinds of terrain is physically demanding, but secretly I suspected she was still mourning the loss of her longtime companion.

"So the lieutenant has you supervising the K-9 teams?" I asked.

Kathy slapped at a mosquito on her neck. "I'm coordinating with Maine Search and Rescue Dogs, too."

She was referring to a volunteer group of experienced handlers whose personal pets had been trained as rescue dogs, taught to sniff out living people who might be trapped or injured, and cadaver dogs, whose gory job was tracking the scent of corpses, including those buried under six feet of dirt or submerged at the bottom of a lake. The mention of the search-and-rescue organization made me remember a question I'd been meaning to ask someone all night.

"Any idea why DeFord partnered me with Nissen?" My eyes were beginning to adjust to the dark.

"He's the fastest hiker here. I'm surprised your aging legs were able to keep up with him. The man's a freak of nature."

"Or just a freak."

Her mouth curled on one side in either a smirk or a grimace.

"You're wondering what his story is," she said. "The guy's an ex-con. He did ten years in prison down south for cooking meth. The folks at Moosehead Search and Rescue tell me he found salvation in the slammer. As soon as they let him out, he took off up the AT like the devil was hot on his trail. I guess he's quite the Bible-thumper now."

I summoned an image of Nissen. His scarred shoulder blades came into focus. "He used to have a tattoo on his back."

"I've never seen the man without a shirt, and I never want to."

"He must have had the tat removed—and not by a plastic surgeon." I had to keep shifting my weight to keep my hamstrings from tightening up. "I'm surprised they let a felon join Moosehead Search and Rescue."

"*You* of all people don't believe in second chances?"

"The guy just creeps me out. Caleb Maxwell told me Nissen's writing a book about the ways people have died on the AT. The two of them seem to have sort of a history."

"Caleb has a lot of history—most of it sad." She scratched her forearm where another bug had bitten her. "I'm getting eaten alive out here. Can we pick this up tomorrow?"

"One more thing," I said. "Who was that guy with a tie in the corner?"

"Special Agent Genoways with the FBI. He doesn't say much."

"Why is the FBI interested in missing hikers?"

Kathy grinned from ear to ear. "You and your curiosity! Enjoy your stay at Ross's, Grasshopper."

That was her pet name for me when I was her young pupil. "Where are you sleeping?"

"The Indian Hill Motel in Greenville. One of the perks of being a sergeant is that I get a private room. Tell your bunk mate I said hi!"

When a search operation is under way in a remote location, the Warden Service stashes searchers wherever it can—in fleabag motels, bed-and-breakfasts, the homes of other wardens, wherever. I parked on the wet lawn outside Ross's Rooming House, grabbed the duffel bag from the backseat, and jumped out of the truck with all the grace of the Tin Woodman after a rainstorm. My joints might actually have creaked.

The inn wasn't a single building, but three: the original white clapboard structure, a newer annex sided with white vinyl, and a separate two-story bunkhouse so ungainly, I had to assume the carpenters had been drunk when they'd raised its roof.

I made my way to the front door of the old inn and, taking note of the sign posted beside it—OUR DOOR IS ALWAYS OPEN—dragged myself inside. Hiking boots were piled in pairs in the big entryway, and raincoats and ponchos hung from hooks along the walls. I did my best to scrape the mud from the bottoms of my boots, then passed through the dimly lit foyer into a spacious front room. Mismatched furniture had been tossed carelessly about the place. In one corner, a woman with long gray braids was snoring in a recliner, an open book (by Barbara Kingsolver) on her lap. Otherwise no one was about, including at the front desk. But I found a piece of paper with my name on it, as well as instructions to make myself at home. Breakfast, it said, would be served at seven. That was past the hour DeFord expected me back at the command post, so I'd likely be eating oatmeal from the Salvation Army chuck wagon. There didn't seem to be a room key.

Nor was there a map to direct me through the rat maze of hallways to my room. I couldn't imagine who my bunk mate could be. Knowing Kathy's wicked sense of humor, I had to expect the worst. Christ, I thought, what if it's Danielle Tate? Was Kathy perverse enough to force Dani and me to share the same twin bedroom? My gut knew the answer to that question. I hesitated before turning the doorknob.

The room was dark, but a shaft of light from the hall showed two beds. One was neatly made. The other contained a half-naked old man. He had a prominent chin, a formidable nose, and a full head of stiff white hair. He seemed to have been asleep but had snapped fully awake when he'd heard the door. Now he turned on the table lamp and squinted up at me.

"Well, aren't you the most mournful-looking object of pity."

"Charley?"

"Who were you expecting?" Stacey's father said. "Queequeg the Cannibal?"

Charley Stevens had grown up around lumber camps. To hear him speak in that thick Maine accent, using lingo he'd picked up from illiterate trappers and Québécois lumberjacks, you might have concluded that he had never cracked a book in his life. But over the years of our friendship, I had learned how deceptively intelligent he was, and I had come to suspect that the old autodidact was better read than some of my English professors from Colby.

"I didn't know you were staying here," I said.

"Figured it didn't make much sense to fly all the way home just to turn around again at first light."

Charley and his wife, Ora, lived a hundred-odd miles to the east, in a lakeside camp, near the village of Grand Lake Stream. Stacey still lived in a guest cottage on their property, ostensibly saving up to build her own house. Given her graduate school debt and how little she made as an assistant wildlife biologist, it was going to take a while.

Charley was wearing a sleeveless T-shirt that showed off his Popeye forearms and the scars he'd gotten as a POW in North Vietnam. He grinned and held out one of his big paws. I tried not to wince when we shook hands. The skinny geezer had a grip like a bench vise.

"Good to see you, young feller."

"Same here." I slung my rucksack on the floor and sat down on the rock-hard bed. The box springs might have bounced half an inch at most. "I take it your daughter called you."

"Stacey thought you might need a little help. She's wicked worried about those two girls."

"Did you talk to her tonight?" I asked.

"Not since I took off. Why?"

"She tried calling me, but I was out in the boonies. When I had a signal again, I figured it was too late to call her back, so I e-mailed her instead."

The old pilot chuckled. "You don't know much about the female sex, do you?"

Charley Stevens had been one of my first mentors: someone who'd believed in me as a warden and a man when I'd done nothing but shown bad judgment. In just four years, he had taught me more about the woods than I could have learned on my own in three lifetimes. He and his wife were, in just about every meaningful way, the parents I'd always wished I had, which made my new relationship with their daughter both fitting and awkward.

I put my head in my hands. "So you mean I should have woken her?"

"All women, in my experience, appreciate hearing that their men haven't fallen off a cliff."

"Should I call her now?"

"I'm not sure if you should be asking your sweetheart's dad for romantic advice," he said with a chuckle. "And I definitely shouldn't be giving it to you. So what's the latest on the search?"

"Samantha and Missy signed into the logbook at Chairback Gap, but there's no trace of them after that. It looks like they disappeared in the valley between Gulf Hagas and the Katahdin Iron Works."

"The KI Road runs through that stretch," he said. "Those girls could have hitched a ride out."

"That's what I'm afraid of."

Charley had a craggy face that spoke of a long life of outdoor adventure. He was the only person I knew who tugged on his chin while he contemplated a problem. "Searching that section of the trail is going to be the devil's own job."

"Do you want me to fill you in on my meeting with DeFord?"

"I'd rather you took a shower," he said. "If we're going to be bed-fellows for the night, I'd prefer you didn't skunk up the place."

And with that, he turned off the light.

I O

When I opened my eyes, the window shade was a pale rectangle in a wall of black. I listened for the sound of Charley's breathing but heard only distant noises elsewhere in the building—footsteps, vague creaks, the sound of water running through pipes. I tried to make out the time on my wristwatch, but the luminous numbers had lost their glow. After a minute, I ventured to turn on the lamp. Charley and his trapper's pack were gone. Somehow he had managed to make the bed without waking me. The sheets were as tight as those on an army cot.

I saw that it was just after five o'clock. My joints were so stiff, I had a hard time bending my knees. My forearm was itching, and I realized it was from the horsefly bite I'd gotten the previous morning at Popham Beach. The memory of the cottage seemed clouded already. I put on the clean uniform pants I had brought with me and then went into the hall bathroom to shave. The porcelain sink had an orange rust stain under the tap and an ancient mirror, cracked and flecked from age. I did my best to avoid glancing into the toilet bowl. It didn't pay to look too closely at anything in this hikers' hostel.

I found Charley in the dining room, sitting across a long table from an old man, drinking coffee.

"Good morning!" said Charley.

"G'morning."

"This is Ross. He's the proprietor of this establishment." He pointed at me as if I were surrounded by people and needed to be picked out. "Ross, this is the young warden I was telling you about."

Mr. Ross wore steel-rimmed glasses, sported a neatly trimmed mustache, and had the sleeves of a crisp white shirt rolled up to his elbows. He looked more like a barber than the owner of an inn for free-spirited adventurers. His rugged features suggested he had once been as handsome as a matinee idol—some women would have said he still was.

"You must be starved," he said, rising to his feet. "How many, and how do you like them?"

In my sleepy state, it took me a moment to realize he was referring to eggs or possibly pancakes. "Just some coffee, please."

Mr. Ross appeared heartbroken.

"You should eat something," Charley said. "The food's a helluva lot better than those store-boughten doughnuts you're going to get back at the fire station."

I noticed that my friend had a yolk-streaked plate in front of him.

"I guess I'd have some of whatever you're making, if it's not too much trouble," I said.

Ross laughed and disappeared into the kitchen.

I poured myself a mug of coffee from the carafe and sat down in one of the mismatched chairs across from Charley. "Are we the first ones up?"

"So far, but Ross said that most of the thru-hikers are early risers. They're all eager to get back on the trail. They've been hearing about the Hundred Mile Wilderness for months. Ross had twenty-one people staying here last night, including a couple of other wardens. I don't know how he and Steffi manage this place, just the two of them."

I rubbed my eyes and took a sip of the strong, hot coffee. "I was out cold last night."

"Has anyone ever told you you snore like a bear?"

"Did I keep you up?"

"My mind was active anyway," he said. "I was preoccupied with those two girls. Ross told me they spent the night here before they set off into the wilderness. He said that the young men were all eager to make their acquaintance."

"I met one of those young men at Hudson's Lodge last night."

"I've been waiting for you to be conscious enough for conversation," Charley said.

While Ross clattered about in the kitchen, I told him about everything I'd discovered at the lean-to and the lodge, as well as the information I'd learned about Chad McDonough's sexual assault charge.

"I feel like I should have brought him back with me," I said.

"It doesn't sound like he would have come willingly," Charley said. "It's too early in the search to assume someone attacked those girls. The first order of business is to keep looking for them until we know for a fact that they're beyond help."

Ross returned with a leaning tower of pancakes.

"I can't eat all this," I said.

"I'm used to cooking for hikers," he said. "The rule of thumb around here is that you figure what a normal person would eat and at least triple it."

Charley kicked the leg of the chair beside me so it slid out from the table. "Have a seat, Ross! Tell Mike here what you told me about Samantha and Missy."

The old man glanced toward the kitchen door. "I should be getting the bacon started. It's going to be chaos here in half an hour."

"Just for a minute," Charley said.

Ross sat down on the edge of the chair, his long legs knocking the bottom of the table. "I only served them meals, and I'm usually too busy for small talk," he said. "Steffi was the one who checked them in. I remember that they were from Georgia and very polite. You don't often see two young women thru-hiking the AT alone. People think it's not safe, and maybe they're right. All I know is that ninety-nine percent of the hikers who come through our doors are good human beings—better than most you meet in the world.

Something about the trail seems to weed out the bad ones. I can't explain it."

The condiments were bunched together on a lazy Susan in the center of the table. I grabbed a glass jar of what I thought was maple syrup, only to discover it was dark, rich-looking honey. The name on the label was Breakneck Ridge Apiary: Nissen's brand.

"Have you ever hiked the AT?" I asked.

"Me?" Ross flashed his handsome grin. "Heck no. Where would I find the time? Besides, I'm too old now, although we had a thru-hiker in here last year who was seventy and fit as a fiddle. All I know about the trail is what I hear from my guests—and Steffi."

"That's right," Charley said. "Steffi hiked the AT herself, didn't she?"

"It's how she ended up in Monson. She stayed here a couple of years ago when Carol—my first wife—was sick." He removed his glasses and wiped the lenses on his sleeve before returning them to his nose. "She came back later, when she heard I was alone and thinking of closing the place. Offered to help out. That was how Steffi fell into my life. I said her trail name should have been Trail Magic, because she bewitched me."

"What do you remember about this McDonut feller?" Charley asked.

Ross raised his eyes to the ceiling in thought and then nodded. "The one with the sombrero."

"That's him," I said between bites.

"He was quite the character! Before dinner, he dumped everything out of his pack and went into town. He came back from the general store with a case of Budweiser inside. I remember him handing out cans of beer like Santa Claus on Christmas and everyone laughing and clapping."

"Did the girls drink any?" Charley asked.

"They did. I remember everyone making a big deal about it because the girls had never tasted alcohol before they started hiking the trail."

"Did this McDonut seem especially fixated on them?"

"Not that I noticed, but I was pretty busy that night. Steffi says I'm oblivious."

Charley tilted his head at me. "Mike, maybe you can show Ross the names you got out of the trail register and see if he remembers any of them."

In my early years as a game warden, I'd often gotten myself into trouble by meddling in matters that were none of my concern. It was an impulse I was trying my best to curb. My career finally seemed to be on the right track, and I didn't want to risk derailing it again.

"Maybe we should leave those questions for the investigators," I said. "I'm sure Pinkham will want to talk with Mr. and Mrs. Ross himself."

The old pilot frowned at me. "What happened to your curiosity?"

Three bearded young hikers entered the dining room and Ross sprang into action. "Good morning!" he said to the trio. "How many, and how do you like them?"

Charley was scowling again.

"What?" I asked.

"I'm not sure I like the new you."

"You mean the one who's not always on the verge of being fired?"

Charley appraised me for an uncomfortably long span of time.

During his tenure in the Warden Service, my friend had acquired the reputation of being a maverick. He'd been an excellent officer in every other respect, but he seemed to delight in pushing boundaries whenever he ran up against them. It was one of the reasons he'd taken a liking to me when we'd first met. Charley had never possessed my insatiable appetite for self-destruction, but he enjoyed taking risks, and I think he saw me as a kindred spirit.

But that was more than three years ago, and I was no longer that reckless kid.

"What?" I said again.

"We should be getting over to the command post."

He got up and bused his dirty dishes, leaving me alone to finish my impossible breakfast. I got out my phone and checked my e-mail to see if there was a message from Stacey. She tended to be an early riser. I was troubled that there was no word from her.

II

Charley and I gathered our packs and said good-bye to Ross in the kitchen. It was a hot, airless room with a dishwasher, two stoves, three refrigerators, and five freezers wedged into it. The smell of frying bacon hung in the air, and Ross was already sweating over a cast-iron pan the size of a trash can lid.

"Steffi will be sad she missed you," he told Charley. "You know how it is, though. I'm the morning shift, and she's the evening shift."

"Give her a hug for me, Ross."

"Just a hug?"

"Anything more and she'd slap me."

We were greeted with birdsong when we stepped outside—the rapid whistles of robins. The sun hadn't yet cleared the hills in the east, but the sky above the lake was streaked with pink and gold, and there wasn't a breath of wind to stir the leaves of the maples. The lake, visible between the sleeping houses, was as flat and blue as stained glass. We walked across the lawn to my truck and climbed inside.

I watched the fuel gauge rise when I started the engine and thought ahead to the many miles I was likely to travel that day. "I should get some gas if the station is open."

Charley made no response. He rolled down the window and hung his arm out. It irked me that he disapproved of my wanting to follow protocol. The old fart was just sulking because I didn't want to be his partner in mischief anymore. Stacey was the same way: not happy unless she was misbehaving.

He put on the dark sunglasses he wore in the air. He'd told me once that he didn't like polarized lenses because they interfered with his ability to see the displays on his control panel. The Serengetis had been an expensive Christmas present from me.

I hadn't asked him where he'd tied up his plane for the night, but as we drove toward Main Street, I caught sight of the Cessna floating beside a dock across the lake.

"Whose dock is that?"

"Someone who owes me a favor."

We passed the run-down Lake of the Woods Tabernacle. The resident pastor must have been an early bird himself, because he had changed the sign in front of the dilapidated building to read PRAY FOR THE LOST. The choice of words unnerved me: *lost*, not *missing*. The implication was of souls gone astray.

The general store at the edge of the downtown area was open and already busier than I would have expected at such an early hour. An orange electric company truck was parked beside a blue Ford shuttle bus, and there were vehicles at all but two of the six gas pumps. A sign on the cinder-block wall announced that hunters could register their kills inside at the tagging station. My guess was that this little convenience store was the most profitable business in an otherwise-unprofitable town.

I pulled up to a pump and turned to Charley. "You want anything inside?"

"See if they have any Beemans."

This chewing gum was favored by pilots of the Chuck Yeager generation. Our private joke was that Charley always asked me to get some, but no stores carried it anymore.

I smiled at him, and he smiled back. Whatever disappointment he'd felt in me was gone. We were friends again.

A battered red Toyota 4Runner pulled up to the pump opposite us while I was filling my tank. It was one of the boxy older models, customized with aftermarket tires for mud running and equipped with a row of spotlights across the cab, perfect for jacklighting deer. The quintessential poacher's truck. A rack of deer antlers was mounted to the grille, as if to hammer home the point.

The driver had a shaved skull and a reddish blond beard. He stared defiantly at me through the window and gave the idling engine one last rev to show me what he thought of my badge. Law-abiding people have a knee-jerk request for law-enforcement officers, but criminals—men and women who have been in and out of jail—learn the limits of our authority and don't worry about being arrested, since it's such a routine occurrence in their lives. I met jokers like him nearly every day in the field.

He hopped out of the elevated cab, giving me a better look at him. He wasn't tall, but he was burly. His skin seemed almost abnormally pale for someone who looked like he spent most of his life outdoors; his head was as white as a goose egg. He wore oil-smeared jeans, a red flannel shirt, and a fleece-necked denim jacket, too hot for this humid weather. A sheathed hunting knife hung from his belt.

"How's it going, Officer?" he asked in a voice that sounded like a bulldog speaking.

I squeezed the handle of the gas pump harder. "Good."

He grinned and, in the process, revealed that one of his canine teeth was missing. "You guys must be up here looking for those two girls."

"That's right," I said with as much friendliness as I could muster. "I don't suppose you know anything about them."

"Just what came over the radio." Felons living in the backwoods always owned a police scanner. "If I didn't know better, I'd say there was a game warden convention in town."

The passenger door swung open and a boy jumped to the ground. I hadn't noticed him before. He had the flattened facial features and upward-slanting eyes of someone born with Down syndrome, which made it hard to guess his age. His skin had a pink tint, and his hair was as fine as rusty threads of corn silk. He wore a Monson souvenir T-shirt and jeans patched with different color fabric at the knees.

"I want to pump," the boy said.

The driver kept his eyes locked on mine. "Get back in the truck, Toby!"

"Gram said I could."

The boy named Toby tugged on the man's sleeve. I couldn't begin to guess the relationship between the two, but they didn't seem like father and son.

The bearded man tore his gaze free. "You'll just spill it again."

"Gram said I could pump."

"OK, Dummy."

Inside my truck, Charley had removed his sunglasses and was watching the driver with a hawklike intensity.

The gas handle jerked in my clenched fist, telling me the tank was full. I shoved the nozzle back inside the pump. The credit card function was broken; a note said I needed to pay inside.

When I stepped through the door, I was hit in the face by a blast of air-conditioned air. The checkout counter was a narrow space between lottery ticket displays, novelty lighters, and shots of high-caffeine energy drinks. A tall man peered out from beneath the overhead cigarette rack. He had iron gray bangs, deeply set eyes, and a rhinestone stud in his ear. He was wearing a blue uniform that didn't fit him. His nameplate said BENTON. He glanced at me silently while nibbling his fingernails.

Two linemen in orange coveralls were gabbing beside the coffee dispensers. They saw my uniform and the gun at my side, and both of them nodded, the way certain men do when they encounter a police officer. I slid a two-liter bottle of water out of the curved shelf in the cooler.

When I returned to the checkout, I found that the old woman who had been making egg sandwiches behind the deli counter was now standing beside the door, looking out through the plastic window. She wore the same shapeless blue uniform as the tall man behind the register. A measuring tape ran along the door frame so that the clerk could estimate a robber's height as he ran outside. It told me that the old woman was exactly five-eight. Her attention seemed to be riveted by something in the parking lot.

"Oh, God!" she said suddenly, putting a plastic-gloved hand to her mouth.

I tried to peek past the deli lady's head. "What's going on?"

"Don't, Trevor!" she shouted through the door.

The bottle of water dropped from my hand and rolled across the linoleum. I had to push the old woman aside to get through the door. Outside, head-spinning gasoline fumes floated in the morning air.

Charley Stevens had the much younger, much heavier man— whose name, evidently, was Trevor—pinned face-first to the asphalt. He was kneeling on the redneck's spinal column, twisting his right arm around his back. Trevor bucked and kicked his legs, but he couldn't dislodge the wiry old pilot.

"Get off me, you old fucker!"

"Now, are you going to settle down?" Charley said calmly. "Or do I have to break your arm?"

"Fuck you!"

Before I could unholster my pepper spray, the boy, Toby, rushed at Charley, trying to pull him loose. I leaped forward and got the kid in a bear hug. He came free with almost no effort on my part. His body felt as soft as a loaf of Wonder bread.

"What's going on?" I said to Charley.

"The boy spilled gas on the ground, and Hay Face started hitting him."

"Fuck you!" Trevor said from the pavement.

"You shouldn't talk that way in front of a child," Charley said. "Now, are you going to settle down or not?"

"Yes!"

"You won't take a swing at me again?"

"No!"

"You're not a very convincing liar. Does the warden have to hand-cuff you, or are you going to take it down a notch?"

"No! I mean yes!"

With a surprising nimbleness for someone his age, Charley Stevens sprang away from the straw-bearded man. Trevor twisted himself into a sitting position and ejected a brown stream of spittle.

"You made me swallow my chew!"

I decided to risk setting the boy free. Toby just collapsed to the pavement, sobbing. I reached for the capsicum canister on my belt. "Put your hands in the air, Trevor."

One side of his head was dented with pebbles, and his beard was powdered with sand. He coughed up more tobacco spit. "Fuck you."

"It's all right, son," said Charley. "I think this feller has learned his lesson. He knows it's too nice a day to spend in jail."

"But he assaulted you," I said.

The old pilot scratched the side of his head and gave me a sheepish look. "It was more the other way around."

I heard a man behind me let out a howl of laughter.

"Do you think this is funny?" Trevor shouted. Angry purple blotches had appeared all over his pale head.

I followed his line of vision and saw that everyone who had been inside the store had spilled out to watch the fight.

"It ain't funny at all, Trevor," the deli lady said. Her voice was parched-sounding. She had the sunken eyes and cracked lips of someone whose vices have aged them beyond their years. Her name-plate said PEARLENE. "Apologize, Benton!"

"Sorry," the tall clerk said, unable to suppress a smile.

She scowled and turned again to the straw-bearded man. "Are you OK? Do you need a Band-Aid?"

"No!"

Trevor pushed himself to his feet. He staggered until he had re-gained his balance. He swept the sand off his jacket and pants with violent motions of his big hands.

"You sure you don't want me to arrest him?" I asked Charley.

"I don't think that'll be necessary. Will it?"

Trevor pointed his index finger at my friend, not needing to speak the words to make his threat known. Then he clambered back into the 4Runner. I had a momentary fear he might try to run Charley down, but instead he began revving the engine over and over. He spun the tires until black smoke billowed from beneath them, jerked his foot off the brake, and peeled out. The Toyota bounced over a curb and swung around until it pointed south. We could hear it a long time after it had disappeared down the road.

The air stank of burned rubber.

"I don't believe Hay Face paid for his gas," my friend said.

I shook my head in disbelief. "How in the world did you manage to take him down? He was half your age."

"Half as slow, you mean."

"I had no idea you were a master of the martial arts, Charley."

"In my day we called it 'Indian wrestling,' " he said.

The old woman came up and slapped my shoulder, hard enough to hurt. "You assholes!"

I stepped away from her attack. "What?"

"They're going to burn down my store!"

"Who is?"

"The Dows!" she said. "You can't just beat up Trevor Dow and think nothing's going to happen. That family is crazy. They don't care if you two are wardens. They don't care about anything. They're going to come back here after dark and burn down my store!"

Out of the corner of my eye I saw a human shape arise from behind the gas pump.

"Trevor? Trevor?"

In the confusion, no one had noticed that Trevor Dow had left the boy behind.

12

Inside the store, Charley and I watched as a kneeling Pearlene wiped Toby Dow's cheeks with a paper napkin. His sneakers, I noticed, were the kind that fastened with Velcro instead of laces.

"There, there," she croaked. "It's going to be OK, honey. Your uncle didn't mean to leave you behind like that. He'll be back here as soon as he realizes you're not in the truck."

Charley and I exchanged glances; we weren't so certain.

Pearlene massaged Toby's small pink hand. "Would you like a Milky Way bar?"

The boy lifted his head. "Snickers?"

She settled back on her heels. "Whatever you want, honey. Benton, can you fetch me a Snickers bar?"

"I've got it," I said.

I walked down the aisle, past a display of moose key chains, beeswax candles, and Monson T-shirts, to the candy. I grabbed a handful of large Snickers bars from the box and returned to the checkout counter. Toby all but snatched the chocolate bars from my hand.

"Those are on me."

"Thanks," said Pearlene, but her tone wasn't exactly full of gratitude.

We all waited for the boy to eat the first candy bar, everyone except Charley, who was studying a bulletin board filled with notices offering livestock for sale, announcements of upcoming bean suppers, and shuttle services for hikers who needed a ride to the trailhead.

Someone had already posted the MISSING poster with the photograph of Samantha and Missy.

Pearlene wiped the smeared chocolate from the boy's lips. "Do you want to go sit on your bucket, honey?"

Toby Dow nodded his head vigorously.

"Come on, then." She led him by the hand through the front door.

I stepped over to Charley and lowered my voice so that I wouldn't be heard by the checkout clerk. "Do you know anything about these Dows?"

"It sounds like they're the resident bullies."

The heavy door swung open, and Pearlene came back inside. She wrapped her bony arms around herself and gave a shiver. "Benton, turn down that air conditioning!" She reached for the packet of Virginia Slims in her breast pocket, then stopped herself. "It seems like a person should be able to smoke inside their own goddamned establishment."

"Trevor Dow has no reason to burn down your store, ma'am," I said.

Charley sighed through his big nose. "I did embarrass him pretty badly."

"That's right!" said Pearlene. "You're exactly right. You're an old man—no offense—and you made Trevor look like a wimp. He's not going to let that go. He knows the story's going to get around Monson. He needs to show this town what a badass he is."

I lifted my cap and scratched the back of my head. "Do you want us to talk to the Piscataquis County sheriff about the Dows?"

"It wouldn't do any good," she said. "Maybe if I pay them off in free beer, they'll leave this place alone."

A prematurely old-looking man set a six-pack of Pabst Blue Ribbon on the counter. It wasn't even eight o'clock, and already he was buying beer. If you stake out most convenience stores in Maine, you'll find the morning rush includes a fair number of alcoholics.

I stared at Charley. "This is the place where Chad McDonough bought his case of Budweiser."

"I expect it is."

"Do you think Samantha and Missy came here, too?"

Charley shrugged.

I glanced at my wristwatch and realized that the altercation with Trevor Dow had caused us to run late for DeFord's morning briefing. I handed my credit card to the tall man behind the counter and paid for the gasoline, the bottle of water I'd dropped on the floor, and the candy bars I'd bought for Toby.

"Can you give me a receipt?" I asked Benton. The Warden Service reimbursed my gasoline purchases.

"Printer's broken," he mumbled.

"That figures." I could have sworn I'd heard it spitting out tape earlier.

After the refrigerated climate inside the store, the heat of the parking lot felt subtropical. As I reached for my keys, I spotted Toby Dow by the side of the building. He was sitting on an overturned five-gallon bucket on which someone had scrawled the words *Mayor of Monson* with a permanent marker, and he was pretending to talk on a cracked cell phone.

I went over to him. "Who are you talking to?"

He stared at me with eyes as shiny as new pennies. "Tom Brady."

"Say hello for me."

He pressed the oversized phone to his cheek again. "Yeah? OK? Uh-huh."

"I'm sorry if I hurt you, Toby. I didn't mean to if I did."

He lowered the broken phone and held out his soft palm. "Pay the toll, please."

"What?"

"Pay the toll, please."

I thrust my hand into my pants pockets and found a quarter. When I laid the coin in the boy's hand, he shook his head. I got my wallet out and found a wrinkled dollar.

"Always heard the taxes around here were steep," Charley said after I'd climbed behind the wheel again. He put on the expensive sunglasses I had given him.

The parking lot behind the fire station was so packed with cars and trucks that we had to leave my pickup on the street.

I'd been afraid that we were going to miss some sort of public address by the lieutenant, but people were still milling about in groups. The game wardens in green, the state troopers in blue, the sheriff's deputies in brown. The volunteers were a motley crew—men and women of all ages—dressed in hiking gear. A few wore blaze orange or reflective yellow vests. The decals and bumper stickers on their vehicles announced their affiliations: Moosehead Search and Rescue, Wilderness Rescue Team, Maine Search and Rescue Dogs. There was even a horse trailer from the Maine Mounted Search and Rescue unit parked at the far end, where the horses wouldn't be spooked by the constant opening and shutting of metal doors.

It all made for a clubby atmosphere, as if we were all gathered for a friendly sporting event instead of a desperate mission to find two lost women. I saw Kathy Frost kneeling down beside a German shepherd, scratching its nape while she spoke with a smile to the dog's warden handler.

In the light of day, my former sergeant didn't look much healthier than she had the night before. Her skin was sallow, almost waxy-looking, but her hair didn't seem so limp. And I still found it strange to see her dressed in hiking clothes at a search instead of in her sergeant's uniform.

"What happened?" she asked. "Did you oversleep?"

"Charley got into a fistfight outside the gas station."

"A what?"

"Tell her, Charley."

Somehow, I'd already managed to lose my friend. As I scanned the crowd, I saw Nissen talking with Dani Tate.

"I don't know where he disappeared to," I said.

"I need to get moving anyway," said Kathy. "We're sending a K-9 team up to Chairback Gap to see if we can pick up Samantha's and Missy's ground scent. Another is going to cross the Pleasant River and go through the Hermitage. Maybe we'll get lucky." She took a hesitant step toward an idling patrol truck. "Oh, yeah. DeFord is looking for you."

"He is?"

"It's about your friend McDonut."

Whatever it was couldn't be good. Suddenly, the pancakes I'd eaten for breakfast felt very heavy in my stomach.

I felt a tap on my shoulder, and turning, I found myself face-to-face with a grinning Charley Stevens. "You'll never guess what I found."

"Surprise," said Stacey.

I couldn't see her eyes behind her oversized iridescent sunglasses, but her mischievous smile made me cough out a laugh. She had tied her long hair in a ponytail, and she was wearing a gray T-shirt with the insignia of the Maine Department of Inland Fisheries and Wildlife, olive drab cargo pants, and hiking boots. A camouflage backpack hung from her shoulders.

I wrapped my arms around her. "What are you doing here?"

"I heard you needed volunteers."

Stacey had participated in other search-and-rescue missions. She was a pilot and a wilderness first responder. I shouldn't have been startled to see her. I pressed my face to her ear and got a loose strand of hair in my mouth. Her body felt warm from standing in the sun.

"I was worried when you didn't answer my e-mail," I said.

"*You* were worried about me? You're the most accident-prone person I've ever met, Bowditch. Tell me again how many bones you have broken?"

"I lost count after ten." I tightened my grip around her waist. "I'm just glad to see you."

She patted my back to let me know that I needed to release her. I blushed when I saw Kathy's and Charley's amused expressions.

"You two go right ahead," Kathy said. "Just pretend we're not here."

She shook Charley's and Stacey's hands before she left. She moved with an unmistakable gingerness. It took me a moment to focus my thoughts again.

"Lieutenant DeFord is looking for me," I said. "Can you wait here?"

"That depends on whether my old man is going to let me fly his plane today."

Charley's hair was white and bristly in the sunshine. "Sounds like too many pilots in the cockpit to me."

"I'll be right back," I said.

I wove my way through the crowd, heading for the mobile command post. As I passed a row of warden trucks, I heard a woman call my name. It was Danielle Tate. The young warden had eluded Nissen and his awkward advances. Her black boots were shining as if she'd gotten up early to polish them, and she was as full of energy and enthusiasm as ever. She wore mirrored sunglasses, which showed me a haggard face I didn't want to believe was mine.

"What's this I'm hearing about coyotes?" Like just about every employee of the Maine Department of Inland Fisheries and Wildlife, she pronounced the word in the western fashion: *ki-yotes*. "Nonstop Nissen told me the girls were being stalked by them."

And I'd thought he couldn't do anything more to piss me off. "They wrote in their last diary entry that they'd heard coyotes outside the lean-to. They never said anything about being stalked."

"Nissen said the coyotes followed them from Cloud Pond to Chairback Gap." Dani Tate tended to speak in an artificially gruff voice, probably as a way to project authority that wouldn't be afforded an officer of her gender and height.

"That's just hearsay, based on what a hiker told us at Hudson's Lodge."

"So you don't think there's anything to it?"

"Absolutely not," I said.

"Crazy rumors always fly around during times like this," Tate said, as if she were a seasoned veteran and not a twenty-four-year-old rookie. "The other one is that there's a serial killer on the AT and the feds have been covering it up."

In my mind I saw the stony face of the FBI agent who had watched DeFord debrief me inside the mobile command post the night before.

"Covering it up how?"

"Saying the deaths were accidents instead of homicides. Not admitting there's a pattern. What do you think about that?"

"I think that serial killers are what we have today instead of wolves," I said. "Monsters lurking in the woods."

"That doesn't mean they don't exist."

"Have you seen DeFord? I've heard he's been looking for me."

"He's inside the RV. Some of us are headed up to Baxter State Park to coordinate with the rangers and interview thru-hikers. But it doesn't sound like you're going with us."

"Where am I going?"

"Back to Hudson's, I heard." She shifted her weight from side to side and pursed her lips. "So, I saw that Stacey Stevens is here."

"That's right."

I waited for her to say more, but she walked away.

So the lieutenant wanted to bring in Chad McDonough after all. But why send me back to the lodge? Why not send a state trooper? It wasn't as if I had established a great rapport with this McDonut.

I knocked on the metal door of the mobile command post and waited, my stomach turning flip-flops. Lieutenant DeFord himself opened the door. He stepped down, forcing me backward.

"There you are, Bowditch. I'm on my way home. I need to take a shower before I meet the plane with the girls' parents in Greenville. Come walk with me."

"Yes, sir."

We started toward his unmarked patrol truck.

DeFord's chin was stubbled, and there were bags under his eyes that hadn't been there last night. I wondered if he'd slept at all. "How was your room?" he asked.

"I was tired enough, it didn't matter where I slept."

"That's good." His mind seemed to be elsewhere.

"I ran into Danielle Tate. She mentioned that you wanted me to go back to Hudson's."

The lieutenant stopped to avoid a state police cruiser passing through the lot. "I need you to track down Chad McDonough."

"He's not at the lodge?"

"Caleb Maxwell said he took off before dawn. He almost slipped out of there without being seen, but he ran into a woman coming back from the showers. McDonough told her he was getting an early start because he wanted to see Gulf Hagas before he hit the trail again. Maxwell didn't realize he'd left until breakfast. McDonough must have known that leaving in the dark would seem suspicious."

I thought back to my conversation with the pudgy section hiker. "I'm not sure he has that level of self-awareness."

"You said he was complaining about his sprained knee still hurting?"

"That's right."

"Well, he left his splint under his bed, so it must have healed overnight."

I knew I should have pressed the kid harder. He'd struck me as a harmless fabulist—those outlandish stories about Jekyll Island and his junior year in Paris—but I should have been more skeptical. I realized now why DeFord was assigning me the task of hunting McDonough down. He wanted the experience to be a lesson to me.

We'd reached the lieutenant's truck. "He's driving a Kia Soul with Mass vanity plates. MDONUT, of course. Ross says he didn't leave the car at the rooming house, and the state police didn't find it at the trailhead outside town. He didn't tell you where he parked it, I suppose?"

Unlike Samantha and Missy, who had been been hiking since

March, Chad McDonough was doing a single leg of the Appalachian Trail, meaning he had to coordinate transportation getting to and from the Hundred Mile Wilderness. "I assumed he'd left his car in Monson," I said. "Maybe he parked it at Abol Bridge, then had a shuttle pick him up and drop him off at the trailhead."

"I'll have Fitzpatrick send a trooper across the Golden Road to take a look," DeFord said.

"What should I do when I find him?" I asked.

"Bring him over to the Greenville HQ so Pinkham can interrogate him."

"What if McDonough doesn't want to come willingly?"

DeFord used both hands to pull himself up into the pickup. "I think he will."

"Why do you say that?"

He kept the door open as he turned the key in the ignition. "An hour ago, we got a call from the Appalachian Mountain Club. A couple camping along the river found something downstream of Gulf Hagas. They turned it in to the AMC ranger at the ford. It was a red tent. Or the remains of one, I should say."

13

After DeFord had driven off, I got myself a cup of coffee from
the Salvation Army wagon and mulled over my assignment.

All along I had thought Chad McDonough was fabricating the
story about the man in the red tent. Cops are so used to being lied
to every day. I knew law-enforcement officers who were incapable
of believing anyone was ever telling the whole truth. I had personally fallen into this trap on occasion and had to remind myself what
a pathological and dangerous way it was of looking at the world.
The possibility that McDonut's story might actually be true hit me
like a bucket of ice water dumped over my head.

The crowd had begun to disperse as different teams got their
orders for the day. I looked for Nissen, hoping to confront him. The
task of finding Samantha and Missy was daunting enough without
rumors going around of four-legged phantoms. But the man was nowhere to be found.

From a distance I saw Stacey rubbing sunscreen on her forehead.
She smiled as I approached, and wiped her greasy fingers on her
pants. I felt bubble-headed at the thought of her having driven all
these miles to join me in the search.

"Where's Charley?" I asked.

"He caught a ride to his plane with Chris Anson. The two of them
were going to talk search patterns."

Anson was one of the Warden Service's three active-duty pilots, a
former Marine who had served in Iraq and idolized Charley Stevens.

Sometimes I forgot that my friend was a mentor to more young men than just myself.

"So you're not flying with him?"

"I was hoping to find some handsome warden who'd be willing to drive me around all day."

I pretended to survey the crowd. "Too bad there are none here."

"That's just what I was thinking," she said with a smile.

As we walked up the hill to my truck, I told her about the assignment DeFord had given me to track down the fugitive section hiker. It was a serious conversation, but I couldn't stop myself from grinning like a teenager whenever we made eye contact.

She climbed into the pickup, sat beside me, and dropped her backpack behind the seat. She sniffed the air loudly. "Did something die in here?"

"Not exactly."

I'd been sprayed by a skunk a few years earlier, and the embarrassment of seeing people hold their nose everywhere I went was coming back to me.

"You might consider getting one of those little pine tree thingies to hang from your mirror," she said.

"Thanks for the tip."

"Always glad to help, Bowditch."

She put on her sunglasses again. They had emerald frames and enormous lenses that had a greenish purple tint, depending upon the angle of the light. "Those glasses make you look like a bug," I said.

"Don't disrespect my shades!" She brought her knee up and pressed it against the glove compartment. "So DeFord suspects McDonut took off when he realized he might be a suspect?"

"He definitely left in a hurry," I said. "When I talked to him, he made it sound like he was going to stick around the lodge. He claimed that his sprained leg hurt too much to hike."

"It sounds like something spooked him."

"Maybe it was me showing up there in the middle of the night."

"Tell me about this guy, Nissen," she said. "You said McDonut knew him."

"Everyone seems to know him. He's famous—or notorious—among the thru-hikers. We met a couple on top of Chairback, and the woman recognized him, as well." I leaned forward to look in my side mirror before pulling into traffic. "The one thing I know is that the guy is a world-class asshole. Dani Tate told me Nissen was going around this morning telling everyone that Samantha and Missy were being stalked by a pack of coyotes."

Stacey snapped her head around in alarm. "What?"

"McDonut said they heard coyotes howling at Cloud Pond. The girls' last log entry at Chairback also mentioned coyotes."

"Wonderful," she said through her teeth. "It's bad enough that the hunters already have people freaked out about coyotes being 'coy wolves.'"

"I thought eastern coyotes had wolf DNA."

"Their skulls and jaws are more wolflike, but it's not like they're out in the woods looking for Red Riding Hood."

In my time as a warden, I had checked the licenses of many coyote hunters and trappers and seen more than a few pelts hanging from hooks. "Some of them are pretty big."

"Bigger than western coyotes, but we're still talking about forty-pound animals." Her voice was getting louder the longer we talked. "I just hate to see any species vilified."

Most of the outdoorsmen I knew in Maine hated coyotes with a passion. Whenever I visited a rod and gun club, I heard horror stories about coyotes chasing deer onto slippery ice or herding them into snowbanks where they could be eaten alive. The reasons for this disdain were primarily selfish, I'd assumed, because the predators competed with human hunters for deer. Truth be told, they were far from my favorite animals, since I myself had seen their bloody work in many frozen cedar swamps.

Stacey was the only wildlife biologist I knew who stuck up for them. She despised the snaring program the department had implemented to control their populations, calling it a waste of money, since scientific research showed that coyotes reacted to such drastic measures by having more pups. If nothing else, the animals were survivors.

I knew that a pack of coyotes had attacked and killed a young woman in Nova Scotia some years ago, but I didn't want to make Stacey any madder by bringing up the incident. "How would you feel about hiking the Rim Trail at Gulf Hagas? McDonut told a woman at Hudson's that he was headed over there."

"Don't you think he was lying?"

"Probably," I said. "But we've got to start somewhere."

Outside of Monson, we passed the place where the Appalachian Trail crosses Route 15 and entered the Hundred Mile Wilderness. There were two Warden Service trucks parked in the lot and a hodgepodge of other vehicles—belonging to volunteers in all likelihood—alongside the road.

"Stop!" said Stacey.

I hit the brakes harder than I'd intended. The impact jolted us both forward against our seat belts.

"What is it?"

"I want to see something."

The engine was still idling when Stacey got out and began jogging back toward the trailhead. I grabbed my keys from the ignition and hurried to catch up with her.

Thousands of people walked this section of the AT each year, but you never would have known it from the path, which was almost a tunnel running through a thick stand of birches, hemlocks, and firs. Green branches pressed together overhead. The trail itself was crisscrossed with tangled roots, worn smooth of their bark beneath the boots of so many hikers. I followed Stacey down from the parking lot and into the cooler dark of the forest. A dank and decaying odor circulated in the shadows—seemed, in fact, to be the smell of the shadows.

The sign where Samantha and Missy had taken their last picture was located in a sun-warmed clearing about fifty yards from the highway. It had been set in concrete to keep vandals from toppling it over. The women must have climbed onto the base to have posed the way they did. To our left was a denim-blue body of water, which the map said was one of the Spectacle Ponds.

Someone had tacked the MISSING poster to the base of the brown sign. Stacey paused before it. She crossed her arms and shivered noticeably, despite having emerged from the murky wood into sunshine.

"Baby Ruth and Naomi Walks," she said. "God, they look so young."

"We're not that much older than they are."

"Yeah, we are."

A dragonfly landed on her shoulder and fluttered its cellophane wings. Its thorax was light brown and it had white shoulder stripes and a black line down its abdomen—a chalk-fronted corporal. Another one landed beside it. Stacey paid no attention to them.

"Tell me about Samantha and Missy," she said.

"They graduated early this spring from Pentecost University in South Carolina so they could hike the AT. After they finished the trail, they were headed to West Africa to do some sort of missionary work."

She blew air through her nose, loud enough for me to hear.

"What?" I said.

"Pentecost was the school in the news last year that expelled a lesbian student when one of the administrators saw her wedding photos on Facebook. They claimed she'd violated their 'Lifestyle Covenant.'" Two more dragonflies landed, one on her bare arm, the other on the toe of her boot. "What else do you know about them?"

"They went to high school together in Buckhead, Georgia, before Pentecost."

"Do they have brothers or sisters?"

"I don't know."

"How are we going to find them if we don't know anything about them?"

It was a good question. "DeFord has been talking to the families. The parents are flying into Greenville this morning. He's gone to the airport to meet them."

"God, I can't even imagine what they're going through."

She turned back toward the poster and started to shake.

"Are you all right?" I thought she might be crying.

She spun around, and all the insects took flight. Her jaw was firm, and her face was flushed with blood.

"I'm *mad*," she said. "And you should be, too. Someone killed those women, and it wasn't a bunch of fucking coyotes. Do you know what I think about when I look at that poster?"

"No."

"I think they look just like me when I was their age. The difference is that I survived."

14

The woods, which had been so dense on either side of the road, began to give way to fields and house lots as we approached Greenville. When Thoreau had visited Moosehead Lake in 1853, lumberjacks were just beginning to range out into the surrounding forests, clearing miles of timber. Horse teams would haul the felled trees to the lake, where steamers would surround the floating logs with booms and pull them to the outlet of the Kennebec River. From there, they would be washed downstream to the sawmills. I often thought of his essay "Chesuncook" whenever I crested Indian Hill and found myself dumbstruck by the shimmering vista before me.

Thoreau had called Moosehead "a suitably wild-looking sheet of water, sprinkled with small, low islands, which were covered with shaggy spruce and other wild wood—seen over the infant port of Greenville, with mountains on each side and far in the north, and a steamer's smoke-pipe rising above a roof." The description still held true, although the loggers were gone, and the last remaining steamship, the MV *Katahdin*, now ferried tourists to Mount Kineo, where they could snap pictures of the rhyolite cliffs rising above the hard blue chop. In Thoreau's days, there was "no village, and no summer road in this direction." Now there were magnificent lakefront estates with Cigarette boats docked out front, a nine-hole golf course, and even plans for a condominium development on the undisturbed shores of Lily Bay.

We drove through Greenville's tiny downtown—just a crossroads with a blinking red light and a string of restaurants and souvenir shops extending out to each point of the compass—and turned right, headed uphill and inland again toward the western border of the Hundred Mile Wilderness. As we neared the Greenville Airport, I caught sight of a familiar yellow Volkswagen Beetle at the side of the road. A gray-haired woman in a green uniform was kneeling beside the back right tire. I slowed down.

Stacey sat up from her slouch and adjusted her sunglasses. "What's going on?"

"It's Deb Davies."

The Warden Service chaplain was a Methodist minister who lived on a back-to-the-land farm, complete with Silkie chickens and Angora goats, down in central Maine. I had a closer relationship with her than most of my fellow officers. Over the years, the Reverend Davies had come to see herself as my personal spiritual adviser, thanks to the many opportunities my supervisors had given me to seek counseling after my puzzlingly frequent brushes with death.

She had short hair, which she stiffened into spikes with some kind of gel or foam. Since I'd last seen her three months earlier, she'd swapped her blue-framed glasses for red-framed ones. This morning, she was wearing her dress uniform and her white clerical collar. I realized instantly where she had been headed when she got her flat tire.

Stacey and I got out of the truck at the same time and met her on the sand shoulder.

"Excuse me, ma'am," I said. "Did you call AAA?"

"Hey there, stranger!"

"It's good to see you, Deb."

Davies turned to Stacey with a tentative smile. "How are you, Stacey?"

The two women formally shook hands. "What's wrong with the Love Bug?" Stacey asked.

"There's a nail in my tire, and I'm already running late."

"You must be headed to the airport," I said.

She blinked and made an exaggerated look of surprise. "I always forget about your deductive powers," she said. "It's not just me meeting the plane. The commissioner is also flying in to welcome Samantha's and Missy's families." She meant Marianne Matthews, who directed the Maine Department of Inland Fisheries and Wildlife.

"That's quite a high-powered entourage," I said.

"I'm surprised the governor's not coming, too." Stacey made no secret of her dislike for the man and his love of all things asphalt and oil.

Deb Davies pretended not to have heard the remark. "Lieutenant DeFord told me you were the one who found the point last seen, Mike."

"It looks that way," I said. "The last record we have of them was at the Chairback Gap lean-to ten days ago."

"I didn't realize they'd been missing that long."

We all fell quiet as she processed the information. Like me, Davies was a veteran of many searches. She knew that the odds of finding missing persons alive after the first two days were slim.

"I can change your tire for you," I said.

But when I lifted up the trunk liner and removed the wing nut, I discovered that the spare was also flat.

"Oh, cheese and crackers!" The chaplain glanced at her wristwatch, and I caught a glimpse of Mickey Mouse with his pinwheeling arms. "That plane is going to be here any minute, too."

"Why don't we give you a lift to the airport," said Stacey.

I didn't want to give Lieutenant DeFord the impression that I was ignoring the assignment he'd given me in order to indulge my curiosity. Stacey clearly had no such qualms.

Deb Davies looked back and forth between us. "Would you mind?"

"Not at all," said Stacey.

The backseat of my pickup was cluttered with all the gear I might use in the course of a week: a sleeping bag, spotting scope, change of uniform, blaze orange safety vest, camouflage raincoat, come-along, hatchet, first-aid kit, wool blanket, my AR-15 rifle and Mossberg 590A1 shotgun, entrenching tool—all sorts of crap. I had to throw half of it into the truck bed to make room for Deb Davies. Her nose twitched as she squeezed inside. She peered around as if she were afraid that I might have a dead beaver hidden under the blanket.

I rolled down my window and started off for the airport.

Deb leaned forward against my seat, close enough for me to smell the spearmint chewing gum in her mouth. "How do you like your new district? It must be a change for you working in the suburbs."

"He misses the woods," said Stacey.

I'd never expressed that thought, but it was absolutely true. "I got to spend a lot of time on the water this summer, at least."

"You looked cute going on patrol on a Jet Ski," said Stacey.

I met Deb's eyes in the rearview mirror. "She's making fun of me for wearing a bathing suit."

"I'm sure all the drunk female boaters liked seeing your pretty legs," said Stacey. "And some of the male ones, too."

She knew I'd been teased about my lake patrol "uniform." It was true that I'd heard some catcalls. I hadn't wanted to admit how much I'd enjoyed tooling around on my shiny Kawasaki STX-15F, playing waterborne traffic cop to the flotillas that plied Sebago Lake on hot summer days. It wasn't why I'd become a game warden, but it had made for a novel experience.

Glancing ahead, I saw a cleared area that I recognized as the end of the runway. I followed the perimeter of the airport property until I reached the entrance. It was more of an airstrip in the forest than a conventional passenger or commercial facility; there was no control tower, just a cluster of hangars on both sides of the landing strip, a firehouse, a fueling station, and a small trailer-like building where the pilots could get coffee. Most of the planes in view had propellers: Cessnas and Cirruses. There was even an antique biplane.

We parked in the dirt lot beside a black warden's truck, a Greenville police cruiser, and an unmarked Ford Interceptor that I recognized as the standard model given to state police detectives. I kept the engine running as Deb got out. Stacey unsnapped her seat belt and hopped to the ground.

"Thank you for the ride," said the Reverend Davies, straightening her uniform lapels.

"It was no trouble," I replied. "Stacey, we should probably get on the road."

"I've never flown into this airport before," Stacey said. "I want to have a look around for future reference. It'll only take a few minutes."

It was more than a pilot's interest, I suspected.

I parked the truck beside the others and followed the two women to the runway. There was no fence or gate to stop us. We saw a group of people gathered around the door of a gleaming Learjet. I spotted Lieutenant DeFord and Sergeant Fitzpatrick, both in their dress uniforms—green and blue, respectively—as well as the taciturn FBI agent, Genoways, in his navy suit. Standing in front of them was Commissioner Matthews; she was a small, sharp-nosed woman with a boy's haircut, wearing a dress the color of a fire engine.

"It looks like the families are already here," I said.

"Crab cakes!" said the Reverend Davies, and hurried off toward the runway.

Stacey started to follow her, but I caught her arm. Her head swung around, lips pursed.

"We need to get going," I said.

"You can pretend you're not interested, Bowditch, but I know you are."

I let go of her arm.

Deb Davies approached the group. We were too far away to hear their conversation, but even from a distance we could tell that she was apologizing for being late. We saw two middle-aged couples step forward to shake her hand.

The fathers could almost have been twins. They both had short brown hair and golf-course tans, and they were both dressed in blue blazers over polo shirts, loose slacks, and loafers. Their bellies curved over their woven leather belts in exactly the same way.

The mothers were opposites. One was as thin as a fence post. She had feathery blond hair that reminded me of pictures I'd seen of women in the 1970s, a long neck and long hands, and a mask of bright makeup. She wore a linen pantsuit and sandals. Based on the hair color, I took her to be Samantha's mother.

The other woman was a short-haired brunette, but the color looked as if it had come from a bottle. She wore a flowery blouse and a pleated green skirt that accentuated the width of her hips. Everything about her—from her pained, drooping face to her slouched shoulders and hanging breasts—seemed to be pulled by a greater gravity than the rest of us were experiencing. Missy's mom struck me as one of the saddest people I'd ever seen.

While we watched, a man I hadn't noticed stepped forward and greeted Deb Davies. He appeared to be in his late thirties and had the build of someone who played a lot of tennis. He was dressed in new-looking jeans, a white dress shirt without a tie, and a gray sharkskin blazer. His hair, styled in a pompadour, was the color of spun gold, and his skin had an orange cast that was meant to look naturally tan but failed to do so. Never in my life had I encountered a person in Maine who looked like him.

The golden man put his arm on Deb's shoulders and leaned his smiling face close to hers, as if they were old friends.

"Who the hell is that?" Stacey asked.

"I think it might be their minister."

"He looks like he's going to a disco later."

Behind us came the sound of an engine. We stepped aside and let an obsidian black Cadillac Escalade creep past. The SUV pulled up to the plane and a man in a black polo shirt and pants emerged. He conferred with the minister—if that was indeed who he was—and began collecting the luggage on the tarmac.

The lieutenant glanced back again in our direction, but I couldn't read his expression. Samantha's and Missy's parents went around the circle, shaking hands again with everyone, and then they all got into the Escalade. The minister lingered on the runway for a moment. When Commissioner Matthews tried to climb into the SUV, he politely waved her away. Then he got into the front seat beside the driver, and the vehicle swung around, heading out.

Again, Stacey and I stepped onto the sunburned grass. As the Cadillac drove by, I noticed that the windows were darkened, but I could feel the eyes of the people inside.

Deb Davies walked toward us. She was looking at the ground and playing with her Mickey Mouse wristwatch.

"How'd it go?" Stacey asked.

The chaplain seemed a bit dazed. "They thanked me for coming but said they didn't need my services."

"So the guy with the hair was their personal minister?" I said.

"He introduced himself as the Reverend Mott. He asked what denomination I belonged to. When I said Methodist, he said that was what he would have guessed."

"What church does he belong to?" Stacey asked. "The Church of Cheesy Hair?"

"How did the parents seem?" I asked.

"They were pretending to be all right," Deb said. "All except Missy's mom. The poor woman looked like she hadn't slept in a week. They're headed over to the Inn at Lily Bay. I'm going to get a ride back to Division C Headquarters with Lieutenant DeFord. He said he'd send someone to fix my car."

"The families don't want your help at all?" I said. "What will you do?"

"Go home, I guess." She bit her lip as the thought overcame her. "This has never happened to me before."

Stacey stared over my shoulder. "Wow, the commissioner is really chewing out the lieutenant."

"She wanted more wardens in uniform here," said Deb. "She doesn't think he understands how important these people are."

"Would she prefer he pull people off the search?" I asked.

The question answered itself. Out on the airstrip, Matthews was making large hand gestures as she spoke with DeFord. Her face was hard and white beneath her helmet of black hair. Good political operator that he was, the lieutenant took every punch the commissioner dished out.

15

Stacey and I headed east on the rutted KI Road, back into the Hundred Mile Wilderness. Impenetrable thickets of raspberries had sprung up in the old clear-cuts. I kept my eyes open, hoping to see a feeding bear.

"I've never known anyone who travels with a personal preacher," she said. "My folks had a Unitarian minister to dinner once. Does that count?"

"I don't think so."

"What about you?"

"My mom would sometimes have priests over to the house in Scarborough," I said. "I remember one of them who got redder and redder the more wine he drank. He kept looking at me whenever he took a sip. Later, I heard a rumor about him and altar boys, but he was never arrested. The bishop just moved him to another diocese."

"Is that why you're an atheist?" Stacey asked.

I couldn't keep myself from laughing. "Who said I was an atheist?"

"You don't go to church."

"Neither do you."

"My church is in the woods," she said with an impish grin. "I worship in a sacred grove of oak trees and mistletoe. I'm studying to become a druid. Didn't I tell you?"

"I don't think the Reverend Mott would approve."

"Definitely not!"

"If we find Samantha and Missy, he won't care what religions we are."

"No," said Stacey. "He'd still say I'm going to hell."

"What about me?'

"The jury's still out on that one."

The truck hit an embedded rock in the road and bumped us into the air.

When we rolled to a grinding stop at the North Maine Woods checkpoint, we found the gatekeeper—a grandmotherly type with reading glasses hanging on a chain from her neck—seated on the steps of her cabin, reading *Guns & Ammo*. Her job was to make sure that anyone who entered the wilderness between Greenville and Katahdin Iron Works checked in and checked out. The landowners didn't want campers secretly holing up in some remote clearing where they might leave trash behind or start a wildfire through carelessness. Wardens and other emergency personnel weren't required to register. The old woman must have already waved through a dozen search vehicles that morning.

The little old lady set her magazine down and rose from the steps as we got out of the truck. Her white hair was done up in braids. She wore a camouflage fleece top, brown cords, and deerskin moccasins, but if she had an ounce of Wabanaki Indian blood in her veins, I was a Pacific Islander.

"You don't need to sign in, Warden," she said.

"I have a question for you if you have a minute."

"All I've got here is time."

I showed her the photo I'd taken of Chad McDonough's driver's license. "You don't have a record of this man coming through here, do you? He'd be driving a Kia Soul with Massachusetts plates. MDONUT."

"Does this have something to do with those missing hikers?"

"I can't say."

She raised her reading glasses up on their chain and squinted at the screen. The sunlight must've made it hard to see, because she cupped her hands to create a shadow. She gave me back the camera and ascended into the building with more energy than I would have expected of someone her age. A moment later, she popped through the door with a clipboard.

"He's not on my list."

"Could he have come in or gone out the Katahdin Iron Works gate?" asked Stacey.

"Chuck and I send our information to each other every night. If he came through, I'd know about it."

I found a business card in my uniform pocket. "If he happens to come by, could you call the state police and ask them to contact me immediately?"

The old woman read my name and peered at me above her square reading glasses. "Are you any relationship to Jack Bowditch?"

I had forgotten my late father's notoriety in this part of the state. In his youth, he had worked all over the western woods—also drank, brawled, and screwed. "Why? Did you know him?"

"No, but my daughter did."

I decided it was a story I didn't need to hear. I thanked her and began to descend the stairs.

"There's one more thing," she called after me. "We wouldn't have any record of your suspect if he came in on foot—or if he was a passenger in a vehicle. We only record the name and license number of the driver."

"Who said he was a suspect?" Stacey asked.

"Why else would you be looking for him?" the old woman said smugly.

The crackle and pop of my police radio was constant as we traveled deeper into the mountains. There were reports of searchers fanning out through the Pleasant River valley. We passed patrol trucks parked at trailheads and groups of volunteers gathered in the shade to plot strategy.

Logging trucks loaded with softwood and dump trucks heaped

with gravel came barreling past, heading into Greenville. By the time we arrived at the Head of the Gulf parking lot, my pickup had been so splattered with mud, it looked more brown than black.

"I've always wanted to see Gulf Hagas," said Stacey.

"You've never been here?"

"No, but I have friends who've taken kayaks through the gorge. They told me there was some big water here."

I sometimes forgot that Stacey had been a rafting guide out west for a time. She so rarely discussed that part of her past. The idea of paddling down these chutes struck me as borderline suicidal—and I am someone who enjoys taking physical risks.

"Do you think Samantha and Missy might have taken a detour to see Gulf Hagas?" she asked.

"It's possible."

"So for all we know, they fell to their deaths somewhere in the canyon."

"They wouldn't be the first."

The gulf had been carved by the spring floods of the Pleasant River in the aeons since the glaciers gave up their icy hold on the land. The walls of the ravine were sheer slate; in places, they rose to heights of 130 feet. Over a three-mile stretch, the river dropped down a series of cascades. Stair Falls, Billings Falls, Buttermilk Falls, the Jaws, Hammond Street Pitch—the waterfalls were named by the log drivers who had once sent pulpwood downstream to feed the furnaces at Katahdin Iron Works. In all seasons, the river was brown with tannins, which are the biomolecules that leach from decomposing pine needles and are used to tan leather.

We fastened on our packs and applied insect repellent to our exposed skin. I reached instinctively for my cell phone, then realized I wouldn't be able to use it anywhere along the Rim Trail. I checked the coverage anyway and was surprised to see four bars. All I could think was that the state police must have brought their portable cell tower into the Hundred Mile Wilderness in order to boost the signals the searchers were using to communicate. I'd noticed it parked behind the Monson firehouse the night before.

I didn't recognize any of the three other vehicles that were parked in the Head of the Gulf lot and assumed they belonged to day hikers who had come in from Greenville to see one of the natural wonders of Maine. One was a nondescript Subaru Outback; the second was a new Ford Super Duty pickup; the third was a Jeep Cherokee with traces of dried shaving cream like frosting on the windows and strings trailing off the rear bumper.

"Someone just got married," I said to Stacey.

"Maybe they were looking for Niagara Falls and got mixed up."

"If you could honeymoon anywhere in the world, where would it be?"

When she threw back her head, her ponytail danced. "Stop it!"

"Stop what?"

"Stop talking about marriage. The last time I got engaged, it didn't end so well, remember?"

I grinned like a drunken man. "From my perspective, it worked out perfectly."

"You like to think so," she said, and kissed me hard on the lips.

The forest floor was flooded from the downpour the previous night, and we had to walk across sawn logs, called "bog bridges," to avoid the biggest puddles. In a few minutes, we came to the Pleasant River. The water was high and brown except along the edges, where foam clung to the half-submerged alders and birches. We were upstream of the gulf. There was no hint that less than a mile downriver were falls so steep, few human beings had ever survived the plunge.

"The water's really high for late September," I said.

Stacey kicked a twig off the bridge, and we watched it rush off downstream. "I guess we won't be skinny-dipping."

We crossed the bridge and saw the Rim Trail on the right. Someone had left an improvised walking stick propped against the sign.

My quadriceps were still aching from my climb up and down Chairback. I picked the stick up, figuring I could use the support.

The trail was flat and easy walking except where we had to balance on bog bridges. There were fresh footprints made since the last thunderstorm, all headed toward the canyon. I counted those of three men—one using a ski pole–style walking stick—and two women. As best I could tell, all of the tracks had been made by day hikers.

Katydids buzzed incessantly in the leaf canopy. Most people I knew confused the insects with cicadas, which emerge from hibernation every seventeen years to drone on in the treetops. Katydids don't take a break: They are perennial annoyances.

In the center of the path near Lloyd Pond, we came across a big mound of brown pellets, each the size and shape of a chocolate-covered almond. Stacey squatted down and held her hand over the pile. She glanced up with a girlish smile.

"Still warm," she said. "That bull moose was just here a few minutes ago."

I thought she was pulling my leg. "You can tell that it was a bull and not a cow just by looking at its shit?"

"See how blocky these nuggets are? Cow pellets tend to be longer and narrower." She jutted her chin at a muddy depression in the leaves. I saw a series of hoof marks, each bigger than my hand. "And look how blunt those tracks are. It's definitely a big bull." She straightened up and glanced at the trees crowding the path. "I bet if I called, I could get him to come in." She took a deep breath and cupped her hands around her mouth.

"Please don't," I said.

The moose rut—or breeding season—was under way in much of the state. I knew how aggressive bulls could get when their testosterone levels spiked. A half-ton blood-mad animal was the last thing I wanted to deal with this morning. I wasn't sure that my .357 could even stop a rampaging moose before it trampled us to death.

"I wasn't really going to do a moose call, scaredy-cat. But that's what you get for questioning the expertise of Maine's most kick-ass wildlife biologist."

I was glad to see her spirits lifting after her blowup back at the entrance to the Hundred Mile Wilderness. Her moods tended to swing hard. I was learning to appreciate the peaks.

"I never should have doubted you."

"Let's go find your friend McDonut." She started off down the path, as eager as a child to see the dangerous waterfalls ahead.

Like father, like daughter, I thought for the hundredth time.

We heard the gorge before we saw it. About a mile south of the dirt road, the path to the river split off from the main logging trail and became more rugged. To get to the gulf, we had to scramble over great boulders slick with moss and painted with blue blazes, pointing the way forward.

Stacey was as nimble as Bob Nissen when it came to climbing, but the chain soles of my Bean boots slipped on the wet rocks. She quickly outdistanced me over the slimy boulders. I found that I had to stay focused on each foothold. I slipped and barely got a grip on a fortunately placed birch sapling.

"How are you doing back there, Bowditch?" she asked.

"I should've put on my hiking boots back at the truck."

I paused for a drink of water from my bottle. As I was drinking, I noticed a faint rumbling noise up ahead. Anywhere else, I might have thought I was hearing traffic speeding along a distant highway, but not this deep in the Hundred Mile Wilderness.

Stacey heard it, too. She peered down the path. "Is that a waterfall?"

"The first one, yes."

Her eyes went wide. Before I could say another word, she took off at a run. I stuffed the bottle into my pack and grabbed the stick from the ground. The binoculars around my neck kept banging into my bulletproof vest every time I took a step.

As the sound of the falls grew louder, the temperature became twenty degrees cooler. A mist drifted like windblown strands of silk between the boughs of the spruce trees. The air had a clean, effervescent smell.

I caught up with Stacey on an escarpment that jutted over the river. The cliff dropped straight down into a churning plunge pool the color of root beer foam. She stood inches from the edge and fumbled for her camera in her backpack with one blind hand. My first instinct was to pull her back from the precipice, but she wasn't a child, and I wasn't her parent. All I could do was swallow my anxiety and trust she wouldn't slip.

"Look at that smoker!" She had to shout to be heard over the sound of the cascades. "Which falls is this?"

"Stair Falls," I said.

I watched while she hung over the cliff, taking pictures of the stepped falls above the gorge and the thundering water below. I was just about to call her name, telling her we should move along, when she popped to her feet. She came toward me, the camera hanging from a strap around her wrist, a solemn expression darkening her face.

"What's wrong?" I asked.

"I was just thinking something crazy," she said.

"Tell me."

"I was thinking that you could've pushed me over that cliff and told the police that I fell. No one could ever prove that you'd killed me. It would be the perfect murder."

"That's a morbid thought! Why would I want to kill you?"

"If you did, I mean."

I put my arms around her and pressed my mouth to her ear, tasting the chemical bitterness of the bug spray she'd rubbed into her skin. "You have a very disturbed imagination."

She blinked several times and let out a humorless laugh. "Matt Skillin really did a number on me, I guess."

"You didn't know what a monster he was."

"That's what's so scary. I thought I loved him—but he had me fooled."

I made my voice soft. "I'm not hiding who I am from you, Stacey. You can trust me."

She pulled free of my arms with an embarrassed smile. "What's the next falls after this one?"

"Billings."

"Is it higher than this one?"

"Yes."

She stuffed the camera into the thigh pocket of her cargo pants and set off ahead of me into the depths of the gorge. I watched her run up a flat boulder that was tilted at a thirty-five-degree angle, wondering what to make of her frightening admission. Then I lost sight of her in the fog-wrapped trees.

16

The Rim Trail was a nightmare to negotiate. The lattice of spruce roots underfoot felt as if they had been greased. I have never suffered from a fear of heights, but there was something unnerving about the way my feet kept slipping, as if an invisible pair of hands had closed around my ankles and was trying to yank them over the drop-off. I imagined the gorge as a malevolent entity intent upon tossing me to my death in the churning water below.

I found Stacey waiting for me at Billings Falls. She was perched on a rock, massaging her leg; the pained expression on her face made me think at first that she'd sprained her ankle.

"I just realized I left that book I was reading back at Popham," she said. "It's a sixty-dollar textbook."

Stacey had a way of losing things, especially when she was distracted, which was often. We'd once spent the better part of a morning searching for keys that were in her back pocket all along.

"I'll call the property manager and have him send it to you."

She stared at me through her dark lenses. "Did that guy strike you as a thoughtful person? I'm sure it's in the trash. Oh well. It's only money, right? There are worse things in the world than losing a stupid book. Way worse things. Right?"

She didn't have to say more for me to understand she was thinking about the missing hikers.

I paused a moment to take in the majesty of the falls beneath my feet. There were a few scraggly trees on the downslope, the last chance for someone falling to save himself, and then thin air for half a hundred feet, until the person shattered his spine on a cluster of boulders. Not that landing in the river would be any better. Anyone who has ever paddled a canoe through Class IV rapids knows that the hydraulics of certain waterfalls make them death traps. The circulating currents can drive capsized swimmers to the bottom and hold them there against the sand until they drown. Some of the most furious falls refuse to give up their dead for weeks. For all we knew, Samantha's and Missy's corpses might be spinning beneath the leaf-flecked water, as limp as stockings rotating in a washing machine.

As we started down the trail again, Stacey called to me over her shoulder. "What were their trail names again—Samantha's and Missy's?"

"Naomi Walks and Baby Ruth. Why?"

"I don't know," she said. "They're odd choices."

"Maybe Missy ate a lot of candy bars."

She clambered to the top of a big rock, pulling herself up by her fingertips until her head was peeking over the top. She froze there for fifteen seconds and then let go, sliding back on the toes of her hiking boots onto the wet mat of pine needles. She pressed a hand to her mouth to hold in a laugh and motioned with her thumb that I needed to take a look.

"What?"

She held a finger over her lips. Then she doubled over, shaking all over with silent laughter.

I moved around her and took a run up the rock face, catching the top with both hands. Slowly, I raised my head.

A young couple was having sex thirty feet down the path. Both the man and the woman had their pants around their ankles, and he was driving into her from behind while she steadied herself with both arms braced awkwardly against a birch trunk. He had one hand on her shoulder while his round white buttocks thrust back and forth. Every now and again he spanked her bare ass.

I dropped back to earth. "It must be the honeymooners."

"They don't look old enough to have gotten married. What's the age of consent in Maine anyway?"

"Eighteen."

She pressed a hand flat over her heart. "Young love is such a beautiful thing."

I peered up into the forest, looking for a detour, but I saw none. The trees were thick as the bristles on a hairbrush, and there were deadfalls everywhere with sharp branches on which you could easily impale yourself.

"We can't circle around them."

"Let's have some fun, then." She tilted her face up at the boughs overhead, giving me a peek at the mole beneath her chin, and let out a shout at the top of her lungs, "Come on, Officer Bowditch! Buttermilk Falls are just a little ways ahead! Don't quit on me now!"

"Stacey."

"We'll give them a minute to get their clothes back on." She counted the seconds on her wristwatch. "You go first. I want to see their expressions when they get a load of your badge and gun."

When I pulled myself up again on the rock, I found myself staring into the startled eyes of two fully dressed young people. The young woman's brown hair was as wild as Medusa's, and the fly on the man's Levi's was unzipped, revealing the bulge of his tighty-whities. Otherwise, I never would have guessed what they'd just been doing.

I hauled myself over the top.

The man had a wimpy mustache, inflamed whiteheads on his cheeks, and dirty blond hair cut in a style that was almost but not quite a mullet. The outline of a pack of cigarettes showed in the chest pocket of his chamois shirt. He gave a meek wave.

The woman's cheeks and throat were flushed with blood. She was wearing a yellow shirt, indigo-dyed jeggings that showed off her long legs—she was taller than he was—and muddy sneakers.

"How's it going?" I asked.

"OK," the man said.

"Nice day for a hike," said Stacey, sliding over the rock behind me. "It's so awesome to feel the blood pumping."

The couple looked at each other, unsure what to make of Stacey's comment.

"Are you guys on your honeymoon?" she asked, raising her sunglasses and resting them atop her head. Her green eyes were full of merriment.

"How'd you know that?" the man asked. He removed the cigarette pack from his pocket and shook a Marlboro out, trying to affect a composure he clearly wasn't feeling. I could practically hear his jackrabbit heart.

"Saw your Jeep back in the lot," Stacey said.

"Yeah, we're camping down to Katahdin Iron Works."

I decided that Stacey had indulged her twisted sense of humor enough. "I'm Warden Bowditch, and this is Stacey Stevens, who's with the Maine Department of Inland Fisheries and Wildlife. We'd like to ask you a few questions, if you don't mind."

"What kind of questions?" the man asked.

"Let's start with your names," I said.

"Mr. and Mrs. Ryan Tardiff," the young woman said, exulting in her new status as a wife.

"What do you think of Gulf Hagas?" Stacey asked.

"It's pretty awesome, I guess." The unlit cigarette hung from his lower lip. He'd made no attempt to light it. "Is this some kind of tourist survey?"

I ignored the last question. "Have you two hiked the entire Rim Trail today?"

"No, we turned around about halfway," Mrs. Ryan Tardiff said. The blush had begun to fade, revealing orange freckles under her eye sockets.

"Did you run into any other hikers?"

"Just a guy at Buttermilk Falls," Mr. Ryan Tardiff said.

"He's the reason we turned around," his new wife said.

Stacey narrowed her eyes. "What do you mean?"

Mrs. Ryan Tardiff glanced to her husband for encouragement, but he didn't seem to pick up on any of her nonverbal cues. "He was acting kind of weird."

"Weird how?" I asked.

Mr. Ryan Tardiff brought out a NASCAR-branded lighter and finally fired up his cigarette. "He was crying."

I retrieved the camera from my pocket and flipped through the saved photographs until I came to the picture I'd taken of Chad McDonough. I held the screen up for them both to see. "Is this the guy? He might have been wearing a sombrero."

"Maybe," Mr. Ryan Tardiff said.

His wife let her mouth drop open in disbelief. "Ryan! The guy we saw was *old*."

"How old?" Stacey asked.

Mrs. Ryan Tardiff scratched the back of her neck. "I don't know. Forty?"

"Oh, you mean he was a senior citizen," Stacey said.

Again, the Ryan Tardiffs seemed uncertain whether she was teasing them.

A crying man on a cliff above a raging waterfall—whoever he was, the possibility of a potential suicide suggested that Stacey and I should haul our asses down to Buttermilk Falls instead of joshing around with the newlyweds. I shoved the camera back in my pocket and found another business card. I gave it to the wife, guessing that her tough-guy husband would never deign to report information to a game warden.

"If you do run across the man I showed you, can you call this number?"

"Is there a reward?" Mr. Ryan Tardiff asked.

"Absolutely," Stacey said.

"How much?"

"A thousand dollars."

I glared at her, but she merely smiled as the dollar signs flashed behind the young man's eyes.

After we'd left the newlyweds, I said to Stacey, "You can't just lie about there being a reward when there isn't one."

"I'm not a law-enforcement officer. I can lie until my nose is a foot long."

The Pleasant River drops more than three hundred feet as it plummets through Gulf Hagas. My knees were definitely feeling the stress of the descent. For the next fifteen minutes, I clung to that walking stick the way an old man does to his cane.

A sign pointed the way down a narrow path to Buttermilk Falls. We emerged from a grove of cedars onto the most jaw-dropping cliff we'd seen yet. There were treetops below us and three tumbling waterfalls. The opposite cliff was even higher, streaked brown and gray, except where daredevil bushes and saplings had somehow taken root in the rocks and were hanging on for dear life. Downstream, an outcropping, shaped like the bow of a ship, teetered precariously over the abyss. On it sat a man with longish blond hair parted in the center. He was bare-chested and wearing brown cutoffs, but he had exchanged his red Crocs for a sturdy pair of boots.

"Caleb?"

The manager of Hudson's Lodge couldn't hear me above the roar of the water, so I called his name again. The jutting ledge he was standing on would have been the perfect diving platform for anyone wishing to jump to his or her death. Maxwell seemed to shake himself out of a trance and then slowly swiveled his head in our direction. He didn't wave or say hello, just rose to his feet in a single motion without using his hands—a testament to the strength of his leg and abdominal muscles.

When we were close enough to converse, I noticed that his eyes were bloodshot. The redness made the aqua color of his irises all the more vivid. I caught Stacey checking out his long shirtless torso.

"What are you doing here, Caleb?"

He returned my girlfriend's smile. "Thought I'd hike on over from the lodge and look for McDonut."

"I take it you didn't find him."

"No such luck." He extended his hand to Stacey. "I'm Caleb."

"Stacey Stevens."

I folded my bare arms across my chest. "So I heard McDonough's sprained knee healed overnight."

"It was a miracle."

"And he ran into a woman as he was trying to sneak out of the bunkhouse?"

"He told her he wanted to see Gulf Hagas before he hit the trail again. There's a cutoff from the AT to the gorge. Lots of thru-hikers make a detour because they've heard of Gulf Glen."

"What's Gulf Glen?" Stacey asked.

He fingered the necklace around his throat as he looked at her. "You've never heard of Simon Garfew? I guess he isn't exactly a household name. There's a poem about him called 'Simon Garfew: A Legend of Gulf Glen,' which some hikers around these parts like to quote." He then began to recite the poem.

> *The Great Spirit comes to the face in the rock,*
> *The moon when the leaves grow red;*
> *And when the round moon shines upon it,*
> *Shines into the Gulf at night,*
> *Shines full and fair upon it, Making it plain and white,—*
> *Whoever waits there, with fasting,*
> *Below the strong face,*
> *With a deer's blood for offering*
> *Always finds pardon and peace.*

"That's beautiful," Stacey said. "Have you found pardon and peace here, Caleb?"

His smile was sadder this time. "No, but I've never tried bringing deer blood with me. There's a story about Garfew—I don't know if it's true or not—that he used to come to Gulf Hagas each fall with his dog to hunt and fish. One autumn, he ventured down into the canyon after a flash flood and was never seen again. Searchers found his dog waiting for him. They tried to catch it, but they couldn't. It wasn't going to leave Gulf Hagas without its master."

"I suppose there are mysterious sightings of a ghost dog, too," I said. The skepticism had given an edge to my tone. Mostly, I was uncomfortable with the way Caleb Maxwell was flirting with my girlfriend.

"It wouldn't be the Maine woods without ghost stories," he said. "I didn't realize the search area for Samantha and Missy stretched all the way to the Head of the Gulf."

"Actually, we're here because I've been assigned to track down Chad McDonough."

"Well, he doesn't seem to have come along the Rim Trail," said Caleb. "I didn't find any tracks coming this way from the Hermitage."

"Odds are that he was lying," I said.

"Chad seemed to have a propensity for embellishing the truth."

"That's a polite way of putting it." I twirled my walking stick in my hands. "I guess it makes sense for us to turn back, Stacey."

"Maybe we'll get another peep show starring the Ryan Tardiffs." Caleb wrinkled his forehead. "The who?"

"We ran into a couple of newlyweds upriver," I explained. "We surprised them while they were having sex."

"Really?"

"They told us they'd seen you down here. They said you were acting weird."

Caleb Maxwell made a face as if he had gotten a whiff of something foul. "What the fuck?"

"They said you were crying," I said.

His eyes flicked away from mine and focused on the treetops behind me. "Why would I be out here crying?"

"I don't know."

His voice came from a deeper place in his diaphragm. "That's totally bizarre. I don't know what they think they saw, but I was just sitting there." He shifted his weight from one foot to the other. "I should probably be getting back to the lodge."

"Full house again?" I asked.

"I figured I could sneak away for a couple of hours to look for McDonut. It pisses me off that I'm not part of the search for those missing women. I've been glued to the scanner since you left last night." An amusing thought occurred to him, and he showed off a set of very white teeth. "So what was your drive back to Monson like with Nissen?"

I lifted my pack straps to give my shoulders a break, then let the weight settle again. "You can probably imagine."

"Yes, I can."

I held out my hand for him to shake. "Take care, Caleb."

"Nice to meet you," Stacey said.

"*Very* nice to meet you," he replied.

We watched Caleb Maxwell vault over a fallen tree that most people would have chosen to crawl under. The next thing we knew, he was gone. The sound of the river seemed louder than before.

"He's kind of a dreamboat," Stacey said.

"We should get back to the truck."

She grabbed my biceps and gave them a squeeze. "Don't be jealous, Bowditch. You know you're my man."

The truth was, I wasn't jealous—not very jealous anyway. I was perplexed. Why had Caleb Maxwell lied to us about being the man the newlyweds had seen crying?

17

The honeymooners must have found another secret spot for their lovemaking, because their Jeep was still parked in the lot when we returned. Stacey paused to draw a heart on the dirty back window.

The faint but fast-moving sound of a plane engine came from the sky. Seconds later, a red-and-white Cessna appeared, flying high above the treetops. I caught sight of the canoe paddles tied to the pontoon cross braces before it disappeared above Gulf Hagas Mountain.

"There goes the World War One flying ace," said Stacey, gazing up at the empty sky where his plane had been.

"I bet you wish you were up there."

She punched me in the shoulder. "And miss all this excitement? No frigging way."

My cell phone rang as we were scraping the mud off our boots. The state police "cell on wheels" tower was such a godsend. The call was from a trooper I didn't know but who spoke in a friendly manner that suggested he knew me. He identified himself as Chamberlain.

"I found McDonough's car," he said. "It's parked at Abol Bridge."

"Are you sure it's his?"

"Kia Soul? Mass vanity plates? Tag reads MDONUT?"

"That's the guy."

"Looks like the car's been here awhile. There are pine needles stuck all over the top."

From the start, I had been fairly certain that the story Chad Mc-Donough had told the woman at Hudson's had been a ruse. He'd never had any intention of visiting Gulf Hagas. He must have feared that, given his criminal record, he would be a prime suspect in Samantha's and Missy's disappearance. We weren't going to find Mc-Donut on the trail. We needed to start looking along the KI Road and beyond.

"What should I do with the car?" Trooper Chamberlain asked.

"Can you put a boot on it? I don't want him driving off before we have a chance to interview him again."

"I don't have one in the cruiser, but there's a guy in Millinocket I can call. You sure this is kosher?"

"The Warden Service will take responsibility. You have my personal guarantee."

He laughed loudly enough for me to hear it over the airwaves. "I'm not sure what your personal guarantee is worth, Bowditch! But let me see what I can do. It wouldn't be the first time a car got booted 'by mistake,' right?"

After Chamberlain had signed off, I told Stacey about Mc-Donough's abandoned car. "I'm going to report in to DeFord. But I want to drive back over to the gatehouse and talk with the woman there again."

"What for?"

"There's a question I forgot to ask her."

She twisted her torso around and leaned back against the passenger door, arching one eyebrow. "Are you going to tell me what it is?"

"You'll see."

She slid back around and snapped her seat belt. "Has anyone ever told you what a tease you are, Bowditch?"

I put my shades on. "A pain in the ass, yes. A tease, no."

* * *

The old woman sat behind a desk in the gatehouse, writing down the registration information for a Mercedes SUV out front, her white braids hanging down on either side of her face. Three middle-aged men in Simms fishing shirts stood before her. Doctors or lawyers, by the looks of them. They politely backed off when I entered the little building.

The woman glanced at me, eyes twinkling above her reading glasses. "Did you get your man?"

"Not yet. I have another question for you, though." I rested my right hand on the grip of my service weapon, as if my hand were tired. "I don't mean to hold these gentlemen up."

"It's no trouble," said one of the fishermen.

"You go right ahead, Warden," said another.

"Would you gentlemen mind waiting outside for just a minute?"

"Not at all!"

I closed the door behind the last of the fishermen. I noticed the MISSING poster tacked to the bulletin board on the wall, next to warnings about setting unauthorized fires and fee information for use of the campsites maintained by the North Maine Woods association. The more I saw of that last photograph of Samantha Boggs and Missy Montgomery, the heavier the weight in my stomach became. It was beginning to feel like I'd swallowed a musket ball.

"You mentioned before that you wouldn't have a record of the man I'm looking for—Chad McDonough—if he came past here as a passenger in a car or truck."

"That's right."

"Do you have records of every vehicle that left the area this morning?"

"The ones who checked out, I do," she said. "But the logging trucks and some of the other commercial vehicles just sound their horns. They'd never get any work done if they had to stop here. The timber companies don't pay us to slow down their operations."

"This might sound like a funny question," I said. "But can you think of any loggers who are in the habit of giving rides to hitch-hikers?"

The woman's eyes flew open, and she put a wrinkled hand over her mouth.

"Is that a yes?" I asked.

She nodded so hard, the reading glasses bounced up and down against her bosom. "Troy Dow always has someone with him! And he came by this morning. I know because he always gives me three blasts on his way past the gate. He works on the road crew for Wendigo Timber, carrying gravel out of the woods to the yard in Greenville."

I tried to pretend that the man's last name hadn't meant anything to me. "Do you have his phone number?"

"I have the number for the yard." She opened a drawer and began pushing papers and pens around. She copied the contact information on a slip of paper, then hesitated before handing it to me. "I hope this doesn't get Troy in trouble with his supervisor. I don't think the company approves of his picking up hitchhikers."

"So he does it a lot?"

Two red sunbursts appeared on her cheeks. "Mostly females. Troy's a bit of a ladies' man. But I don't think he'd refuse a ride to anyone with his thumb out, man or woman. I'd hate it if I caused him trouble. There are some bad apples in his family tree, but Troy is a peach."

"I'll be discreet," I promised her.

Troy Dow was almost certainly related to Trevor Dow, the bearded roughneck Charley had wrestled to the ground outside the general store. I opened the door for the fishermen to come back inside and finish their registration, but one of the anglers stopped me as I tried to slip past.

"We were just talking about those missing girls," he said. "Have you found them yet?"

"Not yet."

"Is there anything we can do?"

"Just call the state police if you see or hear anything. It's the eight hundred number on the poster inside."

"I have two daughters in college myself," the man said, choking up. "I don't know what I'd do if they disappeared."

He coughed to cover his embarrassment at having such an emotional response.

Stacey was seated with her shoulder belt unfastened and her knees drawn up against the dash, as she often did. She'd pushed her sunglasses up so that they rested on top of her head and was studying one of the many MISSING posters I was carrying in the truck. Her forehead was creased with parallel lines.

"What is it?" I asked.

"I don't know. There's something about them—I can't put my finger on it."

We started forward.

On our way out of the forest, we passed the airport again. I glanced past Stacey's head and saw the Learjet parked near the hangars at the far end of the runway. Maybe it was unfair of me to judge the Reverend Mott based on his appearance and mannerisms, but I suspected he was proving to be a complication. Oh, to be a fly on the wall of Lieutenant DeFord's office, I thought.

At the stop sign in Greenville, I hesitated for a moment, feeling myself torn about whether to turn right, toward the Maine Department of Inland Fisheries and Wildlife headquarters on Village Street, or left, in the direction of the yard where I hoped to find Troy Dow.

"I wish we could talk with the parents," Stacey said, staring off to the right.

"It wouldn't help us find McDonut."

"There's something I'd like to ask Missy's mom," she said.

"What is it?"

"Probably nothing. But didn't you notice how horrible she looked? Something is eating her up inside."

"Well, her daughter is missing."

"It's more than that."

I drove slowly through the village, knowing how careless tourists can be when crossing roads, too busy talking on their phones or balancing ice-cream cones. I needn't have worried. The summer tourism season had ended like the tolling of a bell on Labor Day, and the swarms of leaf peepers hadn't yet arrived to take snapshots of Maine's fall foliage. I wished Stacey and I were just out for a drive on such a lovely day. The sky was dotted with cotton balls. The lake looked like someone had drained all the water and refilled the basin with blue ink.

The yard was located in the industrial park on the western edge of town. We turned away from the lake and the old railroad depot. The cracked pavement was littered with shreds of bark and chips of wood from the logging trucks driving in and out. I spotted a sign with a familiar silver-and-black logo up ahead.

Wendigo was a Canadian timber company that had bought up miles of the Maine North Woods and proceeded to evict hundreds of people—including Charley and Ora Stevens—from cabins they had leased for decades. The company planned to sell the waterfront land to housing developers. More recently, Wendigo had been in the news when one of its logging crews was caught cutting down protected cedar groves where white-tailed deer gathered during the winter to escape blizzards and coyotes. The state had ordered the company to pay a twenty-thousand-dollar fine for knowingly breaking the law. But the value of the wood they'd harvested had been many times that amount. And the deer were already gone.

I stopped in front of the office, and we both got out. The air smelled of pine pitch and pulverized rock. A flock of five rusty blackbirds, more brown than black, pecked at the dead lawn. They made a liquidy noise as they took to the air.

Wendigo didn't employ a receptionist, but a man arose from behind a desk and came to greet us as we walked in the door. He wore a black shirt with the company's silver logo. His hair was so blond that it was almost white, and he had one of those all-over tans people get who spend a lot of time boating.

"Something I can do for you, Warden?"

"I'm looking for Troy Dow, if he's around."

The man scowled. "What's he done now?"

Remembering the kind lady at the gatehouse, I said, "Nothing. We're searching the Hundred Mile Wilderness for a couple of missing hikers."

He interjected, "Yeah, we've been following it on the scanner. You find them yet?"

"Not yet."

He lowered his voice so as not to be heard. We were the only ones in the room. "You think Dow might know something about what happened to those girls?"

"What makes you say that?" Stacey asked.

He ran his tongue along his flaking upper lip. "I shouldn't say anything more unless you tell me why you're looking for him."

"We're just talking to everyone who's gone back and forth along the KI Road in the past ten days," I said. "Is Troy here?"

He squinted through a window that badly needed washing. Vehicles were lined up in a row beyond a pile of unpeeled logs. "His truck is still here. It's the red Silverado with those stupid pirate flags on the top. Troy's probably out back, shooting the shit and distracting the other guys from their jobs."

"Can you show us where he is?"

The man motioned with his finger for us to follow him. We passed through the office and down a hall with a kitchenette and a bathroom that gave off the scent of Pine-Sol cleaner. There was some sort of heavy security door in front of us. It made a groaning noise when our guide pushed it open.

We entered a garage bay. The cavernous space was draped in shadows except at the end, where the doors were rolled up and sunlight came flooding in. The air smelled of motor oil and cigarette smoke. Two man-shaped silhouettes stood in the open air.

Our guide's voice echoed off the cinder-block walls. "Who's been smoking in here?"

"Dow," said one of the shadowy men.

"Where is he?"

"Just left."

Somewhere outside, a pickup engine roared to life. I rushed to the open end of the garage in time to see the red Silverado cornering out of the parking lot with both of its pirate flags flapping.

The man beside me let out a laugh. "When Troy saw your warden's truck pull in, he took off like a bat out of hell."

18

Troy Dow had taken off down a dirt track, headed into the thick woods below Moosehead Lake. My GPS gave the name as the Bangor & Aroostook Railroad Road. I'd never traveled the route before, but the map showed only a handful of turnoffs before it hit pavement again, twenty miles to the south in the flyspeck village of Shirley Mills.

I gunned the engine, but Dow had a sizable head start, and he must have souped up the V-8 under the Silverado's hood. The September sun had spent all morning baking the mud into dust, and a brown cloud hung between our vehicles. Unable to see more than fifty feet ahead of the truck, I found myself gripping the wheel tightly, afraid I'd plow into some hapless four-wheeler cruising along in the opposite direction.

"I guess he doesn't want to talk with us," I said.

"Well, you should put your blues on and see if it makes him more sociable."

I glanced at the speedometer—sixty miles per hour—and hit the switch for the light bar and sirens. Before, I'd had no probable cause to stop Troy Dow, but now I could pull him over for speeding.

Stacey must have accompanied Charley on a few high-speed chases over the years, because she gave me the hand mike without my needing to ask for it. A huge smile made her face all the prettier: my sweet adrenaline junkie.

"Piscataquis? Twenty-one twenty-six," I said. "I've got a ten-thirty-three southbound on the B&A Railroad Road in Greenville. Vehicle is a red Chevrolet Silverado. Can't read the plates. Driver's name is Troy Dow. Residence may be Monson. Do you copy?"

The radio gave an electronic burp as the dispatcher responded. "Copy, Twenty-one twenty-six. Do you need assistance?"

"Negative. But I'll let you know."

"Roger, Twenty-one twenty-six."

Stacey's head whipped around. "He just threw something out the window!"

I didn't want to look away from the road, even for a second. "Did you see what it was?"

"Stop the truck."

I stepped hard on the brake pedal, but the pickup kept sliding even as the automatic brake system engaged. The tires rolled along the pebbles as if floating atop ball bearings. ABS is great on paved roads; on dirt, not so much.

Stacey popped open her door and was out of the vehicle before we'd even stopped moving. "Keep going! I'll find what he threw out."

Looking in my side mirror, I saw her leap down into the weedy ditch. Then I took off again.

At the Maine Criminal Justice Academy, I'd taken a class on driving dynamics that had had me zigzagging around orange pylons and sliding all over a closed course. Aside from the days I'd gotten to spend at the gun range, it was the most fun I'd had in the eighteen weeks I'd spent at that brick castle on the Kennebec River. I'd graduated thinking I could outdrive Mario Andretti.

Then I'd gotten into my first real-world chase. I had been on patrol in Sennebec one night when I'd come across a Dodge Challenger that looked like it had just finished two hundred laps at Daytona. The driver blew through a stop sign to get my attention and then spent the better part of an hour tutoring me in remedial auto racing.

Four-plus years on the job had made me a better driver, but I was still no match for some of the backwoods hot-rodders I encountered. Something told me Troy Dow might fall into that category. At the very least, he was familiar with this road. He knew which curves to slow down for and on which straightaways to hit the gas. And he wasn't driving half-blind in a cloud of dust. All I could do was stay on his tail—and hope.

Like most logging roads in Maine, this one had been graded after the snow had melted in the spring, and it had received a fresh coat of gravel. The surface had taken a pounding over the summer from the steady traffic of eighteen-wheelers, pickups, Jeeps, and all-terrain vehicles, and now it grabbed my tires like the grooves in a slot-car track. Pausing for even a few seconds for Stacey to get out had opened up a gap between Dow's truck and mine that seemed to be getting wider with every mile. No longer was I traveling in a glittering brown haze. I glanced at the map on the GPS display and saw an intersection up ahead with a road branching off toward Route 15. If I couldn't keep pace, I wouldn't know if he'd continued straight or taken the fork.

The road entered a wet meadow with a winding brown stream cutting through the sedge. There was a beaver lodge in back with fresh leafy saplings heaped on top. The greenery told me that a family of beavers was still in residence and would be until one of the local trappers set up his Conibears this winter.

Looking across the vast clearing, I saw no trace of Troy Dow's pickup. I despaired of catching him at this point. I could always track him down later at his home—assuming he didn't decide to take an impromptu vacation—but there was a reason why Troy Dow had fled when he'd seen my truck, and I needed to know what it was.

I was weighing the possibility of turning around and retrieving Stacey, in the hope that she'd found whatever Troy Dow had thrown away, when, to my surprise, I came upon the man himself standing beside his parked Silverado. He had a spin-casting rod in one hand and was leaning over the truck bed as if rummaging around for a tackle box. As I slowed to a stop, he glanced up with a smile.

He resembled the Dow whom Charley and I had met that morning, the hay-faced brawler. He also was squat, barrel-chested, and thick-limbed, only Troy had a Yosemite Sam mustache instead of a Yukon Cornelius beard. He was wearing a black T-shirt with the Harley-Davidson insignia, duck pants stained brown at the knees, and the ubiquitous work boots every man who made his living in the woods seemed to own.

I radioed in my location to the Piscataquis County dispatcher and reported that I'd caught the man I was chasing. The whole time, Troy Dow maintained a bewildered expression, as if he couldn't possibly imagine why I might be interested in his harmless, law-abiding person.

I pushed the door open and stood behind it, my right arm hanging along my side, my hand in reach of my SIG. The woods had gone silent at noon. I could feel the heat of the sunbaked road coming through the bottom of my boots.

"Hey, Warden." His voice had the grating quality of a rasp moving along a block of wood. "You want to see my fishing license?"

With his free hand, he reached around his back. My own hand clamped down on the grip of my pistol.

"Stop! Keep your hands up!"

He complied with my command. "What did I do?"

"You didn't notice me chasing you the past ten miles?"

"Chasing me? What for?"

I took five steps toward him and froze. "You took off in a hurry when you saw my truck back at the Wendigo office. Do you want to tell me why?"

"Gee, I don't know. I guess I was in a hurry to get fishing. Honest to God, I never saw you behind me."

"That's because you were going sixty-five miles per hour."

"Was I? I don't think I was. Fifty, maybe. Are you sure about my speed? Were you using one of those radar guns, because I'm pretty sure I wasn't speeding."

Dow knew I might have trouble proving that he'd exceeded the limit along this unmarked stretch of forest road.

"What about littering?" I said. "You tossed something out of your truck about three miles back. What was it?"

"You've got me scratching my head here. I'm not one of those slobs who chuck their beer cans out the window." His bushy eyebrows suddenly climbed a couple of inches on his forehead. "You know what? A partridge did fly up in front of me as I was driving. I bet that's what you saw."

Dow's story was a complete fabrication, but I had to hand it to him: The man was a terrific actor.

"Luckily, there's a way we can be sure," I said. "My partner got out of the truck to see what it was you threw out. Why don't we take a ride and see what she found?"

"I'm not under arrest, am I?"

"No," I said.

"Then technically you can't detain me. I'm thinking I should be on my way."

"I thought you were going fishing," I said.

"That was before you started accusing me of all these misdemeanors. I'm kind of feeling harassed."

I put my hand up as if I'd just heard a noise. "Hold that thought."

I returned to the cab of my pickup and grabbed the mike and held it to my mouth as if I'd just received a transmission that Dow hadn't heard. I moved my lips soundlessly as I stared at him through the bug-splattered windshield. After half a minute, I returned the hand mike back to its hook.

"Well, it turns out my partner found something," I said boldly to disguise my lie.

"What?"

"Let's just say I understand why you didn't want us to catch you with it."

He twisted the end of his mustache. "I think you're trying to trick me."

"I'll tell you what," I said. "You come with me for ten minutes, back to see my partner, and I'll give you a chance to prove the thing we found isn't yours. If you can, I'll let you return to your fishing and forget about the speeding citation, too. Otherwise I'm going to have to poke around your truck a little."

"You can only search for stuff in plain sight."

"That's true—unless you give me permission."

He let out a blast of air through his nose. "Sorry, Warden, but that ain't going to happen."

"How about this, then, Mr. Dow? If you come with me, I'll tell you why I drove all the way over to the Wendigo office to have a word with you."

"You know my name?"

"Yes, sir. I've been looking for you all morning."

"What for?"

"Take a ride with me, and I'll tell you."

What could I possibly have on him? The length of his silence told me there was a long list of offenses. If Troy Dow was the most law-abiding member of his clan—as the woman at the gatehouse had claimed—I could scarcely imagine where that left the rest of them.

"OK," he said at last. "But only because I've got nothing to hide."

He tossed the fishing rod into the back of his truck and walked, bowlegged, toward me. Up close, I could see his eyes twinkling from under those bushy brows. He smelled like he'd recently taken a long bath in turpentine. He squinted at the name tag stitched onto my ballistic vest.

"Warden Bowditch, is it?"

"That's right."

"Troy Dow. Pleased to meet you."

I waited for him to climb up into the passenger seat of my Sierra before closing the door. He smiled at me through the window. I could tell that he wasn't going to drop his affable mask for a second.

He waited for me to turn the truck around before asking, "So why were you looking for me?"

"I'll tell you after we pick up my partner."

We rattled along the washboard road. Eventually, we turned a corner, and I saw Stacey up ahead, standing with her arms behind her back and a big grin that brought out the resemblance to her father.

Troy Dow leaned forward. "*That's* your partner? How do you get any work done riding with a babe like her?"

I treated the question as rhetorical. As we came to a stop, Stacey strolled toward my vehicle, keeping her hands hidden. She seemed to be holding something she didn't want us to see.

I pushed the button to unroll the window. "I take it you found the item Mr. Dow threw into the woods during the chase."

"Oh, yeah."

Troy Dow didn't seem overly concerned about his situation. "Hey, beautiful," he said. "Do you have a sunburn, or are you always this hot?"

"Gee, that's original," she said.

"How about this one, then? Sex is a killer. Want to die happy?"

Stacey groaned and held up the limp gray body of a bird. It was the size of a small chicken, with a black throat and bright red eyebrows. The feathers were fluffed and spattered with blood from where the shotgun pellets had perforated its body.

I turned and looked hard at Troy Dow. "That's a spruce grouse."

"So it is!"

"They're an endangered species."

"You don't have to tell me that," he said. "My uncle shot one of those fool hens once and got a thousand-dollar fine. I bet some poacher mistook it for a partridge and then realized what it was and left it in the woods."

Stacey leaned closer so she could talk to him through the window. "Or he shot it on purpose and threw it out the window when he realized a game warden was chasing him."

"You might have trouble proving that in front of a judge," he said with a genial laugh.

"We saw you toss the bird out your window," I said. "I'm guessing you shot it while you were driving your gravel truck this morning. I bet if we compared the shot inside that bird with the shells inside your truck, there would be a match. You do have a shotgun in your Silverado, don't you?"

"It's a twelve-gauge, and you know what a common load that is. It would be kind of a stretch to call that proof in a court of law. I'm not accusing you of trying to railroad me."

"I have a thought," Stacey said. "Why don't you let me look inside your truck?"

"That's a good idea," I said. "If I don't find any spruce grouse feathers or blood, then I'll let you go with an apology. Otherwise we're taking a ride to the county jail in Dover-Foxcroft."

His eyebrows descended over his eyes. He bit one end of his mustache into his mouth and began sucking on it. "Fuck it," he said, holding his dirty hands out to be cuffed. "You got me."

19

The sun was behind us, the shadows in front.

Stacey sat in the back of my pickup, having given her place to Troy Dow. We'd retrieved his Remington 870, along with an open box of twelve-gauge shells. I'd bagged up the spruce grouse as evidence. Stacey carried the dead bird on her lap with care, the way she might have held a live cat.

"I don't like leaving my truck along the road for any of the local assholes to break into," Dow said with a grumble.

The pickup swayed as I maneuvered it around potholes and avoided the deeper ruts. "If you make bail, you should be out in no time."

"Why are you taking me to jail for a lousy hunting violation? It's not like I gave you any trouble back there. I barely even lied."

"Barely?" said Stacey.

Troy Dow rubbed the heels of his hands on the worn knees of his pants. "It was that kid who ratted me out, wasn't it? The one in the sombrero? I knew I shouldn't have given that fat fucker a ride."

I tried not to show my surprise. I had been waiting to bring up Chad McDonough, unsure that my hunch had even been correct. Now here was Troy Dow admitting to having given McDonut a ride. I needed to be careful about what I said next.

"That's what you get for picking up hitchhikers," Stacey said, raising her voice to be heard from the backseat.

"I knew there was something wrong about that guy," Dow said.

"Why's that?" she asked.

"The way he kept jabbering the whole time. Some people get paranoid when they smoke pot."

"What did he say that made you think he was high?" I said.

"He didn't have to say anything. I could smell it on him. But he kept looking in the mirror like he thought someone was behind us, and then when I stopped for the grouse, he started getting all worked up. He said he was in a hurry. I told him he could always walk back into Greenville. That shut him up for a while."

It had been fun to pretend that Stacey was my partner in solving a mystery and not the woman I was dating. But I was beginning to realize the pitfalls of involving her in an active investigation. She wasn't a law-enforcement officer and had no training in how to deal with potential witnesses to a crime, let alone suspects. I glanced at her in the rearview mirror, trying to hint that she should leave the questioning to me, but she didn't seem to get the message.

"Where did you drop him off?" Stacey asked.

"At the corner downtown. The asshole wouldn't even give me a fucking joint to repay me for the ride."

She leaned against the back of his seat. "Did he say where he was headed?"

"What do you mean?" Dow's wide shoulders tensed. There was suspicion in his voice, but Stacey couldn't hear it.

"Where did McDonough say he was going?" she asked.

As soon as she'd asked the question, I knew it was too late. She'd given us away.

"Wait a second." Dow turned his head slowly toward me, his eyes narrowing. "Who are you looking for—me or him?"

I tried changing the subject to distract him. "So you must be related to Trevor Dow."

"He's my brother. You didn't answer my question. Why are you so interested in that kid?"

Stacey had realized her error and tried to bluff. "We need to get a signed statement from him about you shooting that spruce grouse."

Despite her many skills, she was a lousy liar. I had made a mistake by letting her pretend to be a game warden. Troy Dow was too experienced in the ways of cops to be taken in by such a transparent ploy.

"You're looking for him, and you have no clue where he is." His cheeks turned scarlet above his mustache. "It's got to do with those missing girls, doesn't it? You came looking for me because you knew I'd given him a ride. You didn't even know about that grouse until I chucked it out the window. I knew I shouldn't have taken off when I saw your truck!"

I removed my sunglasses and set them on the dashboard. I wanted him to see the resolve in my eyes. "Why don't you just tell me what he said to you."

His mustache twitched when he smiled. "Let me go, and I'll tell you whatever you want."

"No deal."

"Fine, then," he said. "Take me to jail."

He settled back against the headrest and intertwined his fingers over his bulging chest. He closed his eyes, as if intending to take a nap. In the mirror I watched Stacey bow her head in regret. I wouldn't have wanted to play poker with Troy Dow, I decided.

We passed the Wendigo yard again on our way into Greenville. I had lost my advantage with Dow and was desperate to get it back. I considered stopping at the office, in the hope that he wouldn't want to jeopardize his job by having me parade him in front of his coworkers. But it was apparent that his boss already knew what a miscreant he was, and the thought of threatening the man—however obnoxious he might be—with the loss of his livelihood struck me as beyond the pale.

Moosehead Lake came into view, bluer than the sky and stretching off toward mountains aglow in the afternoon sun. A white sailboat tacked along in the distance, a reminder of summer. But the water looked cold.

As I approached the village crossroads, I had a decision to make. To the right was the road south. The highway traveled through Monson and Dexter before it came to the county seat in the picturesque town of Dover-Foxcroft, where all prisoners arrested in Greenville were taken to jail. It was a two-hour round-trip. By the time we'd have brought Troy Dow in for booking and returned to the search area, it was likely that Chad McDonough would be even farther away.

At the stop sign, I turned north instead.

Troy Dow sensed the change in direction and snapped his eyes open. "I thought you were taking me to jail."

I reached for my sunglasses. "We have a stop to make first."

He sat up. "Where?"

"You'll see."

I followed the eastern shore of the lake for a quarter mile, passing the sign for the Greenville Airport, until I came to Village Street. Up ahead was the Maine Warden Service's sprawling regional headquarters: a collection of tan buildings with green metal roofs. As promised, Lieutenant DeFord had moved the circus here, and now the paved lot behind the sliding chain-link gate was packed with the same vehicles I'd seen earlier in Monson: Warden trucks and police cruisers, vans used by the search-and-rescue teams, horse trailers, and even the Salvation Army chuck wagon, where someone was now handing out tuna sandwiches to the weary volunteers emerging from the woods. Two television news vans with jutting antennas had joined the ragtag fleet.

I found a parking spot beside a familiar black Escalade in front of the IF&W office and turned off the engine.

"What are we doing here?" Dow asked in a low voice.

"I thought we'd get something to eat before I took you to jail. I've heard the food in lockup is pretty nasty. Follow me."

A rack of sun-blanched moose antlers hung above the entrance to the main building. I held the door open for Stacey and Troy Dow. She gave me a questioning look as she passed, but I kept the deadpan.

Dozens of employees of the Maine Department of Inland Fisheries and Wildlife—wardens and biologists—worked out of this office, but on any given day, most of them were in the field. It was unusual to encounter so much human noise inside the building. At the reception desk, I asked a plump blond woman I hadn't met before if I could bother Lieutenant DeFord for a few minutes. She directed a glare at Troy Dow that told me he and she were acquainted—an observation that he quickly confirmed.

"Hey, Megan," he said. "You're looking good. Have you lost weight?"

"Go to hell, Troy."

"Ouch, baby."

Megan tossed her hair as she picked up the phone and pressed it to her ear. "Let me see if the lieutenant is free."

She turned her back so that we couldn't eavesdrop on the conversation. A sudden groan from my stomach caused Troy Dow to break into laughter. I often forgot to eat when I was focused on something; it was a habit I'd had since I was a teenager, sitting all day in a deer stand, listening for the rustle of hooves in the fallen oak leaves.

The receptionist put down the telephone. "The lieutenant said to go on back to the conference room."

"Stacey, why don't you get something to eat. I'll track you down when I'm done."

Her mouth drooped. "Sure," she said after a long pause.

"Hold out your hands," I told Troy Dow.

I unlocked his cuffs.

He massaged his wrists, as if the manacles had caused him discomfort. "So does this mean you're not going to charge me with shooting that bird?"

I motioned for Troy to follow me, and we headed down the hall. The door to the conference room stood open. There were maps, binders, and half-empty cups of coffee on the table. DeFord and the FBI agent, Genoways, were huddled over a laptop, conversing in hushed tones.

157

Genoways shut the laptop before we'd even entered the room. His black eyes had their usual fierceness.

DeFord was still wearing his dress uniform, but there was a sheen of perspiration along his forehead and half-moons under his eyes from lack of sleep. The fluorescent lights didn't flatter him.

"What's going on, Bowditch?" DeFord said. "Oh, hello, Troy."

"Lieutenant."

I should have realized that Troy Dow was a well-known personage among the local wardens.

"Mr. Dow gave Chad McDonough a lift out of the Hundred Mile Wilderness this morning," I said. "He told me that McDonough was nervous and in a hurry to leave. We need to find him, sir. I think he knows something about what happened to Samantha and Missy."

DeFord and Agent Genoways exchanged glances.

"Is that true, Troy?" the lieutenant asked.

Dow settled into one of the chairs and folded his hands across his chest again. His nails were black. "Maybe—but there's a misunderstanding I'd like to clear up first."

I explained to the lieutenant about our wild ride through the forest and the dead grouse Stacey had found in the bushes. "If I let him go, Mr. Dow says he's willing to be of assistance to our investigation."

"Jesus Christ, Troy. Two girls are missing."

"Those twats aren't my concern." His raspy voice had never sounded so unpleasant.

The FBI agent leaned over to DeFord and whispered something into his ear.

The lieutenant shrugged. "Fine. We'll forget about the grouse. Tell us everything—and I mean *everything*—that happened this morning with Chad McDonough, and you're free to go."

The bushy tips of Dow's mustache turned upward when he grinned.

"I picked him up on the KI Road around seven o'clock, over near where the Long Pond Road comes in. I was bringing a load back into town, and he had his thumb out and looked kind of beat-up, so I decided to give him a ride. Like I told Warden Bowditch, I could smell that he'd been toking up as soon as he got inside the truck. His eyes were all red, and he was wicked paranoid, looking in the side mirror the whole way. Gave me a different name from what you've been calling him, too. I forgot to mention that part. He told me his name was Kyle."

"Did he say anything about why he was in such a rush to get to Greenville?"

"He said he'd gotten a call that his father'd had a heart attack and he needed to get home to New Jersey."

"I thought he was from Massachusetts," I said.

"He is," said DeFord. "And his father is deceased. Agent Geno-ways called his house this morning and spoke with the mother." I was eager to hear more about that conversation. But the lieutenant returned his attention to Troy Dow. "What else did he have to say?"

"He told me he hated quitting the AT because he'd hiked the whole way from Georgia in just four months, which was near record time. I didn't believe him, on account of how fat he was. He should have burned off some of that blubber if he'd been climbing all those mountains. I asked him what'd happened to his face, and he said he'd taken a tumble on a wet boulder. I believed that part."

"He was with you when you shot the spruce grouse?" I asked.

Dow paused, as if not wanting to admit his culpability, even though he'd already received a dispensation. "We came up on it in the middle of the road. You know how fool hens are—they just freeze when something scares them. Dumb chickens. I got out of the truck and shot it. He said he didn't know it was hunting season yet. I said I had a special permit because I am one-eighth Penobscot Indian. He asked me which part was Indian, and I said, 'My pecker.'"

He waited for a laugh from us, which did not come.

"Then he started going on about coyotes, and were they danger-ous, and had I ever shot any."

"What did you tell him?"

"I told him that shooting predators was my third favorite thing," said Troy, not needing to name the other two. "I figured he was all paranoid on account of having smoked too much weed when he woke up. I didn't put any stock in what he was saying."

"Where did you leave him, Mr. Dow?" Agent Genoways asked. It was only the second time I'd heard his voice. He had a Baltimore accent.

"In front of the Citgo station. He asked if I would take him to get his car up on the Golden Road—offered me a hundred bucks—but I said I wasn't a shuttle service."

"The state police found McDonough's car parked at Abol Bridge," I told DeFord. "He must've had someone drive him back down to Monson before he started on his trek across the Hundred Mile Wilderness."

"So the last you saw him he was headed north?" the lieutenant asked.

"No, he was just standing in the parking lot, talking on his cell phone, with his backpack on the ground."

"Any idea who he was calling?" I said.

"Someone about a ride, I figured."

"Probably the same person who shuttled him back from Abol Bridge," I said. "There aren't too many people who offer that service around here, Lieutenant. I shouldn't have trouble tracking them down."

Genoways whispered in DeFord's ear again.

"You did a good job today, Mike," the lieutenant said. "But the FBI is going to take it from here."

He might as well have punched me in the solar plexus. I had begun to think of finding Chad McDonough as my own personal project. Now I was being told that my place was back in the woods. There is often a moment when a straight-up search for a lost person becomes a criminal investigation. Sometimes it's only clear in retrospect when the hour has turned. I had a sick feeling that this conversation would be it.

But why the FBI instead of the state police? Calling shuttle vans to look for a person of interest seemed like a job for troopers. Genoways's impassive face told me nothing.

"Can I get a ride back to my truck now?" said Troy.

The lieutenant folded his strong arms across his chest. "We're not a shuttle service, either, Troy. You're just going to have to walk back."

"That's, like, seven miles!"

"You still have some daylight left. You'd better get moving."

A heavy fist began beating against the conference room door. Investigator Pinkham stuck his head in without being invited. His glasses were askew. "You need to get out here, John."

"What is it?"

"The Reverend Mott just slapped Stacey Stevens in the face."

2 0

The lieutenant ran out to the parking lot. People began to hurry past the open door.

Troy Dow gave me a toothy grin. "I want to see this."

"I don't think so."

"The lieutenant said I was free to go. Do you want to come with me or not?"

I couldn't stop him, and it sounded like Stacey might need my help. We followed the other curiosity seekers out into the sunshine. The sudden brightness blinded me. The breeze blew the froggy smell of the lake across the asphalt.

"Who is this person? What is she doing here?" I heard a man yell.

"Reverend, please!" another man replied.

If I squinted, I could make out a scrum gathered around the Salvation Army wagon. I picked out Missy's mother first, the heavyset woman in the pleated green skirt. The distinctive gold pompadour of the Reverend Mott caught the afternoon light. I couldn't see Stacey at all over the heads of the others, but I could hear her voice.

"No, I am *not* going to apologize."

"Would everybody please calm down!" DeFord said. "Wes, can you help me out here?"

"Go back inside, everyone," Wes Pinkham said. "Let's get back to work."

I circled the wagon to get a clear view. Except for Missy's mom, who seemed borderline catatonic, everyone looked livid.

"It was just a simple question," Stacey told the lieutenant.

"What is this woman's position here?" Mott asked. He had a rich, resonant voice, as if his throat were coated with honey. "Are you her supervisor, Lieutenant?"

DeFord stood between Stacey and Mott, like a referee in a ring with two boxers. The reverend had removed his sharkskin jacket at some point since I'd last seen him. His handsome, haughty face was the color of an unripe tangerine.

"The families are already in anguish without being insulted, too," he said.

"I'm sure Ms. Stevens didn't mean to offend anyone," DeFord said.

"Then she needs to apologize." Mott seemed to expand in size as he drew in his breath. "And then she needs to leave."

Pinkham raised his arm to block my way. "Go back inside, Bowditch."

As the person who had brought Stacey to Greenville, I felt responsible for her, but I needed to know what was happening before I intervened. Not that she ever seemed to need rescuing.

"Stacey's with me," I said.

Pinkham's high forehead shone with perspiration. "Then you need to get her out of here."

"I am not going to apologize, because there's nothing wrong with what I asked," Stacey told DeFord.

The lieutenant hissed something at her.

Stacey turned to the families, her arms open, her tone pleading. She had a red mark on her cheek, probably from where the reverend had slapped her. "There's nothing wrong with your daughters. They're not sinners. They're not going to hell."

Suddenly, I knew the question she'd asked the parents—and why the reverend was so incensed.

Beside me, Troy Dow muttered, "This is awesome."

I wanted to slug him, but DeFord caught my eye.

"Stacey?" I said. "Come on. Let's go."

She hadn't noticed me until that second, but I was the only person present to whom she could turn for support. Her only ally. Her mouth tightened, and she began opening and closing her hands, working the blood into her fingers.

"I'm sorry," she told the Boggses and the Montgomerys. "I hope you find your daughters. I will be praying for you."

She put her head down and started off across the lot.

"That isn't good enough!" Samantha Boggs's father called.

I hurried to catch up with her. I hadn't realized that one of the television camera crews had been photographing the confrontation from a discreet distance. A man dressed in a polo shirt and khakis was trying to press a microphone on Stacey, but she practically elbowed him aside.

"Get away from me!"

I followed her through the open gate. She stopped abruptly before she reached my truck, as if she'd reached the end of a leash.

"I don't believe this shit," she said.

"What did you say to them, Stacey?"

"I asked them if anyone had reason to hurt their daughters," she said. "They said no. So I asked if there was somebody who might have hated them for being gay."

"Did Mott actually slap you?"

She touched her rosy cheek. "Can you believe it? He acted like I was some mouthy kid. I would have slapped him back if I hadn't been so shocked."

I glanced back at the lunch wagon and saw Mott and the families glaring in our direction. I knew DeFord expected me to return Stacey to her vehicle back in Monson. It would be better for everyone, herself included, if she didn't stick around the search area tonight. "I think we should get moving."

She yanked the pickup door open and slammed it shut behind her.

I circled around to the driver's side and got in.

"Missy's mom knows, Mike. She knows that her daughter is gay.

I could see it in her eyes when I asked about them. The woman is horrified. She thinks Missy is going to hell." She began fighting with the seat belt. "Goddamn it!"

I reached over and helped ease the strap across her torso. It snapped into place.

"It's so sad and so infuriating," she said. "Samantha and Missy had to hide who they were from their own parents, and now they're probably dead and will never get to tell them."

"I know."

I found myself thinking about Stacey's friend Kendra. She had ink black hair, tattoo rose branches circling her biceps, and a ring in her nostril. To my knowledge, she was the only woman with whom Stacey had ever had a romantic relationship.

"How did you know Samantha and Missy were gay?" I said at last.

"I just knew."

"So you have some sort of gaydar?"

Seconds after the words had come out of my mouth, I regretted them.

"You can mock me if you want. I get a vibe from certain people. I can't explain it, but it's real."

"I'm not mocking you. It was the wrong word. I apologize. I'm just having trouble understanding how you saw that in one photograph. Especially when no one else picked up on it."

"Yeah, because male game wardens are so sensitive to the presence of lesbians in their midst."

"Now who's the one doing the mocking?"

She fell silent. We were climbing the road out of Greenville, passing the Indian Hill Trading Post. Then the forest closed in around the highway and became a blur again.

Black lines squiggled across the gray asphalt before us. Some of the tire marks were the work of hot-rodders who used their vehicles as paintbrushes. Others had been left by inattentive drivers who had lost control of their cars or had veered into ditches to avoid animals. An automated yellow sign sensed our approach and began to flash its amber lights. ATTENTION: HIGH RATE OF MOOSE CRASHES NEXT 6 MILES.

"I'm sorry, Mike," Stacey said after a long silence. "I'm not mad at you. I'm mad at the whole fucked-up situation." She gazed off through the dirty windshield at nothing in particular. "It's just that I see so much of myself in them, you know?"

I wasn't sure if this was a confession. "You mean when you were with Kendra?"

"Yeah. It took me a long time to find myself. I'm still not sure I have."

"Join the club."

"It wasn't just the photo," she said. "It was their trail names, too. A lot of the names people pick are based on private jokes. But the names they chose were just weird. Baby Ruth and Naomi Walks. Both biblical, both humorous. And then I remembered that some people believe Ruth and Naomi were actually lovers."

"I thought Naomi was Ruth's mother-in-law." My knowledge of the Old Testament was spotty at best.

"Yeah, but some of the verses can be read in a way that suggests their love for each other went beyond that. I have no idea if it's really true. I just remember some of my friends saying that there were passages in the Bible that condoned being a lesbian. My reaction was, why should it even matter?"

"The Bible matters to billions of people."

She sighed and slid down in the seat. "My mouth has always gotten me in trouble."

"You're not afraid of speaking your mind."

"Maybe I should be."

Because of the incident with the reverend, I realized we'd never gotten lunch. I didn't like the thought of saying good-bye again, either. "Do you want to grab something to eat?"

"Where?"

"There's that good Cajun place."

"You didn't see the sign out front as we were driving by this morning? It said 'Closed, Out of Food.' "

"I guess all the thru-hikers cleaned them out."

"Fuck it, Mike. I don't want to go home, especially now."

"DeFord will castrate me if I let you stick around. You don't want that, do you?"

"No, I don't." She reached over and rested her hand on my knee. "You can stop worrying about my orientation, by the way. That's one thing I've figured out, at least."

"What do you mean?" I tried to sound convincingly confused.

"I've seen the look on your face since we started talking about Samantha and Missy being gay."

"Who's worrying?"

"Men always worry. They just never admit it."

Busted, I thought.

21

We sped along through birch and spruce woods. Faded asters and goldenrod grew in the ditches beyond the guardrails. White puffs drifted from the late-blooming fireweed and were swept skyward on the breeze.

Just as we were about to enter the dead zone between Greenville and Monson, Stacey got a phone call from her father. Charley was somewhere in the air. His weak cell signal was boosted by the mobile antenna the state police had towed into the Hundred Mile Wilderness.

"Mike and I are driving south on Route 15," Stacey told him. "Lieutenant DeFord kicked me off the search team. . . . No, I deserved it. What's going on?" Her face went white. "Ravens? Where?"

I eased my foot off the gas.

"You're breaking up," she said. "Say that again. Dad?"

I pulled the truck over to a sandy strip along the side of the road.

"Did you lose him? Do you want me to turn around?"

"We need to go back into the Hundred Mile Wilderness." She closed her hand around the iPhone and pressed it to her heart. "He sees a flock of ravens circling a cliff on the east side of Chairback Mountain."

"Has he reported it to the lieutenant?"

"DeFord's sending search teams on the ground to those coordinates."

"It could be anything." My palms began to sweat on the steering wheel. "A dead deer, a dead moose."

My reassurances sounded as hollow to my ears as I knew they did to hers.

As I swung the Sierra around and accelerated back up the hill, I found myself trying to remember the folk name for a flock of ravens. I'd memorized all of those colorful collective nouns as a kid. A group of hawks in flight was called a kettle. A group of crows was a murder. The plural for ravens was on the tip of my tongue. The word finally came to me as we passed the flashing moose warning.

An *unkindness* of ravens.

I pressed the gas pedal to the sand-strewn carpet.

I had to brake as we came through Greenville to avoid hitting a lonely tourist wandering across the street between the Maine Indian Store and Northwoods Outfitters. But as soon as we'd cleared the downtown and rounded the sharp turn at the end of the airstrip, I kicked it into high gear again.

My police radio chattered nonstop. For fear of alerting the media, no one wanted to give away what Charley had found or where the search was now being focused, so the conversations remained vague. But any experienced reporter listening to a scanner would have known something big was happening.

The gatekeeper stood on her little porch at the checkpoint, watching the emergency vehicles speed past. Her wrinkled face was grim. I knew she kept a police scanner on a shelf in her office.

Stacey tried raising her father again, but he was on the line with someone else, probably the Greenville command post. An unmarked Warden Service truck raced up behind me—Wesley Pinkham's silver Sierra—and kept pace as we passed the turnoff to the Head of the Gulf parking lot.

The radio squawked. "Ten-forty-seven," a fuzzy voice said.

Stacey let out a gasp. Charley must have taught his daughter the meaning behind the codes used by state of Maine emergency personnel. The right half of her face was lit by the setting sun; the other half remained in shadow. She was blinking as if she'd just been slapped by an invisible hand.

10-47: Medical examiner needed.

"That shouldn't have gone out across the radio," I said. "Now all those reporters are going to be rushing out here."

"As if this doesn't suck already."

Pinkham flashed his high beams, and I let him pass. His spinning tires sent a piece of gravel flying into my grille. The metal *ping* caused me to wince. I felt embarrassed at myself for caring about something as unimportant as my truck's paint job.

I followed Pinkham's dust cloud into the darkening Hundred Mile Wilderness. We passed a field of stumps where a logging skidder and a dump truck with the Wendigo logo were parked. I wondered if this clearing was the place Troy Dow had been working earlier in the day.

The sign for Hudson's Lodge loomed ahead, but we kept going, past the place where the Appalachian Trail emerged from the trees, past the wading ford across the Pleasant River, and around the base of Chairback Mountain. It was the same route Nissen and I had followed the previous afternoon, but I was stopped from retracing my steps by a state trooper standing in the middle of the road.

I rolled down my window. "Where am I going?"

"Pinkham wants everyone to park down here. You'll have to walk along the tote road. Your guys are about half a klick."

Stacey leaned past me. "What did you find?"

But the trooper had already stepped away from my window, giving his attention to the big-wheeled Toyota Tundra that had come up with his lights on behind me.

I swung the Sierra around and parked it as far as I could off the road, hearing twigs clawing at the passenger door as I scraped the wall of evergreens.

"You're going to have to climb out on this side," I told Stacey.

As I swung my legs down onto the hard road, my eyes traveled upward. The mountain loomed between us and the setting sun. Across the river valley, the hillside was illuminated—splashed with gold, orange, red, and green—but here we were in the dark. Far above our heads, a tiny plane with shining wings circled. I watched for ravens but saw none.

Stacey began hiking up the logging road without waiting for me. I hurried along in pursuit. My sore calf muscles had stiffened up again after an hour behind the wheel. The steep rock face above us was still holding on to the heat it had absorbed during the day, before the sun dipped behind the mountain. The air was warm, almost balmy, but it held an acrid odor, which I associated with autumn in the Maine woods: the smell of rotting vegetation.

"Christ." I stopped suddenly and gazed around at the trees.

Ten paces above me, Stacey heard me and paused. "What?"

"Nissen and I drove past this spot yesterday. The access trail to the Chairback Gap lean-to is at the end of this road." I squinted ahead into the premature dusk and made out a white shape. "That's Nissen's van right there!"

"What's he doing here?" she asked.

The simple answer was that he was one of the searchers. I knew that wasn't what she meant.

"Mike! Stacey!"

Both of us glanced down the road. Caleb Maxwell came striding toward us. He had changed clothes since we'd seen him at Gulf Hagas and was wearing a fishing shirt with the sleeves rolled to his biceps, board shorts, and his signature red Crocs. His hair looked wet, as if he'd just gone swimming or taken a shower. On his back he carried a military-surplus rucksack with a Red Cross badge—a souvenir from his days with Moosehead Search and Rescue.

"I heard the ten-forty-seven at the lodge," he said. "What have they found?"

"We don't know yet," Stacey replied. "We just got here."

I heard a heavy rattling noise and saw headlights come around the bend. It was a Department of Transportation utility truck pulling a trailer equipped with the powerful lights that road crews use for night work. Caleb coughed from the sandstorm it raised.

Nissen stood apart from the other members of his team. They all wore reflective vests, but he was dressed as he had been the day before: in safari shorts, a University of West Virginia baseball jersey, and overlarge hiking boots. We made eye contact, but there was no glimmer of recognition; I might as well have been a total stranger. He took a drink from his canteen, filled his cheeks until they bulged, then spit the liquid onto the fallen leaves.

I spotted Pinkham rummaging around the backseat of his truck. The warden investigator was still dressed like a bank manager on casual Fridays, but he'd exchanged his loafers for a pair of rubber Xtratuf boots. He removed a roll of yellow barricade tape from his backseat. So this was a death scene, just as I'd feared.

He raised his balding head and squinted in my direction. "Bowditch? Good. You can help me with this."

He handed me the roll of tape. The first protocol at a crime scene is always to secure and isolate it.

"Is it them?" I asked. "Is it Samantha and Missy?"

"I need you to chase everyone out of the road," he said. "Push them back to the edge of the clearing. We're going to need prints from everybody here. Tire prints, too, from all the vehicles. This clearing is already pretty well contaminated, but who knows?"

The warden investigator wanted boot prints from every person who had tramped in the soft ground. That way he could focus on unidentified tracks.

"What about me?" Stacey asked.

Pinkham pushed his eyeglasses back up on the bridge of his nose. "You're still around, Stevens? Maybe it's just as well. How much do you know about coyotes?"

"I did my master's thesis on them," she said. "I studied the impact of coyotes on deer populations."

Stacey was lying in order to get a closer look at the death scene, I realized. At the University of Colorado, she had done graduate work researching mountain lions but had never received her degree. She'd been asked to leave the program after coldcocking a tenured professor who'd put his hand on her ass. I felt that I should say something to Pinkham about the deception, but she silenced me with a look.

"Do you have a flashlight?" Pinkham asked her.

"I have a headlamp."

"Come with me then. Follow my trail."

She didn't even glance back as she entered the dense poplars and willows. I saw her headlamp flick on, bob a few times, and then disappear into the puckerbrush. I had to fight the impulse to charge after them, I was so desperate to see the scene myself. I stretched out a length of tape so I could read the printed words: POLICE LINE. DO NOT CROSS.

How exactly did Pinkham suspect Samantha and Missy had died? Was it a homicide or something else?

"Are they dead?" a voice said.

Caleb Maxwell stood ten yards behind me. His arms hung limp at his sides. He was working his hands as if they'd fallen asleep and he needed to get the blood pumping again.

"It looks like it," I said.

"Jesus. How?"

I didn't have an answer, so I didn't give him one.

"Listen, I need to string up this tape along the tree line. Can you tell Nissen and those other guys to back off to the edge of the clearing?"

"No problem. Anything else?"

"Make sure no one leaves. The detective wants to get boot prints from everyone who was in the woods here."

"You got it, man."

I kept picturing Caleb on the ledge above Gulf Hagas. He had lied to us about being the sobbing man the honeymooners had stumbled across on their hike. Had he simply been embarrassed to admit he'd had a breakdown?

As I fashioned a flimsy plastic fence out of the caution tape, I thought of coyotes howling outside the Cloud Pond shelter and creeping up on the women at Chairback Gap. In my mind I saw black shadows darting through the trees, boots tripping over roots, and then a bloodred flash.

"Hey, Bowditch!"

Maxwell waved me over to a knot of people in vests that glowed faintly in the dusk. I ducked under the tape and walked across the carpet of sawdust that covered the clearing from end to end. The searchers stopped talking.

"Nissen was the one who found them," Caleb said.

My eyes had adjusted somewhat to the failing light, but soon I would need to put on a headlamp. Even in the gloom, I could make out my former partner's smug expression.

"I just followed the ravens," Nissen said.

Once again I wanted to smack the man, but I refrained. "What did you see?"

"Those girls have been dead awhile," he said. "Nothing much left of them but skeletons, all torn apart. There are bones everywhere, some missing. The dogs, birds, and bugs picked everything clean. Most of the blood has been washed away by those storms. The rest—their clothes, backpacks—they're just shredded."

Nissen's voice had remained conversational as he described the carnage he'd stumbled across, but I couldn't help detecting an undertone of satisfaction. I remembered what Caleb had told me about their time together on the Moosehead Search and Rescue team, how Nissen had always seemed more interested in being the first to find the missing person. He hadn't cared if the person was alive or dead, just so long as he could claim to be the hero.

"Jesus," Caleb Maxwell said. "McDonut was right."

"We should wait for the medical examiner before jumping to conclusions," I said.

"My God, do you think those poor girls were eaten alive?" one of the volunteers asked.

"I didn't think coyotes attacked people like that," said another.

I lowered my voice. "Let's stop with the speculation. We don't know anything about what happened to Samantha and Missy."

But Nissen was unreachable. "Coyotes killed that girl up in Nova Scotia a few years back."

I poked my index finger against his sternum. "Knock it off, Nissen."

"Why?"

"If you go around spreading rumors, you're just going to hurt the parents."

"I can say whatever I want."

"And I can put you on the ground if you do."

His teeth were the color of a stained porcelain sink. "I'd like to see you try."

A light appeared, like a will-o'-the-wisp floating toward us through the trees. Somehow, I knew it was Stacey. As I stepped around Nissen, he called after me, but I didn't register the words.

Her face was a pale, almost bloodless oval beneath the headlamp. She kept her lips pressed together, as if to keep from vomiting. In my life, I had met few people with stronger stomachs than Stacey Stevens, but I couldn't remember seeing her this stricken.

I crossed the clearing in long strides, felt her bury her soft head in my chest. Every muscle in her body seemed to be clenched.

"Oh, Mike," she said. "It's so fucking horrible."

22

That evening, as darkness fell and we waited for the medical examiner to arrive, I thought about a dead woman named Taylor Mitchell.

On a late October afternoon in 2009, the nineteen-year-old folk-singer was hiking alone on a trail in Cape Breton Highlands National Park in Nova Scotia, Canada. She had come to the Maritimes to promote her new album and had decided to take time between performances to explore the forested plateau above the Cabot Trail scenic highway.

The last people to see Mitchell before the attack were a man and woman who passed her as she was heading up the Skyline Trail. The young woman went a short ways into the forest, then doubled back on an access road to the parking lot, possibly with a coyote already in pursuit.

Just seven minutes after they'd crossed paths with Mitchell, the couple encountered two coyotes on the park access road. The animals trotted toward them along the road, forcing them to step aside, but the hikers managed to take photographs. (A specialist in canine behavior who examined the pictures later testified that the coyotes had displayed an extraordinary lack of fear toward the humans.) These same coyotes are believed to have met the oncoming Mitchell several minutes later. When the couple heard what could have been either animal noises or screams in the distance, they rushed to a telephone to call for help.

A group of four other hikers then arrived in the lot. The man and woman told them about having seen Mitchell earlier and mentioned possible screams they had heard. The group headed out along the access road and soon came across a set of keys and a small knife (possibly used by Mitchell in a futile attempt to defend herself as she was chased back onto the Skyline Trail). In the clearing at the head of the trail, the rescuers discovered shreds of bloodied clothing and pools of blood on the ground. A washroom in the clearing had bloody handprints smeared on the door.

Half an hour after she had last been seen, Mitchell was spotted lying in the trees, with a coyote standing over her body. It took repeated charges by three of the young men to chase the coyote even a short distance away from the injured hiker. Mitchell was conscious and able to speak, but the coyote remained close by, growling. Eventually, a responding officer from the Royal Canadian Mounted Police appeared and fired a shotgun at the animal, and it took off. The rescuers found that Mitchell had been bitten over most of her body, with serious wounds to her leg and head, and she had lost a great deal of blood. She died just after midnight.

That same day, while the trail was still closed to the public, a warden keeping watch at the washroom location shot and killed a female coyote that was acting aggressively. In the weeks that followed, three other animals were dispatched within a kilometer of the Skyline Trail. Scientists determined that three of the coyotes, including the first and last, were linked to the attack on Mitchell by her blood on their coats and other forensic evidence. One of them, a large male, was identified as the dominant lead coyote photographed by the couple. Its carcass also contained pellets from the shotgun of the responding Royal Canadian Mounted Police officer, indicating it was the animal that had refused to move off Taylor Mitchell's helpless body.

The story whipped the Canadian media into a frenzy, with so-called wildlife experts speculating that the young singer might have provoked the coyotes by trying to feed them or by disturbing a den with pups. None of the other proposed explanations for the assault—that the coyotes were rabid, wolf-dog crosses, starving, immature, or protecting a kill—was substantiated by autopsies of the dead animals. In the end, no one could explain why a pack of coyotes had attacked and killed a healthy woman for the first time on record.

I had heard the tragic story of Taylor Mitchell even before I entered the Maine Warden Service, but it was at the Advanced Warden Academy that I learned the details. Like many Maine deer hunters, my instructor at the academy had a visceral hatred for coyotes—which he called "brush wolves." He said he'd seen deeryards in winter that were as red as battlefields from the predators massacring the helpless bucks and does, which were unable to escape through the thick snow. "The only good coyote is a dead coyote," he'd said. And he'd fumed at the know-nothing flatlanders who failed to see the mounting danger these increasingly aggressive animals posed. To him, the sad story of Taylor Mitchell was merely the first chapter in what was destined to become a very long and bloody book.

Listening to Stacey describe the carnage she'd seen—the gnawed bones, still pink with bits of flesh, the hunks of bloody hair stuck to leaves, the clothing torn to ribbons—I remembered my instructor's red-faced warnings. At the time they had seemed irrational. Now they seemed prescient.

I had killed more than a few coyotes in the line of duty, either because they seemed to be rabid or because they were snatching chickens from henhouses. Once, I'd had to put down a hundred-pound Hampshire pig after a coyote leaped over a fence and took a baseball-size bite out of its haunch. I'd also killed a coyote for sport one night when a warden friend named Cody Devoe invited me to hide with him inside a freezing blind, watching a bait pile through a night-vision scope, until the animal came within range of my rifle. The experience hadn't done much for me (the dead coyote, when seen up close, bore a disturbing resemblance to Rin Tin Tin), but I didn't begrudge Cody his fun.

Pinkham and DeFord kept most of the wardens who arrived

away from the scene, except for a handful of veteran officers whom they trusted to secure the area. Standing in the clearing, with the construction lights stretching our shadows across the sawdust like pulled rubber, we engaged in the very activity for which I'd rebuked Nissen. We speculated wildly, and without evidence, about how Samantha Boggs and Missy Montgomery had died.

"Hey, Bowditch," said Warden Tommy Volk. "What's this I heard about coyotes stalking the girls all the way from Cloud Pond to Chairback?"

"I'm not sure that really happened," I said. "It might have been two different family units."

"Family units! Listen to you."

"I knew this day was going to come," said gray-haired veteran Garland Tibbetts, who was a good man in the woods but no one's idea of an intellectual. "I wonder if they was menstruating."

"The girls or the coyotes?" asked Volk with a smirk.

We all glared at him. It was too soon for jokes, let alone tasteless ones.

"If you run from a canine, you trigger a DNA attack response," said Pierre "Pete" Brochu, a warden sergeant who came from a long line of wardens and considered himself more knowledgeable about animals and their behavior than the department biologists. "The girls should have stood their ground. Same as with an ursine."

"An ursine?" said Volk.

"A bear."

"I know what it means, professor."

"Chad McDonough told me they both had capsicum spray with them," I said.

"McDonough? Is he the one they're calling McDonut?" asked Volk.

"Does anyone know if he's been located?" I asked. "I spent my day chasing him."

But no one was interested in my fugitive hiker now that the picked-over bones of the women had been found.

"You see that escarp up there?" asked Warden Garland Tibbetts, jutting his chin at the darkness. "I bet them coyotes chased those poor girlies right off the edge and then fell upon their bodies down at the bottom. Jeezum, I hope those kids was already dead by the time they was eaten."

"Will you please shut up?" Stacey had been sitting quietly on an open truck gate, swinging her feet, not seeming to listen. I'd been trying to give her space since she'd returned from looking at the corpses. "For all we know, Samantha and Missy were murdered."

"I thought you said there were chew marks on the bones," Garland Tibbetts said.

"Their bodies could have been scavenged by the coyotes," she said. "We won't know for sure until the remains are autopsied. You all want to believe the coyotes did it because you already hate them."

The stares of the wardens turned toward the lone female among them.

Pete Brochu said, "Stacey, you haven't seen some of the depravities these animals have committed out in the woods."

"Don't give me that crap. I'm a fucking wildlife biologist."

"Didn't mean to offend."

She gave Brochu the finger and walked out of the light.

The wardens flicked their eyes at one another. They all knew Stacey was my girlfriend—cops can be the worst gossips when the subject is sex or money—and so they refrained from commentary. But Tommy Volk couldn't stop himself from cracking up. The man had impulse-control problems.

When I caught up with her, she had her arms braced against the medical examiner's Dodge camper van, as if she were trying to flip the vehicle onto its side. Her head was down, her arms tensed.

"Somebody murdered them, Bowditch." After briefly using my first name, she was back to her old ways. "It wasn't coyotes."

"How can you be sure?"

"Coyotes don't attack adult women."

"What about Taylor Mitchell, that singer in Canada?"

She let go of the van and straightened up. Her face was hidden behind a veil of shadows. "Those were park coyotes. They were acclimated to people. Wild animals are shy of human beings. You know that."

In my imagination I saw again the bold animal sitting, unafraid, in my headlights.

"What?" she asked.

"I didn't tell you this, but when Nissen and I were driving out of the wilderness last night, we came upon a coyote in the road. It wouldn't move out of the way of my truck. It was like it was taunting me to shoot it."

"Did you?"

"No."

"You know I'm right about someone murdering Samantha and Missy."

"Why don't we wait until the medical examiner studies the remains before making up our minds."

"It could take days or weeks for him to finish his report."

"Pinkham isn't going to shitcan his own criminal investigation," I said. "He's going to keep exploring leads that point to this as a homicide. He won't just wait around for the forensic tests to come back."

"It's still going to take time," she countered. "And meanwhile, everyone in the state of Maine is going to start panicking about 'killer coyotes' on the loose. Even after the medical examiner releases his findings, you know it won't stop the rumors." She shook her head, as if she felt sorry for me. "Two attractive young Christian girls get stalked and eaten by wild dogs in Vacationland. That's a story no one can resist. It doesn't matter if it's true or not. People want to believe in big bad wolves. But only humans can be truly evil."

23

Shortly after nightfall, Lieutenant DeFord pulled most of his men out of the woods. It had gotten too dark to examine the death scene with portable lights, and the medical examiner was concerned evidence might be missed and the area would be further contaminated. DeFord arranged for a contingent of Division C wardens to keep everyone out of that part of the forest. The investigation of the woods at the base of the precipice would resume at first light.

I was prepared to stick around. I traveled with a sleeping bag in my truck, and the thought of leaving Samantha and Missy (or what was left of them) felt like the worst sort of abandonment.

But DeFord took me aside. He held two plastic bags in his hands containing swatches of red-stained fabric. "Where's Stacey?"

I pointed down the logging road to where my truck was parked, out of sight in the darkness. "On the radio with her father."

"I'm thinking you should take her home," he said. "She seemed really shaken up. Pinkham shouldn't have taken her in there, but he wanted to know if the condition of the remains is consistent with a canine attack or if it looked like the corpses had been scavenged."

"What did she say?"

"Inconclusive." He wiped his hand across his bristled chin. "She said they've been dead awhile, though. There are bones everywhere, and some have been gnawed by mice and porcupines."

"Rodents are always the last ones at the dinner table."

He didn't seem to have heard me. "Right now we don't have a

clue how they died," he said, as if to himself. "The coyotes might have killed them, or they might have fallen off that cliff, or we might find bullet holes when we get a closer look at their skulls. And now I have to drive back to Greenville, wake up their parents, and ask them if they recognize a shredded sock and part of a bandana, because all that's left of their daughters is a pile of bones."

"Lieutenant!"

Stacey came running back into the lighted clearing, eyes wide with alarm. She'd removed the rubber band from her hair, which now swung loose on her shoulders.

"What is it?" DeFord said.

"Samantha's and Missy's parents are down at the turnoff. They're trying to get past the troopers."

"Goddamn it."

"It's worse than that," she said. "The Reverend Mott brought along a television crew."

The lieutenant thrust the plastic bags into my hand. "Give these to Pinkham. Then grab some men and meet me down at the road."

DeFord took off at a sprint down the hill. Stacey, as usual, was right on his heels. She always needed to be in the middle of things. I could only imagine the reverend's rage when he saw her face again.

I found Wes Pinkham conferring in quiet tones with a bald man with a neat white goatee and gold spectacles. He was dressed as if he'd come directly from the golf course: navy polo shirt and creased slacks. He was the state's chief medical examiner, Dr. Walter Kitteridge. Both men looked puzzled when I pushed the evidence bags on them.

"What's going on?" Pinkham asked.

"The Reverend Mott has called a press conference at the bottom of the mountain," I explained. "DeFord wants me to get some wardens down there."

I grabbed Brochu and Volk, and the three of us quickstepped down the road. The night was so dark I tripped on a stone and nearly went cartwheeling. Up ahead was a constellation of artificial lights: blue, white, and amber. As we drew near, the scene slowly resolved itself out of the blackness. Two state troopers had parked their cruisers to prevent a television van and the Escalade from driving into the clearing. Close to a dozen people—the families and reporters—pushed against the barricaded vehicles. The freaky illumination exaggerated their faces, making the people look like caricatures of themselves.

Lieutenant DeFord stood with his hands up in the light of the television camera, almost as if he were being robbed at gunpoint. "Can you guys stop taping? I'm not going to give you a statement."

"I want to know where my daughter is!" said Samantha's father.

Reverend Mott had rolled up the cuffs of his dress shirt. "The families have a right to see what you've found, Lieutenant."

Missy's mother seemed about to slump to the ground. Her husband had his arms around her waist, but she was a big woman, and he seemed to be having trouble. She was moving her lips silently, and I realized she must be praying.

Stacey hung back at the edge of the light. Caleb Maxwell stood beside her, shoulder to shoulder. I'd lost track of him after DeFord sent Nissen and the other volunteers away.

In my experience, local television people were generally an obliging lot. They rarely pushed the Warden Service too hard, out of fear of jeopardizing their future access. But the reporter with the microphone had a young face I didn't recognize, and he could smell a career-making story.

"Is it true the girls were killed by coyotes?"

So the rumors were already flying, just as Stacey had feared.

"Oh God!" Samantha's mother said.

DeFord held his hand up to block the spotlight. "Can you please turn that off?"

Headlights approached from beyond the television vans. A police horn barked. The camera turned toward the new vehicle. The unmarked state police cruiser stopped and both of the front doors swung open simultaneously. Sergeant Fitzpatrick stepped into the kaleidoscope. With him was Commissioner Matthews. Neither of them spoke a word, but Matthews advanced fast on the young TV reporter and lifted her brightly painted mouth to his ear. I don't know what she whispered, but the microphone nearly dropped from his hand.

"Turn it off, Randy," he told his cameraman.

The Reverend Mott puffed up his chest. "Mrs. Matthews—"

"I'll be with you in a minute, Reverend." She slid past him. "Lieutenant DeFord!"

The three of them—Matthews, DeFord, and Fitzpatrick—huddled together. Except for Samantha's mother, who had begun to sob, everyone else had fallen silent, waiting to see what was decided. I made my way over to Stacey.

"What a shit show," she whispered.

"How do you think they found out?"

"Maybe one of those searchers called the media."

"Nissen?"

"Reverend Mott!" Matthews motioned him over.

I saw the pastor's golden pompadour nod each time the commissioner finished a sentence. DeFord pointed up the logging road, and they all followed his outstretched arm with their intent eyes. Then they went back to talking.

After a few minutes, Mott returned to the families and gathered them together. Missy's mother straightened her spine. Samantha's mom stopped crying. The five of them formed a circle and held hands.

"Let us bow our heads in prayer," the reverend said, as if speaking to a packed church. "Let us remember the words of the Psalms. 'God is near to those that are broken at heart; and those who are crushed in spirit he saves.' For we find ourselves here—parents and friends of Samantha and Missy—brokenhearted and crushed in spirit. We can't help but ask why you have taken these girls from us, Lord. You who also lost a child and know the agony of grief.

Bring peace to those of us who are suffering and hear our prayers that you grant salvation to our lost children."

Stacey reached up, squeezed my shoulder, and said, "I need to get out of here."

I'd assumed that she would want to keep a vigil with me until Samantha's and Missy's remains were brought out of the woods. But I could see her chest rising and falling, and see her tears, and I knew what I needed to do.

"All right."

She turned and disappeared from the light in the direction of my parked truck.

Mott began to shout, his words ringing through the trees: "Tonight we find ourselves screaming in a screaming wilderness. God, have mercy on us. We are confused and angry, and we don't understand the powerful mystery of your ways. Lead us out of our own darkness and back into the light of your love and grace."

I approached DeFord and said, "Stacey wants me to take her home."

His expression was firm, almost cold, but I knew it was just a mask he was putting on. Being a police officer means that you are frequently a witness to the worst moments in people's lives. In those instances, you do your best to maintain your composure and separate yourself from the other person's pain. Most of the time you hold it together. Sometimes you fail.

Without a word spoken, the lieutenant gave me leave to go.

As we drove out of there, Stacey turned away from the grieving families. They were still holding hands, still saying their prayers. I watched their benediction in my rearview mirror, the glow of the emergency lights growing fainter and fainter as we left them all behind.

News spreads quickly in rural places, quicker than in cities and suburbs even. There are fewer distractions, and so when something dramatic takes place—a selectman is arrested for drunk driving, a farmhouse burns to the ground—the entire community becomes consumed by it. Rumors spread like a contagion. Schoolrooms, diners, and churches become vectors of gossip.

I could almost hear the conversations traveling through the telephone wires along the side of the road:

"Those two girls from Georgia were eaten by coyotes."

"I always said those coy wolves were going to kill someone. Only a matter of time."

"Well, maybe now the state'll get serious about shooting the damned things."

"Too late for those Bible students, though."

Stacey was right: It wouldn't matter if the forensic pathologist determined that the women were murdered or had died from a fall off the precipice. Some people would still believe the coyotes were to blame. This freak occurrence would validate their prior fear and loathing. No scientific proof can make someone stop hating something if their hatred gives them pleasure.

Deer eyes flashed green in my high beams, then disappeared into the thick cover along the side of the road.

"What did your dad say?" I asked when the silence became too much for me.

"He knew when he saw the ravens that it was them." She shut her eyes and massaged the bridge of her nose. "He predicts there will be a panic, and the governor is going to do something stupid."

We passed the gatehouse at the western edge of the Hundred Mile Wilderness and drove through the darkened downtown of Greenville, the only lights coming from the gas stations and lakeside bars. We headed south in silence, both of us lost in our thoughts, until we came to the trailhead outside Monson where Samantha and Missy had snapped their last photograph.

"Did you listen to Mott's prayer?" she asked. "Did you notice the way he avoided saying Samantha's and Missy's names? How he didn't pray for the salvation of their souls? Because in his mind they are already damned."

"I noticed."

"That's right. You notice things."

What does it matter? I thought. In my mind, prayers were for the living, to give the survivors strength and comfort. Let Mott prattle on if it helped the parents. Samantha and Missy were past the point of help. But I didn't want to debate my religious beliefs with Stacey, and I was certain she didn't want to debate hers with me, either.

"Do you want to get a room for the night?" I asked.

She gathered her hair together and knotted it in the back. "I just want to go home."

In the village, we passed the Lake of the Woods Tabernacle. The resident pastor must have also owned a police scanner—either that or one of his congregants had telephoned him with the news—because the lighted sign out front carried a new message to the world:

LOOK OUT FOR THE DOGS! LOOK OUT FOR THE EVILDOERS!
LOOK OUT FOR THOSE WHO MUTILATE THE FLESH!
PHILIPPIANS 3:2

"It's already beginning," said Stacey. "What did I tell you?"

I turned into the driveway beyond the firehouse, where she had left her Subaru that morning. Her Outback was one of the last vehicles there on the trampled field. The steel sparkled with a fresh sheen of dew when the headlights caught it.

An old man dressed in green sat on the ground with his back against Stacey's bumper. He rose wearily to his feet when he saw us pull in. It was Charley, I realized. He must have left his floatplane down at Lake Hebron again. His shoulders sagged, and his forehead was etched with deep lines.

Stacey and her father had a complicated relationship. They had been very close when she was a tomboy who wanted to learn how to shoot guns and pilot planes. That they were so much alike had only added to their estrangement after her mother, Ora, was paralyzed in a crash while Charley had been teaching her to fly. For a long time in her twenties, when Stacey was living in the Rocky Mountains and the desert West, neither of her parents knew what she was doing for work. She had returned to Maine only because she had been forced to leave graduate school and was out of money. She'd carried all her old resentments home with her like so much luggage. Being forced to move into her parents' guest cabin after so many years of independence humiliated Stacey. And her broken engagement with Matt Skillin had only made it worse.

Now she bounded out of the truck the way a child might, leaving her backpack behind. I sat behind the wheel with the engine still running, watching father and daughter embrace.

24

The days that followed seemed to move faster than they had before I'd entered the Hundred Mile Wilderness. It was late September, officially autumn now, with deer season fast approaching, and we were losing the light. In the afternoon it felt like the lengthening shadows were reaching into my soul.

After I left Stacey with Charley, I had driven to my rented house in southern Maine, where the Portland suburbs faded into the woods and cornfields around Sebago Lake, arriving just before dawn. De-Ford disbanded the search team later that morning, after the corpses had been removed from the base of the cliff and taken in a repurposed ambulance to the office of the state medical examiner in Augusta. The investigation into the cause of death continued, but I wasn't to be part of it. I heard that Pinkham wasn't ready to accept the prevailing wisdom that the women had been killed by wild animals, not until the forensic pathologist signed off on the theory. In the meantime, the warden investigator would continue to explore the human element.

Others were less circumspect. As Stacey had predicted, the national media seized on the salacious story of the beautiful young girls eaten by wolves. That Samantha and Missy were so-called Bible students only added to the tale's juiciness. I did my best to stay away from television sets and tabloids, but I couldn't escape the rumor mill that was the Maine Warden Service. I learned from Tommy Volk that the Reverend Mott had gone on the morning news shows as a spokesman for the families. There was no doubt in the preacher's mind that Samantha and Missy had been chased to their deaths by coyotes, and he was open in his condemnation of the state of Maine, as if somehow the searchers were at fault for not knowing the women had gone missing over a week earlier. There was talk of a lawsuit—for what and against whom, I had no idea.

Just as the story was about to be shoved aside by a new wave of fighting in the Middle East, a student at Pentecost University appeared in front of the cameras to tell the world that Samantha and Missy had secretly been lovers. Now there was sex to go along with the violence and religion. The university refused to comment on the rumors, and the Reverend Mott disappeared abruptly from the airwaves.

To quiet the panic and minimize the bad publicity threatening Maine's tourism industry, the governor issued an executive order, placing a bounty of one hundred dollars on every coyote killed around Moosehead Lake. Driven by money, revenge, and bloodlust, dozens of hunters and trappers took to the woods. Biologists were dispatched to tagging stations to receive the dead animals and take blood and hair samples to compare against the evidence found in the forest where Samantha's and Missy's bones were discovered. Stacey was pulled away from the study she had been doing on white-tailed deer and stationed back in Monson.

At the end of her first day collecting pelts, she called me from Ross's Rooming House, where she was staying.

"A German shepherd, Mike." Her voice sounded dry, as if she had yelled herself hoarse.

"What?"

"Some asshole shot a goddamned German shepherd today. He wouldn't believe me when I told him it was somebody's pet, even after I showed him the nails had just been clipped. He just wanted his hundred bucks."

"Oh God, Stacey."

"Troy Dow and his relatives brought in thirty-three animals.

Thirty-three! Some had been snared, others shot. One had an arrow broken off in it. For all I know, they imported half of them from other places around the state. It's like a fucking gold rush here."

"People are scared."

"Scared and greedy," she said. "I met a bunch of the Dows today. Trevor, Terrence, Todd, Tara—there seems to be a pattern. I guess the family matriarch is named Tempest. People think she's a witch because she never comes down off her hilltop. She just sits up there cursing people."

"Have you met Toby yet?"

"The developmentally disabled boy who hangs out at the general store? I asked Pearlene—she's the woman who owns the place— why she allows him to beg money from her customers, and she says everyone is terrified of the Dows, herself included. The whole in-bred clan lives together in a compound in the woods. Supposedly, the settlement is booby-trapped with all sorts of trip wires and explosives. In addition to the usual poaching and drug dealing, they've got a racket going as caretakers for the cottage owners around Hebron Lake. If you don't hire them to watch your place for the winter, they'll burglarize it or just burn it down. It's like the hillbilly mafia up here."

"Take care of yourself."

"Don't worry, I've got my pink canister of pepper spray." She paused when I didn't respond. "That was a joke. But if my body shows up, gang-raped and shot in the head, you'll know who to talk to first."

I pinched my brow between my thumb and forefinger. "That's not funny, Stacey."

"None of this is funny. It's sickening is what it is. Today was one of the worst days in my life. Pickups were coming in stacked with dead animals, one after the other. I've never seen slaughter like this, and people were just gleeful about it. Guys were teasing each other because they'd shot more coyotes than their buddies. Others were pissed off at me that I wouldn't pay them cash and told them they'd have to send in a voucher to be paid. Not one of them mentioned Samantha or Missy, either. Those women were just an excuse for these assholes to commit mass murder—or whatever you want to call it. I don't know if I can do this, Mike. I'm just praying that the medical examiner will come out with a statement tomorrow saying that the coyotes didn't kill them, so that the bounty gets called off."

I hesitated before I spoke. I respected Stacey immensely but was obliged in my job to consider all possibilities. "We don't know what the forensics report will say."

"What do you mean?" She seemed genuinely puzzled.

"What if the results are inconclusive? There's also the chance that—"

"What?"

"It happened before up in Canada. Remember Taylor Mitchell?"

Stacey seemed to go away for a long time. I wondered if the call had been dropped.

"Not you, too," she said at last.

That was when she hung up on me.

The next morning, I met Kathy Frost for eggs and coffee at a breakfast place in Lewiston. She was on her way to have some tests done at Central Maine Medical Center. I didn't ask what kind of tests, but I assumed they had something to do with her having been shot. Some of the steel pellets were still lodged inside her torso and would be as long as she lived.

My former sergeant came through the door of Simones Hot Dog Restaurant. She looked better than the last time I'd seen her—but not much.

"How are you feeling?" I asked.

"Like a road-killed raccoon. Is it that obvious?"

The waitress came over with a coffeepot to fill our cups. She blinked her heavy eyelashes at me and said how much she liked my uniform, causing me to redden in spite of myself. I ordered a chili and cheese omelette. Kathy opted for oatmeal.

"Your gastrointestinal system must hate you," she said.

"I have an iron stomach."

"Wait until you hit forty."

Two old geezers at the next booth were arguing with each other in singsong French. One of them—it sounded like he owned apartment buildings—had a gripe against *les Somalis.*

Lewiston was a former mill town. At the turn of the twentieth century, the textile factories along the Androscoggin River had employed tens of thousands of Canadian émigrés, my great-grandparents among them. In those days, fancy restaurants had signs in their doors saying NO FRENCH ALLOWED, and children at the Catholic schools were slapped by nuns for not speaking English. In time, the mills began to close as the manufacturing jobs went to Asia. Lewiston's population plummeted, until a new wave of immigrants arrived from Somalia. Now it was commonplace to see dark-skinned women in head scarves carrying bags of groceries along Lisbon Street. Inevitably, there were culture clashes. The Lewiston mayor appeared on national TV telling the Somalis to stop coming and draining the city's welfare services. A man tossed a pig's head into a downtown mosque.

The names change, I thought, but hate reigns eternal.

"Stacey is mad at me," I said.

"What did you do now?"

I sat back in the mustard-yellow booth. "Why do you assume I'm to blame?"

By way of an answer, Kathy raised an eyebrow over the rim of her coffee mug.

I lowered my voice so that the Franco men wouldn't overhear. "She's convinced that the medical examiner is going to find that Samantha and Missy were murdered," I said. "She thinks the governor's bounty program is a waste of time and money. She says he's just whipping up fear for political purposes."

"That sounds right to me."

"You don't think it's possible they were killed by coyotes?"

"Possible, but unlikely."

The waitress arrived with our plates. I waited until she had finished refilling our mugs to return to the conversation.

"In that case, who do you think killed them?" I said.

Kathy doused her hot cereal with milk. "They could have just fallen."

"Both of them?"

She sighed, glanced around at the nearby booths and tables, then leaned over her bowl.

"If I tell you something, I need you to keep it a secret. Remember that FBI agent who was at the command post the night you came back from Chairback Gap, the man who never blinked?"

"Genoways?"

"You didn't wonder why he was there?"

I lowered my fork. "Don't tell me the rumors about the serial killer are true."

"Over the past five summers, there have been a series of strange deaths and disappearances on the AT. It started when a young guy in Virginia was found dead in a creek, as if he'd gotten carried away by a flash flood. The only problem was, he had no water in his lungs. The next year, a couple of day hikers in Pennsylvania came across a woman hanging by a bungee cord from a tree. It looked like a suicide, but her family said she had no reason to kill herself. There were similar unexplained incidents in the Adirondacks and Vermont. And then there was the Iraq vet who disappeared in New Hampshire last summer."

I hadn't heard of the other occurrences, but I knew about the missing Marine. He had lost one of his legs in an IED attack in Fallujah and was hiking the Appalachian Trail on his prosthetic limb to raise awareness about the plight of wounded warriors. The man had vanished without a trace in the Presidential Range during a stormy week when New England was being battered by the remnants of a tropical hurricane. The working theory was that he'd wandered off the trail and fallen into a gorge.

"The FBI thinks all these incidents are related?" I asked.

"They aren't sure. Except for the fact that they're all unexplained, there isn't anything to tie them together."

"Other than the northward pattern."

"Right. After Vermont and New Hampshire, Maine would be next. With the hiking season almost over, it was looking like the connection had fallen apart. Then Samantha and Missy disappeared."

I tried a forkful of omelette but the chili had gone cold. "How come this is the first I'm hearing of this?"

"Because the Bureau doesn't want to start a panic. Hundreds of thousands of people hike the AT every year—either the whole trail or just parts of it. What would happen if word got out that a serial killer was loose out there, especially when there's no concrete proof it's even true?"

"The FBI might not have wanted a panic, but that's what they've got. The problem is that people are freaking out over man-eating coyotes."

In college I had taken a couple of courses in psychology, naïvely thinking it might help in my future career in law enforcement, and one of my instructors had given us tests where we were supposed to look for hidden images in television static. Most everyone in the class found something, but it turned out the experiment was rigged. There were no hidden numbers or words. It was all an illusion. The professor wanted to show us how the human brain searches for patterns where none exist. He said it was an evolutionary tool we'd developed to deal with uncertainty and helplessness—a way to find meaning in chaos.

"That explains Genoways's interest in Chad McDonough," I said, pushing aside my half-eaten omelette. "The kid told me he was a section hiker. What do you know about his whereabouts over the past five summers?"

"Genoways didn't share that information with me."

"What motive would someone have to murder strangers and make it look like accidents and suicides?" I asked.

Kathy shrugged. "Kicks? A sense of power? Knowing he was outwitting the hapless FBI? And who says the victims were strangers? The killer might've known one or more of them. He could have murdered the others as a means of misdirection. Didn't you ever read Agatha Christie when you were a kid?"

"I was more of an Arthur Conan Doyle fan."

"Why am I not surprised?" Kathy winced as she settled back against the hard plastic booth.

A depressing thought came to me. "If this is part of a pattern—if the same guy killed Samantha and Missy and the others—then we shouldn't expect the medical examiner's report to settle anything. All the other deaths have been inconclusive."

"It might absolve Stacey's coyotes at least. My guess is it will."

Until that moment, I hadn't realized that the Franco guys who'd been arguing in the booth behind me had left.

"I should apologize to her for not trusting her instincts," I said.

"I'm not going to tell you what to do, Grasshopper."

"That would be a first."

Kathy gave me a wink and returned to her oatmeal. The waitress came by with the bill.

Before I drove back to my district, I sent Stacey an e-mail, asking if she wanted me to drive up to Monson after work. I could help out at the tagging station. Better to offer my apology in person, I thought.

Kathy's news had rattled me. When Dani Tate had brought up the rumors of a serial killer stalking the Appalachian Trail, I had laughed them off as delusional. Human predators were an obsession of Hollywood, but there hadn't been a mass murderer apprehended in Maine for as long as I could remember.

But what if Genoways was chasing a real person, and what if that person was someone I had met?

In my mind, I saw Chad McDonough's half-baked smile again. Where had McDonut gone? There had been no sightings of the pudgy section hiker after Troy Dow had dropped him in downtown

Greenville. The last I'd heard, his car was still parked at the Abol Bridge Campground with a boot on the wheel.

What about his mysterious man in the red tent? Was it just a coincidence that a camper had found a shredded tent in the river below Gulf Hagas?

And then there was Nonstop Nissen, who had volunteered to search Chairback Mountain and had conveniently been the first to find the broken skeletons of Samantha and Missy below one of its cliffs.

Even Caleb Maxwell suddenly seemed suspicious. The manager of Hudson's Lodge had lied to me about being seen crying on a ledge above Buttermilk Falls. Maybe it had nothing to do with the dead women. But maybe it did.

Not to mention the dozens of anonymous thru-hikers on the trail that week, of course.

It was as if I was back in psychology class, staring into a fuzzy television screen, trying to connect the dots, looking for a pattern that might or might not be there.

25

While I was up north, I had received a voice mail from the executive director of a local land trust, asking if I could swing by several preserves the organization managed around Sebago Lake. He said that the parking lots were being used by men engaged in certain clandestine sexual acts.

His message had a pleading, slightly embarrassed tone: "It's really getting out of hand, Warden. We don't want to get people arrested. But a mother was taking her kids for a hike at Standish Cove yesterday, and she came upon two half-naked men doing you-know-what behind a big oak tree. We've tried cutting back the bushes to give them fewer places to hide, but my stewardship director was there this morning, and he found used condoms all over the place. All we can figure is that the lot must be listed on some Internet site as a place for cruising. Can you just stop in every once in a while and chase off anyone who doesn't seem to belong there?"

From Lewiston, I followed the back roads to the Lake Region. The weather had turned cooler, more autumnlike, and there were new patches of gold and red on the hillsides. Sebago looked as hard as a sapphire in the morning sunshine.

I found two pickups parked side by side in the Standish Cove lot: a newly washed and waxed Ford F-150 and a beat-up Toyota Tacoma patched together with Bondo. The Ford had a Fraternal Order of Eagles decal on one of its windows. The Toyota was plastered with bumper stickers with slogans like COEXIST and LOVE OUR

MOTHER. I pulled in beside the mismatched vehicles and turned off the ignition.

In the distance, a red-breasted nuthatch tapped its bill against a tree. Shafts of dusty sunlight angled through the canopy onto the dead needles and fallen leaves. Small stumps, as wide around as broomsticks, showed where saplings had recently been. The land trust had spared only the towering evergreens and a few gnarled oaks. At the trailhead I saw a kiosk, similar to one at the entrance to the Hundred Mile Wilderness. I also noticed fainter paths winding away into the deeper woods. Each one, I suspected, led to a place of concealment.

As I summoned the energy to start beating the bushes, a Cadillac turned in behind me. Glancing in my mirror, I saw the driver's face as he spotted the word POLICE painted on my truck. With a strained expression of nonchalance, he swung the Caddie around in a circle and accelerated back onto the road, never once making eye contact with me.

What a miserable task this was.

Fuck it, I thought. I'm just going to sit here and let these guys finish.

After five minutes, a skinny man with a brown goatee appeared from behind a tree trunk. His jeans were too big for him, and his flannel shirt was untucked on one side. He stopped when he caught sight of my patrol truck, fumbled for a pair of sunglasses, then proceeded confidently toward my half-opened window.

"Good morning!" he said.

"Nice day for a hike."

" 'Tis."

"Have I seen you here before?" I asked, hoping he'd get the message.

He started pawing around for his keys. "Gee, I don't think so. Not from around here, you know. Just passing through. Have a good day, Officer."

His Toyota made a coughing sound when he started the engine. The rusted tailpipe scraped the ground as he drove away. The metal threw sparks when it struck the pavement at the edge of the lot.

Moments later, another man appeared out of the woods. He was middle-aged, overweight, wearing a navy blue suit but no necktie. When he saw me, his face went tomato red.

He took off like a frightened rabbit back into the shadows from which he'd come.

Some wardens—I was thinking of Tommy Volk—might have found the sight comical. All it did was make me feel like a bully. These men were wrong to have taken over the land trust's parking lot for their secret hookups, but I took no pleasure in shaming them.

When I became a game warden, I imagined that my life would be one of nonstop derring-do. I pictured myself wrestling night hunters into handcuffs and going undercover to break up poaching rings. Not once did it occur to me that I would spend mornings policing parking lots for desperate, closeted men. I almost felt sorry for the naïve kid I had been.

I had just left Standish Cove when my cell phone rang. It was Warden Investigator Pinkham.

"We found Chad McDonough," he said. "I thought you'd want to know."

"Where is he?"

"Dead. A guy was picking up recyclables along Route 15 and found his body in a ditch. It looks like he was hit by a truck."

I felt the skin tighten across my forehead. "When?"

"Days ago. Probably around the same time you were looking for him. He had on the clothes he was last reported as wearing at Hudson's Lodge. We found his backpack at the scene—and that ridiculous sombrero. The impact threw him into a patch of ferns about fifteen feet from the road. I don't think anyone would have seen him lying there until the vegetation had died back."

My mouth had gone dry. "Don't you think that's suspicious?"

"Of course I do. But there's no proof the hit-and-run had anything to do with what happened to Samantha and Missy."

"The timing is pretty damn coincidental. McDonough was running from someone, Pinkham."

"You also described him as a paranoid pothead. I know you won't believe this, Bowditch, but I'm not a complete buffoon. I've been doing this job for twenty years without your expert assistance." The words were harsh, but his voice had a merry ring in it, as if he were smiling. "Something else that might interest you," he continued. "We've inventoried the items we found with the girls' bodies—backpacks, clothes, et cetera. The scavengers had torn up a lot of it, looking for food. Guess what we didn't find? Cell phones."

"Coyotes don't usually eat electronic devices."

"Go on."

"You think the person who killed them took their phones. They owned Samsung Galaxies, right?"

Pinkham chuckled. "Tim Malcomb was right about you." He was referring to the Warden Service's acting colonel.

"How so?"

"He said you're smarter than you look. Don't be offended. There are worse things for an investigator than being underestimated. I say that from personal experience. Missy's mom told us that her phone has a Hello Kitty sticker on the back. I'll let you know if something turns up."

After Pinkham had hung up, I puzzled over his comments about the perks of being underestimated. Had he meant that he saw a future for me as a warden investigator? Considering all the black marks against me, I never thought I would get the chance to pursue my dream job.

Stacey needed to hear about McDonut and the missing cell phones. I called her cell twice but landed in voice mail both times. Even though she hadn't answered my earlier e-mail, I decided to send a text: *Just heard from Pinkham. Police found McDonut dead. Hit-*

*and-run on Rt. 15. Looks like he died same day Dow dropped him
in Greenville. Call me when u get this. XO M.*

The state owed me comp days for having worked the search during my vacation. I could think of worse places to hang out than in
the North Woods. I called Sergeant Ouellete and told him I was taking the weekend off. He could reach me at the Monson General
Store, where I would be helping the regional biologist catalog dead
coyotes.

26

When I got home, I changed out of my uniform in favor of jeans and a T-shirt, clipped my badge and sidearm to my belt, and threw my duffel into the back of my patrol truck. By six P.M., I was on the Maine Turnpike, heading north. The sky had taken on a peach-colored hue after the sun had set, and the drivers hurrying home in the opposite direction were switching on their headlights.

Stacey still hadn't responded. I wanted to believe that she was busy with her work, or maybe she was just working through her anger. The worry manifested itself as a ticklish sensation inside my chest.

My phone rang as I passed the exit to Lewiston. I hit my blinkers and pulled into the breakdown lane. When I saw the number on the screen, the itchy feeling spread to my spine.

"I just got a call from Stacey's boss, Tom Waterman," Charley said. "He and I worked together at IF&W on that lynx project up north. He wanted me to hear the news from him."

"What news?"

"Stacey blew up at him on the phone this afternoon. Told him she was done tagging coyotes, and if the governor wanted to hand out bounties, he could come up to Monson and collect the damned carcasses himself."

I could almost hear the conversation in my head: Stacey launching into a blistering tirade, followed by her supervisor's exasperated response. No doubt she had dared him to fire her, knowing the union would protect her job. From personal experience, I knew how hard it was for the state to terminate a problem employee.

"Have you spoken with her?" I asked.

"Ora and I have been trying to reach her, but she won't pick up the phone."

Before I spoke again, I waited a moment and gazed up at the darkening sky. I saw a V-shaped formation of geese outlined against the diaphanous clouds. The term for that flight pattern was a *skein*.

"Maybe she's driven off into the woods to cool down and she can't get a signal. You know how hotheaded she can be."

It would explain why she hadn't gotten back to me.

"The problem is, Ora has one of her feelings."

Woman's intuition had once struck me as an outdated myth. Then I met Stacey's mother. Ora Stevens had empathic powers that were downright spooky.

"I'm actually on my way to Monson."

"Say again?"

"Stacey sounded miserable the last time I spoke to her. I decided to take a couple of comp days and drive up there. I thought I'd help her out at the tagging station."

He murmured something to another person in the room with him. Ora, I assumed.

"Can you give us a call when you find her?" he said.

"How about I have her call you instead?" I didn't want them to worry.

"Good luck with that!" he said. "Stacey can make a mule seem accommodating when she doesn't want to do something."

He didn't need to tell me about his daughter.

The stars were out by the time I left the highway. In Maine the constellations become sharper the farther from civilization you travel, especially on a moonless night like this one. I saw Sagittarius drawing his horn bow, and winged Pegasus taking flight. The Big Dipper hung, as if from its handle, above the northern horizon. That was the direction I was headed. Into the wild.

I filled my gas tank at the truck stop in Newport, feeling the eyes of the people inside—the truckers, clerks, and drunk drivers— watching me. The station burned with a bright, cold light. I put on the expensive Fjällräven climbing jacket my mother had given me the Christmas before she died. I found myself missing her intensely. She had never met Stacey, and so I would always wonder if she would have approved of her. At the very least, my mom would have appreciated knowing I was in love again. It hurt my heart to think that she had passed on when I was still alone, probably wondering to the end whether I would ever find the right woman.

The road to Moosehead Lake passed through a series of derelict mill towns. The windswept parking lots outside the factories had weeds growing through the cracks in the asphalt. Apple trees out- side one stately house dropped their unwanted fruit onto the side- walks for the raccoons to eat. Halloween was a month away on the calendar, but the ghosts were already in residence in Piscataquis County.

I arrived in Monson an hour after leaving the truck stop, my back stiff, my nerves raw from too much caffeine. The town was as dark as the others, but the neon beer lights in the windows of the general store beckoned.

Toby Dow's overturned five-gallon bucket sat beside the Dump- ster, waiting for the mayor of Monson to return in the morning. Stacey's IF&W truck wasn't in the lot, but I hadn't expected it would be. The shuttle van hadn't moved since my last visit; I wondered if it was a permanent fixture. I pulled up beside an empty, idling Dodge Neon. My headlights bounced against the cinder blocks.

The man behind the counter looked up from the register. I rec- ognized him from my prior visit: six-five, gray hair cut straight across his forehead, rhinestone stud, deeply set dark eyes. In his build and affect, he reminded me of Boris Karloff lurching around the set of *The Bride of Frankenstein*.

He had been making change for an underaged girl buying cigarettes. She couldn't have been older than sixteen, but I was not in town to enforce the state's laws against minors purchasing tobacco. She swiped two packs of American Spirits off the counter when she saw my badge and gun.

"See you later, Benton," she said in a squeaky voice, hurrying out the door.

"Take care, Tasha," the clerk said.

When the door closed, I realized that we were alone. The last time I'd been inside the store, country music had been playing over the speakers, but now that he had the place to himself, Benton had opted for the shrill flute of Jethro Tull. I inspected the bulletin board. The missing-persons poster had been torn down, but there was a new notice, emblazoned with the shield of the Maine Department of Inland Fisheries and Wildlife, advertising the hundred-dollar bounty for coyotes.

The clerk examined me with the impassivity of a steer.

"I don't suppose that girl's last name is Dow, is it?" I asked.

"Tasha? How did you know?"

"Just a wild guess." I tapped the badge on my belt. "Do you remember me?"

"Of course I do."

"I don't suppose you know where I can find the wildlife biologist who was here tagging coyotes."

"She left in a huff this afternoon." Benton began chewing his fingernails, or what was left of them.

"She didn't say anything about where she was going?" I asked.

"No, sir."

I couldn't tell if he was slow-witted, lacked all powers of observation, or was lying to me for fun.

"Thanks." I turned toward the door.

"How will you folks know when you find the coyotes that killed those girls?"

"Excuse me?"

He spit a piece of keratin out of the corner of his mouth. "Do they do blood tests or something? Or cut open their stomachs to see what's inside?"

"I don't know," I said. "I'm not a forensics expert."

"A lot of the hikers that've come in are scared to go back onto the trail. They keep asking me if it's safe."

"What have you been telling them?"

He finally showed me a smile. It completely changed the character of his face, almost made him handsome. "I tell them no."

"That's the right answer."

"There are nights when the wolves are silent and only the moon howls."

"Excuse me?"

"That's a quote from George Carlin. Have a good evening, Warden."

What a flake, I thought on my way out the door.

I decided to make Ross's Rooming House my next stop. Stacey had told me she was staying there on the state's tab. With luck, I would find her holed up in her room, cooling her anger with a six-pack of beer.

As I cruised through the village, I passed the boarded storefronts and the illuminated sign of the Lake of the Woods Tabernacle with its dire biblical warning. Then I turned left toward the lake. The old Victorians along the side street seemed to be sinking slowly into their own front lawns. Stacey's truck wasn't parked outside the hiking hostel, either.

I sat behind the wheel and considered my next move. The engine made a ticking sound, like a stopwatch counting down the seconds until something exploded. After a minute, I went inside.

27

A woman behind the front desk took her eyes away from the two bearded hikers with whom she was talking and watched me as I stepped into the parlor. She was tall and broad-shouldered, with a weathered complexion and hard gray eyes like chips of stone. She had reddish white hair gathered together in a topknot. The sleeves of her orange fleece pullover were pushed up to her elbows, revealing powerful forearms.

"Can I help you?" Her voice was as deep as I would have expected, and she had a strong German accent.

"I hope so. I'm Mike Bowditch. I'm with the Warden Service."

"Did you stay with us during the search?"

The two hikers moved aside. One of them smelled so strongly of BenGay it stung my nostrils.

"I did, but I came in late and left early." I cleared my throat. "Is Mr. Ross here?"

"He has gone to bed. I'm Steffi Ross. What can I do for you?"

She was so much more outdoorsy and vital than her husband—more the kind of person I would have expected to find running a way station on the Appalachian Trail.

"I'm looking for Stacey Stevens," I said. "I didn't see her IF&W truck out front. Did she check out?"

"Not unless she left without telling me." Steffi Ross turned to the two hikers listening in on our conversation. Both looked freshly showered. "Have you guys seen her around? The woman in the uniform?"

One of the guys grinned through his blond beard, his teeth barely visible beneath his brushy mustache. "She wasn't at dinner." He had an English accent.

"I think she might have gone to her room," said the other Brit.

"Would you mind if I take a look?" I asked Mrs. Ross.

She brought one of her big hands to her chin. "Does she know you are coming?"

I decided a bluff was in order. "She was hoping I could stay the night with her. How much is it for an extra person in the room?"

She narrowed her eyes, cocked her head, and gave me the once-over with a closemouthed smile.

"Why don't you have a look at her room, *ja*? In case she left. Pay me later for the room if you stay."

"Thanks. What room is she in?"

"Number twelve," Steffi Ross said.

I thought I understood the layout of the building, but there didn't seem to be any rhyme or reason to the room numbering system. After two dead ends, I finally found myself outside Stacey's door. I rapped on the wood and spoke her name.

I listened but heard only music playing in the adjoining room. Phish.

When Stacey didn't respond to my second knock, I tried the knob. It twisted easily in my hand, and the door swung inward. The bedside lamp was ablaze, and clothes were falling out of an unzipped duffel bag on the floor. Her toiletries kit hung from a nail on the wall.

She hadn't left Monson yet. So where was she? I couldn't deny that I found the scene disquieting.

I sat down on the bed and felt the springs shiver underneath my weight. The duffel bag was red, manufactured by L.L. Bean, with a monogram on the side: SOS. I'd never asked Stacey for her middle name. Was it Ora, after her mother?

She hadn't bothered to hang anything up in the closet or put her socks in the drawers of the bureau. Evidently, she hadn't expected to be in Monson long. I stared at the open duffel, trying to resist the urge to rummage through its contents.

SOS.

I rose to my feet and followed the twisting halls back to the lobby. The bearded hikers had retired to the fireplace, where they had joined half a dozen other tanned and longhaired young people. One of them was tuning a mandolin, which he must have carried on his back all the way from Georgia.

Mrs. Ross had a wireless phone pinned between her shoulder and her ear. "Listen, I have to go. Someone is here." She replaced the telephone on its charging stand. "Did you find your girlfriend?"

"No, but her stuff is still in the room. I don't suppose you spoke with her this afternoon?"

She brought her hand to the lower part of her face again. "We talked a bit, sure."

"Can you remember anything she said?"

"You're not stalking this young woman, are you?"

"Would I tell you if I was?"

She let out a laugh that showed me the metal fillings in her molars. "Good point!"

"I'm worried about Stacey because no one knows where she is. Do you remember what you talked about?"

Near the fireplace, the traveling minstrel had begun strumming the strings of his mandolin while a woman passed out pints of Ben & Jerry's ice cream from a paper bag. The hikers were digging their hooked fingers into the containers and lifting gobs of Cherry Garcia and Chunky Monkey into their mouths.

Steffi Ross motioned me into the office behind the front desk. I pushed aside a curtain of beads to enter. She crossed her arms and leaned her rear end against a paper-strewn table with a computer monitor, keyboard, and inkjet printer.

"Your friend was in a bad mood when she came in, *ja*?" she said.

"I had been hearing all day about the scene over at the store. It sounded disgusting. But that is not what we talked about. She wanted to know about that kid who got hit by a truck—McDonut."

So news of the hit-and-run was making its way through the village. I shouldn't have been surprised.

"What did she want to know?" I asked.

"Everything."

"Can you be more specific?"

"I told her McDonut seemed a little strange, but a lot of the people who come through here are odd ducks, you know? He brought in some beer to share. That is something the hikers do. He got a little drunk, you know? But he seemed nice."

Her account matched what Chad McDonough had told me about his night at Ross's.

"Did he seem nervous or anxious?" I asked. "Like he was afraid of something or someone."

"No," Steffi Ross said. "That kid was the life of the party."

"Did she ask you about Samantha Boggs and Missy Montgomery?"

"Naomi Walks and Baby Ruth? *Ja*."

"You're using their trail names," I said.

"That is our practice here. I feel that trail names are more honest, you know, because they are *chosen*. They are closer to who a person truly is."

"What was yours when you hiked the AT?"

Her cheeks flushed, whether from embarrassment or anger, I couldn't tell. "Das Shieldmaiden."

I decided to let it go. "What did Stacey ask you about Samantha and Missy?"

"If I knew the girls were homosexual."

"Did you?"

"Yeah, I could tell right away that they were a couple. They were quite open. They kissed and held hands."

Samantha and Missy had been closeted at Pentecost University, afraid the world would learn about the romantic nature of their relationship. Very few of their classmates had known they were secretly lovers. But somewhere along the hundreds of miles of the Appalachian Trail, the women had found the courage to make their feelings for each other public. They really had been on a journey of personal discovery. The revelation seemed to make what had happened to them all the more tragic.

"What else did Stacey ask you about them?" I said.

"She asked if I could remember any little details. I thought I'd told the police everything."

She removed a tube of lip balm from her pocket. She took a moment to apply it to her heavily chapped lips. I had the impression she was stalling.

"You left something out of your statement to the police," I said. "What was it?"

She let out a sigh that went on for ten seconds. "Naomi Walks and Baby Ruth asked me about churches, *ja*? I told them about the Community Church and the United Church of Christ. 'Or you could check out that crazy tabernacle on Main Street,' I told them."

"Do you think they might have visited the tabernacle on their way back to the trail?"

"I had meant it as a joke. I didn't think they'd actually go there."

"What can you tell me about it?"

"The preacher is nuts! He calls himself Brother John. My husband thinks he might have been a hiker himself. That is how he found Monson. Me, I've never been inside the dump."

Out near the fireplace, the hikers had broken into song. They were shouting along to "Free Bird" while the guy with the mandolin played.

Steffi Ross's throat flushed from her breastbone to her cheeks. "I don't understand the point of these questions. I thought coyotes killed those poor girls."

"We're still waiting for the report to come back from the medical examiner. In the meantime, the investigators are looking into all the ways Samantha and Missy might have died."

"So now the police think those girls were murdered?"

"They're looking at all the ways the women might have died," I repeated.

I had the sense that Steffi Ross felt mad at herself for having forgotten to mention the Lake of the Woods Tabernacle to the detectives. She was expressing her embarrassment to me as frustration.

"But what is your friend's interest in this? Did she know them?"

"Not personally."

"I do not understand what that means."

I wasn't sure that I could explain. "I appreciate your talking to me, Mrs. Ross."

"You might look for her at Shoebottom's. There is a bar that serves drinks. *Ja?*"

A thought occurred to me as I turned to leave. "There is one more thing. Do you ever have outsiders here?"

"I do not understand what that means."

"People who come for supper, who aren't staying at the inn."

"On Saturday nights we serve lobsters for ten dollars. There are some people who come in for dinner, you know?"

"Did you have any outside guests the night Samantha and Missy were here?"

"I think not."

"Thanks anyway."

Lynyrd Skynyrd on the mandolin accompanied me to the front door.

"Wait!" Steffi Ross called after me. "There *was* somebody here that night. Nonstop was here."

"Bob Nissen was at the inn?"

Mrs. Ross placed her hands on the desk and leaned forward. "He trades us honey for lobsters, so he comes for dinner. He likes the attention from all the pretty girls, you know? He is a famous figure on the trail."

"Did he speak with Samantha and Missy?"

"I do not know. Sorry."

"Thanks anyway."

I pulled my collar up as I stepped out into the chilly evening. Somewhere out on the dark waters of Lake Hebron, a loon was giving his eerie, half-crazed call. Why hadn't Nissen told anyone he had been in the same dining room as Samantha and Missy? It was a significant omission, to say the least. As soon as I tracked down Stacey, I would need to have a talk with the legendary thru-hiker.

28

Stacey was a mystery to me in many ways, but I could guess where she had gone after leaving the rooming house.

I drove up the street and parked in front of the Lake of the Woods Tabernacle. I leaned on the steering wheel and looked up at the ramshackle wooden structure, seeing it as if for the first time. The first floor was an old storefront with plate-glass windows that needed cleaning inside and out. Upstairs seemed to be some sort of meeting space: maybe an old dance hall from the days of the river drivers. On the third floor, a lamp glowed behind a shade. The clapboards were flaking blue paint onto the cracked sidewalk. A single match could have burned the whole place to the ground.

Faded lettering on the building identified it as the DOW BLOCK 1894. So the Dows were the original settlers in this neck of the woods. No wonder they acted as if they owned the town. Their ancestors probably had.

As I climbed out of the patrol truck, I readjusted the holster containing my .357 SIG. Looking up at the darkened sky, I saw a few faint stars veiled by clouds, as well as blinking lights I recognized as airplanes traveling to Europe and beyond. A transatlantic flight corridor passed directly over the state of Maine like a superhighway through the heavens. No matter how deep into the woods you went, no matter how far from civilization you believed yourself to be, you couldn't escape the sound of jets or the sight of contrails.

The message on the lighted sign hadn't been changed since my last visit. It still displayed St. Paul's warning to the Philippians about dogs and evildoers. Sage advice, I thought.

I pressed my face to the darkened plate glass, but it was difficult to see more than a few feet inside. The first floor appeared to be some sort of storeroom. I could make out stacks of cardboard boxes and a sagging clothes rack with coats and dresses. Stuffed animals and baby dolls were lined up along a shelf.

A rickety set of stairs had been built along the side of the building: a jerry-rigged fire escape to bring the place barely up to code. I climbed to the third floor, where I had seen the light. A television murmured inside the apartment. I knocked and waited.

After a few moments, the door opened a crack, and a young woman in a shapeless cotton dress peered out at me.

"Hello?" she said with no friendliness.

She was very thin, except for her very pregnant belly. She had acne scars and limp brown hair, but her features were beautiful. A makeup artist would have viewed her face as an exciting canvas.

Warm air, scented heavily with garlic, flowed out into the night.

"I'm Warden Bowditch. I'm looking for Brother John."

A man called from the next room. "Teresa, who is it?"

She slammed the door in my face.

I took a step backward and felt my lower back touch the railing. The wood creaked but held. It would have been a long way to the ground.

Before I could knock again, the door opened wide. A bespectacled man stood before me, dressed in a white shirt buttoned to the throat, creased black slacks, and white athletic socks. His neck was long; his wrists were skinny. He wore his graying hair in a buzz cut, white-walled around the ears.

"Yes?" he said.

"Brother John?"

"What do you want?" There was a twang in his voice that made me think of cattle roaming across distant prairies.

"I wondered if I could ask you a few questions."

He inspected my badge and gun. "Is this an official inquiry?"

I gave him my best bullshitting smile. "No, but I hope you can help me with some information."

He locked eyes with me for an uncomfortably long time. Then he nodded and stepped aside to make way. I entered a brightly lighted kitchen where a pot was bubbling on an electric stove and two cats were eating from cans on the counter. I could hear fake-sounding laughter coming from the television set in the room beyond.

Brother John padded off into the living room. One of the cats, a tabby, sprang onto the linoleum and began rubbing against my pant leg, leaving a residue of gray fur. I nearly tripped over it when I took a step forward.

The furniture in the living room consisted of a threadbare couch and a beanbag chair pushed beneath a reading light. The bone-colored walls were utterly without decoration. A big boxy television balanced on a table. Brother John pointed a remote control at it, and the picture winked off.

The woman had disappeared into the bedroom, but another cat, a calico, was curled up on the sofa. Brother John swatted at the cat, which gave a yowl and leaped onto the floor, hissing.

"Have a seat." He indicated the cat-shaped depression.

I remained standing. "This won't take long."

"I'm going to sit, if you don't mind." He settled himself, stiff-backed, against the couch cushions. "I find this constant harassment wearying."

"I'm not here to harass you, Pastor."

"That's what your colleague said this afternoon."

"My colleague?"

"The woman warden." He pushed his glasses back up on the bridge of his nose. "I had to ask her to leave."

If Stacey had let him think she was a police officer, she could be fired, or worse.

"What happened?"

"I don't want to have this conversation again."

"Did she ask you about the hikers who disappeared in the Hundred Mile Wilderness?"

A cat jumped onto Brother John's lap, and he began stroking it vigorously. "I'm not sure why it matters."

"Why didn't you tell the police that they had been here?" I asked. "You must have known that people were searching for them."

"When they came in that morning, they introduced themselves as Christians."

"They were."

"My congregation isn't some freak show to be mocked. Especially by two homosexuals."

I tried to keep my face blank. "What happened?"

"They laughed at us. So I ordered them to leave."

"You threw them out of your service?" I said.

"'No one who practices deceit shall dwell in my house. No one who utters lies shall continue before my eyes.' Psalm 101:7."

The image I had in my mind of Samantha and Missy was that they were polite young women. I had a hard time believing they would have behaved rudely. But whatever they had been at the start of their journey, they no longer were when they arrived in Monson, at least according to the testimony of Steffi Ross. In reality, I knew very little about these women. Believing that the victims of violence are perfect little lambs instead of complicated human beings is a dangerous fantasy.

Maybe Samantha and Missy had behaved like brats; maybe Brother John had cause to ask them to leave the service. It still didn't excuse his failure to report the incident.

"You should have told the police they were here that morning, Pastor."

"And bring my church under suspicion?" His voice seemed to bubble up from the bottom of his throat like something viscous. "We had nothing to do with what happened to those girls."

"How can you be certain?"

"Because they brought it on themselves through their sinfulness."

"What are you saying?"

"The Lord sent those wild dogs to tear them apart."

Was this the point where Stacey had started screaming? Had she even made it this far? Steffi Ross had warned me that he was insane. It was all I could do not to punch the man in his self-righteous face.

"You really believe that?" I said. "You think their death was some sort of divine punishment?"

"God's justice is not man's justice."

There was no point asking him where I might find Stacey. Even if he knew, this crackpot preacher wasn't going to tell me. I tried to imagine what it must be like living inside his skull, seeing the world through his crazy eyes, but it was too much of a horror show.

I looked down at my hand and saw a fist. "I need to leave now."

"I never should have invited you in," Brother John said, as if I were a vampire. In his twisted mind, I was probably in league with the devil.

Two of the cats followed us into the kitchen. Whatever was cooking on the stove had started to burn.

As he closed the door on me, I said, "Can I give you some advice, Pastor?"

He hesitated. His eyebrows pushed against the tops of his glasses.

"When the state police show up at your door tomorrow, you should try giving direct answers to their questions. Homicide detectives aren't big on psalms and proverbs."

The door rattled in its frame, and the lock clicked. In the silence I could hear the drumbeat of my own pulse. I closed my eyes and tried to collect myself.

The investigators would want the names of every person who had been present at the church that morning. One of them might have been Chad McDonough's man in the red tent. Maybe Samantha and

Missy were the victims of a hate crime, I thought. People were still murdered in this world for being gay. It was a lot more plausible than a coyote attack.

I opened my eyes and gazed down on the village of secrets. In the houses below, televisions flickered behind drawn curtains, and woodsmoke rose like ghosts from chimneys. To the south was the oil-black lake stretching off into the void. To the north were the shadow-draped mountains of the Hundred Mile Wilderness. Darkness seemed to be closing in around the town of Monson. It felt as if the only candle in a room was dying and about to go out.

29

When I got back to my truck, I tried Pinkham's cell, but he didn't answer. I left a message, saying I had new information about Samantha and Missy. In the past, I'd found my offers of help rebuffed whenever I'd tried to assist a major crimes investigation. Detectives never took me seriously. Pinkham seemed different in that regard. The warden investigator hadn't been so quick to dismiss my insights. Had I found a new ally in the department? I would know the answer to that question when and if Pinkham returned my phone call.

In the meantime, my search for Stacey continued.

Steffi Ross had said that the Cajun restaurant on the edge of the town was the place for nocturnal entertainment. I decided to stop in, figuring she might have come here earlier, since she hadn't had dinner at the inn. Besides, I was running out of places to look for her.

A bayou bistro in the North Woods? The idea wasn't so far out. The Appalachian Trail serves as a natural conduit for southern culture to the wilds of New England. And Mainers have a deep love of country music, which always surprises visitors who expect—I don't know—sea chanteys. The way I had always thought of it was that we were just hillbillies with a different accent.

As expected, the place was packed. All I'd had to eat since lunch was some trail mix. Maybe I'd get myself an oyster po' boy.

I locked my SIG in the glove compartment and dropped my

badge in my pocket. In my hooded jacket, jeans, and work boots I looked like just another backwoods barfly. The smell of roasting ribs greeted my nose when I opened the truck door. Lady Antebellum wailed through the window screens, and I saw the orange embers of cigarettes waving in the hands of smokers lined up along the porch rail.

A woman spoke from the darkness. "Hey, Warden!"

She was nobody I knew, just one of the half-drunk smokers. Then I realized that they'd seen me drive up in my patrol truck. So much for anonymity.

I went up the steps.

Every seat seemed to be taken inside. The crowd was a cross section of the North Woods in late September. The AT thru-hikers were recognizable by their flowing braids and beards, tanned skin, and hiking apparel. The locals tended to go for flannel, leather, and denim. I elbowed my way to the counter. A woman wearing an apron and a kerchief around her head was ladling dirty rice onto paper plates. Her face gleamed with perspiration. I took out my phone and pulled up a photograph of Stacey to show her.

"Excuse me," I said.

"The bartender will take your order."

At the bar, I watched a woman with tattoos on her forearms fill a pint glass with Pabst Blue Ribbon. She set it in front of a familiar white-haired man who looked like he had been there so long that he was becoming one with the stool. The bartender seemed to sense my presence without having to look at me.

"What can I get you?" she shouted above the music. Toby Keith had begun to growl over the speakers.

I showed her Stacey's picture. "Have you seen this woman here tonight?"

She glanced at the phone for all of two seconds, then returned to washing glasses. "Sorry."

"Are you sure?"

The old man reached a liver-spotted hand toward my outstretched arm. He was a little fellow, wearing a plaid shirt and blue Dickies held up by suspenders. "Can I see that?"

I turned the screen to him.

"She's the woman who's been at the store this week," he said. "The biologist tagging the coyotes."

"Have you seen her today?"

"Not here." The odor of alcohol leaked from his pores. "I passed her truck on my way into town. I waved at her, but she didn't wave back."

He sounded offended. In the Maine woods, it is considered a politeness to wave at drivers going in the opposite direction, even if they are strangers. It was unlike Stacey to ignore this unwritten rule of the road.

"Which way was she headed?" I asked.

"Over to Blanchard."

What was Stacey doing in Blanchard Plantation? It was even more of a ghost town than Monson. "What time did you see her?"

"Five o'clock or so. Before dark."

I felt a strong arm wrap itself around my shoulders. A man pressed his unshaven cheek against mine and exhaled a blast of beer breath. "Warden Bowditch! Hey, Lindsey, get my friend a PBR!"

Troy Dow's eyes glowed like chips of amber with prehistoric bugs trapped inside. His copper-brown hair was pushed away from his forehead and tucked behind his ears. He was wearing a denim jacket over a long underwear shirt, duck pants, and steel-toed boots.

I peeled his dirty fingers off my coat. "No, thanks. How are you doing, Troy?"

"It's Friday night, and I've got a buzz on. Life is good."

Four men—Trevor Dow and three others—stood behind him. They all had the same light brown eyes and copper-colored hair, but their bodies ran the gamut from spindly to bruising. Pearlene had told me the Dows were legion. I thought about the SIG pistol locked in my truck and the Walther PPK/S I sometimes wore at the small of my back but which was currently secure in my gun safe at home.

The old man on the stool tried to shrink away, but Troy clapped him hard between the shoulder blades.

"Roland! How goes it, bud?"

"Good."

"When you gonna let us take down those white oaks near your house? Those things are fucking hazards. The next nor'easter is going to knock those trees right through your roof. We'll cut them down and haul the wood away, no problem. Five hundred bucks."

"I've been planning on logging those trees myself, Troy," Roland said.

White oaks were one of the most valuable species in the forest.

Troy stood with his feet apart, as if balancing on the deck of a ship in heavy seas. "An old guy like you? You'll just hurt yourself, bud. Let us take care of it. Peace of mind is worth the money. How about we come over tomorrow?"

"I don't—"

"We'll be over around seven." Troy leaned in close again, close enough that I could see potato chip crumbs in his mustache. "Hey, I heard about that hitchhiker. I can't believe someone just ran the poor guy down and took off. What kind of son of a bitch would do that?"

"Your guess is as good as mine."

Troy took a staggered step backward so the others could crowd around me.

"Do you know my brother, Trevor?" he said. "Oh yeah! You do. This is my uncle Trent, and my cousin Todd, and my other cousin, Terrence. Guys, this is that hard-ass game warden I was telling you about."

I addressed the pack. "Gentlemen."

Troy waved a finger at me. "Are you off duty? You look like you're off duty."

"I'm off duty."

Old Roland downed his Pabst, slid off his stool, and made a beeline for the bathroom.

Five against one. I shook my head and started to laugh.

Troy's bloodshot eyes narrowed to slits. "What's so funny?"

"I was just thinking about the woman who works at the gate-house on the KI Road. You've really got that poor woman fooled. She said you weren't like the rest of your family."

"Come on, guys!" the female bartender said behind me. "This isn't the O.K. Corral."

"Maybe we should all go outside," Troy said. "What do you think, Warden? How about some fresh air?"

The Dows would be on me the minute I stepped through the door. Two of them would pinion my arms while a third got me into a stranglehold. I would be at their mercy—to be choked unconscious, knifed in the stomach, or shot with a hidden handgun. Real-life brawls aren't like the ones in movies. Brute force and a willingness to do whatever it takes—gouge an eye, kick in a knee—matter more than martial arts training. The dirtiest fighters are the ones who always win.

Glancing to my left, I saw an empty Heineken bottle on the bar. I might get one chance to break it over Troy's skull before the others tore me limb from limb.

One of the Dow cousins—I wasn't sure if it was Todd or Terrence—reached into his jeans pocket and pulled out a ringing phone. He held it up to one ear.

"What are we waiting for?" Trevor snarled.

I placed my left hand on the bar, inches from the bottle.

The skinny Dow with the phone squeezed Troy by the shoulder. He brought his mouth close to his cousin's ear.

Troy snapped his hairy head around. "What?"

"We've got to get back home!" his cousin said over the music.

Troy sucked one end of his mustache into his mouth. Now was my chance to coldcock him, but I had a feeling Lady Luck had just dealt me a new card.

He spit his mustache out. "To be continued."

"I'm looking forward to it."

The five Dows piled out of the restaurant. Lindsey, the tattooed woman pouring drinks, picked up the empty bottle I had been planning to use as a weapon.

"Are you sure you don't want that beer now?" she asked.

Roland emerged from hiding in the bathroom and returned to his stool. I recognized him now: He was the old man I'd seen buying beer at the store first thing in the morning. He tapped his glass.

"Another, please."

"You don't have to let the Dows bully you into taking down those oak trees," I said.

The old man rubbed his eyes. "I'm not as brave as you."

"Can I give you another piece of advice, then? Grab a ride home with someone. You're in no shape to drive."

Roland nodded, but I knew he wouldn't voluntarily give up his keys.

I left the restaurant, mindful that the Dows could have been playing a game with me and might be lying in wait in the shadows. I decided to risk it. More smokers had joined the crowd on the porch.

"Bye, Warden!" It was the same woman as before.

If I had been wearing a cap, I would have tipped it to her. I made my way out of the lot and along the row of vehicles parked on Main Street. As I neared my patrol truck, I noticed that it seemed to be abnormally low to the ground. There was a reason for this. All four tires had been slashed.

30

The cuts were in the sidewalls, not the treads, which meant the tires were unfixable. I would need to get all four of them replaced. Because I was using my patrol truck for personal business, I couldn't very well call the Warden Service for roadside assistance. I found only one garage listed for Monson. The man who answered the phone said he had to pull a car out of a ditch in Guilford, eleven miles to the south, before he could get to me. I sat behind the wheel and waited.

I took the opportunity to put my holstered pistol back on my belt. I wouldn't be taking it off again soon. Then I decided to call Charley and fill him in on my unsuccessful attempts to locate his daughter. I could only conclude that he'd been sitting up beside the phone, he picked up so quickly.

"I'm still looking for her," I said. "Has she called you?"

"No."

"An old guy at the Cajun place outside Monson told me he saw her truck over in Blanchard a few hours ago."

"What was Stacey doing in Blanchard?"

"It must have something to do with Samantha Boggs and Missy Montgomery."

"Why do you say that?"

"Since she left the store, Stacey has been driving around, asking questions. She's already found one piece of evidence the detectives missed. On the morning they left Monson, Samantha and Missy asked about local churches, and Steffi Ross mentioned the Lake of the Woods Tabernacle to them as a joke. Stacey had a hunch the women might have gone to services there. It turns out she was right. The creep who runs the tabernacle calls himself 'Brother John.' He said he made Samantha and Missy leave because they were laughing during the service and because he realized they were gay."

"I thought the girls were keeping their relationship a secret."

"Steffi Ross said they were open about it at dinner the night before."

"But how did this Brother John know? What did those girls do—smooch in the church pew?"

I hadn't thought to ask that question. "He must have heard about their being gay after the fact. It seems to have added to his sense of outrage. Brother John doesn't exactly approve of same-sex couples. He thinks God sent coyotes to kill Samantha and Missy as a punishment for their wickedness."

"The detectives will want to talk to everyone who was in the church that morning."

"That's what I was thinking."

Four motorcycles roared past my truck, headed for Greenville at an unsafe speed.

"What's that?" I said. "I didn't hear you."

"What if the person who killed those girls hears she's sniffing around town?" Charley said.

"Stacey can take care of herself. You taught her well."

"I'm flying up there as soon as it gets light."

"You don't have to do that, Charley," I said.

"Yes, I do. She's my daughter."

Stacey would be livid when she learned that her father thought she needed rescuing. But what if Charley was right? The person or persons who killed Samantha and Missy were still at large and possibly in the area. So far, the murderer had benefited from the confusion and panic over killer coyotes. What would he do when he learned Stacey was asking questions that might expose him? I hadn't wanted to admit to myself that she might be in real danger.

I went back into the restaurant, ordered a po'boy sandwich to go, and returned to my truck to wait. The diners began to leave the restaurant. I watched Roland climb into a dented Lincoln Town Car and drive away without turning on his headlights. I radioed in his plates to the Piscataquis County Sheriff's Department. If he was lucky, the old drunk would end up in jail tonight instead of the morgue.

The woman in the apron and kerchief came outside. She folded up the blackboard sign with the specials. A minute later, the porch light blinked off.

In the silences between passing cars, I listened to the crickets playing their love songs in the weeds along the road. Soon the frosts of autumn would put an end to their music. When the temperature drops, survival takes precedence over romance.

The wrecker arrived just before midnight. The driver was a big man with a big head. He wore coveralls and sneakers, and his camouflage ball cap seemed to perch atop his hair. He made a circuit of my truck, prodding each of the punctures with his fat finger. Then he straightened up, looming over me like Goliath.

"You're fucked all right," he said.

"I know that."

"Must have been the Dows." He let loose with a chuckle. "Man, I should give those guys a cut of my profits for all the business they send my way."

I crossed my arms. "What are my options here?"

"I can tow your truck back to the garage for the night. In the morning, I'll order you some new tires. Should have you back on the road by afternoon. Do you got someplace to stay around here?"

I had been prepared to sleep in my sleeping bag in the bed of my truck, but the idea of camping out inside his garage held little appeal. "Can you drop me at Ross's Rooming House?"

The tow driver winched my truck up onto the flatbed. He brushed candy and pastry wrappers off the passenger seat before I could sit down. The inside of the cab smelled of Lysol.

As we drove back into town, the driver murmured something to himself.

"What's that?" I asked.

"The store's closed early," he said. "Pearlene is usually strict about staying open until one A.M. so she can maximize beer sales. There's always a rush before closing, since the store's the only place to buy booze and cigarettes from here to Guilford."

"It sounds like there will be some unhappy partiers tonight."

"You think?"

As we passed the tabernacle, I noticed that the upstairs apartment was dark, but the sign was burning with a new message in my honor: GOD'S JUSTICE IS NOT MAN'S JUSTICE. I wondered how defiant Brother John would be when the detectives appeared. I might have to arrange to be there when it happened.

When we arrived at Ross's, I removed my long guns—the shotgun and the AR-15—from the patrol truck and placed them in a big duffel. I dropped my spare uniform, state-issued laptop, and GPS unit into a rucksack. After having my tires slashed, the last thing I needed was for something valuable to be stolen out of my patrol truck while it waited to be repaired.

"You don't have to unload all that shit, Warden," the driver said. "There's a lock on my door."

"I'm not taking any chances with the Dows."

"What do you mean?"

"Where else would I have my truck towed other than your garage?"

He let out another of his big-chested chuckles. "Fair enough."

The driver gave me walking directions to his auto-repair shop—it was a mere four miles away—and said I should call him after nine. We said good night. I heaved the heavy bag over my shoulder, picked up my rucksack with my free hand, and made my way into the hostel.

A couple of hikers were still up, playing cards at a rickety table near the fire, and another was talking on her cell phone in the corner. She was speaking an Eastern European language I didn't recognize. The Appalachian Trail drew trekkers from all over the world.

I looked for Steffi Ross in the office behind the bead curtain, but she must have gone to bed.

Everything was just as I'd left it inside Stacey's room. I eased the bag with my firearms to the wooden floor and sat down on the bed. I looked at the dirty laundry bulging from the unzipped duffel.

Where the hell was she?

I lay back on the blanket and stared at the cracks in the ceiling. When I closed my eyes, I saw Troy Dow's leering smile. I tried to bring up a more pleasant image, but the ugly face wouldn't leave me alone.

I sat up with a start. The overhead bulb was still blazing. I checked my watch and saw that it was nearly five A.M.

Stacey hadn't returned while I was asleep.

It had been close to twelve hours since the old drunk, Roland, had seen her truck. Twelve hours unaccounted for. Both of us had spent plenty of nights in the pitch-black forest and knew there was no reason to fear the dark. But I couldn't imagine what she might be doing out there. In spite of my confident assurances to Charley about his daughter's ability to handle herself, I felt worry nibbling around my heart.

I tried her number again. The duffel bag at my feet began to buzz.

I rifled through the wrinkled clothes and found Stacey's khaki uniform shirt—and of course her phone was in the pocket. She had never given me her pass code, but I didn't have to look at the log of missed calls to know she hadn't heard any of the messages I had left since the previous afternoon.

Out in the hall, someone got up to use the shower.

Roland had said he'd passed her truck when he was coming from Blanchard.

What was in Blanchard?

I set my laptop computer on my knees and pulled up a topographic map of the region. Blanchard Plantation was the next township to the southwest. The Appalachian Trail followed the looping course of the Piscataquis River. It was the route Samantha and Missy had taken on their way into Monson. I zoomed in, searching for any clue that might be hidden in the landscape.

The map showed an oblong elevation south of the river: Breakneck Ridge.

Nissen, I thought.

His business was named Breakneck Ridge Apiary. Stacey must have gone to Blanchard to speak with him. But why? Had she discovered that he was at supper with Samantha and Missy the night before they entered the wilderness? If so, she hadn't gotten the information from Steffi Ross. Until I'd jogged her memory, the Teutonic innkeeper had forgotten about Nissen.

What about the Lake of the Woods Tabernacle? Kathy Frost had told me Nissen had served time in prison for cooking meth. She'd said he'd found Jesus in the joint. A religious zealot, motivated by blind hatred of homosexuals, determined to punish them for their sacrilegious behavior. The man in the red tent?

It made sense why Nissen would have volunteered to search Chairback Gap. If he had pursued Samantha and Missy there—if he had known they were dead—then he would have wanted to direct searchers away from their corpses for as long as possible. The more time that passed, the less evidence would remain for the forensic technicians to connect him to the murders.

It also explained his antagonism toward Chad McDonough. He was panicked that Chad remembered him from supper at Ross's. What had McDonut said? "Good to see you again, sir."

After Nissen and I had showed up at Hudson's Lodge with news of Samantha's and Missy's disappearance, McDonough might have put the puzzle pieces together. He might've realized who the mysterious man in the red tent had been. Instead of telling the authorities what he knew, McDonut had taken off in the dark.

Later a message had gone out over the police scanner that we were looking for Chad McDonough. By identifying him over the radio, we had announced to the killer that we knew the kid might have incriminating information. We'd signed his death warrant, I realized. Pinkham said McDonut had been run down by a truck. What if it had been a van?

Nissen was the first man to discover the scavenged bones at the bottom of Chairback Mountain. He'd displayed no anguish at the discovery. In fact, he had relished being the one to have found the corpses.

At every turn in the search, Nissen had been there. This theory explained everything.

Had Stacey come to this same conclusion? I couldn't believe that she would have been so stupid as to drive out to Nissen's isolated farmhouse if she suspected he was a murderer. But what else would have led her there after dark?

My pulse was racing as I dialed Wes Pinkham's home number in Greenville.

"Yeah?" he said.

"It's Bowditch. We need to get over to Bob Nissen's house in Blanchard right now."

"Huh? What are you talking about? Where are you?"

"At Ross's, in Monson. Listen, I think Nissen might have murdered Samantha Boggs and Missy Montgomery. And there's a chance he's connected to the hit-and-run that killed Chad McDonough, too."

"Slow down."

"There's no time," I said. "I'm pretty sure Stacey Stevens is at his house. If I'm right, she's in danger, or worse. And I just discovered that she left her phone at the rooming house. I need you to pick me up. I'll fill you in on what I've learned in the truck. You need to trust me, Pinkham. You know I've been right about things like this before. We need to go now."

I heard the warden investigator take a breath. "I'll be there in twenty minutes," he said at last.

31

The predawn sky had a fuzzy blue glow that reminded me of a television with no reception. Closer to the ground, the shadows were breaking apart as individual trees sharpened into focus. A goldfinch perched on a wire made its squeaky-toy noise. I waited at the edge of the wet lawn for Pinkham to arrive.

In the empty dining room, I'd wolfed down a bowl of dry Cheerios from a container I'd found on the sideboard. I'd heard Ross puttering in the kitchen but hadn't wanted to trouble him for milk.

In less than an hour, the sky would turn pink above the ragged horizon, and Charley's plane would appear. I had thought of calling him with my revelation about Nissen, but he would be here soon enough. Once he arrived, I would tell him to take a look at Breakneck Ridge from the air and see if he spotted Stacey's pickup.

A truck turned down the road, its headlights slicing the early-morning gloom. When I opened the door, the dome light came on. Pinkham's thinning hair was sticking up in wisps, and he needed a shave. I really had pulled him out of bed. The investigator was dressed in his usual plain clothes—button-down shirt and chinos—but he'd put on his warden's jacket with the badge on the front and the red department logo on the sleeve. He wore his SIG openly on his belt.

The inside of the cab smelled of hot coffee. When I saw that he'd picked up a cup for me, I wanted to kiss him. I slung my duffel into the backseat.

"What's in the bag?" Pinkham asked.

"Guns."

"Dare I ask why?"

The light above my head dimmed after I locked the door. "My truck is at the garage in town, getting repaired. The Dows slashed all four of my tires last night outside the Cajun restaurant. I appreciate your picking me up."

He shifted into drive. "How do you know it was the Dows?"

"They invited me to a brawl first."

"You must have refused," he said.

"Why do you say that?"

"No stitches."

Pinkham took a sip from his Styrofoam cup. I had no need for caffeine with all the adrenaline percolating through my bloodstream, but I joined him.

"I listened to the voice mail you left me," he said. "It's interesting that Samantha and Missy visited the tabernacle, but what does that have to do with Nissen?"

"Maybe nothing."

"That clears things up. Thanks for getting me out of bed."

"Kathy Frost told me that Nissen was born again in prison," I said. "I saw him with his shirt off, and I think he had his jailhouse tattoos removed. I'm guessing that his name is going to show up on the list of people who attend services at the Lake of the Woods Tabernacle."

"You're guessing?"

"For the moment, yes. But here's something I know for sure: Nissen had supper at Ross's the same night Samantha and Missy were there. That's quite a coincidence, don't you think? The man who volunteered to search the mountain where they died—the same guy who found their bones—had a previous encounter with them he neglected to report to the police."

Pinkham kept his eyes on the cones of light projected onto the road. He made a right onto the Blanchard Road, following the shoreline of Lake Hebron into the deep woods west of town. The police radio made a gurgling noise.

"All right," he said, turning down the volume. "You've got my attention."

He listened without interruption as I laid out my theory about Nissen. As I heard myself talking, I kept thinking how much was pure speculation. I was weaving a crazy quilt out of circumstantial threads of evidence. When I finished, I was half-afraid Pinkham would push me out of the truck.

"Has Stacey forgotten her phone before?" he asked.

"She does it all the time."

"So when was the last time you spoke with her?"

"A couple of days ago. We had an argument. I was letting her cool down."

When he smiled, he reminded me of a kindly schoolteacher. "I heard she told Tom Waterman to perform an anatomical impossibility on himself."

"I heard that, too. That's one of the reasons I raced up here."

"And you discovered she'd been nosing around town, trying to prove that Samantha and Missy were really murdered?"

"Stacey has a tendency to get single-minded about things."

"It sounds like you two were made for each other."

Tell *her* that, I wanted to say.

"I can't think of any other reason for her to have gone to Blanchard other than to talk with Nissen. And you have to admit there's cause to be suspicious of him."

He didn't answer, but I noticed the speedometer jump ten miles per hour.

The road was like a groove gouged through the forest. Every mile or so, we passed a lighted homestead with trucks and ATVs in their dooryards and often a BEWARE OF DOG sign out front. It was the kind of road where you prayed not to break down after dark and be forced to knock on doors.

Fifteen minutes after we left Monson, we came to a crossroads where a handful of homes were clustered together. Robins hopped across the lawn of a white meeting house. Flowers were dying in its window boxes, and a frayed American flag hung limply from a pole. We crossed a bridge over the shallow, quick-flowing Piscataquis River and made a hard right after the municipal sand shed. Then we were plunged into the forest again. That seemed to be the entire village of Blanchard.

"What do you know about Nissen?" I asked.

"I see him selling honey and beeswax candles at the farmers' market in Greenville," Pinkham said. "He's not the most sociable human being I've ever met, but I guess that's not news to you. DeFord tells me Nissen knows every inch of the Appalachian Trail. That's why Moosehead Search and Rescue lets him volunteer despite his being a convicted felon. As far as I know, he's never been in trouble since he moved to Maine from down south. I would have heard if he'd ever been pinched for anything."

"Ever hear anything that would suggest he's a religious fanatic?"

The warden detective peeked at me from behind his glasses. "What do you mean?"

"Is he known to be a Christian extremist?"

"I go to church every Sunday—Holy Family in Greenville. Does that make me an extremist, too?"

"No."

We drove on for another few minutes. We had left the last of the streetlights behind.

Without looking at me, Pinkham said, "The worst thing you can do is go into an investigation prejudiced."

"I'll try to remember that."

"We don't know how the girls died yet, let alone why. I think you're trying to come up with a motive that fits your personal bias. You don't like Nissen, and so you want him to be guilty."

"So what if I do?"

"How is that any different from the folks who believe coyotes killed those girls?"

In my head, I tried to articulate a response—of course it was different—but my thoughts kept sputtering out.

"You're right," I said finally. "I don't like Nissen. And I don't know if he's a murderer. What scares me is that Stacey might find out before we do."

Pinkham had the same government-issue GPS unit mounted to his dash that I used in my truck. I saw Breakneck Ridge appear on the screen as a series of elevation lines. I peered out the window, looking for it. At first I couldn't see anything. Then I became aware of an elongated hill looming above the treetops like the humped back of a sleeping animal.

The unmarked turnoff came on us quickly. Pinkham cornered too fast, and the force knocked the side of my head against the window. The dirt road climbed in switchbacks up the north face of the ridge.

Near the top, we came to a muddy field that had recently been a forest. The loggers had left some stumps and a few scraggly trees to comply with the state law against wholesale clear-cutting, but they had taken everything else. Torn pieces of bark and wood chips carpeted the dirt road. The treads of heavy machines crisscrossed the property like so many stitched wounds.

I surveyed the injured hillside with disgust. "Is this Nissen's wood-lot? It looks like it's been scalped."

"No, this is Dow land."

"Wait a minute. The Dows live in Blanchard?"

"Not here," said Pinkham. "Their compound is off the Barrows Falls Road. But the family owns land all over town. Across the line in Monson, too. The Dows settled this whole area back in the 1800s. Every generation sold off a bit more and a bit more. In a few years, they won't even own the land under their own houses."

When I had heard that Stacey had been spotted going to Blanchard, I'd jumped to the conclusion that she'd been headed to Nissen's place. What if she'd been headed for the Dows' backwoods stronghold? I didn't dare say anything to Pinkham after he'd just warned me against letting my imagination whip up conspiracy theories.

Pinkham took his foot off the gas pedal and extinguished his headlights.

"I'm going to park here, and we can walk up," he said.

We followed the road out of the clearing and into an uncut stand of softwoods whose branches interwove above us. One of the oaks decided to bounce an acorn off my head. Far away, I heard the cackle of crows leaving their roost.

Pinkham moved surprisingly softly. His jowls and beer belly had made me forget that he'd been a district warden before becoming an investigator. The man clearly knew how to find his way in the woods.

We emerged into another field, this one rolling and wide. Everywhere I looked I saw white boxes rising from asters, goldenrod, and ragweed. Nissen's beehives. During daylight hours, the air must have been alive with buzzing, but the insects were asleep now in their wooden frames, waiting for the sun to clear the treetops. Then they would begin their incessant work of harvesting pollen.

Pinkham paused in the middle of the road. "Up there," he whispered.

A log cabin squatted against the tree line. No lights shone in the windows. No smoke rose from the stainless-steel chimney pipe. In the gloom, I could distinguish an assortment of outbuildings—various sheds and workshops—but there was no sign of a human presence. I saw a bright orange Kubota tractor. Where was Stacey's truck? Where was Nissen's van?

There were tire marks on the ground—headed in and out. I knelt down and ran my fingers over the subtle ridges. The Warden Service had trained me to read treads the way fortune-tellers do palms. In the right conditions, I could tell what type of vehicles had driven along a dirt road, whether they had been heavily loaded, and when they had last been through. It was a good party trick to show off to my nonwarden friends. Most of the marks I saw had been left by the same vehicle—obviously Nissen's van. But there was another set left by a pickup that had recently come and gone. It had to have been Stacey's.

I took a step toward the darkened cabin, then another. Pinkham called my name as loudly as he dared. I kept walking, my eyes fixed on the ground, following the tracks she had left behind.

She had parked under an old apple tree from which Nissen had harvested the best fruit. In the spring, its blossoms must have trembled with hungry bees. A few misshapen apples still clung to the limbs and other rejects lay scattered about the grass. I kicked aside the rotting cores until an odd-shaped piece of plastic caught my eye. I dropped hard to my knees and cradled Stacey's broken sunglasses in my hands.

32

Pinkham leaned over my shoulder. "You're sure those are her sunglasses?"

"What are the odds that Nissen also wears emerald-green Maui Jims?"

The warden investigator studied the crushed patterns left in the grass by the truck. "It looks to me like she might have dropped them without realizing. I'd say they broke when she ran over them on her way out."

"What if she left them for us as a sign?"

"A sign of what?"

"That she was taken against her will."

"I know you're upset," he said, "but it's a lot more likely that she was just careless. You said she tends to be forgetful. If Nissen forced her to go someplace, then why is his van gone, too?"

I didn't have a ready answer for him. I glanced up at the cabin, which I could see better now that the sun was coming up. It appeared to be a new building; the logs were still orange and the green roof shingles hadn't yet begun to warp or curl. I rose to my feet and handed Pinkham the shattered glasses.

"Where are you going?" he asked.

"I'm going to have a look inside."

"We can't enter the cabin without a warrant. There are no exigent circumstances."

A muscle twitched underneath my jaw. "A possible kidnapping isn't reason enough to bust down the door?"

"There's no sign of a struggle. And I'm not sure what we'd be looking for inside the house."

"Jesus Christ! Can't we just make something up?"

His tone was patient, without a trace of condescension. "I know you're worried about her, Mike. I am, too. Stacey's one of our people. Her old man and I go way back. But if something bad happened to her, you're going to be glad we followed the letter of the law. The last thing we want is to give a judge reason to toss a case out of court."

"You worry about the legal stuff. I have other concerns right now."

Pinkham kept his gaze on mine, refusing to let me inside his head. He handed me back the sunglasses. "Why don't you call Charley and tell him what you found? He can look for her truck and Nissen's van from the air."

"What are you going to do?"

"I don't think a judge would have a problem with me peeking in the windows."

"I want to go with you."

"With all due respect, I don't think that's a good idea."

"Are you afraid I'm going to break a window?"

He didn't answer, but his expression said yes. Desperation was causing me to revert back to my old self. I was going to suggest he call Fitzpatrick and have the state police issue a BOLO—the police acronym for "Be on the lookout"—for Nissen's vehicle. But again, there was no cause. I had never felt so impotent.

I watched Pinkham proceed carefully up the front steps of the cabin. Nissen didn't strike me as the sort of paranoid who would booby-trap his place against intruders, but it paid to be careful. The investigator studied each board on the porch before he stepped on it. He shaded his eyes with his hands to look in the windows but was careful not to touch the glass.

"Anything?" I called.

Pinkham shook his balding head and checked the next window.

I knew Stacey had a permit to carry a concealed weapon because she'd shown it to me when we'd gone shooting together at a gravel pit: a steep-walled excavation outside of Grand Lake Stream littered with broken beer bottles and spent cartridges, where she'd put five rounds in a target the size of a pie plate from fifty feet. I hoped to God that she was carrying that lethal Ruger .38 on her person.

I reached Charley in the air, and as usual we had to shout at each other for him to hear above the noise of his plane engine. He said he was north of Bangor, less than fifteen minutes out. He asked if there had been any new developments since the night before. I did my best to keep emotion out of my voice as I told my tale, but I was undone by my mouth, which had chosen to stop producing saliva.

"You say this Nissen is an ex-con?" he asked.

"He did a stint in the federal pen for cooking meth. There's no history of violence in his jacket, though."

It didn't sound like much of a consolation.

"A white van should be easy to spot from the air," he said. "Not many of those hippie wagons still around."

I paused to get my salivary glands working. "Listen, Charley, do you know if Stacey is carrying her Ruger?"

"Son, I didn't even know she had a permit."

Stacey and her secrets.

Pinkham returned with his hands in his pockets and his brow furrowed. I told Charley I needed to go. He said that I should see his Cessna soon. He'd call me with an update in an hour.

"Anything?" I asked Pinkham again.

"I saw some papers and books scattered on the table. Also two mugs, which suggests he had company. It seems strange that he would have invited her inside for tea. Even stranger that she would have accepted the invitation."

"You don't know Stacey," I said. "She's fearless—not always in a good way."

"I'm not sure what more we can do here, unless you think it makes sense to wait until Nissen returns."

"No." Despite having no idea where to go, I wanted to keep moving. I needed to burn the nervous energy out of my system.

"How about I take you to get your truck?" Pinkham said.

"It's in the garage, remember? My tires were slashed."

"You said it's at Monson Automotive?"

"Yeah. Why?"

He removed his cell phone from his jacket pocket. "How choosy are you about tires?"

"As long as they're not flat, I don't care."

"Let's see if I can expedite your repair. You can thank me by not doing anything foolish."

I wanted to tell the warden investigator that my foolish days were over, but I doubted he would believe me, especially when I didn't even believe it myself.

On our way down the ridge, Charley's Cessna appeared against the rising sun. The old pilot must have seen Pinkham's truck, as well. He waggled his wings in greeting. Usually, the gesture made me smile, but not today.

We retraced our route back to Monson but turned south on Route 15. Before I saw the sign for Monson Automotive, I saw the heaps of discarded tires piled behind the garage. That was why Pinkham had asked if I was choosy about what went on my truck, I realized. In the interest of time, I was getting used treads. I supposed I was fortunate the GMC Sierra was such a popular model in this neck of the woods.

The big man who'd towed my pickup earlier came out through the bay door as we pulled up. He was holding an impact wrench in one hand and covering a yawn with the other. I could see my truck on the lift behind him.

"Hey, Jasper, thanks for bumping my friend to the head of the line," said Pinkham.

"What's the rush on this?"

The investigator hitched a thumb inside his belt and smiled. "The usual thing. Police business."

The big man shook his round head. He had a grease smudge under his eye like football players do and speckles of dandruff on his shoulders. "You frigging game wardens. Everything's a god-damned secret. There's coffee in the office. I should be done in half an hour."

In the waiting room, I filled two Styrofoam cups from the coffee machine while Pinkham inspected the hunting and bikini magazines on the table.

"I guess Jasper doesn't get a lot of female customers," he said with a raised eyebrow.

"Thanks for doing this, Pinkham."

"Maybe I'm just tired of chauffeuring you around."

"In any case, I owe you."

"No, you owe *Jasper*. I hope you brought your credit card."

We sat down to wait, but I couldn't stop checking my watch every other minute. After a while, I got up to use the grimy bathroom. The toilet refused to flush unless the plunger in the tank was lifted manually. I washed my hands for a solid three minutes and still didn't feel as if I'd killed all the germs.

Jasper was standing behind the register when I came out, gabbing with Pinkham.

"Bob Nissen? Of course I know Bob," the big man said. "Replaced the transmission on his van this spring. You don't see many of those old VWs around anymore. What did he do?"

"We're just looking for him is all," said Pinkham.

"Do you know if he has any friends or family in the area?" I asked.

Jasper scratched his scalp, loosing a flurry of dandruff on his shoulders. "I couldn't tell you. Nissen mostly keeps to himself. The only time I ever see him around is at the store. You should talk to Pearlene. I think she buys honey from him to sell. Candles, too."

The gas station truly was the center of everything that happened in the village.

When I reviewed my bill, I saw that Jasper had tacked an extra charge of fifty dollars on for the rush job. I wasn't going to argue about it. I was just glad to be mobile again.

I loaded my bag of guns into the cab of the Sierra and fired up the engine. Pinkham knocked on my window.

"I'll follow you over there," he said.

"Afraid I'm going to do something rash unless you're there to stop me?"

"I was thinking my clogged arteries could use a breakfast sandwich."

The general store was as bustling as ever. Every gas pump was in use. Men in coveralls hurried in and out with cups of coffee and bagged lunches to take to their job sites. The smell of hot grease wafted through a vent.

Toby Dow's overturned bucket waited in its usual spot for its owner to return. The arrangement was probably easier for his family than baby-sitting him all day. As I turned off my engine, an image came into my head of the boy sitting on his makeshift stool, and I experienced a curious sensation I couldn't quite define. I felt a tingle of anxiety, as if the apparition was a warning of some sort, which was a ridiculous thing to think. What did I have to fear from a teen with Down syndrome?

Pinkham pulled his truck up next to mine, and we both got out.

Inside the store, a line stretched from the checkout counter to the beer cooler. Pearlene stood behind the register, rushing to ring up purchases. She was wearing her usual baggy smock and a hairnet pulled down to her eyebrows. Sweat streamed down the side of her face and an unlighted cigarette dangled from her painted lips.

"Morning, Pearlene," Pinkham said. "Looks like you've got your hands full this morning."

"I'm too busy for small talk, Wes. If you want to buy something, get in line."

"There's something we need to talk with you about. It's kind of delicate."

"Can't you see I'm working?"

"Please, Pearlene. This is important." He turned toward the line of customers, each of whom had the expression of someone waiting for a bathroom. "I'm sure these good folks can spare a few extra minutes."

Pearlene scowled at us as we approached. She pushed aside some of the objects cluttering the counter—her cell phone and a can of Diet Coke—in order to lean over it. "You're costing me money, Wes."

He smiled and lowered his voice. "But it's for a good cause. Do you know Warden Bowditch?"

"We've met," she said with no hint of warmth. "If it's about Benton again, I don't want to hear it. We got fined last month because he sold cigarettes to a teenage girl. I told him if it happened again, I was going to shitcan him. So tell me the bad news."

"Actually, we're looking for Bob Nissen."

"He lives out in Blanchard, on Breakneck Ridge. You should try out there." With her tongue, she moved the cigarette from one side of her mouth to the other. "Why? What did he do?"

"We were at his cabin earlier. He's not there," I said. "Jasper, at the garage, told us you were friendly with him."

"Friendly!" She let out a witch's cackle. "I buy honey and candles from the man. We're not bosom buddies, for Christ's sake."

"Is there anything you can tell us about him?" Pinkham asked. "Anything that might help us track him down?"

"You still haven't told me what he did."

"Please, Pearlene."

"You probably know about his speed record," she said. "He hiked the AT faster than anyone. I guess he's a celebrity among the thru-hikers, which is kind of comical, if you ask me. Some of them come in asking for directions to his place. They want to make a pilgrimage out there while they're in the area, but I tell them Bob isn't the type who welcomes visitors. He's chased more than a few of those kids off his property, according to Benton."

"Do you know if he attends church services over at the Lake of the Woods Tabernacle?" Pinkham asked.

"You should go ask that horse's ass, Brother John."

"You don't like the pastor?"

"If he's a real pastor, I'm the Queen of Sheba." Her gaze went to her milling customers.

The detective made eye contact with me, as if to say, Well, this was a dead end.

I leaned against the counter and accidentally overturned a tray of disposable lighters. Some fell to the floor.

"Goddamn it!" Pearlene said.

"I'm sorry."

I began picking up the scattered Bics and putting them back into their display case like pegs in a pegboard. Pinkham stooped to help me. When I touched the case of lighters, the back end slid across the counter and knocked Pearlene's cell phone to her feet.

"Are you always this graceful?" she asked as she bent down to retrieve it.

"I'm sorry."

When she set the phone beside the register again, I saw that it was one of those oversized models, nearly the size of a small paperback. Cracks spiderwebbed the glass screen. I reached for it without thinking.

The case was broken, and the battery was missing. Someone had tried to scratch a little girl's sticker from the back. Most of it had been peeled away, except for what appeared to be a bright red bow. I dropped the phone as if it had scorched my hand.

I looked up at the old woman. "Where did you find this?"

"In the parking lot."

"Pinkham, didn't Samantha and Missy own Samsung Galaxies?"

"Yeah. Why?"

"Their phones weren't found with their bodies, you said."

I pointed at the counter. A sudden light came into Pinkham's eyes. His hands fell to his sides.

33

Pinkham had said that Missy Montgomery's phone was identifiable by a Hello Kitty sticker on the back. Someone had done a poor job trying to remove it—almost suspiciously poor, in fact.

The investigator called Sergeant Fitzpatrick and told the state police detective what we'd found. The cell carrier would have a record of the serial numbers. Whoever had taken the battery had forgotten to scrape off the identifying information inside. We should have our answer in minutes.

I took Pearlene aside while frustrated customers gave up and left without their purchases. She watched them go with a pained expression, as if she could count the dollars being blown away on the wind. She replaced the sodden cigarette in her mouth with another. If she couldn't light up, she was going to try sucking out the nicotine.

"When did you find the phone?" I asked her.

"This morning. I picked it up and brought it inside. Figured it was Toby's."

I'd already told Pinkham that Toby Dow was playing with a broken cell phone the morning I'd met him. At the time, I didn't know the women's phones were missing. I wanted to kick myself for not remembering the kid and his toy later.

Stacey had been at the store the same time as Toby Dow. Maybe she had noticed him talking on his phone. But if she had realized the Samsung might have belonged to Samantha or Missy, she would surely have alerted the police. She wouldn't have abandoned a key piece of evidence, leaving it behind in the store parking lot. And it didn't explain why she would have rushed out to Nissen's place.

Pinkham held his own phone pressed between his ear and his shoulder so that he could jot down the serial numbers of the missing Samsungs. He held his pen poised over his little Rite in the Rain notebook. His tired eyes opened wide behind his unfashionable glasses.

"It's Missy's," he mouthed to me.

"Are you sure this is the phone Toby Dow has been playing with?" I asked Pearlene.

"It was right over near his bucket."

"Do you know where he got it?"

"Probably out in the lot," she said. "People drop things out there all the time when they're pumping gas or getting in and out of their cars. Wallets, phones, sunglasses."

Pinkham finished his conversation with the state police detective and came over to me. "How'd you like to take a drive back to Blanchard?"

"Just the two of us?" I was remembering the crazed faces of the five Dows as they surrounded me in the bar. How many more of those brutes were back at their compound?

"Fitzpatrick is sending backup," he said.

Pearlene removed the unlighted cigarette from her mouth and waved it at Pinkham. "I don't get it. You're saying the Dows had something to do with what happened to those girls? What about the fucking coyotes?"

He placed a hand on the old woman's shoulder and leaned in close. "I'd appreciate it if you didn't mention this to anyone."

The color bled out of her cheeks. "What are you going to do?"

"Just ask the boy a few questions," the investigator said.

"You can't tell the Dows it was me who gave you that phone. If they think I ratted them out, they'll burn my store down—with me in it!"

"It's going to be OK, Pearlene."

"The hell it is!" She clapped a blue-veined hand to her forehead. "I am so fucking screwed."

We left her to contemplate the many terrible ways the Dows could wreak revenge on her business and her person.

"Do you know how many troopers Fitzpatrick is sending?" I asked Pinkham as we returned to our trucks.

"Are you worried about being outnumbered?"

"I'm worried about being outgunned."

Pinkham seemed to know where he was going. As the local warden investigator charged with catching the worst poachers in the Moosehead region, he must have made regular stops at the Dow family compound. My replacement tires, vibrating over the asphalt, made a noise like a wax-paper harmonica. Through the trees, I could see glimpses of Lake Hebron, the water as flat and blue as stained glass in the early-morning light.

Halfway there, we passed a vintage Ford F-100 with a dead coyote tied to the flatbed. The driver had probably spent a long night in the woods, waiting to shoot the animal over a pile of Alpo. He was going to be pissed to learn there was no one to tag it at the Monson General Store.

Unless one of the Dows had run into Samantha and Missy in Monson—or seen them walking along the road to the trailhead—I couldn't see how they would have crossed paths. The idea of hiking for recreation was foreign, if not laughable, to mountain men like Troy and Trevor. The only time they took a walk in the woods was when they were heading to a tree stand or patrolling a trapline.

Troy Dow had been in the Hundred Mile Wilderness on the same day the bodies had been found. He'd been working on the KI Road that very morning, which was how he'd come to give Chad McDonough a ride. He'd also had the opportunity, after I had released him from custody, to go looking for his hitchhiker, once he'd realized McDonut was a witness to the disappearance of Samantha and Missy. Troy Dow might have crushed the poor kid under the wheels of his Silverado to keep him from talking.

Whenever I was trying to solve a puzzle, I liked to use my imagination to re-create the sequence of events. This time, however, I couldn't get the film to play smoothly inside my head. The images kept jump-cutting.

As a theory of what had happened, it just didn't hang together. Nor did it offer an explanation for Stacey's disappearance. To my knowledge, no relationship existed between the Dows and Nissen, nothing that would explain where my girlfriend had gone or been taken.

Charley called me from the air. I rolled up the window and put my phone on speaker, so I wouldn't lose Pinkham.

"I'm over Moxie Pond," he said, shouting to be heard above the floatplane's engine.

"And I'm driving to Blanchard again."

"Back to the beekeeper's place?"

"Pinkham and I are going to talk to your friend, the mayor of Monson."

"Say again?" he shouted.

I did my best to explain to him about finding Missy's phone at the general store.

"That's a new twist in the pretzel," he said. "Do you want me to fly recon for you over that compound?"

"It might spook them."

"I'm sure the DEA makes regular flyovers."

"Keep looking for Stacey's truck. Start at Nissen's place on Breakneck Ridge and range out from there."

Whatever he said next was lost beneath the mechanical roar.

"What was that?" I said.

"How afraid should we be for my little girl?"

"She'd be pissed if she heard you call her that."

"Ain't that the truth!" His tone was light, but I could hear the bluff behind it.

My old friend had done two tours in Vietnam during the war, flying Cessna O-1 Bird Dogs over enemy lines. After a surface-to-air missile blasted off his rudder, he'd managed to ditch in a rice paddy, with only a broken ankle to show for it. Afterward, he'd done a stint in the Hanoi Hilton, where his torturers made sure his ankle never properly healed. Back home, working as a game warden, he had been shot, beaten up, and nearly drowned; he'd been in three more plane crashes, including the one that paralyzed his wife. And not once had I heard him complain about being in pain or ever worry for his own life. In short, Charley Stevens was one of the bravest, strongest men I had ever met. This was the first time I'd ever heard fear in his voice.

As we drove into what I'd come to think of as downtown Blanchard, we turned left, heading southeast along the Barrows Falls Road. We passed a single farmhouse with Rhode Island Reds pecking in the wet grass. Then we were swallowed up again by the green woods.

A state police cruiser was parked along the shoulder. Beyond the car was a huddle of mailboxes. Across the road, a dirt drive led up a thickly wooded hillside. The forest here was damp and dense, crowded with northern white cedars, red maples, and black spruces packed so closely together that the shadows between them appeared to be tangled, writhing things. It was no surprise to me that the woods-wise Dow family had chosen this impassable place for their stronghold.

As I came to a stop behind Pinkham's truck, I spotted an improvised gate—a felled cedar log that would need to be dragged aside whenever anyone wanted to enter or exit the property. Tacked to the trees for hundreds of yards in both directions were POSTED signs, and rusted barbed wire was strung at crotch level between the trunks. To make it absolutely clear how they felt about trespassers, the Dows had placed the rotting head of a longhorn steer on a spike at the end of the drive. Stacey had told me that the locals believed the clan matriarch, Tempest Dow, was some sort of evil witch. I could see how this disgusting fetish might awaken primitive fears.

The trooper straightened up out of his Interceptor and adjusted the strap on his brimmed blue hat. He waited for Pinkham and me to approach. He stood about six-five, all muscle. His name tag identified him as Chamberlain.

"Fitzpatrick is on his way," he said.

"We'll wait for him," said Pinkham. "Chamberlain, this is Warden Bowditch."

The trooper and I shook hands. "We spoke last week," he said.

I remembered him now—the officer who had found Chad McDonough's car at Abol Bridge Campground.

"What's the plan?" I asked Pinkham.

The detective unrolled a topographical map on the hood of his truck. He pointed to a small elevation to our north, rising approximately three hundred feet above the river floodplain. The survey map included a cluster of black rectangles indicating buildings at the top of the hill.

"Fitzpatrick and Chamberlain will go up the drive," Pinkham said. "You and I will approach through the woods from different directions. There are probably fifty people living up there, including the kids. Most of what's up there are mobile homes, but there's an old farmhouse, a barn, a sugar shack, and a bunch of sheds. Lots of places to hide, in other words."

"Are there other ways out of there?" I asked.

"There are ATV trails going in every direction. The last time I poked around these woods, I found piano wire stretched across a few of them at neck height. It's a miracle none of the Dows have beheaded themselves."

I had a bad feeling about sneaking up on men like this unless we were going in force with guns drawn. "Are they just antisocial, or do they have business they don't want discovered?"

"Both," said Trooper Chamberlain. He popped a piece of gum in his mouth, as if the word had left a bad taste.

"The Dows have always grown marijuana," said Pinkham. "They do most of their farming on other people's properties to keep from being busted. I've had summer people who came up in August and found their backyards overgrown with pot plants. Rumor is that the Dows have recently gotten into dealing 'bath salts,' too."

The investigator wasn't talking about the crystals you pour into your tub. He meant the illegal stimulants that cause users to jump off bridges, thinking they can fly.

"No wonder they don't like visitors," I said.

Chamberlain folded his arms. "A few years ago," he said, "a census taker tried going up there to ask them some questions. He came running out in his Fruit of the Looms, covered in pig shit. I told him he was lucky the Dows hadn't made him squeal like a pig, too. He decided not to press charges, needless to say."

A dark blue Ford sedan appeared, coming from the direction of Monson. I recognized it as Fitzpatrick's unmarked police car. It rolled to a stop in the shadows behind my truck, and the state police lieutenant got out. He paused to tuck his shirt into his pants, revealing the holstered pistol on his belt. A bloody piece of paper stuck to his chin suggested a shaving mishap.

Pinkham briefed him on the situation. He brought out the bagged Samsung Galaxy for show-and-tell.

"Are you sure this is the phone you saw the boy playing with?" Fitzpatrick asked me.

"As sure as I can be."

The state police sergeant hadn't placed much faith in my opinions that first night of the search. But events had intervened since then: Chad McDonough was dead, Nissen had disappeared, and I'd discovered the one piece of hard evidence to suggest Samantha and Missy had died by human hands.

"So the question is where he got it," said Fitzpatrick after a pause.

"Let's go ask him," said Trooper Chamberlain.

I gazed up at the trees on either side of the log gate. I was remembering the expression of terror on Pearlene's face whenever she talked about the family's capacity for violence. There are dangerous places in Maine—dark corners like this one—where officers are required to go in pairs except in grave emergencies. In this case, I wondered if even four of us was a prudent number.

"I'm guessing they have game cameras all over these woods," I said.

"That's a safe bet," said Pinkham.

"What about booby traps?" It wasn't uncommon for backwoods pot growers to rig trip wires and explosives in their fields.

"Keep your eyes open, and you'll be all right."

I returned to my truck to change jackets. On patrol, I always carried a Mossy Oak camouflage raincoat and a matching ball cap. I couldn't do anything about the blue jeans, but the light was low enough under the trees. I doubted the color would scream out.

We all exchanged cell numbers and set our phones to vibrate. Pinkham directed me to walk a hundred yards down the road. The plan was for me to approach the hilltop from the southeast while he climbed up the southwestern slope. He laid a hand lightly on my shoulder, the way priests used to after the sacrament of confession, when they'd told me to "go with God."

"Watch yourself in there," he said. "The Dows don't screw around."

"You, too."

The investigator smiled, winked at me, and patted the firearm at his side. Then he went to put on his camouflage.

34

On Fitzpatrick's signal, we all began moving up the hill. I found a sagging spot in the barbed wire that I could step over. I lost sight of the others as soon as I entered the evergreens.

The trees were thickest close to the road, and the forest floor was puddled. The branches scraped my cheeks and flipped my cap off my head. I stepped from slippery root to slippery root, not wanting to put my foot down into a pool of water and find a leg-hold trap hidden at the bottom. Poisonous toadstools sprouted from rotting logs. The heavy boughs were fragrant and wet. You can always tell if deer are in the woods by looking to see if the cedar branches closest to the ground have been picked clean. These were untouched. I was certain that no deer ever escaped the Dows' land alive.

After a few minutes of climbing through the muck, I found myself in a dry grove of hardwoods. Some of the hand-shaped leaves overhead had begun to turn scarlet, and a few of them had already fallen, blown free by one of the recent thunderstorms. The trunks were scaly and crusted with gray-green lichen.

I saw the first game camera mounted to one of the maples at knee height. It was an olive drab box, the size of a deck of cards, with a single lens pointed at an overgrown moose trail. The Dows must have used the video recorder to watch for animals or guard against trespassers—probably both.

Carefully, I made my way around the trunk, collided with a spiked branch, and got a cut on my cheek for my trouble. By the time I was an old man, my entire epidermis was going to consist of nothing but scar tissue. *If* I lived to be an old man. I kept going up the hill.

The fallen leaves were brittle on top but wet underneath, and every once in a while a whole mat of them would slide loose, causing me to slip. I didn't want to rush, for fear of stumbling into a booby trap, but I was concerned that I wasn't keeping pace with the others.

A flash of silver brought me up short. At first I thought I was gazing at strands of spider silk. Then I saw the sharp pieces of metal.

A row of fish hooks, tied to monofilament line, dangled from a branch overhead. They had been set at eye level. Another step and I might've been permanently blinded.

I parted the plastic threads with my hands and moved deliberately up the hill. I saw white Indian pipes growing in the shade, a neat mound of pinecone scales where a red squirrel had eaten its dinner. The treble hooks had taught me that if I overlooked anything, however mundane, I might find myself injured, or worse.

Five minutes later, I saw light shimmering around tree trunks, caught the warm smell of ragweed drying in the sun, and knew I was nearing a field. At the edge of the clearing was an improvised fence. Loose coils of barbed wire unrolled like a child's toy to my right and left, blocking my way.

It took me a few minutes, but eventually I found an opening between two rolls of wire.

A rabbit had tried to jump through the gap, but the animal must have gotten stuck on the barbs. Its soft coat was torn and bloodied. In places I could see the pink muscle beneath the fur.

Strange, I thought. It was a domestic rabbit, not a wild snowshoe hare. Had it escaped from the Dows' hutches?

The question made me hesitate before stepping through the gap. I paused long enough to notice the coyote snare on the opposite side of the fence. It was a noose made of aircraft cable, suspended a foot off the ground. The rabbit hadn't accidentally impaled itself; it had been placed there as bait.

The snare wouldn't have hurt me. Even if I'd gotten a leg caught, I would have been able to snip the cable with the wire cutters on my multitool. But I preferred not to disturb the trap.

A wave of silent warblers passed through the trees overhead, individual birds flitting from branch to branch, indistinguishable except as momentary flashes of color—and then they were gone and the forest held its breath again.

I was readying myself to leap over the snare when my muscles locked up. My body refused to obey the commands traveling from my brain. Something was wrong here.

My father had run a trapline in the western Maine mountains when I was young, and he had taught me to always set two snares for smart predators like coyotes and foxes: one in plain sight, the other concealed. In trying to avoid the first trap, the clever animal would fall victim to the second. I lowered myself onto my haunches, but I didn't see anything on the ground, not a foothold trap or a leaf mat that might have concealed a pit filled with poisoned spikes.

Shafts of sunlight—alive with drifting dust motes—entered the forest from the field. I lifted my head to feel the warmth on my face. That was when I saw it. Five feet in the air, another fishing line was strung horizontal to the forest floor. My breath caught in my throat when I saw that it was a trip wire connected to a bomb.

A Maxwell House coffee can had been nailed sideways to a tree. The monofilament line ran through a hole punched in the plastic lid and was connected, I assumed, to a switch or fuse inside. What else was inside the can? Black powder? Roofing nails? Buckshot?

Booby-trapping your land is a felony in Maine. The danger that a jury-rigged explosive might pose to innocent people who have a good reason to be on your property—firemen, police officers, utility workers—outweighs your right to blow yourself to bits. Not that the law has ever been effective at protecting people from themselves.

"The Dows don't screw around," Pinkham had said. He wasn't kidding.

To be on the safe side, I looked to see if there might be a third trap. But evidently there were limits to the number of precautions the Dows were willing to take to protect their pot fields.

Getting past the snare required some gymnastics on my part. I ducked my head to avoid the trip wire and tumbled forward over the wire noose. I rubbed the leaf mold off the bottom of my jeans as I climbed to my feet. I would need to make a note of the explosive's location so a bomb-disposal officer could remove it.

A shadow passed at the edge of my vision.

"Don't move!" The voice was almost doglike in its timbre.

I raised my hands.

"You're not going to shoot me in the back," I said. "Are you, Trevor?"

"You're trespassing. This land is posted. Law says we can shoot trespassers."

"Game wardens don't need permission," I said, and began to turn around.

"Stop!"

Trevor Dow wore the same outfit he'd had on the day he'd tussled with Charley Stevens outside the Monson General Store: dirty jeans, flannel shirt, Dexter boots. His beard shone like spun copper in the brilliant light of morning. He raised a scoped AR-15 rifle—the kind used to execute coyotes—and pointed it at my heart.

"Did I miss one of your game cameras coming up the hill?" I asked. "Is that how you found me?"

His mouth jerked to a smile beneath his mustache. He was fifteen feet away, and he had his finger on the trigger. It was too far to make a flying tackle.

"It's illegal to booby-trap your land, Trevor," I said. "And making bombs is a felony."

He stared down the scope at me. "Take your gun out. Slowly!"

I didn't like where this was headed. I could only hope that Fitzpatrick and Chamberlain were nearby, and that Trevor Dow wouldn't decide to use me as a human shield if they drew their weapons. But I didn't see what options I had.

His fox-colored eyes bored into mine. "Toss it at my feet. . . . Not that way! By the barrel."

My heavy SIG landed with an audible thud on the dirt. He squatted down beside it. I hoped he would take his eyes off me while he picked up the gun. It might give me a split second to throw myself at him. But Trevor Dow was wise to my plan and began feeling around blindly with one hand. The other remained on the pistol grip of the AR-15, his index finger curled around the trigger.

His mouth jerked again as his hand closed around my gun. He hefted the SIG in his palm, as if trying to guess its weight. "I've always wanted one of these."

The explosion took us both by surprise.

The earth didn't shake. There was no flash of light. Just a *boom*. And then a man's scream.

My head whipped around in the direction of the noise. *Pinkham*, I thought.

In my peripheral vision, I saw Trevor Dow flinch. The hand holding my pistol fell to his side, and the SIG dropped into the weeds. He looked down to see where it had gone. The barrel of the rifle drooped.

Without pausing to think, I hurled myself across the space between us.

My forehead collided with his hip bone, and he let out a gasp. Before he could bring the butt of the rifle down on my skull, I wrapped my arms around his lower thighs and lifted him clear off the ground. Trevor landed hard on his shoulders—I heard the wind propelled from his lungs—but he never let go of the AR-15. A shot fired into the air when his trigger finger clenched.

Lying on his back, Trevor shoved the stock of the rifle at my chest, trying to separate us, but I got hold of the hand guard. He was expecting me to play tug-of-war with him. Instead, I yanked the barrel to my right side while pushing the polymer stock against his temple with my left hand.

He was a strong man, stronger than me, but the impact of the gun against his head caused his grip to slip. Now I pushed the muzzle forward and pulled the stock back. The metal sight knocked him between the eyes.

I pulled back with all my might, knees planted firmly on the ground, and stripped the AR-15 from his grasp.

The motion caused me to fall backward. Trevor was bleeding badly from his cut brow, but he wasn't done fighting. He lunged at me, trying to grab the weapon.

I had just enough time to drive the stock into his chin. There was a sharp crack as the mandible shattered. Blood sprayed from his mouth. He slumped to the ground.

I shimmied away from him until I was far enough away to get the rifle turned around.

"Don't move," I said, aiming at his chest.

He lay on his side, red drool trailing from his lips, a deep wound plastering the hair across his forehead.

"You're under arrest," I said, panting.

I could see his rib cage expanding and contracting as he struggled to catch his breath.

I reached into my back pocket and found my handcuffs. I threw them at his legs.

"Put those on."

"Fuck you."

I raised the barrel. "Do it!"

He fumbled with the cuffs while I got my feet beneath me. My ears were ringing. I watched him close the clasps.

"Now get up."

He put his weight on his hands until he was on all fours. He began hop-crawling toward me as I bent to retrieve my pistol. *The son of a bitch is going to try rushing me!* I circled around behind him.

Defeated, Trevor Dow staggered to a standing position.

"You're under arrest for assaulting a police officer," I said.

"Fuck you."

During the struggle, the world had gotten small. Now I could feel it expanding around me, returning to full size. I heard shouting. Dogs barking. The roar of engines.

Pinkham.

I felt a sudden pull on my heart, strong enough that it might have tugged me across the field. The impulse was to run to see what was happening. But there were other booby traps on the Dows' land, probably lots of them.

I told Hay Face to start walking.

Trevor Dow spat blood into the weeds and began to march. I kept pace behind him, with the tip of the gun raised, fully prepared to drill a hole in his back. We followed the perimeter of the field toward a fenced group of buildings that looked, from a distance, almost like a concentration camp plopped down in the Maine woods.

Looking to my right, I began seeing structures outside the wire: an old two-seater outhouse missing its door; a listing hay barn about to collapse on top of the vintage tractor parked inside; assorted storage sheds. I saw a washing machine with a trio of sunflowers growing up from inside the open lid; cable spools used as picnic tables; and, beside them, a rusted oil tank like a red elephant in the tall grass.

A mustached man on an ATV came racing across the field. His unbuttoned shirt flapped behind him like denim-blue wings. I spotted a deer rifle in a scabbard mounted to the side of the four-wheeler. Troy Dow glanced at us but never slowed to help his brother. We watched him disappear into the woods.

Some thirty or so people milled about in the road up ahead. From a distance I couldn't tell what they were looking at, but their attention seemed riveted. They were men and women, boys and girls. Idling trucks spat out toxic fumes, and barking dogs circulated among the onlookers, excited by all the commotion.

I glimpsed a figure in a powder blue hat through the crowd. It was Trooper Chamberlain. My pulse throbbed in my neck.

Trevor and I weren't far from the oil tank. A pipe jutted from one end. It looked solid enough.

"Over there!" I told him. "Walk to the tank."

I raised the rifle barrel to show him that I was serious. He let out a snarl but did as ordered.

I found the keys to my handcuffs in my pocket and made him extend his arms. I unlocked one cuff, then snapped it shut again around the pipe. A purple bruise had begun to blossom above his left eye.

I turned and began jogging toward the crowd, holding the AR-15 in a port-arms position across my chest. To my right was a jumble of mobile homes, arranged in no obvious pattern inside a tall wire fence. In the center of the compound was a big rotting farmhouse that had once been painted red but now looked mostly gray.

Chamberlain held his .45 pistol with both hands. He shouted at everyone to get back, but the mob kept surging forward. I spotted Toby Dow among the bystanders. The young man was red-faced and sobbing. Many of the smaller children were crying, too.

"Stand aside!" I said.

The crowd broke apart as if I were a grenade thrown in their midst. Suddenly, they had no idea how many cops were raiding their backwoods garrison. A couple of men hightailed it back inside the compound; a few others jumped into their waiting trucks and went shooting off down the road. A skinny boy drove away on another muddy all-terrain vehicle with an overweight girl on the back, her hands clutching his stomach. She screamed something and flipped me the bird.

Chamberlain pointed with two fingers at the tree line behind him. "Pinkham!"

"Do you need help here?"

"No, but he does."

I sprinted along the far edge of the clearing, hoping I wouldn't step into a bear trap. I found Fitzpatrick kneeling beside a big maple. From the rear, it looked as if he was praying to the old tree. Then I saw Pinkham lying on the ground, his skin the color of bone.

There were finger smears of blood on Fitzpatrick's cheek, and both of his hands were red from applying pressure to the other man's wounds. When I got closer, I saw that the bottom half of Wes Pinkham was missing. The improvised bomb had ripped off both legs below the crotch.

35

I wish I could say that Pinkham had died instantly, but Fitzpatrick told me the warden investigator had lived for a few minutes, trying to sit up, not knowing where his legs were, until the light went out of his eyes.

I'd also like to say that I didn't gag. That, too, would be a lie.

I wiped my mouth with the back of my hand. Fitzpatrick was on the phone with Dispatch. He had covered the corpse at his feet with his blue windbreaker.

State police troopers and sheriff's deputies would soon converge on the hilltop. Dozens of game wardens would rush to Blanchard when word got out that one of our own had been murdered. The state police would send bomb-sniffing dogs and a disposal unit from Augusta. Only once the compound was secure would the medical examiner be allowed up to tell us what we already knew: Wes Pinkham had been cut in half by an improvised explosive device.

Fitzpatrick called DeFord next. "Wes has been killed," he said without prelude. "He walked into a hidden explosive on the Dow property." He cleared his throat. "No, he didn't. Wes said the land was booby-trapped, but he'd been in and out of here enough times, he wasn't worried." He paused while DeFord asked a question. "Chamberlain and your man Bowditch. Uh-huh. All right." He held out the phone, which was tacky from the dead man's blood. "The lieutenant wants to talk with you."

"Are you OK, Mike?" DeFord asked.

My mouth tasted of regurgitated coffee. "No, sir. I'm angry."

"So am I." Wes Pinkham had been a mentor to him, too. "What the hell happened?"

"I didn't see it," I said. "I came up the hill a different way. I found another bomb at the edge of the woods—similar to the one that killed Pinkham—but I got past it without triggering the explosive. I must have given myself away in one of the Dows' game cameras, though, because I found Trevor Dow waiting for me with an AR-15. I managed to disarm him and then handcuffed him to an oil tank."

"Good man." The lieutenant's voice sounded distant.

"There's one other thing, sir," I said. "Troy Dow got away. I saw him ride off into the woods on an ATV."

"In which direction?"

"North. Back toward Monson."

"Put Fitzpatrick back on."

I handed the phone to the detective. He pressed it to his ear and turned away from me. Whatever Fitzpatrick had to say to DeFord, he didn't want me to hear.

I looked over at Chamberlain and saw that the mob had dispersed except for a single barking dog, which had decided its responsibility was to continue sounding the alert. The Dows had all vanished inside their trailers or taken flight down secret trails into the woods.

Pinkham had been a good man and a good warden. He'd had a wife, children, and grandchildren. He hadn't deserved to be murdered by cowards like Troy and Trevor Dow.

No one deserved that.

I wanted Trevor to contemplate spending the rest of his life behind bars for what he and his family had done. I wanted to parade the whole goddamned clan past Wes Pinkham's lifeless body. I started walking toward the oil tank to fetch my prisoner. A red haze obscured my vision.

Greasy smoke began to rise from inside the compound. One of the Dows was trying to get rid of incriminating evidence.

A siren wailed in the distance. Half a minute later, a black Ford SUV bearing the insignia of the Piscataquis County Sheriff's Department came screaming up the hill. It slid to a stop on the gravel, and a female deputy jumped out holding a pump shotgun.

"Deputy!" I pivoted so she could see the badge on my belt.

The woman sprinted toward me. She had short brown hair, and she was wearing a ballistic vest over a chocolate-colored uniform.

"I heard there's a man down," she said, already out of breath.

"Wes Pinkham. He's dead. Over there."

"Jesus."

"I need you to do something for me. Do you know Trevor Dow?"

The muscles around her eyes began to twitch. "I know him."

"Well, this is his rifle. I took it away from him after he pointed it at me. He's handcuffed to an oil tank on the other side of that barn. I need you to go get him for me. Here are my keys."

She stared at the keys as I dropped them into her palm. "You don't want to do it?"

"I don't trust myself with him at this point."

More sirens sounded, coming up the road. I turned and began walking with the rifle toward the gate into the compound.

"Where are you going?" she called after me.

"I need to find someone."

"They've already killed one warden. You're going to get yourself shot!"

Wes Pinkham would have told me not to risk my life to locate Toby Dow. But then, it no longer mattered what he wanted. I tightened my grip on the AR-15 and kept marching. It was completely reckless, but I felt armored by my anger.

As I passed through the gate, I could feel their eyes crawling over me. A wheel-rutted lane meandered between the mobile homes, garages, and sheds toward the farmhouse at the center of the compound. It was a rambling three-story structure—no doubt the ancestral Dow manse—and it dominated its surroundings like a feudal castle among grass-thatched huts.

A barn cat trotted across the space in front of me and ducked under a boat trailer.

My gut told me that the worst of the Dow men had fled, afraid to be found violating bench warrants or in possession of firearms as felons. But there might still be a teenaged boy around, looking to make his bones by assassinating a Maine game warden with a deer rifle. And I doubted that the Dow women were harmless.

Smoke spiraled up from a long, flat-roofed building. The windows had been sprayed with black paint, but I could see flames glowing behind the opaque glass. The Dows had constructed their drug warehouse apart from the trailers in the event it needed to be razed in a hurry.

I kept advancing toward the farmhouse. Someone else could worry about the fire. A porch stretched the length of the first floor and was littered with blue and yellow toys, potted tomatoes, and mismatched chairs. Pushed up against the back was a ratty sofa, and seated on it, out of the sun, was a tiny old woman. I knew who she was: the witch of the castle.

She had pink skin the color of a dog's belly and long frizzy hair that had once been red but was now mostly whitish yellow. She wore a biker's leather jacket over a cotton nightdress. Her legs were so short they dangled clear of the floor, and on her feet was a pair of doll-size moccasins. She sipped from a can of Mountain Dew.

Tempest Dow wiped the soda from her thin lips. "Who the fuck are you?"

"Mike Bowditch, with the Maine Warden Service."

"That gun you got looks familiar."

"I took it off your son Trevor when I arrested him."

"Arrested on what charge?"

"Assaulting an officer. You seem pretty relaxed here. You didn't notice an explosion just now?"

When she smiled, she showed how few teeth she had left. "My hearing ain't as good as it used to be."

"One of the bombs on your property just killed a game warden investigator. That's first-degree murder, Mrs. Dow."

"I ain't never been married."

"You and your family are in a lot of trouble, and that's before we start searching your buildings. God only knows what we're going to find. You can help yourself by answering some questions for me."

Her manner was utterly relaxed, as if a man hadn't just been blown to bits outside her fence and a building wasn't going up in flames a hundred feet away.

"I don't know nothing about no bombs," she said. "It ain't my property, neither."

"Whose is it, then?"

"Everything's in my grandson's name. Lawyer down in Dover-Foxcroft said I should transfer it over to him for tax purposes. Keep the government from taking it all when I croak. What will you give me if I answer your questions?"

"I'll put in a word for you with the attorney general," I said.

Tempest Dow knew enough about the criminal justice system to realize how much my word would be worth.

"I'm looking for a young woman," I said.

"You must be hard up if you came here for a date."

I ignored her joke. "Thin, brown hair, driving a green IF&W truck. Have you seen her?"

"Oh, yeah. I know the one you mean. The biologist in Monson. My boys told me about her, said she was a real bitch."

My hands tightened around the rifle, but I did my best to stay cool. "She hasn't been here?"

"No," Tempest Dow said. "What else do you want to know?"

"Where can we find your son Troy?"

She took another pull from the Mountain Dew can, then let out a burp. "He's down in Massachusetts on business."

"I just saw him. He took off on an ATV seconds after Warden Investigator Pinkham was killed."

"You must be confused about who you saw, Warden. Troy's been gone since last night. Everyone here'll swear to it."

I had just about reached my breaking point. "Where's your grandson Toby?"

For the first time, a flicker of worry showed in her expression. "What do you want with that retarded boy?"

"Is he inside the house?" With the tip of the AR-15, I pointed at the door. "How about we go find him together."

She scratched the bottom of her chin with cracked fingernails. Then she tilted back her head. "Tara!"

An obese woman opened the screen door and peered angrily out at me. She had the same pink skin as her mother; her hair was the color and texture of rusted steel wool. She wore a nightgown that revealed cleavage deep enough to hide a kitten.

"What is it, Mumma?"

"Go get your boy. The warden here wants to talk with him."

The breeze shifted and I could smell the smoke again. "You've got a building on fire, you know?"

She turned her head but showed no real interest. "Really? Where?"

"Near the fence. I hope there's nothing precious inside."

She showed me the gaps between her teeth again.

After a minute, the younger woman, Tara, threw open the screen door and shoved Toby Dow onto the porch. "You answer the warden's questions, Toby!"

The doughy young man stood there in his Monson T-shirt, which was a size too small, stretch jeans rolled up half a foot around the ankles, and Velcro sneakers. His thin hair fell into his upslanted eyes.

"Here you are, baby!" Tempest Dow took his soft hand. "How's my little man this morning?"

He opened and closed his mouth soundlessly, like a fish.

The old woman twitched her nose. "What do you got to ask my grandbaby?"

"Toby," I said. "Do you remember me?"

He gazed at the gun in my hands with fear. "We met at the Monson General Store last week. I gave you a Snickers bar."

"Answer the man, Toby!" his mother commanded from behind the ripped screen.

"You were sitting on your bucket," I said. "Talking on a phone."

"What's your question?" Tempest Dow demanded.

"Toby, can you tell me where you got that phone? Did you find it somewhere? Did someone give it to you?"

"It's mine," he said.

"I know it's yours. I just want to know where you got it."

"Phone?" Tempest Dow said. "What phone?"

Suddenly, Toby's face went apple red and tears started streaming down his cheeks. "I don't want to go to jail, Gram."

"You ain't going to jail, baby." The old woman leaned forward suspiciously. "Why are you asking him about a telephone? What's this all about? Why are you trying to trick this poor boy?"

"I'm not trying to trick him. It's just a simple question."

Tempest Dow started to massage her grandson's arm with both of her hard little thumbs. "Tell the truth, baby. It's OK."

"Who gave you the phone, Toby?" I asked again.

"No one!" He was blubbering so hard, the words melded together. "I found it!"

"Where?"

"In the big trash."

"You found it in the Dumpster, you mean?" I said. "At the general store?"

He blinked but didn't speak. But I could tell that was what had happened.

How had Missy's phone ended up at the Monson General Store? She had used it to take that photograph with Samantha at the trailhead sign. Unless she lost it later and someone found it on the AT. They might have tossed it into the Dumpster after the fact. But that still wouldn't explain why Samantha's Galaxy was also missing.

"Is that all?" Tempest Dow said.

A siren wailed and a car rumbled to a stop behind me. I turned to look and saw a state police cruiser. Both doors opened and a trooper—not Chamberlain, but a man who could've been his body double—got out from the driver's side. Fitzpatrick emerged from the passenger door.

"What the hell are you doing, Bowditch?" the state police detective asked, more confused than angry.

"Did the boy answer your question or not?" the old woman barked at me.

I had an answer all right. The problem was that I didn't have a clue as to what it meant. Nor did I know how to explain myself to Sergeant Fitzpatrick.

36

The compound swarmed with state police troopers, deputies, and game wardens. Some of the officers were charged with rousting the Dows out of their holes for questioning. Others were searching the property for unexploded bombs and assorted booby traps. A team of firefighters had arrived from Greenville to extinguish the burning drug lab.

I handed Trevor Dow's AR-15 to a female state police detective who had spilled coffee on herself speeding up from Augusta. We sat in her car, and I gave her a preliminary statement, with the understanding that I would submit a written report in the next twenty-four hours. Afterward, I directed a trooper with a bomb-sniffing dog along the path I had blazed from the road to the field. In the process, we discovered the game camera that had given away my position to Trevor Dow. It was a well-camouflaged Bushnell unit with night-vision infrared and wireless capability to transmit pictures to a remote computer. Aside from the IED I had almost stumbled over earlier, we discovered no more explosives. When I was done, I went looking for DeFord.

The lieutenant was watching the medical examiner take notes with a digital recorder over the remains of Wes Pinkham. An evidence technician in a blue uniform waited nearby to begin his work. There was nothing left of the device to fingerprint or swab for DNA. There was barely anything left of Pinkham.

DeFord looked even more haggard than he had during the search for Samantha and Missy. There were razor nicks on his jaw. He kept rubbing his hand back and forth through his honey-brown crew cut, the way one might stroke a nervous animal.

"There are kids here," he said absently.

"What's that, sir?"

"How is it possible they never blew up one of their own children?"

"Maybe they don't let them outside the fence."

"Or maybe there's a kid's skeleton buried in the family graveyard."

A cache of weapons, a concealed locker filled with drugs, the bones of missing persons—God only knew what we were going to find hidden in this hellhole.

"Where's Fitzpatrick?" I asked him.

"Interrogating Trevor Dow."

I would have thought the lieutenant would have insisted on participating in the questioning. Then I realized that DeFord wasn't going anywhere until his friend was loaded into the ME's van for transport to the Augusta morgue. Anything less would have felt like an offense to the memory of Wesley Pinkham.

"Has anyone picked up Troy Dow yet?" I asked.

"We've got an alert out for him, but he knows these woods too well. My guess is that it's going to be one of the biggest manhunts since—"

He stopped himself, but I knew how the sentence ended: It was going to be one of the biggest manhunts since my father, Jack Bowditch, took off into the Boundary Mountains after being accused of murder. And I knew how that sad story had turned out.

"Charley Stevens is up there somewhere in his Cessna," I said. "He's looking for Stacey's truck."

"She still hasn't turned up?"

"No, sir. Maybe Charley can help us track Troy Dow down from the air. Do you want me to call him?"

"Do it."

"He'll need someone on the ground if he sees anything. You have plenty of men up here now. I'd like permission to assist Charley in the search for Troy Dow."

DeFord studied my face. He understood that my desire to get on the road was tangled together with my concern for Stacey.

"All right," he said.

"Thank you."

"And Bowditch?"

"Yes, sir."

"Let me know when you find her."

The first responders had dragged aside the cedar log at the bottom of the drive, but no one had removed the rotting steer head from its spike. I paused a moment to stare into the empty eye sockets and had the stomach-churning sensation of falling headfirst into a pit. Maybe if we had taken the ghoulish warning more seriously, a good man would still be alive.

I wanted to let out a howl of rage, but what was the point? I'd never believed in the idea that a person could die before his time— as if there was some sort of cosmic plan for a soul that could be foiled. You die when you die. Wes Pinkham was gone, and that was all that mattered.

I dug my cell phone out of my raincoat pocket and tapped in Charley's number.

The connection was poor.

"What's going on down there?" he asked. "I heard the commotion on the radio."

"Wes Pinkham is dead. He tripped a wire on the Dows' land, and a bomb blew him up. He lost both of his legs in the explosion. I'm sorry. I know he was your friend."

He fell silent.

"Charley?"

"Wes was a good man."

"Yes, he was."

His voice disappeared again. I listened to the sound of his engine coming through the speaker.

"Charley?"

"I was thinking about the day his first daughter was born. Wes and I were up on the Allagash, looking for a lost canoeist. That was before there were pocket phones. The colonel had to send another warden down the rapids with the good news. I never saw a happier man than Wes Pinkham that day."

Sometimes I forgot that my old friend was a combat veteran, that he had seen many friends die in the worst-possible ways imaginable. The experience had hardened him to death. He responded to horrible circumstances with a stoicism that might have seemed like coldness if you didn't know how big his heart was.

"Where are you now?" I asked.

"Up over the Hundred Mile Wilderness, looking down on Hudson's Lodge. I'm checking everywhere you and Stacey went in your travels. I was just about to buzz Gulf Hagas."

He didn't have to tell me he hadn't found her.

"DeFord is hoping you can shoot down our way," I said. "Troy Dow took off on a four-wheeler. He was headed north, toward Monson. He might have looped back to the Moxie Pond Trail."

"He'll get into some dense country pretty quick if he goes that way. There's plenty of places to hide himself around Shirley Bog."

"Why don't you backtrack the Moxie Pond Loop on your way south? I'm going to ride back into Monson and ask questions. I'm guessing the Dows have secret deer camps all over the county."

"Good idea. A wounded partridge always goes into a hole."

I'd never heard the expression before. "Is that an old saying?"

"Well, it's *my* saying—and I'm old—so I guess you could call it that."

I wished I had Charley's ability to maintain good humor in the face of bad news. With any luck, I would live long enough to develop that capacity. For the moment, it remained an open question.

"Keep your eyes open for a VW van and a green IF&W truck," I said.

"Will do."

I was about to sign off, when a random question pushed itself into my head. "Whatever happened to the canoeist?"

"Say again?"

"The man you and Pinkham were looking for on the Allagash."

"Oh, he drowned," Charley said. "We found his body wedged under a rock below Chase Rapids. It had been there awhile. The poor bastard looked like he prit'near drank the whole river."

In small Maine towns, convenience stores are the principal hubs of gossip, even more so than post offices and churches. If you want to know anything about anybody, you start at the place that sells tobacco, caffeine, and alcohol.

The Monson General Store was even busier than it had been when Pinkham and I had left. I had to look for a spot on the street because the parking lot was full. I could barely believe that a few short hours ago, the even-tempered warden investigator had been alive, cracking jokes with Pearlene. What a waste. What a stupid, meaningless waste. I caught sight of my reflection in the rearview mirror. My ragged emotional state revealed itself in my overbright eyes and stubbled jaw.

Five people stood in line at the register while Pearlene, still wearing her hairnet and gloves, tried to fix the paper tape. I stepped out of the way of a rotund woman in a hurry. She slammed her bottle of diet soda on the counter.

"Just a minute!" Pearlene said.

"I can't wait no more. I got an appointment at the beauty salon."

After the woman left, I heard Pearlene mutter, "It's going to take more than one appointment."

Until she could get the line moving, I occupied myself by reading the bulletin board. Someone in Guilford had lost a twelve-year-old black Lab named (ugh) Jigaboo. The high school kids at Foxcroft Academy were performing *Once Upon a Mattress* in October. The tear-off flyer offering goats for sale was missing another tag. There was a conspicuous blank spot in the middle of the corkboard. I tried to recall what had been there previously, but I drew a blank.

A man shuffled past with a case of Pabst Blue Ribbon tucked under his arm. It was the old guy from the Cajun restaurant. For the moment, he seemed to be sober. At least he didn't reek of alcohol.

"Roland," I said.

He blinked his crusted eyelashes at me and parted his cracked lips. "Yes?"

"You don't remember me?"

He made a motion to the holstered gun on my belt. "You're a game warden."

"We met last night at Shoebottom's. The Dows were trying to bully you into cutting down some of your trees."

There was no spark of recognition in his milky eyes. He sucked at his dentures, deep in thought. I had a sense that sobriety had ceased to be a natural condition for him. "I'm sorry, but I don't remember."

"Roland, I could use your help," I said. "Troy Dow has committed a crime and is on the run. It's vital that I find him as soon as possible. I don't suppose you'd know if he has any deer camps in the area?"

He shook his head violently. "I wouldn't know."

I could tell he was lying. "If I apprehend him, he'll go to prison, and you'll never have to worry about him again. His brother, Trevor, is already in custody."

A shiver ran through him. "It's a big family."

"Warden!" Pearlene had finally spotted me.

I stepped up to the counter. "Good morning again, Pearlene."

She frowned at me from behind the lottery-ticket display. "Good? This morning has gone from bad to worse. I've got an employee who didn't show up for work. And now I hear you and Wesley Pinkham have gotten the Dows all riled up. Is it true there's a SWAT team up there?"

So word hadn't yet reached the store about Pinkham's death. I was relieved not to have to answer questions about that subject at least.

"There are a lot of officers at the scene."

"Why aren't you up there, then?"

"I'm looking for Troy Dow. I was just asking Roland here if Troy might have some places he goes when—"

"When what?"

I turned back to the bulletin board. "What poster used to be in this blank spot?"

"Christ, I don't know. You think I keep track of every flyer someone tacks up in my store?"

"It was for a shuttle service," Roland said over my shoulder.

"Do you mean like giving rides to hikers out to the Hundred Mile Wilderness trailhead?"

"That and dropping cars off at Abol Bridge."

"There was a blue Ford shuttle van parked outside the store last night," I said. "But it isn't there this morning."

"That's Benton's van," Pearlene said. "He drives hikers around for extra cash."

"And you said he didn't come in for work this morning?"

"Son of a bitch closed early last night, too. I had to hear it from customers who came looking for beer. Now he won't answer his phone. Next time he shows his face, I'm going to tell him he's fired."

It can't be a coincidence, I thought. Benton ran a shuttle service for hikers who needed someone to transport their vehicles to Abol Bridge. Hikers like Chad McDonough. Had he also driven Samantha and Missy to the trailhead the morning they set off into the Hundred Mile Wilderness? Was he the one who had taken their final picture?

The phone.

Toby Dow said that he'd found Missy's Samsung Galaxy in the Dumpster. The boy seemed too simple to fabricate a story like that.

At every turning point in the drama, the mysterious clerk had been present, looming in the shadows, watching and listening.

"Hey, can I pay for my breakfast?" a man in line said.

I pushed myself against the checkout counter. "Tell me about Benton."

"What do you mean?"

"What do you know about him? Is that his first name or his last name?"

Her mouth trembled. "His name is Benton Avery. He's only been working here since June. Came from New Hampshire, he said, but that accent of his sure sounds chicken-fried to me. Told me he moved up here to the middle of nowhere because he likes to hike on the AT. He's a strange guy. I still couldn't tell you if he's a genius or a moron."

A rootless man who lied about where he was from, whose entire being seemed to be a disguise, who haunted the most godforsaken stretches of the Appalachian Trail. Benton Avery isn't a moron, I thought with horror. Not at all.

"Where can I find him? This is important, Pearlene, please."

"He's got a place on Slate Street. It's just outside of town, near the old mines. Just what is it you think Benton's done?"

It wasn't what he'd done. It was what I feared Benton might do if I didn't stop him first.

37

Pearlene said to take the Monson Pond Road north of town until I passed the active quarries of the Sheldon Slate Company and to keep driving into the woods toward the village of Willimantic. Slate Street would be on the left, she told me. Benton's place was at the end.

I picked up the phone and called Charley again.

"Change of plans," I said. "I need you to take a swing over the Monson slate mines."

"Did you get a tip?"

"Do you remember the creepy clerk at the general store? Benton? I think he's the missing link that ties everything together: Samantha and Missy, McDonut, Nissen, the Dows."

"You think Stacey is there?"

"We'll see. I'm driving out to his house now. It's located at the end of a road called Slate Street—you'll see it on your GPS. Look for my truck."

"Roger."

Despite what I'd told Charley, I was having trouble seeing a pattern in the dots. What was the connection between Nissen and Benton? As far as I knew, they weren't friends; Nissen didn't seem to have any. The store sold his honey and beeswax candles, but that hardly seemed like the basis for the two loners to begin a partnership murdering people together.

I thought back to my brief conversation with Benton the previous night at the general store. He had closed up early, Pearlene had said, not long after we'd spoken together. Had I said something to panic him? What was that strange quote he'd spouted? "There are nights when the wolves are silent and only the moon howls."

Maybe he thought he'd given himself away.

What about Stacey, though? It seemed unlikely that Nissen could have persuaded her to accompany him to Benton's house in the middle of the night. The alternative was that she hadn't driven herself because she was incapacitated—or worse. I didn't want to contemplate that possibility.

As Pearlene had said, the road took me past Monson's working slate mines. From my truck window, the pits didn't look as deep as the limestone quarries that pockmarked the face of midcoast Maine. The stone here wasn't powder gray the way it was back in Rockland, but shiny black, and it sloughed off the walls in flat sheets, some as large as tabletops, or broke into sharp chips like primitive arrowheads and hand axes when it fell to earth. The precipices of Gulf Hagas, miles to the north, were formed of these same minerals.

Soon the mines were behind me, and I was back in the birch and maple forest. Tent caterpillars had hit the trees hard, spinning vast webs to protect themselves from hungry birds and to devour the leaves. The insect army had left behind acres of skeletonized branches to mark their relentless march through the woods. Where the sunlight hit them, the gray silk cones seemed to writhe with the undulations of the larval moths inside.

On the GPS display, Slate Street seemed to be little more than an abbreviated fire road. I slowed as the turnoff appeared on the map, hoping that I would hear a plane and that it would be Charley winging his way to the rescue. Every other law-enforcement officer in the county was occupied, sweeping up members of the Dow family. Had I not been so desperate to find Stacey, I might have waited for backup, but I would never have forgiven myself if something happened to her while I dithered around.

Ahead, I saw a green-and-silver sign with the logo of the Maine Forest Council. As I drew closer, I could read the words: MONSON STREAM PRESERVE. APPALACHIAN TRAIL 1.5 MILES. I began punching buttons on the DeLorme. I zoomed out on the digital map to get my bearings. Beyond the abandoned pit mines at the end of Slate Street, a dotted line indicated a northbound path. It was a shortcut from the village limits of Monson into the Hundred Mile Wilderness. If you were pursuing someone who had started on the AT at the Route 15 parking lot (as Samantha, Missy, and Chad had done), you might intercept them between Big Wilson Stream and Barren Mountain. At the very least you could count on catching them at Cloud Pond, provided they camped at the lean-to for the night.

I passed a trailer with two ATVs in the yard and a cat sleeping on the warm hood of a Volvo station wagon. A burned-down house appeared next, its scorched fieldstone foundation all that was left of someone's farm. Then the woods became as dark as a jungle, and I realized it was because the resident maples and oaks were being choked to death by invasive bittersweet. Green vines crawled up the trunks and constricted the branches. The metastasizing leaves pushed skyward, blocking the sun from reaching the lower limbs, until the parasitic plants finally caused the trees to wither and die. The bittersweet would die, too, eventually, but it couldn't stop itself from killing its hosts.

Stacey's truck was parked beneath the tangled mass of vegetation, as invisible from the air as if it were covered by camouflage netting. In front of her Sierra was Nissen's VW van. It, too, was concealed by the canopy. If they had come here together, it appeared they had chosen to approach Benton's home in secret and on foot. Had Nissen been leading her into a trap? And was I about to step into it myself?

I called Dispatch and told the man on the other end where I was and what I'd found.

"You want to wait for me to send someone else out there?" he asked.

"I need to go in now."

"Are you sure that's a good idea?"

"I'll let you know."

I opened and closed the truck door as quietly as I could. Then I removed my service weapon from its holster.

I moved in a crouch along the edge of the road, keeping as much in the green shadows as possible, until I was at the passenger window of Stacey's truck. I peered through the dusted glass but saw nothing amiss inside. The usual half-empty iced-tea bottles and trail-bar wrappers were littered on the floor. I tried the handle, but the vehicle was locked.

Three robins fluttered out onto the road. They had the distinctive bloodred breasts and black bodies of birds moving south out of the Canadian Maritimes in advance of winter. One of them let out a startled *yeep,* and they all took off into the brush. I listened for the sound of Charley's plane engine but heard nothing but the breeze ruffling the bittersweet leaves.

Nissen had stripped the interior of his van of all furniture and cabinets, leaving just a boot-stained carpet and a mattress stripped from a bunk bed. His white beekeeping hood and suit were bunched in the corner beside a blackened smoker and stacked hive frames. A large cardboard box in the back was printed with his company name: Breakneck Ridge Apiary.

With my shoulders hunched, I ran forward until I caught sight of the trail for the AT cutoff. Judging from the undisturbed leaves on the ground and the absence of household garbage in the small lot, the path didn't look like it got much use.

I kept going through the tunnel of vine-strangled trees. There were dark shards of slate all over the road. I began placing my feet softly, heel to toe, the way I did when I stalked deer. *Watch for motion,* I told myself.

The tangled bittersweet formed a web between two oaks. There were enough holes in the foliage for me to see the house beyond. At first glance, it looked abandoned. The clapboards were mildewed where they weren't altogether rotten, and most of the windows were covered with plastic to keep the wind from finding the cracks.

In the dooryard, I spotted the same blue Ford E-450 shuttle bus I had seen outside the Monson General Store. The bus's automatic door stood open, and on the ground beside the front wheel was a heap: cardboard banker's box, polyester duffel bag, European ruck-sack. Someone looked to be leaving in a hurry.

I pressed my body against the snaking vines until I was half-submerged in the leaves. I began regulating my breathing, trying to bring down my racing heart rate. If I could just be patient, I might get an opportunity to draw a bead without having to charge out into the open.

From my hiding place, I could see an old metal gate blocking the end of the road beyond the house and then an overgrown field that dropped below the horizon, as if into a pit. In the hazy distance the land rose again: a bank of bright-colored trees that climbed into roll-ing hills.

A trickle of salt water rolled down my forehead and into my eye. If I could maneuver a ways to my left, it seemed that I might be able to make a dash for the van without being seen from the house.

I was just starting to move again when I heard the howl.

For a moment, I thought I was hallucinating. Then I heard it again. The bloodcurdling noise was more like a man impersonating a werewolf than an actual wild animal's cry. As I listened, the howl transformed into a series of distinctly human laughs. The echoes continued even after the man shut up again.

I straightened up and made a break toward the gate that blocked the road to the slate pits. Concrete Jersey barriers had been set on either side of the gate to prevent access onto the land by motorized vehicles. There was no room to slip between them, so I used my mo-mentum to throw myself over the top and landed hard on my rib cage in the weeds.

I hadn't seen anyone in the field while I was sprinting. I hoped that no one had seen me.

The plants in my face had been crushed beneath human feet. Wet blood clung to the blades.

"Woof! Woof!" was followed by laughter. The barks were deliberately cartoonish. Someone seemed to be playing a sick game.

I raised my head, trying to see above the frayed goldenrod. I crawled forward on my forearms and knees. Some of the weeds had sharp edges that cut the skin on my hands and cheeks.

There was another long howl, followed by a different noise: rock against rock.

"Fuck you!" I heard Stacey scream.

I leaped to my feet. Up ahead a tall man stood atop a berm at the edge of a cliff. His back was to me, but I recognized his profile. In his left hand, raised above his head, he held a stone the size of an orange. In his right hand, hanging relaxed by his side, he held a Ruger .38 revolver.

"Police!" I shouted. "Put down the gun, Benton!"

He opened his hand, and the rock dropped to the ground. But not the pistol.

"Drop the gun!"

"Mike?" Stacey called, her voice reverberating up from somewhere below. "Mike, is that you?"

Benton turned around. One of his eyes looked like a smashed plum.

"Put the gun on the ground!" I said.

I'd only seen him dressed in the blue uniform he'd been made to wear at the store. At home, he had changed into hiking boots, olive drab pants, and a plaid shirt, which was unbuttoned, revealing his gray-haired chest. His posture seemed different, too. His shoulders were no longer stooped. His body appeared lithe and powerful.

I advanced on him, holding my pistol in a Weaver stance, left foot forward, gripping the gun with both hands. "Get on your knees!"

He smiled, took a step backward, and disappeared, as if he'd stepped through a trapdoor.

Stacey shouted my name again, and I rushed forward to the edge of the slate pit.

Beyond the raised berm, the quarry tumbled down thirty feet, a sloping wall of black scree that plunged at the bottom into a dark pond covered, from shore to shore, with dead leaves.

My mind struggled to take in the scene before me. Benton was riding the mini rock slide as if his boots were skis. He had his arms spread wide, the gun still gripped tightly in his hand, and was expertly dancing along the skidding stones, as agile as a mountain goat.

He threw himself into the waist-deep water as I raised my pistol. Stacey had been on her feet, but now she lunged away from him, falling with a splash and kicking out with her legs, trying to swim. A man's shirtless body floated facedown beside her in the pool. I recognized the burned-looking skin on the shoulders where the tattoo had been removed. There was a red hole, larger than a fist, in the middle of the spine, and bloody pulp where his toes had been. The waves Benton created when he hit the surface caused Nissen's corpse to bob up and down like a boat at anchor.

Before I could squeeze off a shot, Benton whipped halfway around and fired. I heard the bullet crack against the slate at my feet. Reflexively, I dropped down onto one knee. It was just enough time for Benton to fall on top of Stacey and spin her over like a man wrestling an alligator. He got his left arm around her throat and held the pistol to her temple. Her body was almost completely shielding him from me; her legs kicked and thrashed beneath the rippling mat of leaves.

Both of them raised their faces to me. His was ecstatic. Hers was contorted in pain. Blood flowed from Stacey's hairline down to her chin, and her shirt had been ripped open, the buttons pulled off, so that I could see her flesh-colored bra. She tried driving her elbow into his ribs, but Benton seemed not to notice the blows.

"Shoot him!" Stacey screamed.

Grinning, he pressed the barrel of the revolver painfully into the side of her wounded skull. She cried out in agony.

"There's no way out of this, Benton!" I said.

"I know," he replied.

The nerves in my gun hand refused to obey the impulses traveling from my brain. I'd missed my chance to take a clean shot and now risked hitting Stacey, if Benton didn't kill her first. Just thirty feet away—and yet it seemed like a mile.

Stacey stared up at me. How to describe the emotions that passed across her face? Anger? Disappointment? Fear? Then her body seemed suddenly to go limp, as if she was deliberately trying to sink herself.

Defeat, I thought.

Benton let out another of his coyote yells, this one directed at me. He wanted me to live with this memory.

"Don't do it!" I shouted.

Stacey lifted her face, as if she were warming herself one last time in the sun. Then I became aware of the buzzing noise in the air above me. Benton's chin tilted up. A plane was flying low above the tree-tops, headed toward the slate mines.

I saw Stacey slide farther down into the water. One of her shoulders began to flop. Was she trying to give me a shot at his throat? I sighted down the length of my pistol, aiming for the exposed half of Benton's head. My arm began to jerk as I tried to aim past Stacey's ear. Hunters call it "buck fever": the jumpiness that ruins the kill shot.

Then Charley's plane banked hard around the open pit. For a split second, I thought the old pilot was making a kamikaze run into the quarry.

Benton forced the revolver against Stacey's head as he craned his neck to follow the diving plane.

I had a chance now. *Steady,* I told myself.

Before I could squeeze the trigger, Stacey twisted around. She brought her submerged right arm up from beneath the floating leaves. I saw something black clenched in her fist. It was a piece of slate she'd found at the bottom. She thrust the sharp point into Benton's neck.

Dark blood spurted from his throat. He cried out, let go of Stacey, and dropped his weapon. With a look of wide-eyed disbelief, he clamped his hands against the wound and fell backward into the water.

Charley's plane pulled up, but one of the pontoons tore the top off a spruce at the edge of the vast clearing. The impact caused the wings to shake back and forth, but somehow he maintained control, lifted the nose, and regained altitude.

Stacey began wading toward the scree cliff beneath me. The water seemed to be holding her back, the way it does in a nightmare when you can't move. I could see her clenched teeth between her open lips.

"What are you waiting for?" she shouted up at me. "Shoot him!"

A red stream issued from between Benton's fingers. If Stacey had cut his carotid artery, he'd be dead in three minutes.

I thrust my SIG back into its holster and leaped onto the sloping cliff. The slate slid out from beneath my boots. Knees bent, hands at my sides, I skied down the cascading black rocks.

I landed feet first in the water just as Stacey made it to the edge. Little waves lapped at our knees. She held one palm up to her scalp to stanch the trickle of blood. I reached out for her, but she recoiled.

"Shoot him! What's wrong with you?"

"He's already dead, Stacey."

"No, he isn't!"

She glanced back at Benton's spasming body. Her pants were plastered with yellow and green leaves. I wanted to hug her, but she kept her distance.

"Are you all right? What did he do to you?" I put my hand out to examine her head wound.

"He hit me in the fucking head." She pinched her buttonless shirt together, as if overcome with modesty. "And I twisted my ankle when I jumped off that fucking cliff."

"You jumped?"

She swung around to face the quarry. "My gun! We need to find it."

But Benton had stopped moving. He lay on his back in the rippling water. The leaves near his head were shining and crimson.

"Bowditch!"

Men stood along the top of the berm above us, DeFord among them. The lieutenant sprang down the rocky wall, keeping the sides of his boots against the incline the way a snowshoer might descend a steep hill. He dropped into the pool beside us.

"Are you two OK?"

"Yes," I said.

"No!" Stacey shouted.

The lieutenant began wading across the pond toward Benton's inert body, using his arms in a swimming motion to assist in moving himself forward.

Stacey pushed her wet, bloody hair out of her eyes. "What are you doing here, Mike? How did you find me?"

"It's a long story."

Before I could say more, DeFord shouted out, "This man is still alive! I need an EMT down here!"

I couldn't believe he was still breathing. Benton must have had a stronger constitution than Rasputin. When I turned to Stacey, I found that her face was contorted with anger. I had assured her that the man who had brutalized her and murdered Nissen would die. But somehow he clung to life. Her lips were pressed so tightly together now, they were almost invisible. There was nothing there for me to kiss.

Meanwhile, Charley's floatplane circled high overhead, wheeling around and around like a watchful eagle.

38

Stacey kept telling us she was fine even while blood continued to seep down her jawbone. I'd given her a compression bandage from my first-aid kit to stanch the wound, but it didn't seem to be working.

"You need stitches," I said.

"I'm not going anywhere until they finish searching the house."

"You're bleeding right through that bandage."

"Give me a clotting sponge, and I'll drive myself to the hospital when they're done searching."

"You're not driving yourself anywhere," Lieutenant DeFord said.

Stacey sat in the passenger seat of the lieutenant's truck with the door open, her legs facing out, so she could keep her weight off her twisted ankle. She wore my camouflage raincoat to cover her ripped shirt. And from the way she was shaking, you might have thought she'd just guzzled a pot of coffee.

Fifteen minutes earlier, the EMTs had rushed off in their ambulance with Benton's unconscious body. A Life Flight chopper would transport the wounded man to Eastern Maine Medical Center in Bangor. His skin had been as gray as a zombie's when he went by on the stretcher. It seemed that Stacey had punctured his jugular vein, not an artery.

Now DeFord and I were listening to her story.

"It all started at the store," she said. "I was so pissed off about my stupid job, I couldn't think straight. I told Waterman I wasn't going to tag another coyote—I was through with his witch-hunt. He said my refusal was grounds for firing, and I dared him to do it. Then I drove over to Ross's to get my stuff."

"You were going to check out, but then you had a conversation with Steffi Ross."

She wrinkled her nose. "How did you know that?"

"I followed you there."

She kept focusing on DeFord, as if she was pissed at me for some reason and couldn't bear to look me in the eyes. "I wanted to hear what Steffi remembered about Samantha and Missy."

I tried to regain her attention. "She told you Nissen was in the dining room with them that night, and she mentioned that they'd asked about local churches—which led you to go to the Lake of the Woods Tabernacle."

Now her mouth dropped open. "What the fuck, Bowditch?"

"Brother John told me you went to see him."

Stacey raised her voice to Lieutenant DeFord. "If he knows all this already, why do you need me to explain it to you?"

I didn't understand where her anger was coming from. After what had happened, I wanted nothing more than to hold her in my arms, but if anything, she seemed to be pulling farther away.

"Because I don't know what made you decide to drive out to Blanchard," I said.

"I drove out there because Nissen was a member of Brother John's church," she said. "He was the one who told the pastor that Samantha and Missy were gay. Nissen had some problems with women. I think lesbians probably scared the shit out of the guy."

"No one knew where you were, Stacey."

"I can take care of myself."

"That's not the point."

"You should have called Pinkham or myself with your concerns," the lieutenant said, not unkindly.

"After the way I pissed everyone off up in Greenville? Would you have believed me if I'd called with a bunch of suspicions and nothing to back them up?"

DeFord scratched the back of his neck.

"That's what I thought," Stacey said.

"I would have believed you," I said.

She stared at me, but I couldn't tell what was going on inside her head. She was in distress; I could tell that much.

"So you drove out to Breakneck Ridge," DeFord said. "What did you find when you got there?"

"Nissen wasn't home. There was no sign of him. I decided to wait in my truck until he turned up, but I ended up falling asleep. The next thing I knew, it was almost dawn, and he was tapping on my window. He nearly scared the shit out of me."

"Did he say where he'd been?" I asked.

"He said he'd had a booth at the Eastern States Exposition in Massachusetts. He'd been there the past few days, he said, selling his honey and candles in the State of Maine Building. His van was full of boxes and stuff. I helped him unload it, and he asked if I wanted to go inside."

"You went with him into his house?" I said. "Just the two of you?"

"Yeah, why? I had my Ruger in my pocket."

"You didn't have any concerns for your safety?" DeFord asked. "You just told us that you suspected Nissen of being a murderer."

She removed the bandage from her head, releasing a new trickle of blood. She stuck it back in place. "Of course I was concerned! But I wasn't going to let fear keep me from asking questions."

Stacey was as much of a bulldog as her old man in that respect.

"How did you get him to open up?" the lieutenant asked. "Bob wasn't very chatty."

"Not with men, maybe. I batted my eyelashes at him. It wasn't exactly a secret that the dude was hard up for female companionship. Why do you think he had meals at Ross's all the time? He went there for the pretty young thru-hikers."

"Why didn't you call me first and tell me what you were doing?" I asked.

She ignored my question and flicked her eyes at DeFord. "Once we were inside, I told him everything I'd learned. He seemed angry at first, said it was none of my business."

"How did he explain his actions?" DeFord asked.

"He said he hadn't told anyone that he'd met Samantha and Missy because it didn't matter. He knew he'd had nothing to do with their disappearance, he said. Why bring it up?"

"Because it was relevant," I said.

Stacey's hand trembled as she moved the bandage and shifted uncomfortably on the seat. "I felt sorry for him living alone out there with just a bunch of bees for company. He showed me this plaque someone had given him for his speed-hiking record. He was like a little kid, he was so proud of it. And he said he was writing a book called *Death on the Appalachian Trail,* about all the ways people have died on the AT since the 1930s. I got a little nervous again when he told me the title."

There was a shout inside the house, and a state police evidence technician hurried though the front door. I could see that DeFord was itching to follow, but he restrained himself.

"How does this connect with Benton?" he asked.

"I asked Nissen to tell me about the murders on the AT," Stacey said. "I wondered if there might be a connection to what happened to Samantha and Missy and the others who died. He was pretty insistent that coyotes had killed them. I think he thought it would be better for his book if they had. But I kept pressing him. He said there had been a serial killer down in Virginia named Randall Lee Smith, who shot two hikers in 1981 and later tried to kill two fishermen. And then he told me about two gay women who were murdered in 1988 in Pennsylvania by a guy named Stephen Roy Carr. Over the past few years, he said, there had been a series of strange deaths and disappearances in the Northeast, but nothing yet in Maine."

I tried to catch Stacey's attention, to no avail. "Who figured it out? You or Nissen?"

"Both of us," she said. "Nissen had started a file on Samantha and Missy. We went through it together, page by page, until we came to that MISSING poster. I must have seen that picture a thousand times, but I'd never thought about the T-shirt Missy was wearing. For some reason, it finally jumped out at me."

Of course, I thought. Toby Dow had been wearing the same Monson souvenir shirt every time I'd seen him.

"You asked Nissen where she might have bought it," I said.

"He said there was only one place in town that sold them."

"The general store."

"That's right. And I said it was odd that no one had reported that Samantha and Missy had stopped there. It seems like the kind of thing someone would have remembered under the circumstances."

"What happened then?" the lieutenant asked impatiently.

Like her father, Stacey enjoyed telling stories and was never in any hurry to wrap them up if she had an attentive audience.

"Nissen jumped up with this big shit-eating grin and said we needed to go somewhere," she said. "He wanted me to ride with him in the van, but I said that I'd follow in my truck because I still had my doubts about him."

"He didn't tell you where you were going?" I asked.

"I thought it was the store. But then he kept driving past the slate quarries, until we got to this place. I think he'd realized Benton was a killer, and he wanted to be the one to get credit for catching him."

Caleb Maxwell had told me that Nissen had always cared about being the first to find a missing person when they were members of Moosehead Search and Rescue. That same competitive, self-aggrandizing nature seemed to have been on display this morning.

"When we got here," Stacey continued, "Nissen came out of his van with an axe. Maybe he didn't own a gun because he was a felon."

DeFord and I laughed at the same time.

"That doesn't stop most of them," he said.

Stacey frowned. "Well, I'm glad you think it's funny. I had no idea whose house this was until I saw that shuttle bus over there; then I realized it was Lurch's place."

The lieutenant raised an eyebrow. "Lurch?"

"Like in the *Addams Family*. It's what I called Benton." She paused as another police cruiser pulled up, this one belonging to the Piscataquis County Sheriff's Department. "I got out my Ruger, and Nissen and I went to the front door. What we didn't realize was that Lurch had been packing up his bus. He must have heard us coming, because he hid behind the seats. When there wasn't any answer at the door, I went to take a look inside the bus. He jumped out and hit me on the head with a piece of wood."

"Who gave him the black eye?" I asked.

"It was me. I didn't go down the first time. I managed to get a punch off, and I think I hurt him. But he grabbed my shirt and ripped off the buttons. So he clubbed me again."

Her voice wavered. "When I came to, I was lying next to Bob inside the shuttle. I'm not sure where Lurch was planning to take us. He must've been hoping to cover his tracks again. I guess it doesn't matter now. He was in the house a long time, and we were alone in the van. We were tied up with paracord, but Lurch didn't know how to tie knots. He must have flunked that part of the psycho test. It took forever, but Bob finally managed to get free. He was untying my hands when Lurch came back. Christ, it was horrible."

She closed her eyes and shivered. "After that, he made us walk to the quarry," she said. "Bob could barely move. Lurch had shot off his toes. That asshole shoved the poor guy over that concrete barrier because he couldn't climb. I thought about taking off, but I knew he would shoot me in the back while I was running—and I didn't want to leave Bob. When we got to the pit, Lurch told us to stand on the edge. He shot Bob first."

"And that's when you jumped?" I asked.

"What else could I do?" she said. "Benton thought it was hilarious. He started howling and throwing rocks at me. I knew there was no way out. I was sure I was going to die."

A state trooper emerged from the house. "Lieutenant!"

"Excuse me," DeFord said.

Stacey hopped to the ground and winced when she landed on her bad foot.

"I'm sorry, Stacey," the lieutenant said, "but you can't go in there. It's a crime scene."

"Just let us know what you find," I said.

"I will."

When we were alone, I said, "Stacey, why did you disappear on me like that?"

"Because you didn't believe in me. I told you someone murdered Samantha and Missy, and I needed your support. I started wondering how much I could trust you if you wouldn't trust me."

I resisted the overpowering urge to touch her face. "I was sure something horrible had happened to you."

"Well, it kind of did," she said with a bitter laugh. "And now, with my luck, that monster is probably going to pull through. I wish you'd just shot him when you had the chance."

"No, you don't."

"Don't be so sure about that."

I reached into the pocket of the coat I had given her to wear and removed the broken sunglasses I'd found on Nissen's lawn. "These belong to you."

She looked at them without recognition for a few seconds before stuffing them back in my jacket pocket. She leaned against the side of the truck and began flexing her ankle, testing the limit of her pain.

"You don't want to know how I found you?" I asked.

"Go ahead."

I almost felt embarrassed telling her now. "The broken cell phone Toby Dow was playing with at the general store—it was Missy's. Benton must have thrown it into the Dumpster."

"Well, that was stupid of him."

"No, it was *daring*," I said. "Those other deaths and disappearances on the AT in the past few years—they had one thing in common. They were all staged to look like something other than homicides. Benton was toying with the FBI, daring them to figure out what he was doing. He probably placed that phone in the trash in hopes it would be found, because the game wasn't thrilling enough for him."

"Congratulations on figuring it out," she said. "It's too bad for Nissen you didn't do it sooner."

I must have looked like I'd been punched in the gut.

Tears appeared in her eyes, and she shuddered. "I'm sorry. That was a horrible thing to say. I'm just a wreck right now. I shouldn't be near anyone when I'm like this."

"What can I do for you?"

"Just let me be alone. I need to be alone."

I watched her limp away, wondering about the last word she had used. Alone for how long? I had spent my entire life trying to escape from my own solitary confinement. The thought of returning to that lonely prison terrified me.

But it would be better to lose her this way, I thought, than to have lost her in that flooded pit. I could still hear Benton Avery's howls in my head and probably would forever. What had driven him to commit such atrocities? Even if he survived, would he be able to tell us, and would we even understand?

I threw my head back and gazed up at the perfect sky. From horizon to horizon, the color was a deep, heavenly blue. Not a single cloud to be seen. On such an unblemished morning, it seemed hard to imagine that such evil could exist upon the earth, not unless you believed, like Brother John, that humanity had fallen from God's grace; that our mortality was the price we paid for our sinfulness, and the two were coiled up together, impossible to ever unravel.

39

The state police found a leather satchel under Benton's bed. Inside was an odd assortment of mementos: a bottle opener shaped like a trout, a woman's turquoise bracelet, a trail map to Bear Mountain State Park in New York State, a shot glass from Bennington College, a Purple Heart medal, and a Samsung Galaxy smartphone with a serial number behind the battery registered to Samantha Boggs. The evidence techs also discovered a police scanner in the kitchen with a pad of paper. Benton had scribbled Chad McDonough's phone number on a note.

DeFord took Stacey to Dover-Foxcroft to get stitches once the evidence technicians and the death-scene examiner were done with their work. It seemed pointless for me to ask to drive her. If nothing else, she needed time to cool down. DeFord later told me that, after they were done at the hospital, her father picked her up in his float-plane on Sebec Lake and flew her back home to Grand Lake Stream. Charley called me that night to talk about what had happened to Stacey. We spoke for an hour, and then I asked him how much time I should give her. He said she would get in touch with me when she was ready.

But she didn't.

The FBI held a press conference, asking for help identifying the man called Benton Avery, since his fingerprints were nowhere in their databases. When they showed his photograph, people from up and down the eastern seaboard called to report having seen someone who looked like him along the Appalachian Trail. He had flipped burgers for a time in Gatlinburg, Tennessee, where he was known as Randall Smith. In Bartlett, New Hampshire, where he'd worked as a carny at an amusement park, people called him Stephen Carr. Benton Avery—or whoever he really was—had a wicked sense of humor. He'd stolen his aliases from two other AT serial killers.

Benton also had an amazingly strong heart. He survived the ambulance ride and helicopter flight to the hospital in Bangor before lapsing into a vegetative state after surgery. As far as I know, a machine is still forcing air into and out of his lungs in a hospital bed he will never leave. I have a recurring dream of sneaking into his darkened room and pulling the plug, only to find that his heart continues to beat.

The medical examiner released his report concerning the deaths of Samantha Boggs and Missy Montgomery. The skulls of both women had been fractured. The forensic evidence indicated they had died from massive blunt-force trauma. What the coroner couldn't determine was what had caused their fatal injuries. They might have had their heads beaten in with a rock, or the fractures might have resulted from a fall from the Chairback precipice. Their other bones displayed unmistakable signs of having been masticated by canine teeth. On the question of whether coyotes might have driven Samantha and Missy to their deaths, the evidence was inconclusive.

Despite the open-and-shut case against Benton Avery (should he ever be fit to stand trial), the rumors continued around Greenville. Some people wanted to believe that coyotes had killed and eaten the Bible students, and they clung to the uncertainties in the coroner's report to justify their fear and hatred. Isn't that the purpose of folktales?

Thousands of people turned out for Wes Pinkham's funeral in Lewiston the following week. He had graduated from Bates College, but there was no auditorium on campus big enough to handle the crowd, and so the Warden Service decided to hold the ceremony at the Colisée arena downtown. The facility doubled as a hockey rink, and the maintenance crew had to lay down parquet flooring over the ice to set up the stage. Even in my red wool coat, I was freezing.

Otherwise, it was a nice memorial. Colonel Malcomb presided over the ceremony, and the Reverend Davies gave the eulogy. The governor spoke, as did one of our senators.

During the service, I tried not to look around, because it seemed disrespectful to the memory of a man I had come to like, but I found myself sneaking glances at those in the audience. I was hoping to see Stacey, but if she was there, she wasn't seated with her parents. I did spot Caleb Maxwell sitting with the other members of the Moosehead Search and Rescue team.

After the service was over, I made the rounds. The mood was solemn whenever we wore our dress uniforms, but it was even more somber because of the affection in which everyone had held Wes Pinkham. I thought Lieutenant DeFord seemed to be carrying himself with admirable stoicism until I glimpsed him sniff a couple of times and turn his face to the wall. When he turned back, his expression was hard and grim once again.

Caleb tapped me on the shoulder. His blond hair was neatly parted in the middle and swept back behind his ears, and he was wearing a black suit with a red tie. He was also wearing his red Crocs, I noticed.

"I heard what happened at the slate quarries," he said. "It sounded brutal. I never thought I'd say it, but poor Nissen."

"Have you heard anything about a funeral for him?" I figured that I would attend.

"He's not having one. His will instructed that his body be cremated and the ashes scattered along the AT."

In death he would become part of the trail that had given his life meaning.

"Is Stacey here?" Caleb asked, glancing around.

"I haven't seen her."

"You're not together?" The question seemed to have multiple meanings.

"Not today we're not." I made eye contact with Danielle Tate, and she came over. "Excuse me."

As was always the case, Tate was perfectly put together; there wasn't a wrinkle in her uniform or a scuff on her spit-shined boots. We shook hands—her grip was strong for such a small person—and she looked up at me from beneath the brim of her olive green fedora.

"Was that the guy who manages Hudson's Lodge?" she asked.

"Caleb Maxwell? Yeah, that's him." I thought she was going to comment on what an aqua-eyed dreamboat he was.

She let out a grunt. "What kind of douchebag wears Crocs to a funeral?"

I smiled and shrugged.

"Some of us are getting together afterward to tell stories about Pinkham," Tate said.

"I didn't realize you knew Wes."

"He was my mentor at the warden academy. Do you want to join us?"

I looked around the mass of red jackets and police uniforms. Kathy Frost waved to me from across the room. "I was hoping to find Charley and Ora Stevens."

"Oh," she said, the light dimming in her gray eyes. The woman so rarely smiled as it was.

"Charley was my mentor," I explained. "One of my mentors at least."

But Dani knew who his daughter was, and how I felt about her.

"Are you going to apply for the warden investigator position?" she asked with characteristic bluntness.

"Me? With my track record? I wouldn't have a shot in hell."

"I heard Lieutenant DeFord mention your name."

"You're shitting me."

Her nostrils flared. "Do you think I'm lying?"

I seemed to have a rare talent for angering women. "I'm just surprised."

She began to walk away, then remembered something. "Did you hear about Troy Dow?"

"The last I heard, he was still on the loose. Did somebody catch him?"

"No, he's dead. He ran into a moose on his ATV. A bear guide found the two dead bodies on his way to check his baits. Poor moose."

"God's justice is not man's justice," Brother John had told me. I'd never viewed a moose as an instrument of the Almighty's will. But there it was.

"Why are you grinning like that?" Dani asked.

"Nothing," I said.

I finally caught up with Charley and Ora. He was pushing her wheelchair down a ramp.

"Is Stacey here?" I asked. "I haven't seen her."

"She said it would be too painful." Ora had snowy hair and flawless skin that didn't need the help of cosmetics. Stacey had been a surprise baby who had arrived just in time to complicate her parents' golden years. "She was going hiking instead to test her ankle. It makes her feel better to be outdoors."

I tried not to show my disappointment, but I was sure that Ora could feel it emanating from my soul. As I said, the woman had unnatural powers of perception.

"What's this I hear about blood on the bumper of Benton Avery's van?" Charley asked me.

"They think it's Chad McDonough's," I said. "The DNA results haven't come back."

"So that poor kid took off from the lodge because he was afraid of Nissen, and he ended up calling a serial killer for a ride."

"It looks that way. Benton was the one who shuttled him from the parking lot at Abol Bridge to Ross's in Monson. So they definitely knew each other. Maybe Benton killed him because he was afraid of being identified as the man in the red tent. Or maybe he just killed him for kicks, like he did all the others. Who knows?"

"That man is the most unusual specimen of God's carelessness I ever came across," said Charley.

"That's one way of putting it," I said.

Ora looked up at her husband with a tender smile. "Did you ever find Doris?" she asked Charley.

"I gave her our condolences. She's hoping we can fly over for supper in a few weeks."

"It won't be the same without Wes there," Ora said.

"That it won't." After a pause, the old pilot began to smile wider and wider. "Wes was always good company. I remember getting sluiced with him one night when we were both young bucks up at Clayton Lake. Back in those days, I was quite a hand to drink rum, but Wes never had any tolerance for the stuff. Next morning, I found him asleep in the outhouse with a big smile on his face and his drawers down around his ankles."

"Charley!" Ora said, smiling.

I tried to join in the spirit, but I kept visualizing Pinkham's dead body lying in the grass. "I wish I'd known him better. He seemed like a good man."

"He was a true friend," Charley said, making it sound like there was no higher compliment.

"Listen, I wanted to talk with you two about Stacey."

Ora touched my arm. "Be patient."

"I just feel like I did something wrong."

"Like what?" her father said. "She's still alive."

"Do you remember when Sarah was attacked when we lived in Sennebec?" I said. "The circumstances were similar, and I had no trouble taking a shot."

"That's because you were young and reckless," Charley said. "You've learned since then not to depend on luck. There's nothing more foolish than firing blind and hoping you hit the bad guy. Real life isn't like a Dirty Harry movie, young feller."

I would have to draw strength from Charley's reassurance that I had acted responsibly. For most of my life, I had confused heedlessness with heroism. Maybe the time had come to get past that.

In the lot outside, I followed the row of identical Warden Service trucks until I found my vehicle parked near the end. Stacey was leaning against the passenger door. She was dressed in a green T-shirt and hiking shorts that showed off her tawny legs. She lifted her sunglasses, looked me up and down, and let out an appreciative whistle.

"Looking good, Bowditch."

"It's just the uniform."

"No, it's the man."

I stepped forward to embrace her. "Stacey, what are you doing here? Your folks said you went hiking."

"I had a change of heart on Tunk Mountain." Her arms went around my waist and very nearly squeezed the breath out of me. "You should have said something about Pinkham that morning at the quarry. When my dad told me what happened to him, I just about lost it."

"I thought you'd had enough trauma for one day."

"You don't have to protect me from the world, Mike."

"I know that," I said.

"Besides, if you'd told me about Pinkham, maybe I wouldn't have been such a bitch." She bit her lip and gave me a sly look. "Maybe."

I held her by the shoulders and inspected the black stitches on her forehead below the hairline. She had made no effort to hide the ragged wound. Her lack of vanity was one of her most attractive qualities.

"You're not a bitch—not usually. You're passionate. Anyone who doesn't understand that doesn't understand you."

"That's kind of you. But I'm not sure it's the truth."

"Did you see any of the service?"

"The end of it. I didn't want to go in dressed like this, so I watched from the nosebleed section."

I scanned the faces of the people flowing past. "We should go find your parents."

"I'll see them later," she said. "Where are you headed?"

"Dani Tate and some of the others are getting together to drink and tell stories about Pinkham."

"Tate, huh?"

"Yeah, why?"

"You know why. But it doesn't sound like you're going."

"I thought I wanted to be alone."

She touched my cheek with the palm of her hand. "But you don't anymore?"

"No."

"How about we take a ride, then?"

I fished my key fob out of my pocket. "Where do you want to go?"

"Let's just drive."

Most of the cars and trucks were headed either downtown or to the Maine Turnpike. I decided to sneak out the back, in the direction of the Thorncrag Bird Sanctuary in the hills above Bates College. Stacey loosened her ponytail, letting her dark hair flap around her face and stream behind her in the breeze.

Clouds piled up like scoops of vanilla ice cream in the western sky. In a few days, it would be October, and my life would change again with the turning leaves. The boaters would tow their boats out of the water, and I would put away my Jet Ski and cover it with a tarp. On the first day of the month, bow hunters would creep to their secret tree stands, and men who had won permits to kill moose would start cruising the back roads with loaded rifles and cans of beer wedged between their legs, scouting for trophy bulls. For the next two months, I would spend long hours dressed in camouflage, stalking the woods for armed and dangerous men. But right now, all I could think about was how beautiful the day was.

"I heard a rumor the legislature was going to overturn the governor's coyote bounty," I said.

"That's one good thing that came out of this. The only good thing."

"Have you been back to work yet?"

"Not yet. It turns out that being attacked and nearly murdered by a serial killer qualifies you for workers' compensation. Who knew? The truth is, I haven't wanted to deal with the questions about Benton Avery. It's still hard to talk about."

I took this as a hint to change the subject. Sooner or later, we would need to discuss what had happened to us in Monson, but I trusted that she would let me know when she was ready.

"I ran into Caleb Maxwell," I said. "He asked about you."

"I'll bet he did. He called me at home last night. I'm not sure how he tracked me down."

My foot kicked the gas pedal and we rocketed forward, nearly bumping the car ahead. "What?"

"He didn't come right out and say it, but I'm pretty sure he wanted to know if we were a couple, so he could ask me out."

"I'm going to turn around now," I said. "I need to go punch him in the face."

"You have nothing to worry about," she said. "He's kind of a sorry figure, if you ask me."

"Sorry how?"

"DeFord told me about him. I was curious why he'd left Moosehead Search and Rescue, since he seemed to miss it so much. His fiancée committed suicide at Gulf Hagas a few years ago. No one knows why. She didn't even leave a note, just threw herself off a cliff one morning. They recovered her body trapped in one of those grinders. And now Caleb goes there all the time and visits the place where she died. I thought you knew the story."

"No," I said. "Are they sure it was a suicide?"

She patted my knee. "Every death is suspicious to you, isn't it?"

"It's a bad habit of mine, thinking that way."

"You just can't help yourself."

I remembered the brown-haired woman in the photograph on Caleb Maxwell's desk, how even her brilliant smile had seemed tinged with sadness, as if even in that seemingly happy moment she was aware of what was ahead, and I knew that my suspicions were misplaced. "That explains why Caleb was crying when the newlyweds saw him on that ledge." A shiver ran through me at the thought. "I can't imagine what it's like, having someone you love kill herself with no explanation. No wonder he roams the Rim Trail like a grieving specter."

"I wonder if he's ever tempted to jump himself."

"What?"

She unfastened her seat belt and drew her knees up against the dash. "If all you had to do was let yourself fall into the abyss, and you could be with the person you loved again, wouldn't you consider it?"

"I'm not that confident in the hereafter."

"So if Benton Avery had killed me, you would have kept on living, huh?"

"Am I supposed to say yes or am I supposed to say no?" I asked. "What's the right answer?"

"The right answer is always to keep on living."

She leaned across the console and tucked her head into my shoulder. Her body felt sun-warmed against mine. She smelled of the same suntan lotion she had worn at Popham Beach. I felt myself being transported there again, back to the cottage. She pressed her ear to my chest, closed her eyes, and listened to the steady beating of my heart.

AUTHOR'S NOTE

This book is a work of the imagination, and it should go without saying that every character and event in it is fictitious. I drew inspiration from real places, not least of which was the town of Monson, Maine, a beautiful and big-hearted community rightly loved by AT thru-hikers. I have taken liberties in its depiction and in my rendering of other locales in and around the Hundred Mile Wilderness.

Thank you to the Appalachian Mountain Club, specifically the helpful staff at Gorman Chairback Lodge & Cabins and Little Lyford Lodge & Cabins: the best base camps for anyone wishing to explore Gulf Hagas. And thanks also to Simon Rucker of the Maine Appalachian Trail Land Trust for answering my last-minute questions about the area.

Certain books informed the composition of this one: Bill Bryson's *A Walk in the Woods* (of course); Michelle Ray's *How to Hike the AT: the Nitty Gritty Details of a Long Distance Trek*; the *Appalachian Trail Thru-Hiker's Companion*, published by the Appalachian Trail Conservancy; *The Maine Woods: A Fully Annotated Version* by Henry David Thoreau, edited by Jeffrey S. Cramer; and finally, my trusted companion throughout this series, Robert E. Pike's *Spiked Boots*. The National Geographic Channel documentary *Killed by Coyotes*, which tells the tragic, true-life story of Taylor Mitchell, was an important resource in my revisions.

As always, I am indebted to the Maine Warden Service, in particular to Corporal John MacDonald, who provided me with crucial information about the service's search-and-rescue operations.

My agent extraordinaire, Ann Rittenberg, offered support and advice along the way—thank you, Ann.

I am grateful to my editor, Charlie Spicer, publisher Andrew Martin, and everyone at St. Martin's Press and Macmillan Audio. Thanks also to Beth Andersen for her proofreading help.

Lastly, I would like to thank my wife, Kristen Lindquist, for her encouragement, insight, patience, and love—all of which I needed during the writing of *The Precipice*.